ANTARCTICA

Other Bella Books by Katherine Rupley

Calculated Risk

About the Author

Katherine Rupley lives in California with her wife and cats. She's an avid reader, runner, photographer, and dark beer drinker. When she's not posting pictures of her cats online, you can find her at her keyboard writing and editing (or playing word games).

http://www.KatherineRupley.com
Instagram: Katherine RupleyAuthor
Twitter: @KatherineRupleyAuthor
Bluesky: @KatherineRupley.bsky.social

ANTARCTICA

Katherine Rupley

BELLA
BOOKS
2024

This is a work of fiction. Names, characters, businesses, places, events and incidents are either the products of the author's imagination or used in a fictitious manner. Any resemblance to actual persons, living or dead, or actual events is purely coincidental. The publisher does not have any control over and does not assume any responsibility for author or third-party websites or their content.

First Edition - 2024

Editor: Ann Roberts
Cover Designer: Melodie Pond
Author photo credit: Yvonne Whitcomb

ISBN: 978-1-64247-523-4

PUBLISHER'S NOTE

Acknowledgments

Antarctica has always fascinated me. When I was a child, our neighbors, Dr. Harold Muchmore and his wife, Donna Muchmore, did research at the South Pole. Their stories captivated me. My wife and I traveled to Antarctica right before the pandemic. The cruise showcased nature, science, and history with a series of lectures and on-deck experiences. I talked with several people about the continent's fragility and its impact on our planet. Nobody owns Antarctica and a forward-thinking treaty governs its use and protection.

I owe many people thanks for making this book a reality.

Terry Wolverton and her workshop, Crafting the Story, helped me with the messy first draft. Thanks to all the workshop crew, especially Carrie, our writing dates made a difference.

My GCLS Writer's Academy (WA) class 2021-22, headed by Dr. Finnian Burnett, introduced me to a group of wonderful writers (Dillon, Sue, Laura, Kate W, Beth, Carolyn, KP, KL, Dana, Claire, JD, Sandy, Cameron, and Dianna, who we lost, RIP). The wonderful WA teachers taught me more about writing.

A big thank-you to my WA Mentor Susan X Meagher for reading my book through twice and helping me refine my thoughts. She kicked my butt when I whined and pushed me to finish the novel.

Big thanks to Dillon, Carrie, Sue, Laura, and Kate W for writing discussions and all the rest. My alpha readers Steve and Cate's Editing. My beta readers Dillon, Susan X, Sue, and Dana. Proofreaders Deb and Jayne.

All the people at Bella Books who have done so much to make this book the best it can be. My editor, Ann Roberts, who gave me sound advice and helped me get my ideas to come alive on the written page.

Finally, my mom and dad for instilling in me a love of travel and exploration, and my wife Deb for going on adventures with me.

Dedication

To the explorer in all of us

CHAPTER ONE

Siberia-October

The tires skid sideways, throwing me against the ancient Toyota Land Cruiser's door and straining the makeshift seat belt. Equipment shifted in the back, and Laura, my current assistant, grunted. The back tires spun and the front wheel couldn't find purchase despite the truck's four-wheel drive. I could feel the back tires sinking into the tortured Siberian earth. Throwing the gearshift into neutral, I cut the engine.

"Boards in the back," I said as I released my seat belt and shoved the door open. Laura followed my lead on her side.

Last week, the temperature had been in the low fifties, with smoke so thick it was almost painful to breathe. A week of rain had dampened the fires but not put them out. This week started with a snowstorm that would turn into a blizzard in the next few days. And still the fires smoldered and flared. The ground was soft, where the thick layers of peat had burned and formed pockets for the blowing snow, creating small pools of mud and debris. The smell of burning peat still filled the air but it was cleaner, sweeter than the acrid smoke of the vast landscape flaming for miles. The snow was slowly lessening the smoke and heat.

Still dangerous, though. I could sense the heat through my boots even as the snow swirled about my head. I reveled in the feel of the heat and the cold, the strangeness of nature so at odds with the feeble efforts of man. Mother Nature had a bizarre sense of humor.

The wind bit and the sun, hazy on the horizon, gave off a blue light. The sun would set soon and the temperature and visibility would plummet. We needed to get out of the mud and back to the huts before nightfall—in twenty minutes.

"You gonna help?" asked Laura.

"The truck isn't going anywhere unless we can give the wheels some traction. Just wedge the boards in front of the back tires. I'll be there in a minute. I need to get a few more air samples."

"You and your damn samples."

"What was that?"

The sounds of equipment being moved and the wood planks being slid from the cargo section covered any reply she might have made.

Laura would get the boards in place, and I would get the data I needed. Eighteen minutes left. Four minutes to collect the data.

Four-and-a-half minutes later, the truck pulled free of the morass and back onto the snow-covered peat. Avoiding the sunken divots that pockmarked the field was akin to a chess match where a misstep would put us back in the gray-yellow frozen patches of sludge. The wind picked up and snow swirled around the vehicle.

Steam was rising from the snow in multiple locations, creating new depressions. Last year, they believed the Siberian winter would kill the fires. However, the peat below the frozen landscape had held its heat and fully formed wildfires had sprung back to life with the late spring heat. Zombie wildfires. Crazy name for a crazy phenomenon.

"Dr. Peterson?" Laura asked over the creak and groan of the truck.

"How many times do I have to tell you to just call me Jo?"

"Our permit is void after tomorrow. I don't want to end up in a Russian prison. Dr. Zharkov was very firm about our departure."

"The plane out is at six thirty a.m. You'll be on it." Out and safe from politics and the coming storm. It was the best I could do.

"Will you be going with me?" Laura sounded hopeful.

"It's the mail plane with only room for one passenger. You'll be taking our data out."

"Aren't you scheduled to present at the World Meteorologists Conference in Dubai?"

She was right. But what was a conference compared to a real weather event? There was nothing to say I couldn't do both. I could feel the smile on my lips as we pulled up to the hut, the last light fading to black. Eighteen minutes. Dr. Zharkov's warning was just that, a warning. He didn't want to report me. He wanted me out of his hair. Out of sight, out of mind. Plus I knew I could get the visa extended. "I'm going to ride a Yakutian horse. And there's an interesting blizzard heading this way."

As I exited the vehicle, my mind filled with the crunch of the snow beneath the horse's feet and the condensation of my breath in the frigid air. Solitude and no responsibility.

My coat pocket vibrated. I snatched my satellite phone from its resting place. Few people had my number—only immediate work contacts, which I deleted regularly, and my one friend, Ty.

I stared down at the screen. A picture of a smiling woman looked up at me. I swiped to answer. "What?"

"And hello to you too." Ty's voice was clear and chipper as if she was standing next to me.

"You know I'm on assignment," I grumbled.

"And I know your assignment ends today and your visa expires tomorrow. Or were you thinking of overstaying your welcome?"

Laura watched me with interest, her brown eyes magnified by her thick glasses. I never got phone calls. I turned away and walked toward the back of the vehicle. The snow was coming down harder. I shivered and pulled up the hood of my parka with my free hand.

"You know me so well. Still, you don't normally call me when I'm in the field. What do you need? Am I getting credit notices again?" As I didn't have a place of residence, I used Ty's address for snail mail.

"What? I can't call and talk to you?"

Anything I said would be used against me, so I stayed silent.

Papers shuffled on the other end of the line. "What do you know about the Antarctica Treaty?"

Antarctica. I shoved my hand into my coat pocket. The one continent I hadn't been to yet. "Signed at the height of the Cold

War, the treaty went into effect in 1961 to protect the continent from exploitation, to be used exclusively for scientific research and other peaceful pursuits. I think there were twelve original signers, though only the US, Australia, Russia, Argentina, and the UK have territories which have never been formalized. It's been signed by a bunch of other countries over the years. No mining, no military actions, and the agreement to keep it pristine. How'd I do professor?"

"Not bad," Ty said. "You missed the part where the treaty comes up for review every two years. There is renewed interest from the State Department and the National Science Foundation in the polar regions. In the Arctic, the Northwest Passage is opening earlier and earlier. Russia and China are building icebreakers. In Antarctica, the Chinese have built four research facilities in the Australian zone, with another coming online soon."

I shook my head. "Whoa. That's a lot of information. What's this got to do with you?" I wasn't seeing the connection. Ty worked for NASA, not for the NSF or the State Department.

"I'm leading a scientific team that will winter over in Antarctica. Isolation, small area food production, and ice sheet movements."

Winter over in Antarctica. How cool was that? "That's great." It was great and I was jealous, except for the leading part.

"NSF Polar Expeditions Division that manages Amundsen-Scott Pole Station has been in conversation with some private companies. GICE Corp. has been trying to get a space research mission focused specifically on Mars to study a variety of topics in extreme conditions. They talked and decided on this Antarctica mission. There will be three teams, of which ours will be one." GICE stood for Ganymede, Io, Callisto, Europa, named after Jupiter's four largest moons. It was run by Cid Balkner, a billionaire with money to burn.

"Why Antarctica?"

"Most of the studies, including isolation studies have been done where there's an out. There is no out at the South Pole. No one can get in or out for seven to eight months."

That's one of the reasons it was so fascinating to me. Harsh conditions and isolation. And the weather. "Congratulations! You deserve to lead the mission."

"Wanna go?"

My heart leaped.

"Before you get too excited, it would be part of a ten-woman team. The commitment is just under two years."

The pressure in my chest increased but not in a good way. Too much time with too many people.

Ty's voice was soft but firm. "I need you, Jo. You have skills I don't have. You see things and have an attention to detail that I lack. Plus, you call me on my bullshit. I need that. The fact that you're a meteorologist helps. The team needs that, too."

"You don't trust me to show up?" I paced behind the truck. The sound of my footfalls and the motion gave me some small comfort.

"Oh, I think you'll show up."

"But…" I sighed. "I can hear it in your voice."

"You chase shiny things," Ty said.

"Antarctica is pretty shiny."

I could almost hear the wheels turning in Ty's head. "I'm not asking you to climb into a confining box of expectation. Your adventurous spirit, brilliance, and way of looking at problems are what I want. I don't want you to hide who you are."

"You just want a commitment." It wasn't a question. I knew what she was asking. Commitment wasn't my strong point. Weather was transitory and so was I. "You know I'm not good with people."

"Wrong. You *are* good with people. People just scare you."

I huffed. "You scare me."

Ty laughed. "I need an answer. We've got several months of training, planning, thirteen months at the Pole, and then time for the debrief."

The pressure in my chest was building again. NO was on the tip of my tongue.

"I know you haven't committed to anything since grad school and even that was touch and go," she said. "Jo, I pulled your ass out of the fire with Dr. Franklin three times. When you took off that last time to chase tornados, I was sure she'd washed her hands of you."

"Tornados are interesting. I didn't want to lead that grant proposal Dr. Franklin wanted, even if it got my doctoral thesis approved. When do you need an answer?" I wanted time. And a way out.

Ty was silent for a few seconds. "I need an answer now. Training starts soon and I need to get the physicals set up for you."

"I'm in Siberia. I have things to do." There was more than one physical? Pressure moved from my chest to my head, my flight mechanism on high alert.

"I've booked the first part of your physical for the end of next week," she said.

"Hey, I have a life. I can't just drop everything." I rocked from side to side.

"Your visa expires tomorrow. You need to come home." As if sensing my edginess, she added, "Jo, you can't keep running."

I wasn't so sure about that. All I had to do was disconnect the line. Bad connection. Not my fault.

"Jo, breathe. You can do this. I need you." Ty's voice was calm and trusting.

And there it was. Ty needed me. Ty, who had always been there for me, needed me. *I could do this.* Ty, who trusted I'd help her, as I couldn't help myself. What was two years? Twenty-four months. Seven hundred and thirty days…Did I have to round up? Was there a leap year in there somewhere? My heart was beating too fast. Breathe. *Ty needs me. I can do this.* She'd surprised me on purpose, not to scare me away but to make me choose to support her. She'd baited the hook well.

"Okay." It came out weak and without conviction. I understood the terms. I said it again. "Okay." Agreement. The pressure in my chest hadn't lessened. I still wanted to run but Ty was right. And I hated it when she was right.

"Okay," Ty said.

My two okays meant I had bought in. Ty's okay meant she'd taken me at my word. I was a runner, not a liar.

CHAPTER TWO

Houston-November

I stared at the envelope on my desk. Who sent letters anymore? The letter was addressed to me with Ty's address. Picking it up, I glanced at the sender. Natalie Peterson. My aunt and the woman who had taken responsibility for my twelve-year-old self when my parents had died. A dull throb started behind my left eye. Did I want to know what it contained?

Ty stepped into the doorway of the cubicle. She glanced at the letter and then at me, a question in her eyes. Ty must have put it in my office. She looked like she wanted to say something, but a pale-skinned woman with medium brown hair and beautiful green eyes trailed her. Her slender form looked like a stiff wind could blow her over. "Jo, I'd like you to meet Amy Simons."

"Amy." I stood, glad for the distraction, and tossed the unopened envelope into the trash can. I wasn't interested in what my aunt had to say. Not now, after so many years.

Ty waved to Amy as if presenting a prize on a game show. "Amy is the engineer on our team. I was telling Amy about the sensors you've been working on for detecting ice movement." Ty kept her eyes on me and didn't look at the envelope. There wasn't anything she would say in front of Amy. "She can help you work out the bugs in the electronics and help improve the data collection software."

"Great." I feigned enthusiasm. I had been tinkering with stuff my whole life. It surprised most people I wasn't an engineer. My dad's smiling face flared in my mind, but I shook the thought away. I wanted adventure, not a desk. And my sensors didn't have any bugs. My anxiety was building. I focused on Ty's words.

"Amy is reviewing all the electrical and mechanical test systems that will support our mission experiments. Jo, I know you've worked up some prototypes. Amy can help get them manufactured and available for all the mission habitats. Looks like GICE may want to buy your designs if you can get the 'Amy' stamp of approval."

"Great!" Selling the design would build my cash reserves. Staying long-term in a hotel was expensive and I couldn't impose on Ty. "Speaking of money. Medical tests are complete." That included the psych eval which sucked. They had asked lots of questions which I had answered. I had years of experience getting around questions I didn't want to answer. "And I filled out all the HR paperwork. Does that mean I'm officially getting paid for this gig?"

"Yes, and for more than you're worth, especially given that room, board, and travel expenses will be covered for more than a year. You can afford to rent an apartment for a couple of months. You might actually enjoy not living out of a backpack." Her phone buzzed. Ty checked the display and grimaced. "I'll let you and Amy talk. I've got a meeting. More logistics."

As Ty strolled away, I turned to Amy, who hadn't moved since the introduction. The GICE cube farm was a balmy seventy-two degrees and I was comfortable in a polo and jeans. Amy was dressed in tailored, lined dark slacks and a matching jacket over a white, long-sleeve shirt and an emerald sweater peeking out from the sleeves of the jacket.

"Aren't you warm?" I asked. I felt hot just looking at her.

"No, I'm very comfortable, thank you," she said, cocking her head as if questioning my judgment.

"Right. Pull up a chair and I'll show you the schematics of my design. I think you'll find what I've done interesting."

Two hours later, Ty came back and found us in the break room, still discussing the pros and cons of 3D printers versus standard manufacturing processes for printed circuit boards.

"I see you both are getting along like a house on fire," Ty said. "What do you think Amy? Good design?"

Amy contemplated her now empty cup. "I think the design has merit."

I sat back, stunned by the comment. After my initial review of the design, Amy had asked question after question with only minor variations. The minutia that only paused for her trips to get more coffee exhausted me. Even after the endless questions, she'd only added a few comments and one suggestion that improved the reliability of the sensor package and could be easily implemented.

"Outstanding." Ty gave me a broad smile and a thumbs-up. "Thank you so much for your time, Amy. I appreciate you meeting with Jo on such short notice." Ty gave me a side wave, which meant I was to leave with her. "I need to talk over a few things with Jo."

"It was great talking with you, Amy," I said, following Ty out of the room to the far side of the GICE cube farm.

Once we got out of range of the room, I started to speak. Ty waved me off and headed for her hard-walled, temporary office, the carpeted walls dulling the pecking sounds of keyboarding and conversations. She closed the office door and leaned against her spotless desk that held only a laptop, monitor, and a few office supplies. The room was a shoebox and had none of the panache of her office at Johnson Space Center, which overlooked the NASA campus and was full of memorabilia and photos.

"What was that about? You know, Amy drinks black coffee like it's water and she's dying of thirst. She wasn't even jittery. That much coffee would kill a normal person. And when did, *it has merit*, become equivalent to outstanding?" I asked as I threw myself in Ty's guest chair.

"Amy is intense." Ty ran a hand through her shoulder-length brown hair. "She's got matching PhDs in electrical and mechanical engineering from MIT and she checks everything twice or three times. Intense. But if she says your design has merit, then it's outstanding."

"Does she eat?"

Ty frowned at me. "Yes, she eats. No smack talk about your teammates."

That was fair. I had taken enough obnoxious comments about my height and if that was why I became a meteorologist, because I'd know before anyone else when it was raining. I couldn't turn around and mock Amy for being skinny. "Her credentials are impressive. I can deal with her. She's quiet, listens, and asks good questions. Still, is she a good fit for the team? Are you ready, or should I say, is the team ready to be in close quarters with intense Amy for the thirteen months we'll be in Antarctica?"

"Good question. I think the answer is yes. One great, albeit intense, engineer means I can have two biologists with different specialties." Ty picked up the single pen on her desk and began flipping it between her fingers. "Food on Mars or the moon is going to be a big deal. There have been several studies, but I want to take the best of those studies and take them one step further. Miho Pierce and Sam Rodriguez are my chosen researchers. Both have practical knowledge and are good people. Miho is fairly low key and Sam is fun."

"What about Ingrid Johansen, your ex from the Swiss language school?" I'd seen her name on the list. "Are you ready to be in close proximity to her for thirteen months?"

"That's ancient history." She waved a dismissive hand at me. "I invited her for her skills as a geophysicist. Cid likes to collect beautiful, smart people."

Cid Balkner, GICE's CEO, did things no one else imagined and had the money and political clout to make things happen. But he wasn't shy about trashing people or organizations he found lacking. If rumor was to be believed, he'd ended several promising engineering careers for no other reason than he could.

"Speaking of the rest of the team…When am I going to meet them?"

"Soon. We have six Americans, one Norwegian, one Scot, and one German. Elisabeth is the youngest at thirty-two. Ingrid is the oldest at thirty-seven."

"I'm assuming that you include us in that count."

Ty nodded.

"That's nine."

"Yes, I can count. The doctor we had broke her leg skiing. Upper management has found us a new doctor. They think she'll be a perfect fit. However, I don't know anything about her at this point. They've been cagey about the whole thing. She's coming in from the National Science Foundation."

"Sounds interesting. Is she a ringer?"

Ty snorted. "No, like Ingrid, she's got real-life skills and credentials that Cid will admire."

"Real world experience is good. I don't know how well I'd deal with stuffy academics. But CEO opinions aside, you know credentials and internal team compatibility are two different things, right?" I pointed at the pen flipping between her fingers. "You nervous?"

Ty glanced down and stilled her hand, pen between her pinkie and ring finger. She laid it carefully on the desk. "Ten strong-willed women in less than sixteen hundred square feet of living space surrounded by snow and ice for thirteen months. What have I got to be nervous about?"

"You said Miho was easygoing. That leaves nine willful women."
Including an ex.

"You'll get your chance to meet them and decide for yourself," Ty said with a grin. "In two weeks, we have team building and survival training in Switzerland. A chance for you to show how much you love the snow and cold."

"December in Switzerland. Awesome. Can I fly in early and get some skiing in?"

"Ingrid asked the same question. No skiing. We've already lost one team member to the sport. Be content with team building on a glacier." Ty looked at me steadily. "And Jo. You're going to have to deal with your aunt at some point." She passed me the letter I'd thrown in the trash.

CHAPTER THREE

Switzerland-December

Even though it was December, I was sweating, a mixture of fear and nerves, as I made my way out of Genève Aéroport's customs area and to the meeting point. Ty said Ingrid Johansen, geophysicist extraordinaire, would be there to gather the group. The blond-haired woman in the Ray-Ban sunglasses leaning against the Hyrim Luxury Van counter, holding a sign that said Antarctica or Bust, was a walking advertisement for healthy Scandinavian living. She was at least three inches taller than my own five foot eleven. She saw me coming toward her and her brow wrinkled before her face shifted into a welcoming smile. I noticed the frown before the smile and it didn't do a thing to ease the butterflies in my stomach. I reminded myself of my promise to Ty to play nice and moved forward.

"Ingrid?" I said somewhere between a question and a statement as I reached out to shake her hand. The internet pictures hadn't done her justice. Ingrid was drop-dead gorgeous. Silver-blond hair framed sharp cheekbones, sky-blue eyes, and full lips. She had hurt Ty and I was predisposed to dislike her.

She nodded and took my proffered hand.

"I'm Jo. Jo Peterson." I stammered. I never stammered.

"Welcome. You are the first to arrive today, Jo Jo Peterson," she said in crisp, slightly accented English.

"Just Jo," I mumbled, hoping we weren't going into a comedy routine.

She wasn't looking at me but staring over my shoulder and I turned to see Ty heading toward us. I was relieved to see her friendly face. I was always more comfortable with people I knew. Okay, I was more comfortable with Ty.

"Jo!" Ty moved the last few yards, pulled me close, and whispered into my ear. "Did you read the letter?"

I snorted and set her away from me. She knew I hadn't but kept reminding me of it. Ty was always curious. I usually was too, but not about this letter. It brought up too many memories best left unremembered.

Ty gave Ingrid a quick, tight smile. Ingrid looked like she was expecting a hug as well, dropped her arms, which had been rising, and scowled at me. I wasn't sure if Ty noticed the exchange.

Ty gave me the once-over as if she hadn't seen me two days before. "Jo, you look good."

"You look good yourself. How was your flight?"

Ty didn't answer as Ingrid waved at a group of three women heading toward us. Amy was in the lead with a backpack that looked like it weighed more than she did. Two women flanked her, a stocky black-haired woman with a light bronze complexion and huge smile and an athletic black woman with intricate cornrows and an air of exasperation.

The stocky woman seized Ty and swung her around. They both laughed.

"Sam, put me down. Meet Jo and Ingrid," Ty said, her hands on Sam's shoulders.

With a final squeeze, Sam put her hand down and smiled at Ingrid and me. "Samantha Rodriguez, but you can call me Sam. Only my *abuela* calls me Samantha and only when she's mad." Her voice was warm and smooth and brought an answering smile to my lips.

Ty turned to the other two women. "Dianna, how was the trip in from Windhoek? Did you solve Namibia's problems?"

"*Yebo*, that's Zulu for 'yes' if you're curious. We provided answers, but not how they expected. Chinese infrastructure support comes with a price beyond access to a country's natural resources. The Chinese bring in their own workers, shutting out the local economy and keep the technical knowledge private. The Nambian government pushed back. Now the locals have the skills to run the rigs themselves." She turned to me and thrust out her hand. "I'm Dianna Moore. I'll be handling all the heavy machinery and maintenance efforts." Ty had mentioned to me that Dianna's skills had come from hard work and a genius with mechanisms. She only needed to read a manual or see a repair and she could figure out the problem on that mechanism or similar systems.

Her callused hand was warm and strong. She waited a beat as I gripped her hand, as if curious about how firm my handshake would be. As I had experienced many times, some people, usually men, tried to establish dominance with a handshake. Because of my size, she was expecting the same from me. I merely smiled, returned her steady grip, and said, "You'll be keeping us alive. I appreciate you already."

She eyed me speculatively before giving me a barely perceptible smile and nod before turning to Ingrid.

"Amy, good to see you," I said. "I see you packed light."

Amy gave me a quizzical glance before turning to Ingrid.

"I'm Amy Simons. I will be working with Dianna on all of our electrical and mechanical systems."

"Pleasure." Ingrid gave Amy's slight form a once-over before turning back to Ty. "The others are already at the hotel. Elisabeth has been in the bar the entire time discussing beer with the very patient staff." The disapproval was obvious in her voice.

"Elisabeth sounds like my kind of person," Dianna said, a genuine smile forming on her full lips.

"Don't be such a stick in the mud, Ingrid," Sam said. "Is Elisabeth drunk or merely inquisitive? You know her parents are brewmasters in Heidelberg, right?"

That was something I hadn't known, but I loved a good beer and was eager to get back to the hotel to have some for myself. I was more curious why Ty didn't step in to defend Elisabeth. She needed to deal with Ingrid and get everyone on equal footing. Ty was the leader, manager, people person. Why wasn't she using this moment to pull the team together? Was she afraid of Ingrid? Or didn't she see the tension?

Ty gave the airport concourse one last glance before she turned to Ingrid. "Is the van ready for us?"

Ingrid inclined her head.

"Then let's get to the hotel and join Elisabeth for a beer."

Ingrid flashed a blue-eyed glare at Sam before turning to Ty with a smile. "This way."

The hotel bar was busy and noisy with a small band playing an eclectic mix of American music. I hesitated at the entrance. The group had just finished a light ballad when the red-haired guitarist spoke into the mic. "This next song is 'This is the Life' by Amy MacDonald. She's from my neck of the woods in Glasgow." The redhead struck a chord and the band followed her lead as she began singing.

I scanned the room. Ty, Dianna, Sam, and Amy were seated at a large table in the center of the bar. A dark blond-haired woman of medium build, that I assumed to be Elisabeth, held court, holding a beer up to catch the warm glow of the table sconces. Each of the women had a flight of six beers in front of them, varying in color from pale to dark amber.

My stomach felt like lead. Tomorrow was soon enough to meet these people. I moved to leave and stepped into the path of a petite woman with shoulder-length, jet-black hair, in jeans and a blue form-fitting sweater. She put her hands out to prevent herself from plowing into me and the motion caught Dianna's attention.

"Hey Miho, Jo," Dianna called over the singer. "Join us for beers. Elisabeth really knows her stuff."

I cringed and smiled apologetically at the red-haired singer who ignored the whole byplay, completely wrapped up in her song. Too late to retreat. The supposedly mild-mannered Miho walked toward the group and I followed.

"No beer for me," Miho said. Her voice was husky with a neutral American accent used by network news reporters. "Beer gives me a headache. I'll watch and stick with water." She looked at me and stuck out her hand. "We haven't met. I'm Miho Pierce, biologist."

I introduced myself without the awkwardness I'd felt with Ingrid. Dianna raised an eyebrow at me and pointed to a flight of beers next to Ty.

"I'll play. I love beer." I took the seat she'd indicated as Miho sat to my right. It would give me somewhere to focus my attention.

Elisabeth nodded to the both of us. "Hi. I'm Elisabeth, communications and programming. Good to have you join us before we get really going. The first beer," she lifted the glass in her hand, "is a Lagerbier pale lager, which has a light hoppy flavor with a lower alcohol content compared to some of the heartier beers we'll try tonight. This is a very popular beer in Switzerland. It pairs well with most foods." She lifted her glass and we followed suit. "*Zum Wohl!*"

"Zum Wohl!" We clinked the bottom of our glasses and chorused back.

The beer was nice, cold and crisp. The light hops suited me after being overwhelmed by high hop IPAs that were all the rage in the US. I preferred a Bock or a dark lager to an American IPA.

Elisabeth continued with her lecture on beer and pairings. Ty ordered a traditional Raclette with additional meats to sop up some of the alcohol we were consuming. Miho ordered a hearty vegetarian stew for herself.

Ty had left to check with the hotel on the next day's activities, and Sam leaned toward me. "What's up between Ty and Ingrid? Were they an item?"

I wasn't expecting the question. "Why do you ask?" I stalled for time.

"The airport. Ingrid was watching her the whole time, and Ty was avoiding any interaction. Ty doesn't usually avoid confrontation."

"Yeah, well, they have some history. I don't have the details. You'll have to ask Ty or Ingrid." I'd said more than I wanted but I'd been truthful.

Sam noticed Ty returning and changed the subject. "What's your deal? Meteorologist?"

"Yep. I specialize in extremes."

"How do you know Ty?" Elisabeth said, leaning closer.

I smiled. "I've known her since college."

Ty caught the tail end of my sentence as she rejoined the table.

"How did you meet Ty?" I asked Dianna, wanting to get the topic off me.

Dianna smirked and flipped a thumb at Miho. Miho smiled at Dianna and flipped a thumb at Sam. Sam grinned broadly and took a seated bow.

Ty laughed. "Sam and I go way back. We grew up in the same neighborhood in Chicago. You might say her family kind of adopted me. When I started this project, I asked her to come on board and she helped me find Miho and Dianna."

Sam pointed a finger at Ty. "Hey, you make it sound like nepotism. I earned my place on this team."

"Yes, you did. Your studies on sustainable farming in small spaces are key to our mission," Ty acknowledged with an incline of her head.

"Okay, back to beer." Elisabeth grabbed the next glass in the flight.

About midway through my fifth of the four-ounce beers and a few health bites of cheesy potatoes, I poked Ty. "Where is Ingrid? Or Rue? Or this mysterious doctor? Has she flown in yet?"

Ty turned in her chair and pointed to the red-haired guitarist. "Rue would rather play than drink beer. Like a good Scot, she prefers whiskey anyway. Christina Sohn, our doctor, will be here tomorrow."

Dianna leaned over. "I think our doctor is coming in from Somalia. They needed her for some complicated surgery in a military hot spot."

My interest rose at this statement from Dianna. "She military?" I asked, curious if the team needed someone like Christina.

"No, not military, just real steady in tense situations," said Dianna as she turned to applaud Rue and the band.

I added my applause. "Rue is the guitarist? Wow, she's really great. And Ingrid?" I pressed. Ty was going to have to deal with Ingrid at some point. It wasn't like she was on the other side of the world, like my aunt.

Ty's shoulders twitched in a semblance of a shrug and turned her attention to Rue. I knew all about avoidance.

The petite singer from last night was already busy working on her laptop in the grand ballroom when I entered for the morning meeting. Her deep auburn tresses framed her face as she concentrated on whatever was on her screen.

"Hi, mind if I sit here?" I pulled the chair out from the table and introduced myself.

She looked up at me with a green-eyed stare as she pushed her glasses up on her nose. Her features were soft and her Scottish heritage was rich in her voice as she acknowledged me with, "Fair morning to you. I'm Rue McKinney. I'll be handling the information management and data processing for the study."

I tried not to be obvious but eyed the massive spreadsheet on her computer. It appeared to be a compilation of names with columns of data listed out.

"What are you working on?"

"Big data," she said without taking her eyes off the screen.

"It looks like the team information," I pushed.

"It is." She swiveled toward me, sighed, and pushed a hand through her hair, tucking an errant strand behind her ear. "I'm trying to run correlations between the team members. Likes, dislikes, personalities, classes, countries visited, languages, sexual preferences, books read…you know…data."

"Are you finding any interesting correlations besides good voices and racing stats?" I asked, especially after hearing the words *sexual preferences*. It was going to be a long winter with these women, and it would be good to know the lay of the land.

Others entered the room and took seats around the conference table. There were a few scattered conversations as the women got coffee from the service by the door.

"Later," Rue murmured as her gaze traveled over the group, her hand reaching out to shut her computer.

Ty entered, talking with Elisabeth animatedly in German. I'd have to let her know that wasn't good since not everyone spoke the language and it stressed division instead of inclusion. It was great that Elisabeth spoke four languages, but thinking of Rue's data analysis, I wasn't sure how helpful that would be in team building. Teams were built on shared goals and a common purpose, with greatness added for working in diversity. I was eager to see how Ty had constructed this team.

As the rest of the team filtered in, a woman I hadn't met entered with a to-go cup of coffee from a nearby café in her hand. She was of average height but seemed to fill the room with her presence. Energy in motion. Her long, dark hair was curly and her beautiful dark eyes swept the room before settling on me. I couldn't look away. Her eyes held mine. She moved with a dancer's grace across the room and took the seat beside me, placing her cup in the center of the waiting coaster. "I'm Christina Sohn. I hear you are the meteorologist and psychologist on this expedition." Christina stated this as fact and not a question. I cocked my head to the side in question, but before I could say a word, she continued. "You studied with Dr. Angelica Falcon? She has some interesting theories on isolation effects on women versus men."

Her gaze had an intensity that made me want to squirm. Fight or flight. A couple of classes didn't equate to being a psychologist. I hoped she wasn't expecting me to be the shrink on this adventure. "I'm familiar with her work. I'm Jo Peterson, extreme weather meteorologist."

She offered her hand, which was warm, soft and strong in equal measures. A surgeon's hands. My pulse sped up as she held my hand a beat too long.

"Team, let's get started," Ty called, pulling my attention away from Christina and back to the front of the room where a large projector screen was hanging from the ceiling. It looked odd in the otherwise baroque appearance of the room and its furnishings. "Thank you all for being here and making my dream a reality." She laughed then. A happy sound. "Okay, what I really want is an all-expense paid trip to winter in Antarctica, but this eight-day survival trek through the Aletsch Glacier is a team-building exercise to see if this group is the right mix. I think it is, but someone might want to bow out after spending a week together." She let the words sink in and gazed around the room. "Wintering over in Antarctica isn't for everyone." I wondered if that last comment was directed at me or Ingrid?

Ty waited a beat before continuing. "Similar to Antarctica, the glacier in Switzerland is a protected site. We'll be packing everything in and out, no exceptions. That includes all waste products."

There was a general groan from the room.

Ty smiled. "We'll be taking a couple of sleds, but yes, the grand two-bucket system, one for liquid waste and one for solid waste. Get used to it, ladies. This isn't the craziest thing we'll be asked to do."

"Merde," Elisabeth said. Her German accent made the word sound funnier than the tired joke was worth.

I chuckled dutifully with a few of the others, noting that neither Christina nor Ingrid joined in.

"We're going on this little survival jaunt to help us meld as a team. We'll have a few sessions in Houston together before we head to Christchurch in November, but this is our first opportunity to come together as a team. Although we'll have a sat phone, just like in Antarctica, we'll need to rely on each other." She looked around the room catching each person's eyes before her gaze landed on Ingrid and skittered away. She quickly moved on to the more mundane matters of what to bring and when to meet up for the trip out to the glacier.

What Ty didn't explain was how we were going to be organized. Ten strong, intelligent, competitive women. Maybe she didn't think it would be an issue.

CHAPTER FOUR

Switzerland-December

Falling, limbs flailing, and a sudden jolt. The climbing harness cut into my waist and shocked the air from my lungs. The muscles in my back and shoulders tightened painfully as I scrabbled for the braided nylon rope, as if by sheer will alone, my gloved hands could stop me from falling farther. My heart pounded in my chest. My body swung and my back hit the ice wall once before my climbing cleats crunched into the icy wall, my ragged breathing coming in gasps. Blood thundered in my ears.

I tried to slow my breathing, filling my lungs with the icy air. My mind raced. Was I hurt? One minute I was the tail end of a ten-person chain of people hiking on the Aletsch Glacier, the longest one in Switzerland. The next minute, I was stuck like a limpet on a crevasse wall. How could the simple retrieval of an aid ladder, screw me so badly?

Four days into this trip and nothing had gone right. I wasn't used to being around so many people for so long. Was supporting Ty worth the irritation? Was Antarctica? How had I let Ty lure me into this cluster? Ty's cooperative approach wasn't working with these Type A women. They were turning this trip into an all-expense paid Swiss party on ice. I wanted to scream at Ty to just pull it together. I just wanted to scream.

Cracking ice brought me back to the present. The layered winter wear had given me some protection against the fall but I could feel bruises forming but no sharp pains, nothing broken. I looked down. I couldn't see the bottom of the crevasse, and the ladder I'd tried to retrieve was long gone. Relief flooded through me, knocking out the frustration.

"Jo, are you okay? Are you hurt?" Sam's powerful voice came from above me. It sounded panicky like it wasn't the first time she'd yelled down.

"I'm here," I said. My voice sounded thin and weak. "I'm okay!" *Was I okay?*

I heard several voices above me, indistinct.

"We'll get you out but it's going to take a little bit of time," Sam called. "Hold tight. We'll get you out."

I didn't want to wait to be rescued. It pissed me off that I fell. Being at someone else's mercy wasn't acceptable. I knew the minute I knelt for the ladder that it was a bad idea. Too close to the edge. Rookie mistake. Dianna could have braced me for the ladder recovery. How could I ignore my own good sense? I couldn't be bothered to ask for help? Dianna and Elisabeth had been arguing the virtues of Belgian beers. Just one more of many arguments. I rationalized they weren't paying attention. Thank God Dianna was quick on her feet, or I would have pulled her into the gaping divide with me. Thirty feet of rope be damned. It had all happened so fast.

Countless images raced through my mind during the fall. My dad's smile. My mom's laugh. My assistant Sharon's face when she got the news she'd be working with me. Years of my aunt's emotionless face watching me. I shook my head. I need to concentrate on the here and now, not wallow. Ty was trying to meld us into a team. It wasn't working. If the team building failed, I wouldn't have to fulfill my commitment to Ty. Maybe I wanted her to fail. Maybe that was why I hadn't used my ice axe for stability before reaching for the ladder. Self-sabotage? No I didn't much care about the mission but I wanted my friend to succeed. Her dream was important.

Ice broke free beneath my left boot and my body swung into the wall. I pushed out with my right foot, centered myself and kicked hard with my left foot, driving the boot cleats hard into the ice wall. The left cleats held and I repeated the action with my right. I took a deep breath. I couldn't wait any longer. The cold was leaching heat from my body. Ice crackled around me. One way or another I had to get out of this hole.

I assessed my gear. My ice axes were still secured to my back and various other gear, including several lengths of strong, thin climbing cord—cordellete—that I used for anchors, was still safely attached by carabiners to my harness. I heaved a sigh of relief. Assuming the team above had me securely fixed, I could self-rescue.

As if in answer to my question, I heard Dianna's voice, strong and reassuring. "The ice is bad up here. It's going to be at least a half hour before we can pull you up. We need to stabilize the ice lip and create a firm anchor. Do you need anything? Are you hurt? Did the ladder hit you?"

"I'm okay. No injuries! I need to stay warm. I'm going to work on a self-rescue while you all figure things out up there." The rope dropped a bit. I yelped. "Hey!"

"Sorry! I said the ice was tricky up here. Go ahead but go easy."

Even the few minutes I spent getting myself together had sapped additional heat from my body. Ice climbing was out. Dianna was right. The ice was unpredictable. I didn't want to fall again. Wasting no more time, I started the setup for a prusik self-rescue. If the last few days gave any clue, rescue by the team would be awhile.

My mind on task, I unclipped a meter length of cordellete from my belt, tied it in a double fisherman's knot to provide a strong loop, and then created a prusik hitch by looping the doubled cordellete around the climbing rope that was the only lifeline between me and the abyss. My fingers were stiff inside my gloves. It made me clumsy, but I slowly wrapped the cord three times around the thin rope, looping it each time, making sure the fisherman's knot was offset and didn't create a weak point. I checked to see if I had formed a clean knot that looked a little like a big smile with a tongue of rope hanging out the mouth. With my waist prusik complete, I used a locking carabiner to attach it to my main harness loop.

I stopped for a moment and called out. "How are y'all doing up there?" The rope hadn't slipped again since the exchange with Dianna, and I was feeling a little more secure in my blue-white prison. It was silent except for the occasional popping and cracking of ice around me. No sounds from above. The light was fading as the afternoon wore on.

This time it was Ty who answered my call. "We're building a snow anchor up here, but Ingrid and Sam are in discussion on the best way to do this."

Great. Sam and Ingrid had been at loggerheads since the start of this week's adventure. Both were skilled at mountaineering techniques and neither was willing to give an inch. I heard the exasperation in Ty's voice, letting me know that the discussion was probably an argument and wouldn't resolve any time soon. I wanted her to take charge. Maybe it wasn't Ingrid. Maybe Ty had ulterior motives. Perhaps this was her form of team building. She was sneaky like that.

"Got it!" I called back. I was here to support her, but I wasn't going to just hang out while the team got their act together.

I unclipped a second two-meter cordellete from my harness. Folding and twisting the line, I completed the foot hold, attaching the loop to my harness via the locking carabiner. As I worked, my fingers warmed, making it easier to manage the cords. After putting the loop around my boot, I gave it a good tug to make sure it was secure and a final push on the carabiner to make sure the lock was engaged. Then I was ready to start up the rope.

"Ty!"

"Jo?"

"I'm going to start my self-rescue now."

There was a brief pause, then Ty yelled down to me, "Go slow. I'm not sure how good the temporary anchor is with the soft snow. What's not soft is icy."

As I rocked myself forward a little in my harness…the first step was always the hardest as everything adjusted…I set my stomach muscles, pushed and stood, pushing the prusiks one at a time up the rope. First the waist and then the foot. The prusik slipped. Blood pounding, I readjusted. Repeating the process, I made it about two feet up the rope with each step. Stand, push the waist prusik, then the foot prusik, repeat. Soon I was sweating, the lip of the crevasse within hand distance.

I called out to Ty. "Can you pull me the rest of the way or am I going to do this completely alone?" What were they doing up there?

Ty laughed. The first genuine laugh I'd heard from her on this trip. I could see her standing several feet from where the rope crested the edge, safely back if the ice lip had given way. "It's fun to watch a pro in action." She turned to the others. "Hey ladies, stop arguing and grab the rope. Jo's at the top and just needs a final pull to get over the edge."

Moments later, air exploded forcefully from my lungs as I was yanked over the edge of the crevasse onto a safe expanse of snow. I lay on my stomach, gasping for breath, trying to recover from the intensity of the pull. Christina came running, her black curls spilling out from under a thick woolen beanie, backpack already pulled off.

"You okay? Anything hurt?" Her hands roamed over my extremities with professional ease. She didn't wait for my reply.

I rolled over. Christina's intelligent, dark eyes assessed me. She was sexy and I wanted to reach for her and pull her down on top of me, her nearness and my near-death experience making my hormones explode. Instead, I pushed her hands away as I sensed the audience around me. She ignored my attempts to get away and continued her practiced review, oblivious to my raging hormones.

"Did you all have to put your backs into it?" I asked, my voice sharper than expected as I tried to ignore Christina's searching hands. The clean scent of her hair filled my nose as she leaned close. "I was almost at the top."

Ty chuckled. "This team doesn't do anything by halves. Anything we can do, we can overdo."

"Sorry about that Jo. When Ty said pull…well, several of us just grabbed and pulled," Elisabeth said, her slight German accent coming through in her excitement. "We were really tired of listening to Sam and Ingrid pontificate about snow anchors. We have two if you're interested. If you fall again, we can bring you up quickly."

"No broken bones," Christina said, pulling out a small flashlight from her pocket.

I tried to sit, only to be held in place by a firm hand. She flicked the flashlight in my eyes, two quick slashes, all business. Her beautiful, dark eyes missed nothing and made me nervous in ways I didn't want to examine too closely. Hormones.

I blinked rapidly. "I'm fine, really."

Christina looked to Ty. "No concussion. I'll want to assess again tomorrow."

"Patient here," I quipped. Both Christina and Ty ignored me.

Christina moved back and I could finally sit up to see three sets of people watching me. The team that had pulled me up comprised Elisabeth, Dianna, and Miho. Ingrid, her lips in a familiar scowl, stood over her snow anchor and towered over Rue beside her. Rue glanced at Ingrid, and then gave me a mischievous smile before she ducked her head. Over at the other anchor were Sam and Amy. Sam glared at Ingrid while Amy, dressed in an overabundance of clothing making her look like the Michelin man, checked out the anchor at their feet.

It seemed everyone was picking sides, even with the practical problem of saving me. Looking at the groups, I wasn't sure my self-rescue had won me any favors. At least I was out of the ice prison and relatively safe until the next crisis. We were all competent women. Anyone in this group could lead. Sam and Ingrid had pushed and Ty had stepped back, letting it happen. It was indicative of the entire trip and that pissed me off.

The surrounding light continued to fade as the late December sun sank below the tree line. The temperature around us was beginning to plummet and clouds from the east began a fast march toward us, as if chasing the fading sun. I shivered as the wind picked up.

"Let's head down to the tree line where there are some protective boulders," Ty said, shouldering her pack. "We're losing the light and we may have a storm tonight."

Ingrid scowled and looked like she was going to object but everyone was already pulling on packs and following Ty's instruction.

I got to my feet and followed suit. I shared a tent with Elisabeth and Dianna, the beer-drinking twins. It was good that I liked beer as it seemed to be one of their favorite conversation topics. Heading to the area Ty had indicated, Elisabeth picked a spot sheltered from the wind by several large boulders. Dianna pulled out the stakes and I took a few and went to the other side of the tent. We worked together, setting up the tent and staking it firmly against the winter elements. It took genuine effort as the cold leached heat and energy. Once the structure was up, we gladly threw our gear and ourselves inside.

"Who do you like for leader?" Dianna asked, her dark complexion made darker by the later afternoon shadows.

I looked up in surprise. No one had been quite this candid yet on the subject.

"Sam," Elisabeth said without turning from her pack.

"Why's that?" I asked, my head cocked to the side as I stared at her back.

"Because I can't stand Ingrid's arrogance."

"I think you'd be a good leader," Dianna said. "You listen and ask questions."

Elisabeth nodded her agreement.

"Not me, buddy," my reply emphatic and swift. "No way. I just fell into a crevasse. I don't think that's the best path."

Dianna and Elisabeth both laughed, though I wasn't sure if it was my vehemence or my words that caused it.

"Why not Ty?" I asked, not wanting to deal with the fear that didn't dissipate with their laughter. I didn't want to be responsible for anyone else, let alone a group of dynamic, accomplished women. I was here to support Ty. I tried to steady myself against the urge to run or hide.

Dianna pulled items from her pack. "I'd go with Ty if she took charge. She just seems to be waiting for us to give her the lead rather than taking it. Telling us to set up camp is the first time she's just made a decision and led."

"I agree," Elisabeth said. She unfurled her sleeping bag and crawled in, leaving only the wool beanie exposed. "You'd think I'd be good with the cold, having grown up in Heidelberg, but the cold just leaches in here." Her voice came out muffled by the layers over her face.

"Better get used to the cold," Dianna mused as she unrolled her own bag. "It's going to be nothing but cold at the pole."

There was a faint scratching at the tent flap. "Debrief on today's activities in Ty's tent in five," came Miho's voice through the fabric.

We all chorused acknowledgment, though Elisabeth grumbled as she struggled to free herself from her sleeping bag.

"This should be interesting," Dianna muttered. "Let's see if Ingrid takes over the conversation."

"I hope Sam or Ty step up and squash her," Elisabeth said emphatically. She pulled the flap open and we followed her out.

The wind was fierce. There would definitely be a storm tonight. Ty had called it.

Ty shared the largest tent with Christina, Miho, and Amy. There was enough room for all of us, but it was a tight squeeze. Ingrid, Sam, and Rue were already seated. Sam and Ingrid were on opposite sides, with Ingrid studiously ignoring her and her glares. We shuffled in and filled the available spaces. I moved next to Ty and gave her leg a friendly pat. It was warm and slightly humid inside the tent with all of us present, so we loosened our outer gear.

Ty waited until we settled before she began. "I won't keep you long as I'm sure we're all hungry and tired from today's adventure." She nodded to me. "What happened, Jo? Dianna said you were there and then you weren't."

I could feel all eyes on me. The light from several solar lanterns gave the group a soft glow. "I was pulling in the ladder and the snow edge gave way."

"Wasn't Dianna supposed to help with that?" Ingrid asked, an edge to her voice.

Dianna, sitting on my other side, looked like she was going to say something. I laid a hand on her leg. "It was my fault. I didn't stop and ask for help."

Ingrid looked on the verge of attacking the point again.

Sam jumped in first. "A good lesson learned." She looked at me and a tight smile plastered on her face. "The lesson?"

"Ask for help, don't take chances, always have a buddy," I said. And plant an ice axe for stability. "I knew that's exactly what I should have done as I was going over the edge." I turned to Dianna, who watched me with sad eyes. "Sorry I didn't ask for help. But how did I not pull you over the edge?"

Dianna's face turned fierce and she grinned, showing her white teeth. "When I felt the rope tug and pull me backward, I pulled my ice axes, hit the path spread eagle, and drove them into the ground. Just like Sam explained." She looked over at Sam and they exchanged a nod. "I still slid some before they really caught, soft snow and all."

"You saved my life," I smiled. "Thanks."

"If I'd had my mind in the game, you wouldn't have gone over at all."

"No harm, no foul," Ty said. "Okay, we lost a ladder and we'll have to report that. I've checked the activities for the rest of our outing and we shouldn't need it. What else did we learn today?"

"That Ingrid and Sam can both build unused snow anchors," Elisabeth said. "Ty, with respect, why did you let that happen? If we had combined forces, Jo wouldn't have had to rescue herself. Hell, if we'd stabilized the edge, we could have just pulled her up like we did when she self-rescued."

Heads swiveled and nine sets of eyes focused on Ty. The temperature in the tent seemed to rise.

Ty ran her hand through her short brown hair and sighed. "My style is to ask questions and lead through group exchange. Obviously, that style doesn't work for leading a trek. There isn't time to stop and ask for opinions. Today was a bit of a cluster. When we get to Antarctica, there will be issues when we have time to work things through and times when I'll need to just take command. I know that Ingrid and Sam are both up for the challenge of leading. I'll step down if you don't have confidence in me, but I think I can get us to Antarctica and prove that an all-woman team has what it takes to make this study a success. That's our ultimate goal." She looked at each member of the team.

I felt the need to stand up for Ty. "I'm good with your leadership. You're one of the reasons I joined this group and I think the mission is beyond cool."

There were murmurs of agreement around the tent. I saw Sam watching Ingrid for the slightest hint that she was going to take over, but Ingrid seemed content now that Ty had pushed forward. It was then that I understood Sam was good with Ty's leadership. She just wasn't going to roll over and let Ingrid take it. Something to watch for, as I liked Sam and didn't completely trust Ingrid, not where Ty was concerned anyway.

The morning after my misadventure was cold, clear, and beautiful. The storm had dumped a couple of feet of new snow. The wind had kept me up most of the night, and my mind spiraled on the confrontation in Ty's tent. Would Ty's plea for unity sway the team?

Ingrid and Sam were working together, digging out the sleds. They were each working on a different sled and seemed to be in competition to see who could dig her sled out first. Rue was busy starting the large gas-powered stove. It appeared that my teammates and I were the laggards this morning.

"Thought I'd let you sleep a little after your fall yesterday," Ty said, joining me. "Christina wants to check you out. Elisabeth, can you help with the sleds and Dianna please help Rue with breakfast? The tent can come down after Jo's checkup. I'd like to be out of here in an hour if we can get the stove water boiling."

Elisabeth shoved Dianna playfully. "You get the easy duty."

"Trade you," Dianna said, shoving Elisabeth back as she pulled on her North Face jacket and followed her out of the tent.

"Please ask Amy to help," Ty called after them as Christina walked up. "Let me know if there are any problems, Christina. And you," she stabbed a finger at me, "answer her questions. No holding back."

What am I? A child now that can't be responsible for myself or honest with the far too attractive doctor?

Christina moved easily around Ty, stepped into the tent, and zipped the door shut. "Okay, so how are you this morning?"

I started to say fine but this wasn't the time to prevaricate. I could state the facts and get this over quickly. I peeled up my smart wool shirt and pointed at the bruising around my waist. "Some bruising and some stiffness in my shoulders and hips."

Her cool fingers on my bruised right hip was pleasant and almost comforting. This surprised me as I was extremely ticklish and jumped whenever anyone even reached a hand toward my middle. It was one of the reasons I didn't like being touched casually by someone I didn't know, but her touch was firm, moving carefully—almost sensually—along the line of the bruise. I suppressed a shiver.

Her head was close to my chest and her black hair so close I could smell a light floral scent. She moved back to look me in the eye. "Are you up for the hike today?"

"Yes," I said and looked back into her dark, penetrating eyes. I could feel myself getting pulled in and quickly looked away, pulled my shirt down and tucked it into my snow pants.

Christina watched me dress. "Did you have bruising on your legs from the straps?"

"Yes, but the worst of it is on my hips," I said and pulled on my jacket. "I'm really fine. I'll monitor today and if I'm having problems, I'll let you or Ty know."

"From Rue's spreadsheet, I see you're not married. Are you seeing anyone?" she asked. Noting my surprise at the question, she added, "Ty said you had to answer all of my questions."

I chuckled then clutched my side. "Not seeing anyone. You?"

"No, Ty didn't say I had to answer *your* questions. You sure you're okay? Don't want to be medevacked out? Could be fun riding in a helicopter."

"You just want a free ride out. I'm fine." I raised my hand, my middle three fingers up and my thumb holding my pinky down. "Girl Scouts Honor."

Christina grinned. She shook a finger at me. "I'll be watching you."

I fluttered my eyelashes at her and her lips curled into a smirk. There was a warmth in my chest that hadn't been there before.

And that was how the rest of the trip went. Ty's declaration stopped Ingrid and Sam's war for leadership. They still sniped at each other but that seemed more personality-driven than hostile, almost like an old married couple who found a form of affection. They actually seemed to go out of their way to get in each other's space, which constantly amused the rest of the team. Even though Ty still seemed on edge, the team-building trip had done its job.

CHAPTER FIVE

Houston-July

"Don't you ever tire of the bullshit?" I asked without heat. The beer I was holding did not go with the one dress I owned—a black, mid-length, strappy number I'd kept for occasions such as this. The three-inch heels were already pinching my toes. I should have worn the flats but I so enjoyed towering over men.

"Suck it up. These events pay your salary," Ty said, elegant in a low-cut topaz dress with a topaz pendant hanging between her breasts to draw the eye. A change of pace from her normal slacks and button-up shirt.

"Remind me why we aren't lovers?"

Ty laughed. It was full-throated and the sound vibrated in my bones.

She was a beautiful woman, but neither of us was interested in a relationship. No chemistry. And I didn't really think she was over Ingrid. It explained Ty's issues with confronting her. I'd always heard makeup sex was the best, though Ty had sworn off a relationship—with Ingrid or anyone else—for the duration of the mission.

"Remind me why I'm here and when can I leave and get out of these stupid shoes?"

With a champagne glass in hand, Ty gestured around the room. "Cid needs to show off the teams to a lot of rich people. He wants to use this study as a jumping-off point for the commercialization of space. To do that, he needs support from rich or politically influential backers."

The hotel ballroom radiated glitz. Thirty-foot white drapes framed floor-to-ceiling windows that showcased the Houston skyline. Crystal chandeliers hung from the ceiling, casting a shimmering glow on the guests. Men in sleek dinner jackets and women in elegant couture mingled among the six opulent serving stations, offering a tantalizing array of gourmet delicacies, accompanied by an equal number of well-stocked bars. A six-piece orchestra played soft background music to accompany the murmured conversations.

There were three areas within the ballroom, one for each of the study teams. Cid wanted no contact between the groups, even here at this glad-handing. The investors could mingle freely, but all the teammates except for the leads had to stay in our respective corners.

Ty's eyes turned to the doorway as there was a pause in the conversation. There was tension, hunger, and anger in the searing look she gave Ingrid, who entered the room on the arm of Cid Balkner. She towered over the power broker, looking every inch the ice queen in an arctic blue dress with one shoulder bare. As she turned, the smooth skin of her back lay equally bare under Cid's meaty hand.

Sam stepped up next to me. "I think Ingrid's the only one who likes these events. Do you think he knows she's a lesbian?"

"Probably not. I see you escaped your handler." I traded my empty beer bottle for another as a server went by.

Sam stared around the room. "Just remember, you can't hide in this back corner all night." She tipped her wineglass to me and strolled back into the milling crowd.

Once Sam left, I turned to Ty to get her mind away from Ingrid. "What's this about commercializing space? Isn't it too early for that?"

"You'd think. But, the current NASA administrator knows government funding will be insufficient to do all the studies, testing, and training, let alone the actual mission without corporate sponsorship and push. Thus, I am wheeling and dealing with these people and that's why I get to go to all the parties. Be glad you're only forced to come to this one." Ty took another sip of champagne. "This is divine and something I will miss in Antarctica."

"I'd been meaning to ask you, not that I'm looking a gift horse in the mouth, but l still don't understand why Antarctica? This study could be done in so many more accessible environments and much cheaper."

Ty shrugged. "Cid's vision was to have separate teams living in isolation, each devising and proving renewable food systems while monitoring climate and geological phenomena. The backers are all on board. Studies like HI-SEAS have tremendous value, but there is always a safety valve. If there's a serious problem, someone can simply evacuate them. Not so with Antarctica. The investors want a place where the outcomes are serious and not easily managed, hostile, separate environments. They want to see how this affects the stress levels. Christina will monitor, as will I."

"I'm not complaining. Wintering over in Antarctica has always been a dream of mine."

We watched the crowd move like starlings on a summer evening.

"I went to a conference on space colonization last year." Ty watched the bubbles in her champagne glass.

"And what did you learn?"

"That the US is way behind in its thinking about the future, and China and Russia are playing the long game."

When I didn't comment, she faced me and continued. "Take the Arctic. The Northwest Passage is thawing earlier and earlier every year. Call it climate change, global warming, natural progress, I don't care. Earth's oceans are warming and the normal, whatever normal is, weather patterns are transforming. Russia and China are moving to exploit these changes: building icebreaker ships, planting flags, deploying troops, and doing training exercises in places where it's prohibited. And no one is stopping them. Treaties only have force when they are enforced."

"So what are you saying?"

"I'm saying that unless the US gets its act together, Russia and China, but mostly China, will have moved so far forward into these spaces that only an actual war will stop them. Without will, diplomacy won't have any effect. The US isn't the power it used to be. We don't have the will."

"Should we police the world?"

"Great question and I have no simple answers, but I know that the Russians and the Chinese do not look at human rights, individual rights, the same way we do." She took a slow sip and added, "China came late to The Antarctica Treaty. They signed on in 1983. Since then, they've built four Antarctica bases in Australia and claimed territory for another one coming on line in a few months. There's been indications of mining surveys. If we can't hold the line in the Arctic, how much '*will*' do you think we'll have if China pushes the boundaries in Antarctica?"

"This isn't our problem, is it? Our mission is to research food crops and to study the effects of global warming on the South Pole ice sheet, all while living under isolation in a hazardous environment."

"You're right." Ty finished her glass of champagne.

"Right about what?" Christina slid in next to me. She wore a dark, sea-foam green dress that clung to her curves. Her dark hair, normally tied back, cascaded in a thick wave over her bare shoulders. She reminded me of Sandra Oh on *Grey's Anatomy* with her dark eyes and full lips, but with more intensity, if that was possible. Energy seemed to vibrate off her.

I took an involuntary swallow and choked as beer went down the wrong pipe.

Sam pounded me on the back, which did little to help. "Look who I found."

"I just came by to let you know I'm headed to Tangiers for a month or so. I'll be back before the team heads to Christchurch." Christina swept a hand through her hair as she gave me a once-over and smiled. "I hate these types of events."

We gazed around at the theater playing out around us. People vied for Cid's attention as he shepherded Ingrid with him from group to group. Miho, Dianna, and Rue congregated around a snowy-haired woman with too much jewelry, who gestured wildly. Amy sat at a table with her phone in her hand. And Elisabeth was chatting up the bartender at the craft brew station.

A thin woman with dishwater blond hair and a slash of red lipstick that didn't suit her sallow complexion drifted over and spoke directly to Ty, ignoring the rest of us, like we didn't exist. "I need the logistics presentation checked and on my desk Monday."

Ty's shoulders tensed. "It's already on your desk, Evelyn. I don't know that you've met everyone on the team. Samantha Rodriguez, one of our biology specialists. Dr. Christina Sohn, our team doctor. And Jo Peterson, our extreme weather meteorologist. The rest of the team is around here somewhere."

Evelyn Cable was our mission lead in Houston, responsible for supporting us when we were in Antarctica. Yet she'd never taken the time to meet with any of us. Ty had worked with her on a previous program and had spoken highly of her. However, I'd seen some of the crap reports and presentations she'd left for Ty to check. I wasn't impressed. The work was subpar and full of mistakes, forcing Ty to handle her work and Evelyn's too.

"Pleasure, I'm sure. I need to talk with Cid. I'll see you in my office first thing Monday," she ordered before she stalked away.

"What's up with her?" I probably shouldn't have said it, but the woman pissed me off, treating my friend like an engineering flunky.

Ty's lips tightened and she cast me a warning glance before redirecting her gaze to our team doctor. "Christina, there's a lot to do before Christchurch. There are training exercises to complete and medical supply lists I need."

"I'll have access to a computer. John will have my contact information."

"Did I hear my name?" John Steinman said. He was tall, with pale blue eyes and blond hair. In charge of all the teams, he had taken the time to meet with us as a team and individually. The interaction was brief and superficial, but at least he'd made an effort.

"Do you think it's a good idea for Christina to be gone during this critical time?" Ty asked.

"There's an emergency, and Christina is the best person to handle it. I'll make sure she has time to complete anything critical before your departure." His tone conveyed no room for further discussion. "Christina, I need a few words before you catch your plane."

Christina nodded to us before following John out of the ballroom. I stared after her.

"I need another drink," Sam said.

Ty waited until Sam was out of earshot. "Did you know Rebecca wanted to take Christina and give us Dr. Connie Charles?"

"Rebecca Cassidy, the mission lead for the mixed team?"

Ty pointed across the room to a short woman in a red dress. "Yep."

"Did she say why?"

"Dr. Charles is more seasoned and a better fit for our team," Ty said.

"Do you believe that?"

"No."

"Then, stay strong. John Steinman brought Christina on specifically for us."

Ty nodded, looking thoughtful.

"That it?"

"Are you aware of the emails?" she asked. I shook my head and she said, "There have been protests against our women's team. Bad press for GICE. There have been discussions that our team's mission should be canceled."

"What's Mr. CEO say?"

"Cid looked like he might agree until John defended us. John also came down hard on Rebecca. Christina is staying with us."

"Do you think Rebecca and George will get Cid to cancel? John is great, but..." I looked into Ty's tired eyes. "What did our team manager, Evelyn, say?"

"John is standing up for us. He holds more sway with Cid," Ty said. "Evelyn was silent."

"Is this where all the cool people are hanging out?" a man's voice boomed. George Weller, head of the men's team, had come by my lab several times. His questions concerning my sensors were thoughtful, if a little annoying. I could never tell if he was asking questions to gain information or challenging my knowledge. "You all know Todd, my right-hand man?"

Todd Schwartz was a beefy guy who didn't fit well in the off-the-rack suit he was wearing. He worked for George and was nice enough. I'd heard him talking fondly of his wife and kids when I'd passed him in the breakroom.

"George, Todd. Are you enjoying the party?" Ty snagged another champagne flute from a server.

"Cid's still working some money issues. Beggin' your pardon, girls, but I'm not real happy with this last-minute add of John's. I think two teams are all that are needed for this study. What do you say, Todd?"

Ty stepped in before Todd could offer an opinion. "It's *women*, not girls, George. And we have discussed this several times. It is necessary and we are going." Ty turned to Sam and me. "Please excuse us. I see Cid signaling us to join him." She strode toward the head of GICE Corp, not waiting to see if George and Todd would follow her.

"Um, sorry girls, I mean ladies." George turned and, with Todd trailing in his wake, followed Ty.

"Ladies. Really? I'm glad I'm not team lead," Dianna said, coming up to stand next to us. "At least Ty is sticking up for us. She's got the patience of a saint. I'd have slugged a few people by now."

I nodded, glad Dianna had heard George's comments. Ty's deft exit reminded me of my own graceless one earlier in the week.

Ty had come in from a marathon meeting with the Houston mission leads and dropped into my guest chair. "I'm not cut out to be the leader of this group."

Since Switzerland, I'd been carrying the same concern. Ty was great at logistics and organization, and she could handle the politics, but that wasn't leading. She was more concerned with everyone getting along than making the hard decisions.

"Hey, Jo," Sam said, striding up to my cubicle. "What's the web address for that plant recycling system you mentioned last week?" Seeing Ty, she added, "Hey, Ty."

I accessed the site and sent it to her. "Check your email."

"Thanks." Sam patted the cubicle wall and left.

"Everyone comes to you for information and advice. Even me." Ty's voice was thoughtful. I could feel her appraisal.

"Whatever you're thinking, stop."

"What?"

"Just stop."

She pursed her lips and frowned at me. "I'm allowed to think."

"Remember me? I know how your mind works, and I'm not interested."

"You'd be a good leader for this mission," she said still assessing me. "It's going to practically run itself."

"Right. The politics would kill me. You thrive in the minutiae. You'll do fine with leading the group."

"Jo, at some point, you're going to have to get over…"

"Stop! We're not talking about this." My words came out in an angry hiss.

Ty raised her hands in a placating gesture. "Their deaths weren't your fault, not your parents, not Sharon's. You know that, don't you? Nobody could have predicted those events."

I stabbed my finger at the cubicle opening. She raised her hands once more and offered a look of sympathy that made me want to grind my teeth. Then she left.

Rubbing my hands over my face, I tried to wipe the words from my mind. It was my fault my parents were gone and Sharon was on me too. A temper tantrum had saved me from the car ride that had killed my parents. A few minutes difference either way and there never would have been an accident. And Sharon died on my watch. My team. My first team. The sound of roaring water filled my ears. An embankment crumbling. Sharon smiling before she was gone. Too close to the river. Too close. Sharon had died because of a decision I'd made. Or failed to make. They had died because of me.

I leaped up and charged down the hall, taking the opposite path to the stairwell. I had to get out. I needed to be somewhere else. I wasn't going to be trapped into making decisions again, taking responsibility for others. No way. The emergency door loomed in front of me. I was tempted to just shove through, alarms be damned, but instead I turned sharply and headed back up the steps, down the corridor, fluorescent lights turning on with my passage. I could see Ty's lone office light on but ignored it as I stalked down the main stairwell and into the half-lit lobby. I flashed my badge and exited the building, heading toward my car, keys already in hand, ready to quit this program.

Then I stopped.

I could feel my body tremble with the need to keep moving. I took a deep breath and then another. I had made a promise. Running wasn't an option. When I had accepted Ty's offer, I had accepted helping her. Not leading. Never leading.

Tonight, as I'd watched Ty converse with Cid, I knew she was the right person to lead this mission and I wouldn't let her weasel out of her role as the head of this team. I owed it to her.

There was more at stake than just this mission. Ty needed someone she knew and could count on. She had history with the others, but it was to me she turned to consistently. I would be on my guard and supporting her against whatever happened.

CHAPTER SIX

Christchurch, New Zealand-November

Three months later, we flew into McMurdo Station on a Tuesday in late November. It was becoming a reality, this journey to Antarctica. I was eager and excited in equal measures, followed by feeling deflated as the weather prevented us from leaving. As far as I knew, Christina was still in Tangiers, but John Steinman had assured Ty she would arrive in time. It felt like our lives were hanging in the balance. Every morning we'd woken up believing that today would be the day to leave for McMurdo, only to get the news that between extreme cold and poor flying conditions, no flights were going out. After four days of waiting, my cell phone rang, waking me from a deep slumber after nights of sleeplessness. Knocking my phone off the hotel nightstand, I fell half out of bed, grabbing for it. Caller ID identified Ty and I swiped to accept the call.

"Hey." My voice sounded groggy from sleep.

"Pack up. The bus taking us to the Christchurch Airport will be here at seven a.m."

"Christina?"

"She will meet us at the airport."

I whooped, but Ty had already hung up.

Christina's arrival had been a source of concern. Endless debate by GICE mission staff had ensued about what it would mean for the team and the mission if she didn't arrive. John had said she'd make it. If Christina didn't make it, I wasn't sure that any of us would be getting on the plane to Antarctica. Ty had received an email from Cid, no doubt orchestrated by Houston mission leads Rebecca and George, Evelyn's counterparts supporting the other teams, questioning whether it was acceptable to start the mission without a doctor present. So many things could go wrong and not having a doctor present raised the stakes. John's calm attitude had kept the other Houston-based mission leads' rhetoric from escalating. I just felt a wash of relief.

And then anticipation. I missed Christina. She was irreverent and funny and didn't take herself too seriously. And she smelled divine. *Where did that come from?*

Needing to talk to someone, I called Elisabeth. She answered on the third ring. Her loud yell had me pulling the phone from my ear.

"Got the call from Ty, I take it?" It was becoming real in my mind that we were finally going to start the real mission. No more waiting. No more wondering.

"Yes, yes, we're finally getting to go," Elisabeth said. "This is exciting." I heard an indistinct voice in the background.

"Your friend from last night still there?" I asked.

"Yes, yes. He's leaving." There was a deep male laugh and then a door clicked shut. "Can we talk later? I've still got to shower and call my mom."

Parents. Family. Friends. I didn't have anyone I wanted to call. Images of a stoic police officer standing in my childhood home murmuring the dreaded words, "Your parents are dead. I'm so sorry for your loss." I shied away from the images conjured by my tired mind. I could call my aunt. My mind flitted to the letter in my backpack. I hadn't thrown it away, probably to torment myself. Thoughts flicked to the rage on my aunt's face as she threw my suitcase onto the lawn. No I wasn't ready to go there, not yet. Maybe never.

With a last look at my backpack, I took my final long hot shower. I love showers, but in Antarctica, every drop of water had to be melted and collected. I knew showers were going to be short and few. I stayed in the hotel shower, luxuriating in the heat and pounding water for over fifteen minutes before reluctantly turning the water off. I toweled my hair dry and put on what would be my go-to clothing, cargo pants with large pockets on the thighs for miscellaneous gear and a long-sleeve, Merino base layer.

I could feel myself getting antsy, so I checked my gear yet again.

On the plane, I'd have on my fleece jacket, down jacket and our extreme cold weather gear for when we landed at McMurdo. They didn't include the survival gear in the personal fifteen-pound carry-on allotment, nor what I carried on my person. With that thought, I stuffed my cargo pockets with a few Snickers bars, two extra camera batteries, three plane-size bottles of vodka, a small, lined journal, and a couple of pens. I could have put these in my carry-on but I was already at the limit. I shifted my stowed gear carefully so my pockets didn't bulge too badly.

On the bed were my discards—extra packaging, an unopened liter bottle of vodka, some extra clothing that would be left at the hotel in long-term storage, a feature of the hotel, which many Antarctica travelers used. It was as good as it was going to get. I knew there would be things I never used and other things that I wish I had brought, but I was tired of rethinking it all. I was antsy.

There was a pounding at the door. I pulled it open to find Ty standing there.

"Do you have any extra memory cards?"

I waved her in and sorted through my pack. I had decided I couldn't have too many thumb drives or memory cards, and they packed easy.

She took what I offered but didn't leave. "Jo, are you ready for this?"

"I'm packed and was just getting ready to go down and grab some breakfast."

I waved to the large duffel on the bed, knowing full well that wasn't what she was asking. She was asking if I was ready to be isolated without room to run or hide for thirteen months. She stared at me. She hadn't come for the cards. She was checking on me like a good leader should. The moments dragged at me.

"I'm good, Ty. You can count on me." I wasn't going to bolt. I just didn't know if I was ready.

With a last long look, she left. I stared at the bed and then began storing the discards in a small duffel wondering again what I'd really gotten myself into.

I half dragged, half carried my eighty-five-pound bag out of my hotel room and down the hallway to the luggage cart. Two bags were already loaded and I turned, hearing heavy, even treads coming up behind me. Ingrid's bag was as large, and I'm sure as heavy as mine, but she had it easily slung up on her shoulder. She smiled as she pulled her duffel from her shoulder and laid it carefully on the pile. Not saying a word, she took mine, and without difficulty, set it on top of hers. She wore gear similar to mine—cargo pants and a Smartwool shirt, which she made look elegant rather than slapped together. Her pants pockets lay flat and didn't have the chipmunk look that was noticeable in mine.

"Breakfast," Ingrid said, her voice clipped as she motioned to the stairs at the end of hallway, as two more hotel doors opened, disgorging our fellow teammates.

"Sounds good unless you plan to play sherpa," I said, nodding at Elisabeth and Miho, who were dragging their bags toward the cart. Miho's bag looked as big as she was and I wasn't sure how she was going to manage.

Ingrid grabbed Miho's duffel and added it to the pile. I helped Elisabeth load hers on the cart.

"We're headed to breakfast," I said.

"Excellent," Miho said, nodding her thanks to Ingrid. "I had to get out of my room or I'd try to add one more thing and I'm over by almost a pound now."

Breakfast was a boisterous occasion. The hotel started breakfast at five thirty a.m., which was unusually early for a tourist hotel, but this one catered to military and Antarctica travelers with early flights. Ty had beaten us down and was sitting with Dianna at a table for ten. There was a buffet of eggs, yogurt, fruit, breads, cheeses, and other breakfast foods along one wall of the large room, food we wouldn't have available to us during our next twelve to thirteen months of isolation.

The space was full of other diners, including what looked like another expedition group busily packing in their last few calories before heading to the airport. There would be a hundred of us on the plane, mostly summer crews. I had to remember it was summer in the southern hemisphere. These people were heading to work the round-the-clock shifts moving cargo, and maintaining mechanical and electrical systems, as well as the scientists responsible for the numerous experiments currently in progress. And then there was us—the three Mars isolation teams taking thirty of the precious seats.

We hadn't spent any time at GICE with the other teams. Other than casual hellos in the GICE hallways, we hadn't mingled. No shared training. No attempts to make friends. The mission managers didn't want there to be any comradery or relationships between the teams. No desire to unite in Antarctica under isolated conditions. No place to run if things got tough or messy.

"I heard we're traveling with some of the new astronomers searching for meteorites on the ice. They were talking last night about the extreme rock hunting they'll be doing for the next month," Miho said, helping herself to the fruit on the buffet tables. "Frank, the guy I was talking with last night, said that Antarctica gets several hits every year."

"Antarctica is pretty big," I said. "I doubt we'll see strikes near our hab."

We finished filling our plates and moved to join Ty and Dianna. We still had an hour before the bus departed, but it seemed that we were all in a hurry to eat, get our leftover gear checked in, and ourselves to the meeting location.

"Anything new?" I asked Ty, around a mouthful of eggs.

She shook her head and took a sip of coffee. "The weather cleared unexpectedly. I got the notice a few minutes before calling you all. The officer I spoke with told me that the flight could still be canceled if the weather changed but to get the team to the airport departure area by eight a.m."

Delays were normal. Though a month into the season, a four-day hit was long and expected to be longer when the weather report was issued yesterday.

"Anything from Evelyn?" I asked. "I know you had some last-minute concerns. Did she get back to you on the new threats?"

Miho's head came up. "What threats?"

"There was some recent email traffic with obnoxious statements about a woman's place being at home." I ducked my head in embarrassment, thinking of Miho leaving her kids with her mom to come on this mission.

"Nothing I haven't heard before," Miho said. She pushed her plate away and stood. "I'm going to go check on our bus."

"Smooth," Dianna said, shaking her head at me.

"Hey, it was directed at all of us not at Miho specifically," I said. "But yeah, that was stupid of me."

We were finishing up when the rest of the team, minus Christina, arrived. Elisabeth came over to the table.

"Bag trouble," Elisabeth said, waving a hand toward Amy, who was busy reviewing her muffin choices at the buffet. "We had to do an intervention to get her to give up her gear."

The group laughed. Everyone had learned how meticulous Amy was with everything. She created lists of lists. Amy laughed about it but that didn't keep her from checking things multiple times to make sure calculations and measurements were precise and accurate. I'd wondered more than once if it was compulsive behavior, but I hadn't felt like it was any of my business. I wasn't the lead.

The bags to be checked were already on board the airport bus when we filed through the lobby. Each of us took turns checking to see that our bags were in the bus's stowage area. Amy checked twice, physically touching each bag and the luggage tags.

The ride to the airport was uneventful and the plane was waiting for us, as expected. Several other groups were milling about the area calling out greetings and huddling around bags. I looked for Christina but didn't see her in the crush of people. When it became evident the plane personnel weren't going to weigh the carry-ons, I pulled everything out of my pockets and stowed it in my backpack.

All outerwear gear had to go through a final vacuum and boot scrub before boarding. The Antarctica Treaty was very specific about bringing foreign contaminants onto the continent. We had already signed an agreement indicating that our stowed gear had been cleaned and vacuumed of any potential hazards. I expected that they would irradiate the gear before it was loaded onto the plane.

After a final briefing, welcoming us to Antarctica via massive video screens placed strategically in the gate area, we made our way through a security checkpoint and down to the bus that would take us to the plane. The Boeing C-17 Globemaster was a beast carrying each of the teams, plus scientists and support personnel coming to work at McMurdo, or Amundsen-Scott Pole Stations. Every seat was filled with standbys ready to take slots if someone was dumb enough to miss the flight. The plane carried about seventy-seven tons of cargo, including some provisions we would be taking with us to Pole Station.

Dianna marched beside me, her smile infectious. "Are you ready?"

Truth be told. I was scared. The knots in my stomach had knots. My last chance to run.

"I'm okay."

She shook her head at me. "No, you're not. Have you heard or read about the South Pole Traverse?" I shook my head. "Getting provisions and cargo to Amundsen-Scott Pole Station is expensive. They built a 955-mile compact snow road between McMurdo and the South Pole. It takes forty days minimum to traverse. One way."

"And that's cheaper than flying? You'd think paying for people and fuel to drive for eighty days would be expensive."

"Flying is expensive. The habitat modules are large at twenty-by-forty feet with five modules for each group, including the power plant, which is several tons. The ice road was the best bet."

"I'm just glad the habs are already set up."

"Oh, we'll have plenty of setup left."

We clambered off the bus and walked between the cones to the plane. I was sweating again. It was summer in Christchurch and fifty degrees, but we had been warned that the plane had minimal heating so I had dressed accordingly. But it was more nerves than temperature that had me on edge.

Dianna looked up at the plane that would be taking us to McMurdo Station. "Have you ever been on a C-17 before?"

"Nope. It seems massive."

"Great planes. We used a few to carry supplies into Namibia. They can land on really short, harsh runways."

"Dianna."

She turned her gaze from the plane to me. "Yeah?"

"Thanks for distracting me."

She bumped my shoulder. "Get on the plane."

The interior of the C-17 was configured with four rows of seats. Two rows were along the exterior walls, with a back-to-back seating configuration down the middle of the plane. The two aisles were wide enough for two people to pass carefully, but there were no storage bins and backpacks and other gear made moving around hazardous. The only windows were in the main airplane doors. I entered the plane and quickly found a seat between Rue and Dianna on an interior wall.

After fastening my seat belt, I looked up to see Christina. She looked great. Dark hair wild above her angular face. She looked tanned and relaxed. Her warm smile at me made my body temp rise. No chance to talk as the crew directed the passengers to take their seats and hear the safety procedures before takeoff.

Then, I spent the next four hours surreptitiously watching Ingrid and Christina, who were across from me, in the center aisle. The seats were relatively comfortable with wide armrests but they didn't recline at all. This was a military plane, not a commercial flight, and it was noisy, so talking with my immediate neighbors wasn't really an option. I couldn't sleep and was too wound up to read, although I pretended to do so as I snuck peeks at Ingrid and Christina. Both of them fascinated me.

Ingrid was beautiful but in an unattainable, too perfect way. What had brought her and Ty together? Ty was so down-to-earth and approachable. Ingrid was anything but that, from her clipped British accent to the way she seemed to look down on everyone from her towering height. Maybe I was just jealous that she was taller than me. They didn't seem to have anything in common. Ingrid and Ty were like oil and water, mixing only when shaken together, only to separate again just as quickly. Ty still wouldn't talk to me about it. How would they deal with the forced proximity? Not well if the past few months were any indication. Ingrid's eyes had tracked Ty's movements whenever she was near. Ty had maintained a professional demeanor—focused but distant.

Christina was mysterious. She seemed at once a part of the group and yet above the fray. When she was present, I felt attuned to my body, hyper-aware of my clothes against my skin and the heat in my face when she'd glance toward me. She was also beautiful but in a more exotic, sensual way. Her eyes were so dark as to be almost black, yet were full of intelligence and mischief.

Back during a training, I had caught Christina switching Ty's black coffee for Miho's triple sugar coffee while chatting them up. Her sleight of hand was so smooth and her face so intent on their joint conversation. She had seen me come in and had given me a sly wink. I was so surprised I'd had to stifle a laugh. Then Ty and Miho had taken sips from their switched coffees, with Ty practically spitting it across the room. I laughed out loud. Miho had grimaced and set the cup down.

I snuck another look at the two women. Christina must have felt my eyes on her, as she lifted her head from the medical journal she'd been reading. I quickly looked back down at my own reader but I could feel her watching me. She was the one I found most intriguing. She seemed aloof and watchful but able to intuit exactly what someone needed at the perfect time. I snuck another peek, and she gave me a half smile before returning her attention to her medical journal.

I could feel my face burning and I looked over at Ingrid, who had seen the exchange and was watching me as well. I wasn't sure how to feel about that. Ingrid wasn't interested in me but her stare was disconcerting. My closeness with Ty didn't sit well with her. Christina hadn't indicated one way or another, but I knew her last relationship had ended before the trip to Christchurch. The gender hadn't been indicated. My internal radar was pinging gay but a mistake could be embarrassing, not that anything could or should happen during the mission. Christina was the mission doctor and I was there to support Ty. If only my body would listen.

Rue woke up from her nap and poked me in the side.

"What?" I asked.

"How long was I asleep?" The noise in the plane's hold was loud and I could barely hear her question.

I checked my watch. "At least four hours."

She nodded and yawned, closing her eyes once again. Rue could sleep anywhere, regardless of the noise and vibrations around her.

I poked her in the side and her eyes popped open. "You've slept enough. I need data."

She gave me an appraising look. "What data?"

"Personal," I whispered.

"What?"

Both Ingrid and Christina looked up at Rue's loud question.

I sat still, eyes on my book, and after a few moments, they both went back to their reading.

"What kind of data?" Rue asked, her voice pitched such that the noise of the plane muffled the words.

"I want to know…Is Christina gay?"

"Look, I briefed you all in Houston two months ago on everyone and sent all of you my perfectly correlated spreadsheet." She gave me a look and then looked over at Christina.

"I didn't see her sexual preference listed."

Rue shrugged and gave me a look like a disapproving teacher. "Not everyone filled out their forms."

After we'd signed on to the mission, Rue had given each of us a questionnaire to fill out. It had been optional and somewhat annoying. I had filled out about half before I had given it back to her. Two months ago, Rue had given us a rundown of information on people. Correlations on our likes and dislikes. Seemed everyone loved *Star Trek* and *Star Wars*. We had one vegan, Miho; one vegetarian, Dianna, and two pescatarians, Ingrid and Ty. An even mix of introverts and extroverts. Miho was the only one with kids. Dianna and Miho were both divorced. The rest of us had never been married. Sam and Rue came from big families. Seemed Amy had filled hers out fully and Christina hadn't. I had gotten tired of filling it out after page ten. Who cared if I liked pickled beets?

"You told us that Amy was pansexual," I said.

"She put in on her questionnaire. It's open source." Rue closed her eyes. "Christina didn't, so it's her own business. Ask her if you want to know."

Before I could wheedle more information out of Rue, an announcement from the main deck blared through the hold. "We'll be landing at McMurdo Station in twenty minutes. Please put on your cold weather gear and secure for landing."

I pulled on my thick, padded outer pants, then the blue extreme cold weather boots, otherwise known as bunny boots, then topped it with the orange parka with simulated fur hood, and lined gloves, all standard issue from the NSF who operated Pole Station.

The landing at Ross Island Airfield, a compacted snow runway, was hard and fast. I was glad for all the gear as the outer door opened and the icy air swirled into the plane. I collected my stuff and pulled the hood over my head, snugging the gaiter over my lower face, and the goggles over my eyes before following Ingrid off the plane. Her elevated height made her an excellent windbreak. Christina was at my back.

Ty pulled us out of the exiting crowd and we huddled close for perceived warmth. The plane broke some of the wind coming across the frozen landscape. It was definitely a lot colder than I had ever experienced and I could feel tiny ice pellets hitting every exposed part of my face, like sand in a desert wind.

"We've got four hours before our flight leaves for Pole Station, so be back here in three," Ty said. She turned and pointed toward a Lockheed LC-130 sitting off to the side of the runway. "Our next plane is being serviced and might complete earlier. If you want a T-shirt from McMurdo, go get it at the gift shop. Yes, they have a gift shop, if you can believe it. Eat something in the cafeteria. I need someone to stay with me to make sure our gear gets transferred properly."

I was freezing but both Dianna and I stepped forward immediately. "I'll help," I blurted before Dianna could.

Ty looked at us both. She nodded to me. "Thanks. Dianna, can you be back in two hours? We'll need to monitor the loading as well, and I'd like a quick break before we head out."

Dianna nodded and then headed into the main McMurdo Station building with the rest of the team.

Ty watched them leave with their backpacks and then turned to me. "So how was your flight?"

"Same as yours I expect."

"Really?" She eyed me. "I slept, except for the few minutes I watched you watching Ingrid and Christina."

As my face was almost fully covered, she couldn't see my blush, though I could feel my face heat up. Maybe I should spend the next thirteen months blushing. At least it kept my face warm. "I find them both interesting people," I mumbled through all of my layers.

"Just don't play them off each other," she said, looking over to where American military personnel were pulling luggage from the C-17. "It won't go well for any of us."

She pushed her goggles up on her head and her steady brown eyes focused on my goggles. "Be careful. Ingrid is very possessive. I'm not sure about Christina but she doesn't seem the kind to share either. I'm the leader of this merry band and am going to stay out of the sexual fray. Ingrid knows that." She shook her head and turned back to watch the cargo handlers. "I think that was part of the trouble at our team building exercise in Switzerland. She wanted me to react…and didn't like it when I didn't."

Her mention of Christina set me wondering. I wanted to read a lot into her comment. However, as her friend and sounding board, I needed to focus on her relationship with Ingrid. "Did you talk with her about it?"

Ty watched as the plane maintenance crew joined the cargo handlers. "No."

"Why not? Thirteen months is a long time to be isolated with a woman you aren't talking to."

She looked like she was going to say more but one of the military types was waving her over. She slid her goggles back over her eyes and started toward him. I trailed in her wake bending into the wind. Geez, it was cold. And this was summer.

CHAPTER SEVEN

En Route-November

"Do you think they'll like the bears?" Miho showed me the T-shirts, stuffed animals, and patches she'd purchased at the McMurdo gift shop for her kids.

Though the LC-130 was configured like a commercial plane, the next leg of our journey to Pole Station was still noisy and cramped. I sat next to Miho, who was staring critically at the presents she had bought.

"Are they going to get confused with the Arctic?" I asked back with amusement. "No polar bears in Antarctica."

Her eyebrows knit in concentration. "Guess I should have gotten the penguins."

"They'll love the bears. How old are they? Do you have pictures?"

She glowed with motherly pride. "Alicia is ten and Brandon is eight." She pulled pictures up on her phone and held it out to me.

As I took the phone from her and eyed the pictures, she leaned toward me, swiped through them. "Brandon is into reading and skateboarding." She paused at a picture of a cute kid, in board shorts caught mid-action doing a board flip, black hair flying. She swiped again and stopped at a picture of a miniature version of herself, an elfin face with big dark eyes surrounded by shoulder-length black hair, her hand reaching for a cookie on a tray. The picture seemed to catch the child unaware, with a mischievous glint in her eye. "She was sneaking a cookie after I'd told her to wait until after dinner."

I glanced at Miho's face and saw her smile grow tender. "How do they feel about you being gone for so long?"

She glanced up at me and then back to the phone as she continued to swipe through pictures. She stopped at one with the two kids holding a poster with an older woman behind them. The poster read "We'll miss you Mommy." A tear ran down her face and she wiped it away quickly. "They'll be with my mom." She took the phone from me and continued looking at pictures.

"How do you feel?" I asked tentatively.

She shut down the screen and pushed the phone back into her bag.

"I need to do this. Raising sustainable plant food in small spaces is incredibly important and it's something I've studied for years. The study of physical changes caused by isolation is also central to the mission. Being a mom, how I deal with the stressors is vital for the formulation of future missions. This is groundbreaking stuff. Just because I'm a mother doesn't mean that I should put my life and work on hold."

There was a defensiveness to her voice, as if she was reviewing a list of reasons she repeated to convince others and maybe even herself.

"I think it's going to be hard regardless. I don't have kids and the thought of being isolated from all the things I do and having limited contact with friends and family...seems daunting. Not being able to call someone spontaneously but having to plan the call. Based on our training simulation, we've got less than four hours of daily satellite coverage, and most of that's for work conversations. Having to wait twenty minutes between our send and their response. And certainly, no quick trip to the store to pick something up. Isolated...as if we were really on Mars." I smiled at her. "Having kids just adds one more layer to that isolation," I finished lamely.

She nodded and then turned away from me to look out the window.

I sighed inwardly. *Great job Jo. First day out and you're already adding to the isolation.*

Miho turned back to me and patted my hand on the armrest between us. "Thanks for letting me know I'm not the only one who is thinking about being separated from my loved ones. Can I talk to you about it if I get overwhelmed?"

I nodded, turning my hand over and giving her hand a light squeeze before releasing it. "Of course, I'm happy to listen."

Amundsen-Scott South Pole Station Antarctica wasn't what I expected. Well, it was and it wasn't. I wasn't expecting to feel the elevation of 9,301 feet above sea level in my lungs. It wasn't overwhelming, just very noticeable as I swung my backpack to my shoulders and followed Miho out of the plane into the bright white landscape. Our habitat module, or hab, was located about two miles north of the main base. Close but not too close. It was weird thinking "north" since pretty much everything was north when you're at the South Pole.

Once again Ty pulled us together as soon as we were off the plane. It was colder than it had been at McMurdo. The pilot had announced the temperature as minus thirty degrees Celsius with winds at five knots, which, with some quick math, came out to about minus twenty-two degrees Fahrenheit with a nice wind chill factor that probably pulled the felt temperature down to minus thirty- or forty-degrees Fahrenheit. And this was summer. It was hard to imagine the cold as the sky was a brilliant blue. Ty looked ready to speak and then looked at our goggled faces and shook her head and waved us to follow her as she headed for the main Scientific Research facility that seemed built on massive pylons protecting it from drifting snow. It was a two-story industrial gray complex with big square windows. An American flag flew proudly from a pole planted next to a sign that read Geographic South Pole.

Ty led us up the steps through a door with a heavy latch into the anteroom, then through a second door into an area for outerwear, where we divested ourselves of our orange parkas, goggles, gloves, and assorted hats. It was like the old scene of people getting out of a VW bug. Finally, she led us up a second staircase to a long hallway with group shots of each year's winter over crews. I wanted to stop and stare but she pulled a door open and we all filed into a regular, could be anywhere, conference room.

Christina moved to one of the enormous windows and looked outside. The rest of us took seats around the big conference room table.

"Can you join us?" Ty said to Christina.

Christina turned to look at her then back to the view out the window. Reluctantly, she took a seat at the table between Dianna and Elisabeth.

"Okay we're here! We move out to our hab module after dinner. We'll have three days of exchanges and checkout before we go into isolation." Ty surveyed everyone, meeting my eyes briefly before moving around the table. "We've all been training for this and our 1,200 square feet of space should have the same equipment except for what you've brought with you in your backpacks and eighty-five pounds of personal gear. Make sure that everything is there. Go over your checklists and then switch with someone and go through theirs." She took a deep breath and then expelled it slowly. "We're here. Let's make history."

After fielding a few questions, Ty said we were free to wander until dinner at six or 1800, given we were going to military time, the move to the module at 2000. Since it was only dark for about a half-hour, time was going to stop mattering very much for the next few months.

Miho hurried out of the conference room to mail her Christmas gifts to her family at the station post office. The rest of the group broke up to go explore. I joined Christina who was back at the window.

"What do you see?" The white landscape looked cold and desolate with a few outbuildings and the circle of national flags around a striped pole with a crystal globe on top.

"I was thinking of all the people who have come before us," she said her eyes fixed on the horizon. "All of their hopes and dreams. Some realized, some not, some in ways they never imagined." She turned then and looked me in the eye. "Why are you here?"

I wasn't expecting the question and was tempted to give a flip answer. She just watched me, looking like she could see the wheels turning in my head. I looked back at her and then out the window. "A lot of reasons, to support my friend Ty, the adventure, the challenge, the science, being the first." I turned to face her. "But I think I really came to find myself."

She nodded. With a final glance out the window, she said, "Let's go explore."

CHAPTER EIGHT

Amundsen-Scott South Pole Station-November

Christina and I spent the last few hours exploring Pole Station. It was amazing what they had crammed into this building made to withstand the ice, snow, and wind. There was a huge gym with windows high on the walls that were covered over with cardboard to protect the telescopes against light pollution during the dark months.

"Do you play an instrument?" I asked Christina as we peered into a small but impressive room full of musical instruments: guitars, digital keyboards, horns, percussion equipment, including a full drum set, and amplifiers. In addition to everything else, there was even an assortment of recording gear. Christina's information had been sparse in Rue's spreadsheet.

"Love music too much to butcher it," came her reply. "I enjoy listening to music. Jazz is my favorite: Miles Davis, Nina Simone, Diana Krall."

"I saw Diana Krall in concert. Smooth voice."

She smiled, and we continued on, finding an empty arts and crafts room with a couple of sewing machines and assorted material for projects in various cardboard boxes and plastic bins. There was a library and a large TV room with overstuffed chairs, a few couches and a shelf filled with VHS tapes, DVDs, and CDs. The collection had accumulated over time, media people had brought to the station in their personal gear, as the Wi-Fi reception was still too poor for streaming video.

We didn't get to visit the living quarters as the staff was between shifts and people were busy getting ready or putting gear away. It was a twenty-four-hour operation. The station was interesting and had a lot of outstanding features but it had a lonely feel. There were definitely people about, but we only saw them in ones and twos, working or moving with purpose through the building. No sizeable groups. Individuals with a lot of space. Something we wouldn't have at the hab. *I could hide here.*

After we exited the laundry, Sam and Miho were coming down the hall.

"Did you see the greenhouse?" asked Sam, her voice booming off the long corridor walls. "Fantástico!"

I shook my head. "We haven't gotten there yet. You both look stoked about it, though."

"Their garden is small but they've done a good job and there's a great variety of fresh produce," Miho said. "They even have a couple of comfy chairs. I guess it's the only humid place down here."

"The air is so dry," Sam said. "I can almost feel my throat getting scratchy and my skin drying out."

"Same. I hope there is beer with dinner," Elisabeth said, coming up beside me.

"I'm ready for dinner," Christina said. "Did you find the galley?"

"Sam not know where food is?" Miho scoffed.

Sam gave the smaller woman's shoulder a friendly pat. "Just because you don't eat."

"I eat," Miho countered, waving a hand down her slender frame. "I just don't have much room for it. And the selection is usually slim for a vegan."

Sam shook her head. "I'll never understand how you get enough protein on a vegan diet. How can you live without tacos, enchiladas, burritos?"

Miho stared at her. "You realize all of those can be vegan? Right?"

Sam and Miho were still arguing as we headed down a hall with Sam still extolling the virtues of cheese and eggs. The noise of people and aroma of baking bread and garlic let us know we were headed in the right direction. The rest of the team had already claimed a table. Sam and Miho pulled up chairs to join them. Christina continued to stand. She did that a lot, stood apart from the group. I started to say something when Ty's voice caught my attention.

"… Captain Nelson Von, the head of the men's group, said that their team would be heading out at nine p.m. Colonel Barbara Ride, the head of the mixed group, is heading out at seven p.m."

The other teams clustered around the room. They, like us, looked new to the environment in pristine outfits and staring around like tourists, and somehow separate from the normal flow of the station.

"Will there be any communication between the teams before we lock down?" Ingrid asked.

It seemed an odd question as we hadn't interacted with them back in Houston.

"Only here," Ty said. "Once we enter our living space, our only contact will be with the station coordinators. Go get dinner, socialize if you'd like. This is the last time you'll see people other than our group for a long time. Be in your gear outside at eight p.m." With the last statement, Ty got up from the table and went over to the buffet line.

Christina headed over to the mixed team table and I followed her. The group seemed very clean-cut, almost military.

"Hi, I'm Christina Sohn, doctor for the women's team. I'd like to introduce myself to your doctor if that's okay." Then she noticed the woman seated at the end of the table. "Dr. Connie Charles."

A tall, black woman stood and came around the table, her hand outstretched. "Dr. Sohn. Long time, no see." What started as a handshake turned into a hug as the two women embraced. It seemed they knew each other.

I waited to see if Christina would introduce me but she didn't. Instead, she and Dr. Charles wandered over to a lone table near the back of the cafeteria. I turned back to the table.

"I'm Jo Peterson, meteorologist for the group. Do you have a counterpart for me as well?" I asked the few remaining members of the mixed team.

Two of the guys swiveled their eyes to me. Both remained seated, the bigger of the two waved me over. The remains of dinner in front of them. The rest of the mixed team got up with their trays moving to the cleaning station.

"I'm John Campbell and this is Peter Fuller. I'm the meteorologist with a second doctorate in biology. I'm fascinated by plants growing in unimaginable environments. Pete here is our shrink." John appeared to be a beefy guy with a red face that looked like he enjoyed making jokes at other's expense. "I need Pete's services regularly," he added, surprising me.

Pete shook his head with a smile and stood to shake my hand. "It's true." He was slim, with glasses, a narrow face and straight nose, that made him look like he spent a lot of time with books, yet he still looked fit and capable. I wouldn't have taken him for a psychiatrist.

"Have you seen the meteorology lab here?" asked John.

"No, we didn't get that far and we didn't want to intrude on real work."

"I think they like the interruptions," Pete said. "It's manned twenty-four-seven here. The data obtained on the ground and by the orbiting satellites is amazing. Cold, colder, and coldest." He waved at the monitors that hung at strategic locations throughout the galley. "Key items always up, temperature, wind chill, and when the next satellite service is available... Oh, and what's on the menu. Very important for morale."

I laughed. "Yep, sunny with a side of cold, with fried chicken served up like Grandma used to make. Meals give us a frame of reference and social familiarity."

"The satellites operated by NASA and NOAA?" I asked, referencing the lesser-known National Oceanic and Atmospheric Administration. "What about the Russians and the Chinese?" I thought I knew the answer but was curious as to what the guys would say.

John and Pete exchanged a look that I couldn't interpret.

"The Russians have several satellites, but I don't know about the Chinese," John said.

Pete nodded in agreement, then added, "The Chinese don't have a polar-orbiting satellite yet, but a launch is planned several months after our missions are completed."

I hadn't known about the Chinese launch, but before I could question them further, I felt someone come up behind me.

"Connie says they need to head out to Destination Alpha, which is where we came in earlier," Christina said.

Both guys quickly looked at their watches and jumped up, grabbing their trays.

"Good meeting you, Jo," John said.

"See you in thirteen months," Pete said.

And they took off to put their trays, dishes, and trash away, leaving the area at a fast clip.

"They seemed nice enough," I said.

"It was good to see Connie. She's got some of the same concerns I do."

"What concerns are those?" I asked, noting she used Dr. Charles's first name and wondered how she knew her.

"We don't have much time. How about dinner?" asked Christina, moving toward the buffet and changing the subject. "I hear the mac-n-cheese is made fresh and is excellent."

I knew she was ignoring my question. From experience, pushing her further won't get me any answers. She was an enigma. A mystery that captivated me, and I had a year to decipher her secrets. The trip was looking up.

CHAPTER NINE

Amundsen-Scott South Pole Station-November

At 19:30, Christina, Sam, and I arrived in the main Pole Station coat room. The rest of the team was there, shrugging into their cold weather gear.

"It's only a two-mile drive, but it doesn't take long to get cold," Ty said.

"Temperature has dropped ten degrees since we got here, and the wind has picked up a little," I said as I grabbed my fleece and started my own process of adding layers.

Miho groaned.

Ingrid laughed. "I guess you won't be spending much time outside the module." The laughter didn't sound forced. It surprised me. Ingrid was always so uptight.

"We will get some limited time outside the modules," Ty said, repeating information we already knew from training.

Ingrid looked over at her. "Not everyone should have to go outside if they don't want to go. Leaves more time outside for those who enjoy fine weather." The stiffness was back in her clipped tones. Ingrid's Norwegian heritage was coming out. She seemed to relish the cold more than most of us.

I agreed with Ingrid, though I didn't say anything. Cold weather was exhilarating, but there was a difference between playing in the snow and Antarctica cold. It seemed like the ultimate test.

Having accessorized, we trooped out of the station and down the stairs to the waiting vans. A tall man, obscured in heavy winter wear, had a stepstool against the open sliding door. The snow tires were huge and the oversized vans were above the ground by a solid three feet. Our backpacks went into the cargo area, and they had already delivered our stowed gear to the hab.

The trip to our hab was quick and bumpy on what looked to be a little-used road cut into the snow. The driver had the heater blasting and I was just getting warm when we pulled up to the front of our new home. Similar to Pole Station, the hab was up on pylons above the snow and made up of two outer bays, which were ten by ten on each end, making up our entry and emergency egress sections, with five twenty-by-forty-foot modules in between. Four modules made up our living and working areas while the last module served as the power plant and storage. Twelve-hundred square feet of living space. Crunching the numbers, it came out to be a hundred and twenty square feet per person—a space smaller than my old room as a kid. It left little room to move around without bumping into someone, unless someone wanted to hide out in the noisy generator room or among the boxes of supplies. We'd be living on top of each other for a year.

We piled out into the cold again, grabbed our backpacks and waved goodbye to the drivers. These were the last people outside the team we'd see for a long time. I watched the vans leave with a feeling of loss and abandonment. My avenues for escape had diminished one by one. Anxiety warred with excitement. I stood still and observed around the white expanse surrounding the modules, breathing in the cold, icy air.

The other habitat modules were located such that there was no line of sight between them and our hab, nor could we see Pole Station. We were supposed to be isolated and that meant no visible neighbors to give a friendly wave. The wind whipped the snow around, pushing it up in waves against the pylons that supported our new home.

For all the snow, it was dry here with a humidity level less than most of the great deserts. In an average year, there was less than three centimeters of snowfall. Due to the frigid temperature, the snow that fell stayed and was pushed around by the winds that could bury buildings, and thus, the reason the hab was up on pylons. The South Pole was actually on an ice sheet that moved about ten meters or thirty-three feet every year. One of the reasons I was so important to the group was the concern over cracking ice shelves due to hydro-fracturing, which would cause faster melting and rising sea levels. I would monitor my specially designed sensors planted around the area and coordinate with Ty and Ingrid on the data. Ground shifts were crucial to studies of ice flows and more immediately could warn of us of any destabilization of our tiny habitat.

Ingrid had moved to the opposite side of the hab. Her shoulders thrown back and head high as she gazed at the snow-covered landscape. The snow seemed to have little contrast. It was almost nine p.m. and it looked like midday, the sun high overhead. As we got closer to the winter solstice, we would have no night at all. It made distances in the snow seem strange. As I moved to follow Ingrid, I tripped over a wave of snow I hadn't seen because of the brilliant sun and no shadows.

"Whoa, okay there?" Dianna moved up beside me and caught my arm before I could face-plant in the snow.

"Thanks." I got my feet sorted out and waved toward a building forty meters from the hab. "What do you think of the fuel shed?" The outbuilding was small and squat and covered the underground fuel storage tanks needed to power the generator during our stay. Two wide pipes sat above the snowline, delivering the fuel to the generator. I studied them carefully, as they were critical to the mission. Without power, the hab would quickly equalize to the outside temperature.

Dianna grinned. "Looks like a good place to hide when I get sick of y'all. But I don't think it's climate-controlled, so I hope I don't have to spend much time there." She shivered.

Ty called out for us to get inside. The outer door was designed like an industrial grade walk-in refrigerator, except this one was to keep the cold out instead of in. Through the thick doorframe was a six-by-ten-foot area, leading to a second latched refrigerator door into a coat room already full of cold weather gear. Dianna, Ingrid, and I divested ourselves of gear using the cubby system designated for each of us, similar to an open gym locker—storage on top for gloves, hats, and goggles, with several pegs for hanging items and a place for bunny boots at the base. It was warm in the room, and I was glad to have all the gear off. The hab would be kept at about sixty-five degrees, which seemed chilly, but when compared with outside, seemed downright heavenly.

Going through the next door, I entered what was the first of the four main modules. The first module was our living and galley area. There was a big screen TV on one wall and couches and chairs to accommodate the entire group with a galley kitchen area for food prep and a couple of tables for meals. The color was a cheerless, industrial gray, but there were a couple of inspirational posters in frames on the wall. Leaving Dianna and Ingrid to investigate the galley, I moved on to the next area via a corridor down the length of the modules. I saw a sign for aeroponics and medical. Crossing into the next section, I noticed a sign marked science and then restrooms. Indistinct voices could be heard as I moved into the sleeping berths.

Ty stood at the entrance to our rooms. "Hey, Jo. You're bunking with Sam. Room four around the corner on the right."

I nodded and shouldered past her in the tight space to the first door on the right. It was open and Sam was already stowing her gear under the left bunk bed. She turned as I entered.

"I gave you the right-side bunk. I want you to be right at least some of the time," she said, smiling.

"Thanks. You know how I like being right, except when I'm leaning left." I smiled and held up my hands to let her know I was kidding. And I saw her eyes twinkle at my lame comeback that let me know I was off the hook for another round of falls. I swung my backpack up on the platform bed above a desk and storage area, a duplicate of the one on the left.

A month after our meeting in Switzerland, she watched me take a header over a bench I hadn't seen and decided I was a klutz. Since then, she had taken me under her wing and was training me in a hybrid Aikido style, having determined that I was hopeless in formal Tae Kwon Do. I wasn't a klutz. The rigid forms just didn't suit me. Too much structure and conformity. But I enjoyed the time with Sam. And if I couldn't learn how to defend myself to Sam's satisfaction, at least I had mastered how to fall.

Sam was always light on her feet, her stance open and ready as if she expected an attack from any of her four brothers, three sisters, and too many cousins to count. Someone was always pulling a stunt on someone. I think that was why she had black belts in several disciplines of martial arts. Be prepared was her motto and she had a weirdly calm intensity.

My gear bag had been stashed under the platform near the cabinet that made up one of the platform bed's pillars. A short counter lined the space between the two platforms with a couple of chairs to form a simple work area. A large rectangular window covered in cardboard was above the counter.

"To keep out the ever-blinding sun," Sam said. "I'm glad we went with the two-person rooms rather than the singles. I get a little claustrophobic, and with the split shifts, we won't tread on each other too much."

"I hear the mixed team went for the one-person rooms." I shook my head. "I'm with you. Space is good, though I expect the Mars explorers will probably get the single space for two people."

"I hear you. I'm on first shift, so I'm going to hit the sack. Six a.m. is going to come early and I'm tired." Sam yawned so hard her jaw popped.

Stifling a yawn of my own, I checked my watch and noted that it was after ten p.m. or 2200. I was on the late shift which was now until 0630. I wished I'd gotten some sleep on our flights into McMurdo and South Pole Station. Shaking my head, I dumped my gear, pulled a pair of sneakers out of my bag, and headed back into the corridor. It was time to explore the science and office area.

Ty was coming out of her room at the end of the module next to the emergency exit. The exit was basically a repeat of the front entrance but with pre-packaged emergency gear, food, and clothing, one large pack for each of us. Ty waved as she came toward me, indicating we could talk once we had exited this module. I turned and headed out toward the restrooms, stopping when I got to the science area and went inside.

I hit the wall switch and the largest space, the front living area, was cast into bright light. A workstation with an outgassing hood, numerous drawers, and cabinets stood on one wall with several computer stations and laptops in docking stations with large monitors lined up against another wall. There was another large table in the center of the room at waist height with a couple of stools neatly placed underneath. Cabinets filled up the remaining walls in the room. It was familiar and calming, a replica of our training room in Houston.

I went over to one of the computer stations and flipped the unit on. I could hear Ty entering behind me, her footfalls quiet on the linoleum-like floor. The GICE Corp. logo popped up and I logged into the system.

"Want to go over the science lab checklist?" she asked.

"Let me check the weather forecast and then we can get started," I answered, clicking through a number of links to drill down to link into the expected sensors that had been placed around our new home. Excitement flowed through me at the thought of finally seeing my motion sensors working as designed. The devices I'd painstakingly described to Amy my first day in the office. As the page refreshed, eight sensors refreshed. Two did not. My two. I refreshed the screen. No change. The other sensors showed the expected temperature, wind speed and direction, pressure, humidity, and dew point. Other than the wind speed having picked up, everything appeared similar to what I'd reviewed at Pole Station just hours before, except my sensors didn't appear to be functioning.

"My two sensors are out," I said, turning to Ty who had logged onto the last computer in the row of four. "I'll need to go check them out. I may need help from Amy and Dianna." I shifted trying to recall the schedule. "They're on day shift?"

"Day for now, although I expect our schedules will change and morph as needed with some overlap of schedules. They'll be working through any mechanical or electrical problems together for the next few days. I don't want you going out alone." She reviewed documents on her own screen and frowned.

I wanted to argue with her. I had waited a long time to see these sensors working in Antarctica. But her frown stopped me. "What's up?"

Her brow smoothed out and she shook her head. "A note from Evelyn. Nothing important." She locked her monitor and came over to my station to review the sensor data. "What can we expect for the next few days?"

I shrugged. "Nothing of consequence. Cold with a side of freezing but nothing to complicate what we need to do. We might have a storm coming in three days." I pointed to the two sensors where the data was stale. "Our two bad sensors. Those will need to be checked and possibly replaced. What's our spare situation?"

"Let's go through the checklist and see. I put in for three spares per sensor, given the weather and the reliability analysis, but if we're digging into the spares already, that doesn't give me confidence. They told me that the systems had been checked out completely three days ago."

We spent the next three hours going over the science lab checklist. We found seven items missing—all the spares for my motion sensors and a chemical compound needed for repairing electronics.

"That doesn't bode well," Ty muttered, glancing up from the tally she was keeping on the computer system. "These are items we need. The devices are sensitive and should've been stored in this lab."

"No, it certainly doesn't," I said as I pulled out the box of spares for the other sensors. I felt the need to "pull an Amy" and do a third recount. "Should we check the storage area next to the generator room?"

"Let's go check with the other team and see what they've found." Ty saved her work and locked the computer screen. "Christina should be in the medical area with Miho going over that area's checklist."

Together we exited the science area in module four and went through the hatch to module two that had the medical and aeroponics sections. The hallway was dark as large pieces of cardboard covered the big windows which lined the walls on each side of the modules. It gave the corridor a somewhat claustrophobic feeling.

"Light sensitive experiments during the winter," she said, noticing me studying the cardboard. "The light doesn't matter now when it's basically twenty-four hours of daylight, but it will in the winter." She waved a hand at the windows. "We can remove them in the hall until early next year if we want. In our sleeping quarters they are basically a must unless you sleep sound in full light."

"Just had this conversation with Sam. Interesting the effects light has on moods, though," I replied. "I like it very dark when I sleep. But I love waking up to the light."

"Most people do," she said as she pushed open the door to the medical area.

Miho had a clipboard in hand and was making notations. Christina was taking items from a long stainless-steel table in the middle of the floor and storing them back in various cabinets along the wall. They looked up as we entered.

"We're missing items," Christina said without preamble. She waved to Miho who dutifully started reading out the missing items.

"...sterile pads large, and finally, diphenoxylate-atropine." Miho's recitation had been longer than our seven items.

"Dipheno what?" Ty inquired. "What's that for? Never mind, did you find any extra items? Some spare sensors?"

Miho checked her list. "We have one extra box of medium-size sterile pads." She ran her finger down the list quickly. "That's all."

"Have you completed your review?" asked Ty.

Christina and Miho both nodded.

"Let's switch," Ty said. "Go review the items in the science lab. A checklist is on the wall. I did it online. So you can review without our influence. Jo and I will review in here."

Christina started to protest and Ty cut her off. "It looks like we have a problem and I want to see if it's real."

Christina shook her head as she followed Miho out. "Don't mess up my system."

Ty turned to me. "Let's see what we find."

Three hours later I found myself yawning as I sacked out on the couch in the module one living area. Christina was on a nearby couch with an arm over her eyes. Miho and Ty were comparing notes. It was still an hour before changeover and we were all groggy and cranky.

"I think it was on purpose," Christina said, not moving from her spot.

"We can't be sure," Miho said, reviewing the checklist in her hand.

"Regardless, we're short critical supplies and we need to have them replaced immediately," Ty said. "Unless we find them in the storage module."

"Not where the medical supplies are supposed to be," Christina grumbled.

"It's our main supply area for food, and non-critical supplies," Miho said, rubbing her bleary eyes.

"We'll know more tomorrow," Ty said, a hand going to her mouth to cover a yawn. "The first-shift team will check the storage area and aeroponics. Oh, and the galley." She laughed as she pulled open the large industrial refrigerator door and eyed the contents within.

After a quick meal, we headed to the sleeping berths. Ty was going to stay up and brief the day shift. I had been up for way too many hours and was losing focus. I still needed to do a little unpacking before I could sleep and wanted to get to it.

Sam was up and dressed when I got to the room.

"Glad you're up," I said as I eased into the room. "I didn't want to wake you. Ty's got coffee ready in the galley."

"Hola, chica," Sam said as she pulled on her sneakers. Her Spanish was perfect but her accent was all Chicago. "Get used to this shirt, you're going to see a lot of it." She was dressed in jeans and a pale blue, long-sleeved T-shirt.

"Ditto," I said, hunching as I moved under the platform to sort through my gear bag. As the platform edge was six feet off the floor, I wouldn't hit the top, but old habits die hard. I unloaded the clothing from the bag into the drawers and cabinets. "I have two weeks of shirts. There will be a lot of recycling of clothing."

"Anything I need to know before I leave you to your unpacking and sleep?" Sam inquired as she placed a large-framed picture on the desk. It joined several other frames, all full of family and friends.

"Missing items in both the science lab and in medical," I said.

"That's not good," Sam said.

I pulled my grandmother's quilt from my bag. Even with weight restrictions, I'd known I had to have it with me on this adventure. Gram had been an adventurer when it was a woman's place to stay home and mind the house.

Sam wandered over. "Wow, what a beautiful quilt. Family?"

"My grandmother. Gram made it for me on my tenth birthday," I said. *Back when life had been normal.* I tossed it across the mattress. "She was an amazing woman, climbed mountains, rode a mule down to the base of the Grand Canyon, and went on one of those

Cook's tours down the Nile. She inspired me. She made this from fabrics she got on her travels."

"She must be proud of you."

"She died when I was eleven." I smoothed the quilt with my hand. "But yeah, she would've loved this adventure."

Sam squeezed my arm and I shook myself from my reverie and glanced down at my watch. "Ty's briefing first shift in about thirty minutes. You may want to catch some breakfast before it starts. Good luck with your counts. I hope you find the missing items."

Sam nodded and left.

I stared at the remaining items and decided I was too tired to figure out where I wanted everything to go. I pulled on a T-shirt and loose shorts and climbed into the elevated bed. Pulling my Grams' quilt around me, I let myself wallow in my loneliness and frustration. My exhilaration at using my sensors, studying movement at the South Pole, contributing to the mission in a meaningful way, hung in the balance. Other than Ty, these people were strangers and I couldn't avoid them. I missed my grandmother. She understood my need to contribute and my fear of failure.

CHAPTER TEN

Hab-November

I woke up groggy and disoriented. I'd been dreaming of running through snow and ice, searching for something I couldn't find. The room was pitch black and I reached out to feel the wall. Cold metal. I traveled so much it took me a minute to place myself. The memories flooded back thirteen months in one place. This would be home, no escape. A wave of anxiety hit.

I reached behind me and found the bed light. Snapping it on, I yanked my hand back in front of my shut eyes to protect them from the flash of light. Slowly, I opened my eyes again and sat up. The ceiling was high enough that I didn't have to worry about bashing my skull. I grabbed my watch on the shelf behind my head, noting the time 1400, 2:00 p.m. I'd slept for seven hours. I was still tired but knew I wouldn't get any more rest.

After a quick trip to the facilities, I updated the required online journal entry, leaving out the dreams but noting my anxiety. Then I sorted through the rest of my gear and stowed it away. There were few items of note besides the quilt, Gram's quilt. I looked up at the warm, welcoming patchwork of fabrics. It gave the room a splash of color. I felt sadness at her loss and my own loneliness peaked.

Before my parents were killed by a drunk driver, she had already passed away from a stroke. I couldn't help wonder what my life would have been if she hadn't died and I'd lived with her instead of my aunt. Grams had understood me like no one else.

"Joey, don't take their words to heart. You are water to their earth. Movement is in you and conformity comforts them. Don't let their fears stop you from living."

I could hear her voice so clearly. I closed my eyes and almost felt her presence. Footsteps in the hallway brought me back.

Movement was what I needed. I couldn't go for my normal run, but I changed into some running gear anyway and headed for the module with a living area that doubled as the gym— treadmill, stationary bike, a couple of mats and weights. Ty was already on the treadmill running at a steady pace. I got on the bike.

"What's the word?" I asked, starting to pedal.

"No spare sensors." Ty spoke slowly as her legs churned. "Found the medical supplies."

Maybe that was what I was trying to find in my dreams. "Can we get spares from Houston? After all I went through, I'd like my sensors." I could feel my frustration coming out with each word I spoke. Evelyn had said all equipment would be shipped. I should have packed them myself, eighty-five-pound weight limit be damned.

"I've already sent Evelyn an email requesting them."

I snorted. "Did you copy John?"

She jumped to the sides of the treadmill and glared at me. "You really have a poor opinion of Evelyn. It's her job to work through these problems for us in Houston and find solutions."

"Right. I'll bet you a dessert that she doesn't do anything," I countered as I kept pedaling.

She jumped back on her treadmill.

"Christina will be happy that you found her stuff." I was still upset but Ty had done what she thought best and I'd have to leave it at that for the moment. "I hope they stocked air fresheners or this room will reek inside a week."

"Air recyclers."

"Anything else missing besides the sensors?"

"Wait for the briefing," panted Ty as she pushed the speed on the treadmill.

I flipped on the bike's video screen, put on a Pyrones hill climb, and pushed hard on the pedals. I needed to burn some of the tension and stress out of my system. My dreams and the long day before had left me frustrated and uncertain about this mission. Ty's unwillingness to include me in her thought process added to my anxiety. I couldn't solve problems without information. I gritted my teeth and pushed harder up the imaginary hills in front of me.

Showered and wearing my standard cargo pants and thermal top, I entered the module galley for breakfast, which was the first shift's dinner, and the briefing. These time differences would take some getting used to. Christina and Miho were already seated at the small table in the galley, instead of the big table in the living area, eating fresh fruit and yogurt, both of which would be gone shortly. No fresh anything after we locked down, except for what we could grow in the aeroponics area in module two. Other than tomatoes, no fresh fruit, only canned, frozen and freeze-dried.

TV sounds came from the living area next door.

Nodding a greeting, I grabbed a plate, sat, and pulled the bowl of fruit toward me. I wanted to enjoy it while it lasted.

Ty was standing, leaning against the stainless-steel counter, a coffee cup cradled in her hands. She had on black dungarees with a crease, a light-colored collared shirt, and a green cable-knit sweater—her Antarctica uniform. She cleared her throat and we all looked up expectantly.

"The day team completed the survey. Jo's sensors are still missing. And we're down some food stuffs but otherwise we have everything."

Christina raised a finger.

"Yes, Christina, medical supplies were in a box labeled TP. Rue set them aside for you to move to medical."

Christina nodded and went back to eating.

"What, no witty comeback on the location of the find?" Ty joked.

Christina shook her head.

"We have got a problem, though. Evelyn responded to my email on the sensors and they can't get any to us before our isolation starts."

"What? That's unacceptable." I jumped up. "What about the other groups? Do they have them? Do they have spares?"

We were all watching Ty now. Logistics was her specialty. And the politics too. Another reason I was glad I wasn't leading,

"They have their allotments but no extras."

"How about after isolation starts? They should be able to manufacture more before the weather changes. Can't they get them and just leave them on the porch like Amazon?" I asked, beginning to pace. There had to be an answer.

"I asked. There are specialized parts in the sensors that aren't in stock. Something about unique design items and lead times. They can't get them to us before the planes stop flying."

"What about the other groups? I'm willing to trade other spares." I knew I sounded whiny but I couldn't help myself. I stopped pacing and stared hard at Ty. "We're on an ice shelf. I need those motion sensors."

She shook her head. "All the groups are missing spares, though the other groups have a full complement of working sensors in place. We're the unlucky group with none."

"Can I plug into theirs? The sensors come with a wireless feature."

"I'll check again but what I was told was that using that feature limited the sensor life and was a no-go."

"Damn." I really wanted to hit something. "Did you get this from Evelyn?"

"Yes."

The protest died on my lips when she continued. "John confirmed it as well."

"Maybe you can get Dianna to put something together," Miho said. "She's supposed to be a genius at jerry-rigging systems."

"That's a good idea, Miho. Jo, talk to Dianna, see what she and Amy can come up with," Ty said. "Amy studied your design. Maybe they can fabricate something. You were arguing with her about 3D printing versus traditional manufacturing for hours. I hear your concerns and share them but unless you want to cancel, I think we're stuck with what we have."

"I need something reliable and sensitive," I grumbled. "I built those sensors specifically for what I needed here at this location with these conditions. Accurate ground movement details. The other teams didn't even ask for them. And now they won't give them up or share data."

I turned to Ty. "I think this makes the mission riskier. As I said we're on an ice shelf and the data I've been reviewing shows an alarming trend. The Ross Ice Shelf has shown increased activity with additional ice streams."

Ty raised her hand. "I'll ask GICE to get the other sites to transfer their data in their daily feeds. The data will be a day or two old but should give you some warning if there is a problem."

I nodded, still not happy. I was pissed and I wanted to blame someone. Evelyn was my top candidate as she had been more impediment than advocate over the last few months. Ice movement and flows were no joke. I had seen what earthquake-like fissures had done in Alaska, swallowing entire homes. Our hab modules' pylons were sunk fairly deeply but they were also new. There was no knowing whether the engineers and construction teams had taken into account all aspects of potential ice movement, especially given that some of the ice flow problems were accelerating and potentially unknowable.

Ty checked her watch and then looked at me, concern in her eyes. She knew I was on edge with nowhere to run. "Dianna and Amy should still be up. Their shift is over but it's only 1830. They're probably still in the science lab."

"Nope," Dianna said, peering through the large opening between the living area and the galley. A car crash sounded in the background before it was cut off. "Heard the last bit." She glanced over at me. "You need sensors?" Amy's head appeared next to Dianna's.

"Ice motion sensors," I said. My voice was tight. I was holding on to my anger by a thread. "Something to give me sensitive data on any movement in the ice around our hab module. I need the data to plug into our system and let me know if there is any motion in the ground or ice. Placed two feet to ten feet under the hab. That gives readings of anything over one centimeter of movement." My gaze flicked between Dianna and Amy. "Amy knows my design."

Dianna was silent for a few moments. "Come on Amy, we got some tinkering to do." As they vanished around the corner, Dianna's warm voice and Amy's staccato replies could be heard as they headed past the galley and down the passage to the science lab in module four.

"We did get all the interesting metal components, wires, and electronics that Dianna wanted. Do you know that she had me add a thousand-piece kid's erector set to the spare list?" Ty laughed. "They still sell sets even though the company officially went out of business in 2000. I'd be surprised if any of the other teams got that."

"What's an erector set? Sounds a little lewd?" Miho asked.

Christina snickered.

"It's a box of various metal strips, gears, motors, nuts and bolts. Basically, it's a building kit of metal parts for kids to build robots and vehicles," Ty said. "Okay, moving right along, Dianna and Amy will work that problem. Finish up your breakfasts and get settled into your workstations. Final reports to GICE are due tomorrow but I'd like to be ahead of the game. Also, we still need to do the outside visual inspections."

"I'll pass," Miho said with an exaggerated shiver. "I'm just thawing out from the ride here." She was dressed in a deep green turtleneck, heavy fleece pullover, and tan corduroy slacks, her hands buried in the pockets.

"I'll go," I said, taking my dishes to the sink to clean. "I'd like to get a feel for the weather firsthand. I was too tired last night to appreciate much."

The snow swirled around us as we pulled open the outer door. It was 2100 hours and the sun was high in the azure sky, which belied the frigid temperature. I pulled my hood tighter around my face. A gust of wind pushed us back as we made our way down the open metal stairs.

"I want to check the failed sensors." I moved ahead of Ty and toward module three, the power station. It stuck out on the side of the hab like a boxy growth. I knew one of the two sensors was located underneath the heaviest part of the module. The power station was responsible for keeping us warm, creating our water, and powering all the systems in the other modules. The main plant could easily take care of our needs for the duration and the secondary backup system could take care of about seventy percent of our needs for four months, longer if we cut back to absolute minimums.

The construction teams had sunk a huge supply of jet fuel about two hundred meters off the power station beneath the squat outbuilding. There were two large-diameter pipes to a reservoir with a week's supply just off the module. Near those pipes were the first of my two failed motion sensors. I had concerns that between the construction, pipe layout, and shelf ice this would be a place where potential movement would be the most serious. Maybe the sensor failure was as simple as a bad wire.

The first sensor's molded ceramic casing looked like someone had taken a blowtorch to it. It was near one of the welds between pipe fittings but still far enough away that it shouldn't have been exposed to the heat from the welder's blowtorch. The second sensor near the back of the habitat was cracked, like someone had taken a hammer to it but it could just as easily have been improper manufacturing allowing moisture or something similar to cause a fracture in the casing due to the extreme cold. Suspicious yes. But explainable.

Ty came up beside me. "Interesting. Miho would say the welder made a mistake. Christina would say they did it on purpose."

"Regardless, it's not a loose wire that I can fix. This requires a complete replacement."

"Maybe Amy and Dianna came up with something."

I blew out a breath of air that created a cloud in the frozen air around us. I wanted to kick something but kicking snow wasn't worth it and the pipe fittings would hurt.

"I know you're frustrated," Ty said. "I'll make another call. Miho was right, though; Dianna is a wiz at this kind of stuff, and I'll get NSF to forward us the data from both other stations and from Pole Station."

"I'm inclined to think sabotage. One destroyed sensor could be a mistake, but we found the other sensor broken as well. That one seemed like it had been kicked." I looked back toward our crew quarters.

"Do you want me to put that in my report? Sabotage?"

This time I did kick a pile of snow. The loss of the sensors wasn't the end of the world. Ty would get me the data she promised. Why was this making me so angry?

"Probably not the best idea. If it was sabotage that puts them on guard that we think there is an ongoing problem. If it wasn't sabotage and we make a big deal, then we're women overreacting." I turned to Ty and shrugged. "Even if it was sabotage, Evelyn will downplay it and George will say we're overreacting."

Ty nodded. It looked like she'd already reached that conclusion and was just waiting for me to say out loud what she'd been thinking.

"Nothing more to be done unless Dianna and Amy can create something for me." I knew the frustration was evident in my words. "I'm going to walk around the area for a bit and wear off some energy, the stationary bike just doesn't do enough for me."

"I'm going to check the outside fuel and pressure gauges. Don't go too far. As you well know from your own briefings to the group, storms can come on fast."

I nodded and took off at a brisk pace to walk around the modules and check out my other sensor. The only sounds were the wind and the brushing of my oversize snow pants as my stride took me to the emergency egress side of the module. On a large post, planted in the snow at my eye level, was a series of sensors, monitors, and gauges. The wind gauge spun furiously, which was consistent with the feel of the air on my face. It felt good. The wind and the cool were a balm against the anger I felt. No one else's area had been messed with. I raised my face to the wind and let the cold cool my resentment.

I loved extreme weather. When I was six, we visited my aunt in Oklahoma. My aunt and I were alone when the tornado siren went off. My parents were gone for the week, leaving me in her care. She built a fort of beanbag chairs, quilts, pillows, and towels in the hallway at the middle of the house. She had me grab my favorite stuffed animals and books while she went for cans of soda, bottled water, snacks, a flashlight, and an old-fashioned transistor radio. Shutting all the doors to the rooms along the hallway, we settled in to wait.

The nest was comfortable and very secure to my six-year-old mind. She tuned the radio to the AM news station, which described the tornado's path as it hopped and skipped through the city. There was no predicting where it would go next. Looking back now, I know my aunt must have been frightened, maybe even overwhelmed by the responsibility of keeping us safe, but she didn't show it. My aunt rarely showed any emotion. Even then.

When it was over, her back fence and several trees were gone. The tornado had missed the house by less than fifty feet, leaving a path of destruction one street over. I had been thrilled at the adventure. My parents had been terrified seeing the devastation. My aunt moved away from Oklahoma shortly after that.

I loved the weather with all its infinite diversity. I saw myself as an adventurer battling the elements and the weather as an unknown world to be conquered or as a source to test my strength against. My aunt hated anything that disrupted her careful schedule. I was a disruption. When she'd learned I was queer, that was a bigger, unwelcome disruption to her ordered life. I thought again about the letter. What did we have to say to each other that we hadn't already said?

I was tired of fighting so hard for everything. I had pitched the ice shelf movement study to GICE as part of this mission. I had asked for the special sensors that I had designed and Amy had collaborated on. All of the work I had done setting up the programming and data structures using primary source material was for naught. Now I would get the data secondhand. I could be sitting in a pub in Glasgow instead of here. When I felt my eyes stinging from the moisture freezing on my eyelids, I rubbed a hand across my face and took deep breaths, once again trying to numb myself from the anger and frustration. I needed to be professional and a team player. I couldn't let old hurts cloud my vision or put this team at risk.

I turned to see Ty coming toward me. If she noticed my inner and outer turmoil, she didn't say anything. Her eyes flicked to the instruments on the post.

"Any other issues?" Her voice was muffled through the scarf she had pulled up over her mouth and nose.

I shook my head. Ty must have known I was frustrated but she didn't call me out on it. I appreciated her giving me my privacy, but I felt a wave of sadness. I wanted to reach out and tell her about my anger and my fears, but I knew that it wouldn't change anything. So, I let the moment pass.

CHAPTER ELEVEN

December-Antarctica

Three days later, the storm hit and isolation started. There was a rhythm to our days. The team mingled during the overlaps of individual living schedules with work shifts. A schedule of cleaning assignments had been set up. No maid service for us. I could tell from the start that trading bathroom duties would be high on the list. What could be termed "breakfast" and "dinner" had become overlapping times in our shifts to exchange details about our work during the days and nights, transferring information and discussion issues needing to be worked or managed.

It was during one such dinner, the night shift's breakfast, I got my sensor. Rue had made lasagna and the team had gathered in the galley to enjoy it. The aroma of garlic bread and pasta permeated the air, making me salivate. Dianna and Amy presented me with a metal sphere on a long pole with various wires hanging from it and my focus changed completely.

"The new motion sensor?" I rotated the jerry-rigged ball in my hands. "Light."

"Yes, if this gives you the data you want, we can build two more with the parts we have." Dianna pointed to the LEDs on the device.

"We can't be sure of the reliability, and I know it isn't as sensitive as what you designed; however, I think it will give usable data."

Amy stood by, shifting from foot to foot behind Dianna. The engineer didn't look happy.

"What's up Amy?" I shifted my gaze from the device to her. She looked paler than normal, which was saying something. I wanted to ask her if she was okay but her words distracted me.

"It's not ready. There are improvements we could make to increase precision and reliability."

Dianna shook her head and sighed, as if they'd had this discussion many times already.

Amy looked over at her and refrained from further comment.

"We'll keep tinkering on the next version. I wanted to get you something to Beta test." Dianna's glance flicked to Amy. "I work better with trial and error."

Amy's eyes were on the mechanism. "I've reached out to GICE to give me access to my lab files." She shook her head. "I forgot to copy those files before I left."

She seemed angry with herself, rubbing her forehead and frowning more than usual. I had yet to see her smile. Or laugh. As she never forgot things, I could understand her frustration.

"What files did you forget?"

"I know you wanted the devices traditionally manufactured. I still thought 3D printing was the appropriate method." Amy glanced up at me before returning her gaze to the sensor in my hand.

"You created a 3D print file for the sensors?" I was amazed. The sensors were complicated. A 3D design would take some serious programming work and time.

"Yes, I had even printed a prototype. There were still three modifications I needed to make." Her gaze was still on the mechanism as if she couldn't meet our eyes.

"That's great, Amy. Why didn't you tell me about it?"

"You said you wanted them manufactured. I hadn't respected your request."

"Has GICE sent the files?" Dianna rubbed her hands together as if she couldn't wait to get started. "I haven't had a chance to set up the 3D printer yet, but it should be quick."

Amy shook her head. "The files are encrypted in my folder on the GICE server and Evelyn says she can't give me access. Something about security permissions and closed compatibilities."

"What? That's crap." Dianna stared at Amy in shock.

I shook my head disgusted. "Par for the course. Evelyn hasn't been helpful so far. Why would she be now? Ty, can you try to get access through John?"

Ty had been listening to the exchange as had the rest of the crew. "I'll see what I can do."

Christina nodded. "I'll send a request in as well. I don't know why Evelyn would stonewall us like this."

Amy looked up hopefully. Ty looked surprised and then thoughtful. I was curious. What back channels did Christina have? Did it matter? I wanted the sensors.

"If you can't get access, do you think you could re-create the 3D files?" It was my turn to be hopeful. I felt sure Amy had an eidetic memory. The thought that Amy and Dianna could 3D print the sensors made me want to do a happy dance.

"I can try."

"Thanks. Both of you. I really appreciate this. In the meantime…" I waved the device in my hands. "Can you help me set up this amazing sensor ball and check it out?"

Dianna laughed. "Sure. My thought was to plant it near your existing weather station and utilize some of the circuitry there. Easier, efficient, and more reliable. It won't be next to the fuel station, but still, it's better than day-old data." Dianna took the device from my hand. "Let's eat and then we can go outside."

"Storm hit about two hours ago. I'm surprised you haven't felt the wind gusts against the hab." I waved my hand toward the corridor as I sat at the table. The lasagna had already made the rounds but there was still plenty left. Even if it was breakfast for me, I wasn't turning lasagna down. "Should blow out tomorrow. Visibility is less than ten feet at the moment, so I think after breakfast tomorrow. Sorry your dinner, my breakfast."

Christina looked at me over a fork full of lasagna poised to be eaten. "I was concerned you'd elect to go out anyway. Air crystallizes in your lungs at temps below minus forty degrees without protection."

I nodded, knowing the information was for the group more than me. Christina and I had discussed the various aliments associated with the cold weather in our GICE training assignments. The others may have heard the information, but Christina and I had both seen the effects and it wasn't pretty.

"Tomorrow is soon enough," I said, eating salad with some of the last of the fresh lettuce we would have until our aeroponics garden started producing. "How is the chess tournament going?"

Dianna grinned and sat down next to me just in time for the lasagna to be passed to her. After taking a healthy slice, she passed the casserole dish to me. "Ingrid is kicking butt and taking names. The only person giving her a run for her money is Amy. Hey Rue, lasagna looks and smells terrific."

My knowledge of chess could be contained in a thimble, though I could talk a good game from binge-watching old episodes of The *Queen's Gambit.* Everyone had to play and I had lost in the first seven moves to Amy. It was pronounced a miracle I had lasted that long.

After breakfast-dinner, I settled behind my computer in the science lab and worked through the data provided by Colonel Ride, Ty's equivalent on the mixed team. There were no irregularities in the data, but it looked stale. Worthless. Nothing yet from the men's group. I logged the data. I'd be glad to have readings of my own to review and hoped the sensor Dianna and Amy had crafted would be adequate for the job. Until we could get the 3D files or Amy could re-create them, I was stuck with the other team's data or the sensor ball. I could feel the anger in me rise again, thinking about the other teams having my sensors. I took a couple of deep breaths, the exhalations loud in the quiet room.

Both Sam and Miho were good at data reduction. They could help me figure out the method, but I knew they were working hard in aeroponics. Sprouted seedlings were being transferred to the water cascade area. Miho made the announcement at dinner that fresh lettuce would be available in about two to three weeks. I had high hopes Miho and Sam, our stellar biologists, would get the strawberries growing soon. Miho had taken supplemental classes in botany and wanted to re-create the potato planting from the book *The Martian by* Andy Weir. It had caused no end of laughter in the summary sessions before we left. We had agreed we needed to try the potatoes and see how it would go. It had taken some real finagling to get it approved. Ty and Sam had managed it with Miho pushing from behind.

I decided to track down Christina instead and see what she thought about the numbers. Her place on the second shift had more to do with her being a night owl than any great need for medical aid in the late hours. Ty had left Christina to her own schedule as she was basically always on call. Most of the team called her Doc, and she seemed pleased with the moniker, but I continued to think of her as Christina. The term Doc had too many other connotations—dwarves, OK Corral, "What's up, doc?" and illness.

Knocking twice before entering, I found Christina on the floor in Lotus position on a large, flat pillow in the corner. Her hands were resting on her thighs, palms facing upward. A single eyelid slowly opened to look at me, then closed. I sighed. Do I just leave or was she almost done? Almost in answer to my question, Christina released a slow breath, placing her hands together against her chest, and bowing toward the floor, like formally to a teacher. Then she opened her eyes and looked up at me.

"Meditating?" I asked.

"As often as I can," she replied calmly. "It helps me destress and focus on the transitory nature of life."

"No one's had any medical problems so far. What's stressing you out?" I asked, not sure I wanted to get into a philosophical discussion about the transitory nature of life.

She smiled at me, the light in the room giving her eyes a bright glow.

I felt a warm shiver go through me. Ty had warned me about playing with fire. I could feel my cheeks warming and blurted out, "I've received the data from Colonel Ride and wanted to review it with you." I pulled my laptop protectively in front of me. "If the other team gets me the data, I need to work out placement versus sensor data between our three sites. I thought maybe you could peer review my setup and give me your thoughts?"

She eyed me from her seated position and then seemed to levitate to her feet. It was so graceful. One moment she was seated and then she stood relaxed before me. Taking the laptop from my suddenly nerveless fingers, she opened the device to review the data and spreadsheet I had created. Her brow creased in concentration. She set the computer down on the metal table in the middle of the lab, pulled out a stool and sat.

"The data looks stale," she said after a minute. "Have you talked with Rue?"

"I thought the same. And no, Ty's got Rue working on other things. I thought you might have some time." I paused to see if she'd say she didn't have time. Christina was even more of a puzzle than Amy. The briefing notes on her background just listed her education and credentials, which were impressive. Graduated from medical school and completed her residency at twenty-two. Fast and impressive. "I didn't expect to see a lot of movement just not the *exact* same number repeated to two decimal points. I'm going to ask Ty to request temperature data from the device."

Christina nodded and continued to review the spreadsheet, noting the distances and motion listings.

"Not much to do yet," Christina said, looking up at me. I still stood motionless just inside the door. She pulled out a second stool and patted it. "I don't bite," she said and then smiled. "Okay maybe I do…but only on request."

Vibe confirmed. My eyes must have conveyed my roiling emotions because she laughed. It was an infectious, full-bodied laugh. I startled myself by laughing with her. The mood broken somewhat, I moved to the stool she indicated.

"At the moment, the only thing I need you to chew on is some data."

"Too bad," she murmured.

I ignored the warmth that spread through my body in response to the purr in her voice. "My programs were set up to accept data directly from my sensors, not from the crap I'm getting from the teams." I was proud there was no tremor in my voice.

She swiveled side to side in thought. "What do you expect to get out of the data? An early warning system? Proof of climate changes?" Her eyes were intent on mine, this time with scientific curiosity instead of teasing sexuality.

"Both," I said. "I'm hoping that through the culminated data, I can formulate expected movement over time and maybe find a trend, as well as pinpoint sudden movements that could signal danger to us or the other groups. We have an emergency channel through GICE for just those contingencies."

It was Christina's turn to nod. "I think I see some opportunities to work the data. Let me think on it. In the meantime, you might as well get your weekly check-in taken care of while you're here."

Her eyes were still serious, though there seemed to be a shade of mischief in their depths.

She took my vitals, all the while keeping up a steady patter of questions. She seemed more interested in my answers than in the readings on the various gauges and devices. I realized quickly she was trying to determine my state of mind. Our bodies had been so thoroughly checked in training that I doubted any of us would get sick this soon into our work, but our minds were funny things. We verbally committed ourselves to this journey. Now the mental exercise was real. Were our minds adapting? Would that change over time? As Ty's sounding board and information mole, it was my job to watch for changes in the group too.

"How do you find my state of mind?" I inquired, wanting to catch her out.

She gave no outward reaction to my question.

"Why are all the introverts on second shift?"

She glanced up at this question.

"I mean you should be working first shift when accidents are more likely to happen and when there are more people around to monitor."

"You were closer with your first inference." She turned to type some notes into her computer.

"A doctor who doesn't like patients?"

"Individuals are usually okay. It's crowds I'm not fond of. I'm on call all the time, so my shift really doesn't matter." She turned back to me. "How about you?"

"Ty asked me to be on second shift. My work can be done at any time. I don't really need others."

"And Ty?"

"She doesn't sleep much and didn't want to put others out. She's the one I'm most worried about." I jumped off the table and pushed my sleeves down.

"Do you find it interesting all the lesbians, with the exception of Ingrid, are on second shift?

It was my turn to eye her speculatively. Question answered and the sexual tension I was feeling was real.

"We have Miho on second," I said. "She's not a lesbian."

"Yes, another of the introverts, but Miho is probably one of the easiest going of our lot. A mom figure with infinite patience."

"Mom yes. She's on a high when she hears from her kids and a low when she doesn't. Patient...I'm not so sure. She has a tendency to avoid conflict, though. Do you believe the sensor debacle was intentional or a mistake? She thinks it was a mistake."

Christina leaned back against her desk and folded her arms. "What do you think?"

A deep, ragged breath came out before I answered. "I want to think it wasn't on purpose but it's too...I don't know. The breaks were too pat. Welding misses, really? The guys on the welding teams are too good, too professional. And Ty was told all the systems were checked out three days before we arrived. Not ordering enough spare sensors? Maybe GICE Corp is testing us...me. All I know is I don't like it." I had too much energy and I didn't know where to focus it. "I just know I don't like it. The whole thing gives me a bad feeling."

"What's the worst that could happen?"

"Anything from a river of water destroying the structural integrity of the hab, to the hab being swallowed up and dropped into an ice sink hole," I said.

"How likely?" Christina asked, now looking slightly alarmed.

"Ten years ago, I would have said not likely at all. Now a landmass the size of Rhode Island has broken off the Antarctic Ice Shelf and is floating freely in the Drake Sea. Change is happening too rapidly to determine what the new normal is," I said. "I expect a problem. I just don't know how big, or when, or where it will come from."

"And stale data from Colonel Ride doesn't help."

"Nope."

I felt close to tears. It was a lot to handle. I felt the weight of responsibility pressing down on me, coupled with the knowledge that I couldn't run from the problem.

"Do you wanna hug?" Christina asked.

I only nodded. I usually didn't like to be touched. Christina's touch in Switzerland had been soothing. My eyes misted. I wasn't prone to these emotional outbursts. I wasn't sure where it was coming from. The tensions of the past week were getting to me—a series of attempts to understand and work through problems with undesirable solutions. I hadn't been getting a lot of sleep. Maybe I wanted the physical contact. It had been so long.

She moved across the few feet separating us and carefully enfolded me in her arms.

I rested my head against her shoulder. I was a few inches taller but it didn't matter. I didn't want to cry. I didn't make any sounds, but slow tears rolled down my face to be absorbed into Christina's soft, long-sleeved T-shirt. "It's stupid. I can't control the environment. Whatever will happen, *will happen* even if I have the motion sensors."

Christina ran a hand down my back, soothing me. "But without the sensors, you've lost a semblance of control. I have a feeling you don't like to be out of control. And you feel responsible. To you, lack of information means you can't protect us."

Her hand felt good against my back. I could feel the heat from her body. I had been cold and I felt some of her warmth transferring into my body. I snuggled closer, soaking it in, wanting to extend the moment.

She leaned back, her arms still around me, and looked into my eyes. "I'll help you with the data."

Anything further that might have happened didn't as the door opened and we popped apart like a lit firecracker.

"Hey, Doc, I need those reports I asked you for earlier. Can you put them in our joint Dropbox?" Ty asked as she came into the room, her head down, focused on her tablet.

Christina moved toward her desk and started fiddling with her computer. I didn't move from the spot where I'd landed when we split apart.

Ty glanced at me, then at Christina and then back to me. "You're upset." She turned to stare at Christina, then again back to me. "What's wrong? And don't brush me off. I want to know what's going on here."

Christina turned on her. "Doctor-patient confidentiality."

"I'm the team leader. If there is a problem, I need to know about it."

"We were discussing the missing sensors, which you know about," I said, jumping in before Christina could respond.

Christina leaned back against her desk, arms folded. Her face a blank canvas, even her expressive eyes were closed off.

Ty looked frustrated but knew she was on shaky ground. Christina had played the medical card. Whatever she wanted to know, she couldn't push if we weren't going to talk about it. "If there are problems, I need to be aware of them."

"I've put the data and report you requested in your Dropbox," Christina said, all business. "Is there anything else I can help you with?"

With a final glance toward me, a hurt look in her eyes, Ty shook her head and left the room.

Christina moved toward me. "You didn't need to tell her anything."

"She's my friend."

"A friend with benefits?"

"No." I felt as if I'd sucked a lemon. "It would be like kissing my sister."

The mood was broken. My tension was back but it was mixed. I wanted to re-create the moment with Christina. It had felt good to be held, to feel the warmth of her body and her breath on my neck. But I also felt like I had betrayed Ty. I was here to help her succeed, not get into a romance with a teammate—an off-limits teammate, who was also the doctor. Another big no-no.

Now Christina was looking at me, with her penetrating stare. Her head tilted and her shoulder-length black hair swaying with the motion, as she watched my face, as if trying to see my thoughts.

"I'd appreciate any help you can give me with the data." I fell back on what I knew, moving further away from our moment of closeness.

Christina looked like she was going to reach for me and I stepped back. I didn't know what I wanted and I wasn't ready to play with fire. Starting a relationship in this closed environment was a bad idea. Christina might be content with a fast and free relationship. Her earlier statement about me liking to be in control was way too close to the mark. It was probably why I hadn't had many relationships—too skittish, too controlled. Let's face it, too afraid of myself and my emotions.

"What's going on in your head, Jo?" Christina asked. She had stopped moving toward me, her hands by her side. "What are you afraid of?"

I started to say nothing but knew it for the lame response it was. I cleared my throat and said in a calm voice, "I don't think this is a good idea."

She eyed me and leaned back against the stainless-steel table. It wasn't a very big room and she felt too close to me. I resisted the urge to step away again or flee. Then she smiled. It was a smile full of mischief and understanding at the same time.

"What isn't a good idea? Helping you set up your system?" she inquired. Placing a finger to her full lower lip, she tapped lightly. "Working up the data from all the sites?"

I watched her lips and that gently tapping finger. My heart seemed to beat in time with the finger's rhythm. I could feel my control slipping. I took a breath.

"I'd be delighted for your help with the motion tracking system." I tried to modulate my tone. "I guess I thought you had other ideas. My mistake."

I turned quickly and fled down the hallway, her laughter trailing me.

CHAPTER TWELVE

December-Antarctica

Over the next several days, Ty was very formal with me, keeping her distance and talking only about work-related topics. By the third day of this treatment, I'd had enough. I beat her to the gym and jumped on the treadmill. I knew it would drive her nuts.

Minutes later she arrived and stopped in the hallway to stare at me. She then continued into the room and carefully placed her towel and water bottle on the stationary bike. I continued to run at an even clip. The thump, thump, thump of my footsteps sounded loud in the room. I waited until she was on the bike and the whine of her pedaling sounded steady before I started my pitch.

"So, you're not talking to me anymore?" My pace was too fast for conversation, but I wasn't going to give her the satisfaction of dialing it down. I still wasn't fully acclimated to the elevation at the Pole.

"What do you mean? I haven't stopped talking to you."

"Yeah, 'Can you send me that report?' isn't really a conversation. More of a job assignment," I panted out. "Don't treat me like Ingrid."

"You need to work on your breath control," Ty said, ignoring my jab. She really was mad.

"I need to work on a lot of things. Enough about me. What's up with you? Why the third degree the other day? You know I'm concerned about the sensor data. We were talking about possible outcomes and I got myself riled up. No big deal."

"So why couldn't you just tell me that?" Ty glared at me.

"Do you really want to know why?"

Her eyes were on the bike's video screen, though they looked unfocused. Then she sighed. "No, I really don't want to know."

"We used to share everything." I pushed a little. Ty was important to me. My best friend. Hell, possibly my only real friend. She was the reason I was here.

"Jo, you know I'm the lead here. I can't play favorites."

"Maybe it's time to talk about the reason you wanted me here," I said, pushing the button to slow the treadmill's pace. "You know something's up, don't you? Or you suspect something."

Sam and Elisabeth came into the room in workout clothing, laughing.

Sam saw us on the equipment and plopped down on the couch. "You should have seen Ingrid's face when she found the dishes in her bed."

"Just wait until Rue finds the toilet brush in hers." Elisabeth waved to us as she joined Sam on the couch. "You guys going to be much longer? I need to get my exercise in. Please say you'll be here for a while." She smiled like a five-year-old trying to get ice cream for dinner, all teeth and wide eyes. "I'd rather watch than sweat."

Ty slowed her pedaling. "I was just finishing." She collected her towel and water bottle. "Jo, I'll catch you later." She paused in the doorway, turning to Sam and Elisabeth. "Watch it with the practical jokes. They might come back to haunt you."

Now I knew something was wrong. Ty had just started. What had I said to make her want to leave so soon or was it Sam and Elisabeth's arrival? Something was definitely up. But at least we were talking again.

The soft knock on the door startled me, as my concentration was fixed on the Lee Winter thriller I was reading. Before I could answer, Ty slipped into my room. She put a finger to her lips and after checking the hall, quietly closed the door behind her.

"These rooms have some sound proofing, though I know most of the team is in module one socializing," she said, her voice soft but clear. "I knew I'd find you hiding back here in your room."

I appreciated that she only mentioned hiding and not running. "You know me so well. What's up?"

"I wasn't totally honest with you before we left Houston." She pulled Sam's chair out from under the elevated bed and sat.

I didn't say anything but put my tablet down.

"Before the trip started, I received several threatening emails and one letter."

"What? You specifically? You only mentioned the company getting them." I was ticked. Ty had mentioned that she wanted me to keep my eyes open, but she hadn't been specific. I took a deep breath. Focus. "From whom?"

"I know I should've told you. I'm sorry." Ty stared at the wall unable to meet my eyes. "It wasn't clear who the emails were from. They were spam-like, you know? Everything looks like it's from a real sender, except when you look closely, you can tell it's not. Something the system security should have picked up and didn't—and addressed to me specifically. The letter was from the Patriarchal Society."

My stomach clenched. I had heard of the Patriarchal Society. Some Planned Parenthood clinics and women's shelter bombings were attributed to them. Several members had been tried and convicted but the sentencing had been minimal. All I could think of was good connections or payoffs. "What was in the letter?" I asked.

"A lot of nonsense about how space exploration was meaningless and a drain on government resources. Also, a detailed breakdown of how many scientists were wasting their talents on manned spaceflight instead of solving current world problems. The letter was very logical. The emails more threatening."

"Threatening how?"

"A lot of crap about a woman's place is in the home. And there shouldn't be a women's team at all."

"Aren't all our emails checked against approved senders?" I knew the message itself was private but spammers and trolls would be weeded out.

Ty shrugged.

"You think they're the source of the sabotage?" I stared at her. I could feel my forehead creasing as I thought about what she'd said. Then shock. "You think it's internal to GICE or one of us?"

She watched me for what seemed like a minute and then nodded.

I blew out a breath. I stood up and paced the three steps to the door and then back. "Who?"

"I don't know."

"You have suspicions," I said this as a statement not a question.

"Yes, but nothing concrete." Before I could ask, she said, "And I'm not going to share those suspicions. Enough has happened to put me on guard, but I don't want to tell you something that is wrong and make a bad situation worse."

I sighed. "Are you aware of any other incidents beyond the motion sensors?"

"Your data."

"My data." We said almost in harmony.

"Shit. That means either GICE or Elisabeth. She's responsible for all the communication coming in and out." I paced the floor again. "I'd rather it be GICE Corp."

"I hope it's no one and I'm wrong. Ingrid, Miho, and Rue all had access too. Even Christina had access, though I really don't believe she has any interest in sabotage."

I had the good grace to blush.

Ty smiled. I was once more caught by her beauty and poise, even sitting in cargo pants on a simple desk chair. She looked sad and worried. That wasn't like her at all. It was clear the stress was getting to her.

"Why did you tell me?"

"When I first asked you on this trip, I told you that I needed your counsel and someone I can trust," Ty said simply.

"What? I'm not a crazy?"

"You're an open book. You wear your emotions plainly. That is one of the reasons I didn't share this information. I also know that you are, pardon the words, a straight arrow."

I stopped pacing the small three-step march back and forth across the room and stared at her. "So why now?"

"I got another email. This time from GICE Corp. It seems someone has called our bluff and mentioned the concern about sabotage. The NSF wants GICE to pull the plug. I need your professional take."

"You mean, are we in danger? Which danger do you want me to counsel you on...the saboteur, the threats, or Antarctica?"

Ty was about to speak when we heard laughter in the hallway. Ty looked at me. I grabbed a deck of cards from my desk and quickly dealt us a hand of rummy. I was just finishing the deal when Sam strode in the room still laughing.

"You missed Elisabeth's Ellen DeGeneres impression," Sam said.

Ty folded her hand and stood. "Well, I'm sure you'd like to get some sleep, Sam. I'm going to head back to the lab. I have some paperwork." And she was gone.

"Sorry, I didn't mean to break up the card session."

"Don't worry about it. She was beating me and I'm already in for enough extra chores as it is."

Sam grabbed her toiletries and headed back out the door. I settled back into my own chair but found it uncomfortable. The room felt claustrophobic. I needed more space to get my thoughts in order. Grabbing my laptop, I headed out and down the corridor. I thought of going to the science lab but decided Ty would be in there and I need time to think before I gave her a response.

What was my professional opinion? How much danger were we in and from whom? Interesting questions to be sure. Was I the right person to be giving this advice?

I headed down the corridor connecting the modules and ended up in the galley. Miho was sitting at the table with Ingrid. Neither looked especially pleased to see me. Their heads were close together and they were muttering over a piece of paper that Miho held.

"Hey," I said by way of greeting. "What's up with you guys this evening? Exchanging Christmas lists?"

Miho flushed and quickly folded the paper and slipped it into her pocket before Ingrid could grab it. Ingrid had stood when I came into the room, and her outstretched hand fell to her side.

"Not Christmas?" I inquired with my best clueless look. "Secrets for world domination?"

Ingrid and Miho exchanged a look, which was funny in itself as Ingrid was so tall and Miho looked like a child beside her. Miho's face was inscrutable. Ingrid's was defiant, even angry.

"Miho was showing me some details on her potato farming plans," Ingrid said, the sound of her voice without inflection as if to show bored indifference, which belied the frown on her face.

Talk about not wearing your emotions so plainly. Ingrid wasn't doing a very good job either. I pushed.

"Potatoes make you angry?"

"GICE wants to shut down our mission study," Miho said quietly.

My face didn't change. I didn't feign surprise; I knew it wouldn't work.

"You knew?" Ingrid barked out, her hands clenching into fists.

"How did you both find out?"

Again, they exchanged a look. Ingrid slumped back into her chair.

"I room with Elisabeth," Miho said.

"And?"

"Elisabeth showed me Ty's email from GICE Corp," Miho rubbed at a smudge on an otherwise pristine table.

"No privacy? I'm sure it was marked for Ty's eyes only." I said, noting the look of consternation on both of their faces. "It was bound to get out anyway. Hand it over."

Miho started to object and Ingrid just nodded. With reluctance, Miho pulled the paper from her pocket and passed it to me. I set down my laptop and took the paper.

"Paper?" I mused as I opened the sheet. "How did you get paper? I thought everything on this mission was supposed to be electronic?"

"Elisabeth has a printer for making drawings for Dianna and Amy," Ingrid said.

Evelyn Cable <evelyn.l.cable@GICECorp.org
To: Tyson.a.blackwell@NASA.gov
Ty,
Cid Balkner and the mission leads are concerned about the missing and broken sensors at your site. This on top of the emails you received before leaving for the mission, makes me worry about your safety. Unless you tell me something different, I may need to pull your team out. Decision will be made on Friday. Logistics to follow.
Evelyn Cable

"Kinda wishy-washy. I wonder if she really has buy-in or is just trying to get Ty to quit but doesn't have approval from John and Cid." I looked up to find them both watching me. "Who else knows besides Ty, us, and Elisabeth?"

"I think that's it." Miho continued to wipe the now nonexistent smudge.

"If half the group knows, the rest probably do as well. Do you guys think the mission should be pulled?"

"No," Ingrid said immediately, her voice loud in the confined space.

"Miho?"

"I can see both sides. It is our lives after all. I don't want to run out on this mission but if someone is intent on harm…"

I watched her as she fidgeted in her seat. Before I could question her further, Sam walked in with Elisabeth and Rue close on her heels.

"Did you hear? Are they going to pull us out?" Sam asked, anger apparent in her voice. "What kind of bullshit is this?"

I nodded to myself. The GICE email wasn't a secret. Was that on purpose too? A way to sow additional chaos and discontent. On a more immediate note, this email was my ticket out of this situation. I'd done what I promised: helped Ty get this mission to Antarctica. What more did I need to do? Still…

I leaned back against a galley counter and folded my arms, my mind playing through scenarios. "They aren't pulling us out yet. I think currently it's more of a question than a demand."

"We all knew there were risks going into this study," Rue said, pushing her glasses up on her nose, her green eyes staring at the group. "Why do they want to pull us out? Are they pulling the other groups?"

"Good question," Ingrid said. She rose from the seat, her tall form creating a sense of presence in the room. "Anyone know the answer?"

The hum of the refrigerator and air filtration system were the only noises.

"Why are they pushing us out?" Elisabeth asked. There was none of her normal humor in the question. No sly innuendo. No hint of sarcasm.

"We have a choice," I said, trying to stop the downward slide and talk myself into staying. "We aren't being forced out. The email was a question to Ty, whether she believed the mission was at risk. It doesn't mention the other teams. Elisabeth, you think it's just our team?"

It seemed as if the group's eyes clicked to Elisabeth. She blushed under the scrutiny and shrugged.

There were murmurs in the group. With six of the ten inhabitants standing in the galley, and all the anger and frustration bubbling off the group, the room felt crowded. These people were used to having data at their fingertips and not being in control was causing the emotions to rise.

"We need more information," Elisabeth said, stating what we were all feeling.

Ty entered the room. As she made her way across the galley to the table, conversation died as we saw her face. Her hair was spiked up as if she had run fingers through her hair repeatedly. Her eyes were too bright and her face was pale, almost blue. The room fell silent as she faced the group. Ingrid stood and took a step toward her.

"Amy is dead," she said.

The room exploded with questions, cries, and moans.

"What?"

"How?"

"Where?"

Ty raised her hand and the questions stopped. "Christina is with her in the aeroponics lab. And no, I need you all to stay here. Aeroponics is off-limits to everyone, including me, unless Christina requests your support. We don't know yet what happened."

There were more questions and Ty shook her head, her topaz eyes bright with unshed tears. "Once Christina has her findings, I'll hold a group meeting in the common area. Right now, I need to notify GICE." She sighed heavily. "I know you've all heard about my private message from Evelyn. And yes, we're the only group being targeted for cancellation."

There were murmurs around the room.

"Did someone hurt Amy?" Miho asked quietly.

"As I said, Christina is with her. I don't have any information beyond that to share with you. If you want out, Evelyn will arrange transportation." Ty's voice, even though the message was delivered quietly, rang in the room. "I'm going to find out what happened. I'm staying."

She pushed through the group toward the door. Elisabeth reached out and made a grab for her arm, which Ty evaded.

"How can you be so callous?" Elisabeth said. She had put a comforting arm around Rue who was quietly sobbing. Rue shared a room with Amy and they had bonded over a love of puzzles and scrabble.

"I care…cared about Amy…and I care about each and every one of you, but I won't be pushed out by bullies or saboteurs or even a death…even an unexplained death. I will winter over here and I will get the data needed to show that women are capable of surviving anything." She turned to look at each of them, slowly and with intent, stopping finally at Elisabeth. "I will find out who is trying to sabotage this work."

She left the room. No one attempted to stop her.

I was as shocked as anyone. Amy had been a quiet, competent presence. It took her a while to make a decision, hell we had made jokes about it, but once she had made the decision, you knew you could stake your life on it. Her intensity and drive for perfection had been striking. I hadn't gotten to know her well, but she had been kind to a fault, always thoughtful. She hadn't deserved to die by accident or with intent.

"I can't believe Amy is dead," I stated into the turmoil. The last time I had seen Amy she'd been rubbing her head. Had she been ill? Should I have said something? The image of the river bank and Sharon flashed through my mind. Another friend died. Was it my fault? Could I have done something? Thoughts of my parents leaving the house, angry at me for my stubbornness. I shook with the effort to force back the memories. "I don't know what is going on. I don't know what happened to Amy but I don't think she would have wanted us to give up. She wanted this mission as much as anyone." My voice lacked conviction, though the words came out steady. I didn't want to stay. I wanted to run. Ty was staying. Would they let her if more people on the team decided to leave?

Ingrid nodded. Sam and Rue looked less sure but nodded too.

Miho glanced around the room. "Was it murder? Who could have done it?"

"We don't know anything yet. Let's not start speculating or accusing each other," Ingrid said.

Rue spoke into the suddenly quiet room. "Amy was so excited to be here. When you asked her to work on the 3D design for your sensors, she was so focused. She was angry she hadn't brought the design with her, but excited by the opportunity to make a difference. She spent all her spare time on it." Rue removed her glasses and used her shirt to polish them. When she put them back on, her eyes still brimmed with tears. "I don't think Amy would have wanted us to give up, either."

I felt a shudder go through my body. Fight or flight. An opportunity to run. "I don't think we should make any hasty decisions. Based on the weather and historical data, we still have ten weeks before the last flight out for the season. Let's focus on Amy and our mission."

I could hear the murmurs behind me turning into adamant conversation as I strode from the room. I needed to find Ty. I wanted to let her know my suspicions and even if it was just the two of us, she shouldn't be alone. As I started down the corridor, it occurred to me Dianna hadn't been in the galley. She and Amy had worked together closely and had bonded over old movies they watched together in the common area. Where was Dianna?

CHAPTER THIRTEEN

December-Antarctica

Christina was just coming out of aeroponics. She looked beat, her black hair pulled up in a messy ponytail. She stepped into the hall and closed the door softly behind her. Her head bowed. I stopped, wanting to go to her, but hesitating. Ty came out of the science lab next door to the aeroponics and saw Christina and then me.

She approached Christina and asked, "What can you tell me?"

Christina rested her hand on the aeroponics door as if it was the only thing keeping her upright. "I don't know. Preliminary says heart attack but there are other signs also. And before you ask, I don't think it was poison. There needs to be a full autopsy. I could do it but I don't have the equipment needed for all the analysis. I don't know that Pole Station has all the equipment either. I took some swabs and I can analyze what I found in her hand."

"Her hand?" Ty frowned.

"She had a plant in her hand when she died," Christina said, fatigue and sadness plain in her voice. "For all I know of botany, it could be tomato leaves."

Ty glanced down the hall at me, knowing I had heard all of Christina's pronouncements. "Can you keep all of that to yourself?"

Christina's gaze, which was focused on her hands, looked up sharply at Ty, eyes flashing, a comment on her lips. Then she noticed me for the first time.

I nodded. I understood the question was for me, not Christina. From Christina's change of expression, she understood as well and the retort died on her lips.

"I can't have you do the autopsy." Ty shook her head even as Christina appeared ready to argue. "We have two biologists and an amateur botanist on site, but I don't want to involve more people at this time, not even to identify the plant. We're all too emotionally involved. I've contacted Evelyn. Medical personnel from Pole Station will be here in about two hours." She checked her watch. "Make that an hour and a half."

"Do you have a way to lock the room?" Christina pointed to the aeroponics area door, which didn't have a lock.

"No, one of us will have to stand guard." Ty glanced between the two of us.

Before either of them could say anything else, I asked, "Have either of you seen Dianna?"

Ty's eyes went wide. "She wasn't in the galley with everyone else?"

I shook my head.

"Christina, did you check the door to the storage area and power plant?"

It was Christina's turn to shake her head.

"Jo, I need you to check her room, the science lab, and anywhere else you think she might be." Turning back to Christina, "You need to stay here and guard the entrance to this room. I'm going to go through aeroponics to the storage and power plant module. I'll keep clear of Amy, but if Dianna's back there working..." Ty shrugged. "I need to get her out of there."

"At breakfast she said something about the power plant needing some maintenance...," I said.

If someone had hurt Amy, Dianna was at risk too. Dianna, the one who had saved me from the crevasse, who had come through with the motion sensors with Amy, and who I'd laughed with just that morning. One death was too many, two would be unconscionable. My gut churned.

"Go look in all the other possible places." Ty waved her hand in a shooing motion. She turned to the door Christina had closed so carefully and opened it.

I took off down the hall. I knew I wouldn't find her. As she liked to call it, the engine room was where Dianna was. Her special refuge.

When I got back from the fruitless search, Dianna was in the corridor sobbing in Christina's arms.

Christina looked at me over Dianna's shoulder. Her helpless expression spoke volumes as she awkwardly patted Dianna's shoulder. Christina, who had been so good with my breakdown, wasn't handling Dianna's racking sobs very well.

I rushed over and laid a hand on Dianna's shoulder. She turned to me and hugged me tightly, tears running down her face. I wished I had the luxury of crying or letting my emotions join hers. My own emotions roiled.

I had seen death before, the death of someone close to me killed by a random act of weather, of God. Or my bad decision. Why had I set up so close to the river? I had seen the land start to give. Sharon's face as the embankment slid into the raging current of the river. Her yelling as I moved, as if in molasses. Watching it all play out and being able to do nothing.

I shook off the memory of Sharon. I needed to be here now. I had to be strong in the moment. If I let Dianna's grief pull me in, I couldn't help Ty or anyone.

God, I wanted to run.

My mind swirled. What was this? An accident? An undiagnosed medical condition? Please let it be anything but an intentional murder—and one of us a killer.

CHAPTER FOURTEEN

December-Antarctica

The forensic team from Pole Station, or what they had cobbled together as one, had come and gone. Amy was now officially in their hands, along with the plant and all of her gear. Ty had balked at this. She wanted a chance to go through Amy's personal gear, but the Pole Station team had just ignored her, bagged Amy's possessions, and taken everything away. They hadn't said much other than to ask where Amy was and which room was hers. Silent and efficient.

Everyone was in the main room when they carried Amy's body out on a stretcher. No one had spoken. Rue and Miho had tears running down their faces. Christina, Ty, and Ingrid looked stoic. The others stared wide-eyed. I felt guilty, like it had been my fault, though I wasn't sure how.

"There is nothing to be learned tonight. The Pole Station doctors will perform an autopsy before shipping the body back to Houston. GICE hasn't communicated any of the other problems we've been experiencing to the authorities there. John and the mission leads will review the findings once the doctors complete their work and determine if further action is required." Ty sighed and rubbed her eyes. "Dianna, everything good in the engine room?"

Dianna nodded.

"Right. Okay. Good." Ty paused and glanced around the room. "Take the night off people. We have enough sensors in this place that if something needs attention, we'll know about it. Rest. Get some sleep. Listen to some music. Talk with a friend." She looked at me and then dropped her gaze to the floor and left the room, shoulders hunched. There was some general grumbling, but no one stopped her.

I stood stunned for a moment then chased after Ty, catching her outside the science room. "You can't just leave it like this. The team is grieving. They need you to lead, not hide." I pulled her into the science room. "I know you hate confrontation."

"Hide? Really? I'm not running," Ty spat.

I held up my hands. "Look, Amy's dead. We don't know how or why. I think the team needs you to help them get through this. To give them a reason to want to stay." I could feel the tremors in my hands, and I pressed them to my sides. I didn't want to stay. Amy had died and I had a golden opportunity to get away from Ty and her mission, Christina's heat, and all the trouble that seemed to have followed us to Antarctica. I needed her to convince me.

Ty must have heard the plea in my voice because she stopped and really looked at me. I don't know what she saw but her voice softened. "This wasn't your fault, Jo. You didn't cause Amy's death."

"You can't know that. Maybe a decision I made killed her."

"More likely a decision I made Jo, not you. If someone is trying to stop us, this is their opportunity. Someone on the team just needs to walk away and it's over." Ty shrugged. "If Amy was murdered, and I can't believe that's true, it wasn't one of us. I can't...won't believe that."

"For what it's worth I agree with you, but you still need to work this through with the group. Don't let this fester."

Dianna was in the hall waiting for me when I came out of the lab. Her face still showed the ravages of the earlier emotions, her eyes puffy and sad.

"What do you know?" she asked. "I know you saw something."

I shook my head slowly maintaining eye contact with her.

Rue and Ingrid were heading toward the sleeping quarters and gave us a curious glance as they passed.

Dianna waved me to follow her and headed back up the passage to the living area. I followed reluctantly because Dianna was hurting. This was why Ty needed to do something.

"Please," Dianna said, turning to face me. "Amy was my friend. We didn't agree on methods but she loved technology and finding solutions." Her hands twisted together as if she was doing all she could to keep it together.

"I'm sorry, Dianna. I don't have anything to share. Ty and Christina are keeping the information close. I don't know why Amy died. I don't know if Pole Station, GICE, NASA, or the NSF will share any information with us. Or when. The only thing I know is that February fifteenth is the last flight out. I know everyone decided to wait for more information but I don't know what conversations Evelyn and Ty will have." I could feel my lips tighten in a slight twist of a smile. "Ty will fight to keep some portion of the crew in place." I gave her arm a squeeze. "But I *do* know you are critical to the mission. With Amy gone," I released a long breath, "with Amy gone, you are the only person who can fix all the systems."

Dianna shook her head as if negating my words.

"I know others can fix their own systems, but you are the only one who knows the power system and water reclamation system."

Dianna shook her head, again, and regarded me helplessly. "No, that's not what I meant. What if it was something I did?"

I just stared at her uncomprehendingly. Only the low thrum of the air circulator could be heard in the now empty common room. My mind swirled with possibilities. Dianna hadn't played into any of them.

"What could you have possibly done? And why do you think that?"

"I was messing with the power plant. Maybe during my flush, some fumes went back into aeroponics. I had my filtration system on per requirements, but I didn't check to see if aeroponics was clear."

"How much bad air could you have generated? How long was the purge?"

Dianna looked thoughtful. "A minute, two max."

"Wait a minute, the door to aeroponics was closed." I looked at Dianna and she nodded. "And you had the exhaust fan on full, per protocol?" She nodded again. "So how could the fumes get into aeroponics?"

"I smelled fuel when I came back into aeroponics. When Ty came to get me and we came through the lab, I smelled jet fuel." Dianna looked frustrated and guilty.

"Can you explain to me how jet fuel could have leaked into aeroponics, if you followed all protocols? Wasn't that system checked? Weren't all filtration systems checked the first week we were here?"

"Yes, I checked them myself. And Amy checked them three times after I did. I joked with her about it," Dianna said, her voice full of sadness and anxiety.

"Amy would've known the smell. She's too careful. She would've left and turned on the air filtration system before re-entering the lab. Two minutes wouldn't have been enough time to cause death anyway. Are you sure it wasn't on your clothes, your hands, or a rag?"

Dianna perked up at this. "I was wearing gloves. I'm always careful with life support systems and contamination. I don't remember taking them off. That could be it. Ty surprised me in the power plant when I was checking fuel levels. Do you think that's it?" She looked like she wanted me to declare it was true.

"Christina didn't mention any smells. Neither did Ty," I said and laid my hand on her arm once more. "I don't think you had anything to do with Amy's death."

She sighed in frustration. "I was always razzing her for being so anal. She drove me nuts. Who is going to check my work? I wouldn't trust any of you cretins with a ruler, let alone a screwdriver. I miss her already."

"Get some sleep. Amy knew how much you cared for her. You'll just have to pick up where she left off and check everything four times to make up for it."

Dianna gave me a weary smile before she headed off toward the sleep module.

"Well isn't that interesting?"

Christina's voice came from a cushy chair against the corner of the room. Someone had pulled it away from the others and created a small reading area where a reader could be separated from the general chaos.

I walked over to her. "Dianna didn't kill Amy."

"Jet fuel fumes didn't kill Amy," Christina amended, and then seeing the frown on my face said, "No, Dianna didn't kill Amy or she's in the wrong business. Dianna wears her emotions on her sleeve—like you do—regardless of how she tries to play it cool."

"Are we all amateur hour to you?" I asked, irritated by her statement. "You keep everything so close to the vest. No one knows what you think or what you want. Did you kill Amy?"

Christina snorted. The sound came out loud in the room and was so unlike her. "What possible motive could I have for doing away with Amy?"

"That's not an answer. I don't know what motivates you."

"Did you know about the emails Ty got before we started this adventure?"

"Not until a couple of days ago." I felt like I was more out of the loop than I should be.

"The emails were hostile to the mission in general and Ty specifically," Christina said, lifting herself out of the cushiness of the chair with less than her normal grace. "No other team got those messages, though our missions are all the same."

"How do you know that? You think it was directed at us specifically? And why are they so hostile to scientific research?"

"I don't think it's the study per se. I think it's expending money on women scientists with the possibility of an all-women exploration team off planet. A whiny piece about how we should be saving the planet and mothers of future generations."

"That's not new."

"They outed her at work." Christina watched my face.

I shrugged. "Ty's boss already knew about her."

"Yeah, but the rest of the people with money didn't and they almost pulled her from the mission. Not good publicity. Dykes in Antarctica. Dykes in Space. Blah, blah."

"Really, is GICE or NASA or the NSF so...so..."

"Why yes, they are. It's all about perception." Christina laid her hand on my shoulder. "Good publicity means money in the coffers; bad press means cuts and management changes."

I felt out of my league. Was I so blind to all the politics and ministrations happening behind the scenes? I wanted to step into her arms and let her hold me. "What does all this have to do with Amy's death?"

"Amy was angry about the emails." Christina dropped her hand and stepped back before I could say or do anything. "You know how she was, checking and rechecking. I think she found something."

I blew out a breath. "Makes sense. She was meticulous. If she found something, it was gospel."

It was Christina's turn to nod.

Noises in the corridor had me turning to find Ty striding into the room followed by Ingrid.

"Any more from GICE or the NSF? From Evelyn?" I asked, stepping away from Christina's warmth.

Ty stopped short and Ingrid had to sidestep to avoid crashing into her.

"Isn't this fun? All the lesbians in one room together," Ingrid said, the clipped accent strong in her voice.

Ty gave her a withering stare.

"What?" said Ingrid, hands raised in a "who me" gesture.

"Evelyn wants us to be packed up and ready to go this Friday," Ty said. "I told her we were staying."

"And?" Christina asked.

"I got John to run interference and we have until the end of January," Ty said.

"To pack or to figure out what's going on?" I asked.

Ty shrugged. "I think if we can figure out what's going on and figure out who's behind it, as well as assure GICE and NSF Polar Research management that we can complete the study, then we'll get to stay."

"Aren't they afraid someone else will get hurt?" Christina asked with a raised eyebrow.

"From now on no one goes anywhere without a buddy," Ty said. "I'm pairing everyone up."

"Who's the threesome?" Ingrid asked with a sly smile.

"Stop already," Ty said, her voice tired.

"How are you going to pair us up?" I asked.

"Miho and Christina, Elisabeth and Dianna, Rue, Sam, and Ingrid," Ty said, staring at Ingrid.

It made sense since it kept the day and night shift together.

As if hearing my thought, Ty said. "We're going to stop 24/7 operation. We'll do a long day split. Start by seven a.m. and end at midnight or so. Work as needed. I'll announce the change at breakfast tomorrow. I think the split shift doesn't help the research or the isolation."

"That leaves you and Jo," Christina said. "Why not put me and Jo together? Miho seems harmless and Jo and I have been doing some work together."

"It's the quiet ones that'll get you," Ingrid smirked.

"Can you be serious for once?" Ty snapped, rubbing her forehead as if she had a tension headache.

"I am serious," Ingrid said all trace of the smirk gone. "Look, Miho has gone from being a quiet person to practically hibernating. Is it the work? Her response to isolation? Or is something bothering her?"

"Has she been getting any mail from her family? Emails? Video?" Ty asked.

There was a collective shrug from the group. We hadn't been paying attention.

"Christina, I still want you to pair with Miho. See if you can draw her out and find out what's going on with her," Ty said. "But watch yourself. All of you be aware of your surroundings and don't go off alone. Ingrid, you're still on the earlier shift even with the shift change. Get me up if there's a problem. Don't hesitate."

"You hardly sleep as it is. You might as well be on both shifts," Ingrid said, looking at Ty and shaking her head.

Christina nodded toward Ingrid and then glanced at Ty. "Exhaustion isn't going to help the situation."

All I could think as I felt my own exhaustion was four lesbians against the world. God I hoped it wasn't Christina or Ingrid. I knew it couldn't be Ty. My shoulders slumped but braced when I saw someone coming down the corridor. I had positioned myself in the common room to watch for the approach of the rest of the team when Ty had gotten serious. "Hey Sam," I said with a little too much exuberance. Modulating my tone, I added, "You're on kitchen duty tonight?"

Sam looked the picture of misery. Her hair was a mess and it looked like she'd slept in her clothes. She shuffled over to the group without any of her usual flair or energy.

I walked over and patted her arm. She smiled without warmth.

"What is it?" Ty asked, apparently sensing something was wrong beyond the recent events.

"I can't sleep," Sam said her voice almost inaudible. "I keep hearing my last conversation with Amy."

"Have you eaten anything since yesterday?" Christina asked.

Sam stared at her like she didn't know what the words meant, a puzzled frown creasing her brow.

Christina stepped forward, took Sam's arm, and steered her toward the galley. Looking back over her shoulder, she said pointedly, "I think we could all use something to eat."

We followed Christina into the adjoining galley. Taking my cue from Christina, I started an easy, all-purpose meal of scrambled eggs, made from freeze-dried eggs, and toast. Food would do us all a world of good.

"What conversation did you have with Amy?" Ingrid asked Sam, sitting down next to her.

Christina appeared like she was going to object to the questioning but Ty silenced her with a look.

"What?" said Sam, her eyes blurry and unfocused.

"You mentioned you couldn't sleep because of the last conversation between you and Amy," Ty said gently. "Can you tell us what the conversation was about?"

Sam glanced around as if expecting to see someone, maybe Amy, then she looked at Ty. "Amy wanted my help. She kept asking me to help her."

"With what? What did she want you to help her with?" Ty asked.

Sam shook her head.

"She didn't tell you what she wanted help with?" Ingrid asked sharply.

Sam looked around her in confusion.

Ty frowned at Ingrid and took the seat on Sam's other side, reaching out and laying a hand on her arm. "Where were you when she asked for help?"

Christina put a glass of orange juice in front of Sam. Sam stared at it like it was a lifeline and drank about half before setting it down. Sam seemed to revive a little with the juice. I placed a plate of scrambled eggs in front of her and Ty.

Sam stared at the food. She seemed like she was going to push it away but the smell of the fresh meal must have hit in the right spot, so she picked up a fork and took a tentative bite. After a couple of bites, she put down the fork and pushed the plate away. She sighed heavily.

"We were in the common room," Sam said with a nod toward the room next door. "She had just come in from outside. She still had frost on her eyelids." She stared around at us, stopping when she saw Ingrid.

I nodded at her as did Ty. Ingrid just watched her.

"She said she needed my help. Then Miho, Rue, and Ingrid walked in and she got quiet and then she left the room," Sam said, looking straight at Ingrid. "That's the last time I talked with her." She paused. "What's going on? Does this have anything to do with the email?"

"What email?" Ty asked, suddenly tense.

Ty glanced around the room but I shook my head as did Christina. Ingrid just watched Sam, her blue eyes unwavering but wary.

"What was in the email? Who was it from?" Ty asked.

"It was from a guy claiming to work at her ex-husband's company, stating she should be home taking care of her children, not isolating for some stupid study for an impossible trip to Mars." Sam continued to watch Ingrid. "You saw the email. I know you did."

Ty looked at Ingrid.

"It was some kook going off," Ingrid said, avoiding Ty.

"Why wasn't I told about this?" Ty asked Sam and Ingrid, her topaz eyes flashing.

"I don't think Miho meant to show it to anyone," Sam said, looking suddenly ashamed. "I saw she was upset and read it over her shoulder. I called her on it. That was two days ago in the science lab."

"And Ingrid was in the lab?" Ty pushed.

"Miho, Ingrid, Rue, me...oh, and Amy," Sam said slowly as if trying to place each woman in the science lab. "Miho told me it was nothing. But she looked frightened."

"You know her ex-husband works for SpaceGenesis," Ingrid said.

Ty stared at Ingrid. "No, I didn't know that," she said. "I thought he worked for Lockheed."

"He did. Recently he switched jobs. He took a position on SpaceGenesis's board of directors," Ingrid said.

I searched my memory. Ty had mentioned SpaceGenesis, or SpaceGen, as one of the companies looking at investing in the study. NASA had turned them down. SpaceGen's charter was a mixture of science and religion, with the science being secondary to religion. Ty's comments had been withering. One of the executives at the cocktail party had insinuated her only role was to bear children and she was taking a job from a real man.

I glanced at Ty. "NASA turned them down. Did GICE?"

Ty seemed to remember the incident and her temper was rising. I could see it in the flush on her face and the narrowing of her eyes. She wasn't the only one getting threatening emails.

Christina came up behind Ty. "We need to talk with Miho. We don't know anything other than she got a hostile letter and her ex now works for SpaceGen. It could mean anything."

I wasn't so sure. The tears Miho had shed on the plane when she had spoken of her kids seemed genuine. It was possible there was more to it than simply not being able to see them. She had said her mother was taking care of her children, not her ex-husband.

"Did Miho's ex have visitation rights? Was the divorce hostile?" I asked.

"It wasn't hostile," Ty replied. "You all had background checks, though her paperwork did have her ex with Lockheed. The move must have been very recent. I should have been notified. It sounds suspicious. This is a commercial venture, not a government operation, but still…I agree we need to talk with Miho. Anyone know where she is?"

CHAPTER FIFTEEN

December-Antarctica

"Found her."

Ingrid's call brought Ty and me down the hall. In the end, Ingrid found Miho in the room they shared. Miho was curled in a fetal position facing the wall in their room. Ty kicked us all out, telling us to get some sleep. Ingrid protested. It was her room and how was she supposed to sleep without a bed? Ty ignored us all and closed the door in Ingrid's face. Ingrid flung her hands in the air and stomped back toward the galley.

Considering I was Ty's buddy and Christina was Miho's buddy, we were both out of luck in following Ty's request to stay paired up. It was late, even though the light was still bright through the hallway windows we'd pulled the cardboard from. I asked Christina to join me in the science lab, so I could check the sensors and whatever satellite information had been sent by GICE. The data from the other team had gotten better, though delayed. The early data was stale because they hadn't had the sensors turned on. After the battle I'd gone through to get the sensors and the other teams' unwillingness to share, I realized their reluctance was a lack of interest in the data or a lack of understanding of how to utilize the data. Either way, I was sure they weren't making use of the sensors or the data. I was pissed.

Downloading the latest batch of sensor data, I used the data filters Christina and Rue had set up. I hadn't wanted to bother her when I had asked Christina to help, but Christina had gone straight to Rue. Now reading the data was easy and the information from Pole Station, the two other modules, and from our jerry-rigged system devised by Dianna and Amy, slid easily into the spreadsheets. My heart twinged at the thought of Amy, and I sent her a silent thank-you.

The color-coded squares and graphs populated quickly. Where yesterday's information had maintained the same nominal green, today the red and orange stood out from the screen in stark relief. Grimacing, I saved and then reran the entry feeds on a second spreadsheet. A second wave of orange and red appeared.

"Crap," I said.

Christina, hovering at my shoulder, pushed my hand off the mouse and started clicking through the various tabs. She smelled divine, hints of jasmine and something I couldn't place.

"Not good." Christina released the mouse back to me.

Shaking myself free of her spell, I began a slower more methodical read through the screens. Pole Station was our benchmark. The data was from the previous season and the last four months of this season. It showed the normal movement for this time of year. Seasonally the ice sheets moved thirty meters a year.

I had learned a lot about Antarctica ice sheets. There were actually two main ice sheets that capped Antarctica—a small, warmer West Antarctica Ice Sheet and the massive and frigid East Antarctic Ice Sheet. These ice sheets had formed over the last forty-five million years. The East Antarctic Ice Sheet was relatively stable and had been for the last three to five million years through various climate scenarios. The West Antarctica ice shelf, which included the Antarctic Peninsula, was the one experiencing rapid glacial melting and collapsing ice shelves. This was the one at risk of irreversible collapse and what my sensors and the sensors from other studies, including the University of Wisconsin-Madison Antarctic Meteorology Program, were trying to monitor and study.

Pole Station was one of three permanently manned stations on the East Antarctic Ice Sheet, the other two stations being Russia's Vostok Station and Europe's Concordia Station. Monitoring snowfall and ice sheet movement was an ongoing project for all these locations, and now us, too. Usually, the movement was stable and predictable, but that wasn't what the readings were showing now. Pole Station appeared good, as did the men's mission group, located closest to Pole Station and farthest from us. Our movement data, as well as the mixed group's data, showed our respective areas moving very differently than what should have been occurring. Col. Ride's group was moving five percent faster. Our numbers showed a serious eight percent faster. The numbers were still small but the percentages were alarming.

"Do we have any satellite data to corroborate the changes?" Christina asked, moving over to another terminal and logging into the system. She had pulled her black hair up into a quick loop bun, which highlighted the elegant curve of her neck and sculpted cheekbones.

"Ty requested the data, but I never heard whether her request was approved." I sat back and stared over at Christina. Her proximity was intoxicating. I needed to move. "I want to take a walk around the perimeter. You up for a stroll?" I asked casually, as if walking outside in Antarctica could be considered a nice stroll.

I had already checked the weather outside. It was clear for the moment. The sun still shone almost continuously, as it would until mid-March when it would go to a kind of civil twilight, progressing on to a nautical twilight, then astronomical twilight, then full night for two and a half months. There were protocols to follow to simulate a true isolation study. Specific tasks for maintenance, samples, and the like. We didn't have to don fake spacesuits, but still buddy checks and notifications were required. This was usually limited to Amy, Dianna, and Ingrid, with an occasional foray by Ty to supervise or obtain additional information for NASA or the NSF, who were using our collected data. I had been out to set up the sensor with Amy and Dianna but that had been a while ago.

"We going to ask or just go outside?" Christina asked. Her tone was noncommittal.

"Let's just go. Ty is with Miho. Your partner is with mine. And I think I might know what Amy was looking at before she died," I said, standing up and heading for the science lab door.

"I know you're aware of the risks. Is this really wise? Going outside without notifying anyone? Buddy system aside, Antarctica isn't something to be trifled with." Christina's voice held genuine worry.

"I don't want to bother Ty. I don't want Miho to know what we're doing. Do you want to wake someone up?" I asked.

Christina turned to the desk she had left and went over to the large printer. Pulling a sheet from the tray, she wrote a few lines and placed it at Ty's workstation. We all had our spaces in the lab, though there had never been anything formally stated. Ty's workstation was in the farthest corner of the room. "Ty should see it when she finishes with Miho. Miho doesn't usually come over here." Christina nodded toward Miho's area, which was at the front of the room.

"Fine. Let's go before I change my mind and agree with you. We have a couple of hours before the weather gets dicey, and I want to check out the fuel storage area. I'm afraid of what we're going to find. I want to get this over before the others start waking up for the day shift."

"Two hours." Christina's fingers tapped her thighs. "Okay, let's do it."

I was nervous. I had done enough storm chasing in my life to know when the risks were high. Going outside in these frigid temperatures was always a risk. I had told Christina our window of opportunity was short. She heard me. A storm was coming but I wanted to do these checks before the wind destroyed the evidence I thought I'd find. My stomach was in knots. We just needed to be fast.

We suited up as quickly as we could, given all the layers we had to add. The gauge on the door said it was minus twenty.

I handed Christina several hand warmer packs and shoved several more into my coat pockets. She looked at me questioningly but didn't argue, shoving the offering into her own pockets. She pulled on a polar fleece beanie before pulling on a second down cap with flaps.

We both pulled up our hoods, and looking like puffed-encased travelers, stepped into the vestibule, which was thirty degrees colder than the coat room. Snow had piled up inside the outer door even with it being firmly latched against the outside. I took a last look at Christina, who nodded at me before opening the door and walking outside.

The cold hit me like a wall. The sky was bright, though there were clouds forming in the distance. It had been a while since I'd been out, the last time checking my instruments and gauges. I could feel the ice crystals forming on the gaiter I'd pulled up over my nose and mouth. I decided against activating a hand warmer in each pocket and started down the stairs, thinking movement was the best defense against the cold. Standing still just meant more time outside and I wanted to find what there was to find and get back into the warmth and safety of the hab as quickly as possible.

The brightness was deceptive, causing me to stumble over a few of the snowdrifts as I headed toward the main jet fuel tanks. Those were buried but the pipes to the secondary tanks were above ground. The wind had removed most traces of human presence but as we neared the main tank, I could see faint tracks close to the primary feed pipe. I stepped closer and began a slow inspection of the pipe and welds.

"What are we looking for?" Christina asked.

"Check the ground along the pipe and tell me what you find."

I was concerned there was a problem with our fuel or fuel system. I wasn't sure what I would find, but if Dianna had smelled jet fuel, and Amy had been outside just prior…It didn't explain why Amy was clutching a plant. No plants grew at the Pole that weren't grown indoors, in environmentally-controlled rooms. The plant had to be a red herring. Amy had been found in aeroponics after all. *Reaching out as she fell.* I couldn't think about that now. I wanted to make sure our power system was stable. If it was broken, I wasn't going to be able to fix it. I was more worried there was something in the system that could harm our infrastructure.

We all had training in the major systems. Since our lives depended on the power system, particular focus was paid to temperatures and flows. Temperatures were my thing; that's why it had stuck in my head. AN08 jet fuel had special additives, giving it a freezing point of minus forty-seven degrees Celsius (-52.6 degrees Fahrenheit). If the heating system failed, or if there was a leak, the entire system could be compromised. There were backups on all the systems for normal wear and tear—not intentional sabotage. Jet fuel would never be used on Mars or on any space expedition.

Hydrogen, yes. Jet fuel, no. Another reason this mission was so strange. Again, my mind was going down rabbit holes. I needed to figure this out.

The outside gauge read less than twenty pounds of pressure. I could hear the low hum and setting my gloved hand on the nearest pipe, I could feel the slight vibration as the fuel moved through the pipes. The tanks were buried beneath us, but there was a small building with stairs down to the tanks. I strode over to the door of the building and pulled it open. It was unlocked. I didn't know if this was the way it was supposed to be or if someone had been here before me and hadn't relocked it. No one was supposed to be near our site so it shouldn't have mattered.

Stepping inside the small room, I flipped on a light switch. Other than the three filtration masks hanging on the wall along with an axe, a fire extinguisher, and a couple of large flashlights, there was nothing else in the room except for a set of spiral stairs down into darkness. Taking a filtration mask, I slipped off my goggles and balaclava and placed the mask carefully over my nose and mouth, shivering as the cold plastic touched my skin. I pulled the goggles back on and adjusted them. I felt a stab of fear and then squashed it down. There were no boogie men waiting to jump out at me. No creepy music played in the background. My mind was so focused on my fears and the filtration system, that I jumped when I heard Christina enter behind me, reaching for her own system.

"Are you sure you want to join me?" I asked. "Shouldn't one of us remain up top to make sure nothing happens?"

"You mean if someone locks us in down here?" Christina asked, her voice muffled by the multiple layers and the filtration system over her nose and mouth.

I let out a sigh, fogging my mouth covering.

"Thought so," Christina said. "Let's just get this over with and get back to our warm module."

I nodded and surveyed the circular stairway. I grabbed one of the flashlights. It felt heavy and reliable in my hands. I flicked it on and checked the light before heading down the stairs. The stairs took about eight turns before I stepped onto the metal floor of the fuel storage area. I found the lower-level light switch and turned on the lights. The room was huge but not especially roomy for people, as it held six large cylindrical tanks—three tanks in two rows—

with a large machine pump at the end and a four-foot walkway in between them. It was cold but warmer than the outside by about twenty degrees and without the wind, it felt significant. I pushed my goggles up on my forehead and looked around.

Now that the room was lit, I turned off my flashlight and began a slow walk down the walkway between the tanks, looking carefully at the floor, the tanks, and ceiling as I went. Christina kept her flashlight on and checked out the corners around the room. The hum of the machinery that pushed the fuel up the lines and to our module sounded loud but normal. I pushed my air-filtration mask down and took a quick sniff. The room smelled of machine oil, metal, and a hint of fuel. Not strong, but present.

I called to Christina, "I don't think we need the masks."

After seeing her nod, I walked to the end of the aisle between the two sets of tanks and checked the gauges. The fuel and machine oil smells were stronger here. The tanks on the right side of the room were full and the gauges showed everything in the normal ranges. The tanks on the left side were a different story. We'd been on site now for a month, and we should still be on the first tank, but the gauge showed it was empty. And so was the second. So either we didn't get a complete fill, we were using more than was planned, or we were losing fuel for another undetermined reason. I was worried that there was a fuel leak.

"Find anything?" Christina asked as she came up behind me.

"We're short on fuel." I pointed to the individual fuel gauges for tanks one and two. "We should still be on the first tank. Do you think they didn't give us a complete fill or do you think there's a leak?"

Christina slid her goggles to her forehead and peered at the gauges and then looked at me. Her eyes were dark and I could see where the goggles had left slight impressions around her eyes. "Ty definitely needs to be told about this. I didn't find anything out of place, but I don't know what to look for. I didn't see any strange packages strapped to the tanks or anything that says 'bomb here.' But the fuel smell is stronger. Dianna mentioned a jet fuel smell."

"Yeah, Amy would've known what normal looks like," I said, looking around one last time. "Let's get out of here. There's a storm coming in."

As we left the storage area, I gave the room one last sweeping look. The tanks looked sturdy and the fittings looked new or at least newer. No signs of rust or wear. It all looked so normal, but it didn't explain the missing fuel. If we were using fuel at a higher rate than expected, we would run out, and it would happen when we were completely isolated. No power meant no water, no heat, no light. Death.

When we got back to the small, ground-level room, the noise from the wind had picked up and the wall shook. We quickly divested ourselves of the filtration systems and returned the flashlights in their wall mounts. I pushed. The door didn't budge. I panicked, shoving frantically.

"I can't get the door open."

Christina came over and pushed with me. The door moved slightly and then came thudding back. I almost sighed with relief, not that it lasted long. I was terrified someone had locked us in, but the truth was scarier. The storm was upon us. It was early or we had spent too much time getting ready and then below ground. Either way, this storm wouldn't blow over for twelve hours. I didn't think we could survive the cold for that long unless we exercised to keep our temperature up, and we hadn't brought any food. I was kicking myself. I'd done it again. Like Switzerland, I had to do it myself. At least this time I had Christina with me—if I didn't get her killed.

"We need to get back to the modules," I said. "Our choices are limited here."

"I'm surprised they didn't put an emergency station kit up here or in the room below," Christina said, looking carefully around the bare room. Her goggles still were perched on top of her head. "We could bunk down and wait the storm out." Her eyes twinkled in the light from the single bulb illumination.

My heart sped up. I had just gotten myself under control from the fear of being locked in this room and kicking myself for not paying more attention to the time. I turned away from that twinkle, scared of what I was feeling. Too many feelings. I felt my emotions turn to anger and I hit the door with so much force that it opened slightly and then the wind caught the edge and flung it the rest of the way open making a loud thunk as it hit the outside rail. Before it could bounce closed, I moved through the doorway, searching the horizon for the modules. The snow swirled and Christina stepped next to me, her goggles lowered over her eyes once more.

I pointed to the entrance module, which was indistinct and getting more so with every passing moment. "We need to move and get there as fast as we can. No deviations." We had a hundred meters of open, snow encrusted, near-whiteout conditions to get through.

Christina pushed the fuel house door shut and grabbed my gloved hand. I could feel her tight grip even through the layers of gloves I had on. We moved at a brisk pace, keeping our eyes targeted on the edge of the module. The wind-driven snow on my goggles blinded me. I raised the hand not connected to Christina and wiped away the snow. I didn't want my goggles freezing and screwing up the sight I still had.

We had crossed about half of the distance when the wind picked up, making the snow dance, and pushed us off course. I could feel Christina stumble and I took my eyes off the prize for just a second. When I looked up, I couldn't see the module anymore. But I knew we had a line of four modules. If we kept going, we'd hit the habitat. Unless we missed the hab entirely. The modules were raised off the ground by a series of pylons. We could walk right under the buildings and end up lost in vast wilderness that was Antarctica. I was scaring myself. We just needed to stay on course and keep moving.

Snow and ice were finding pathways down my tight outer clothing and my shivers escalated. Wrapping an arm around Christina, we stumbled forward making slow but steady progress in the direction of what we believed was the entrance module.

I almost hit it before I spotted the outline. I wanted to cry out with joy but just tugged Christina toward the entrance. Just another twenty steps and we'd be at the front door. Twenty steps to warmth. My teeth were starting to chatter. Christina shuddered beneath my arm. Ten steps. The wind was cruel and pushed against us, making each step harder and harder and leaching more warmth from our already taxed systems.

Then we were there and we tugged furiously at the door, wrenching it open and stumbling into the vestibule. Once we were in, I pulled the door closed and latched it shut. Snow had made its way inside with us and several more inches covered the floor. I was too tired to care.

Suddenly, the second door opened and Ingrid reached out and bodily pulled us into the changing room.

Rue was behind Ingrid and shut and latched the second door, sealing the cold out.

"What were you thinking? *Were* you thinking?" Ingrid's voice was clipped and angry.

Christina and I just stood there, numb to the words. I was so tired.

The next few hours were a blur. I remember waking up with my grandmother's quilt pulled snugly around my shoulders. The room was dark. It took me a minute to remember where I was and what I'd been doing. I lurched upright, only to feel an arm pull me back into a soft form behind me. I tried to twist in the embrace to see who it was that held me, but the arm kept me firmly in place.

"Relax," a soft voice murmured near my ear, creating a puff of air that made my body tingle. "You're safe."

The voice had a cadence that relaxed me then sent shivers down my spine. *Christina.* I wanted to snuggle in. Thought returned, and I rolled out of her arms and sat up. I was clothed in a warm set of sweatpants and sweatshirt; I turned to find Christina in a simple T-shirt, her lower half covered in my grandmother's quilt. She gazed up at me, her chin now resting on her palm.

"What?" she asked. "Never woken up in bed with a woman before?"

My thoughts were all over the place. I couldn't put two words together and my spluttering caused her to chuckle.

"Relax," she said. "Our body temperatures had dropped a few degrees. We decided it would be better to share warmth than use medical means. You were a little out of it. We didn't want to drown you."

"Who is this *we*? You're the medical expert."

"I made the call. Ty, Ingrid, and Rue all agreed it was best," Christina said. "You were really out of it. Have you been getting any sleep?"

I ignored the question and moved to climb out of the bed, only to stop again as there was a brief knock on the door before Ty walked in.

"You're awake," Ty said as she handed me two cups of steaming coffee.

I didn't know what to say. Having my best friend and mission lead handing me a cup of coffee while I was in bed with the team doctor gave me acute embarrassment. I was a private person currently on display. The fact the situation didn't bother Christina in the slightest just added to my chagrin. I wanted to put my head in my hands, but my hands now held hot cups of coffee. I groaned. Reaching back, I handed Christina her cup. Her nipples stood out against her T-shirt. I wrenched my gaze to her eyes. She merely smiled at me as if she could read my thoughts and sat up to accept the cup I offered.

"Two fuel tanks are empty and there is the smell of jet fuel in the fuel storage area," I said, setting the coffee cup on the ledge. My stomach was queasy.

"Yeah, Christina filled us in on your findings yesterday." Ty leaned back against Sam's platform bed frame. "That and the information about Dianna smelling jet fuel in aeroponics. Wish you hadn't risked both your lives out in that storm. At least you had Christina with you this time when you fell off the ledge." She gave me a hard stare.

I could feel the heat rise in my cheeks and knew my fair skin was showing an incriminating blush.

"Have you talked with Evelyn?" I asked. "What did Miho have to say?"

"Miho's husband has been sending her threatening messages. He wants her to sabotage the mission. She hasn't done any of the nasty tasks he asked her to do," Ty said, raising her hand before I could ask. "She showed Ingrid, Rue, Sam, and me the messages. We did a thorough search...she hasn't done anything wrong but she's scared. She thinks something she did caused Amy's accident."

"Accident?" I turned to Christina for confirmation.

Christina nodded. "Per the autopsy, she had a brain aneurysm. She may have had a minor stroke between the mission exam and the trip here. They found the antigens in her blood and think COVID was a factor. Kind of a one-in-a-million problem as her medical record was clean. If someone found her sooner, I might have been able to do something." Her eyes turned almost opaque, letting me see the sadness within her.

"You've read the report. It's legit?" I asked. I wanted to comfort Christina but I was trying to get my mind around the information. I needed someone to blame. At the same time, I was relieved it wasn't one of us.

When she nodded, I turned back to Ty. "And what about the fuel? Leak or on purpose?"

"We hadn't received our final fuel yet. Amy was checking the levels for me. The final fuel load is expected in the next couple of days. It's all above board. I wish you'd talked to me before you went out and took such risks."

Stunned, I rubbed my hand across my face as I tried to understand what they were telling me.

"Did you get the satellite data? The higher movement both here and at the mixed team's site is still strange." Too much was going on for me.

"No satellite data but Evelyn said the files from the mixed-team were probably old or corrupted," Ty said.

"So, everything is explained?" I asked. "Why do I feel we're missing something?" My hand waved as if trying to conjure something from the air. "What about the broken and missing sensors?"

"That might have been done on purpose. We found hints in Miho's husband's emails." Ty stepped away from Sam's bed frame and glanced at her watch. "Team meeting in twenty minutes. You may want to wash your face and put some clean clothes on." She headed toward the door and then turned back. "Maybe spend some time coming up with a good explanation for leaving the hab."

I wanted to crawl back in bed and pull the covers over my head. I felt like I was repeating destructive behavior. So much for learning my lesson in Switzerland. I didn't think the team would be as forgiving this time. Behind me Christina sighed and then reached out to rub my back.

"It's partially my fault. I should have questioned you before letting you drag me outside."

"Yeah, well I should have shared my concerns about why I wanted to retrace Amy's footsteps. I was so sure I'd find the reason she was killed," I said feeling miserable. "I thought she was murdered. I was thinking the worst of one of our team."

"You should have been clearer about the storm coming in. You made it sound like it was hours away, not minutes," Christina said, removing her hand from my back.

I felt her roll away from me and climb down the ladder. I wanted to argue. From the information I had, the storm wasn't supposed to hit for three hours, but weather was like that. I had been so single-minded in my pursuit. I knew weather could kill. Watching Sharon die had pushed me to run faster and faster. It was hard not to blame myself when something went wrong, like watching that rogue wave cut through the exposed bank, taking a human life in the blink of an eye. There, then gone. The urge to run was strong. In the hab, there was nowhere to run except into the cold. No options. Christina could have died due to my actions. My decisions could have gotten us both killed. I had been monumentally stupid. I had no excuses. My gut churned.

"No excuse." I watched as she came to stand in front of me. "I have no excuse. I was wrong and I put your life in jeopardy. I'm sorry."

"You put *both* our lives in jeopardy. One quick conversation with Ty and we wouldn't have gone out."

"I was so afraid the evidence," I said, using air quotes, "would be erased if I didn't go right then. I should've said something. I should've shared."

"We have a lot of really smart people in this group," Christina said in a flat voice, watching me beat myself up. "We're supposed to be in this together. Isn't that the point of this study?" She glanced down at her own watch and tapped it. "Ten minutes."

She left me sitting on the edge of the bed, my legs dangling in the air. My life felt like it was dangling in the air too. Her words had been harsh, but they weren't undeserved. I had dodged a bullet with the storm. It could easily have killed one or both of us. Mother Nature didn't care that you were trying to do the right thing.

CHAPTER SIXTEEN

December-Antarctica

The team was in the common room when I entered five minutes late. I had taken the time to clean up, though I hadn't come up with any good rationale to explain my behavior over the last few hours.

Ingrid and Sam sat next to each other on one couch, reviewing a sheaf of printed emails and talking animatedly. They had come a long way from their animosity in Switzerland, but I hadn't noticed, being so caught up in my search for the saboteur. My consuming anger and frustration had blinded me to the group dynamics. Rue, Miho, and Elisabeth huddled around a computer in a quiet discussion on the second couch. Christina, separate as always, stood leaning against the counter of the passageway to the galley. Her gaze followed me as I entered the room. Her face didn't give me any hint of what to expect.

Ty, who was talking with Dianna near the door, looked alert and well-rested. I had sensed her nervous energy for so long that now when it wasn't there, it seemed glaring to me. She had been under so much stress and my frustrations hadn't helped. Had so much happened since Christina and my trip outside that the anxiety and worry had been put to rest? I was still reeling from the news that

Amy's death was an accident. I was glad…relieved, but I couldn't seem to get past the idea that it seemed too pat. Wouldn't she have known she had the potential for an aneurysm? Was it genetic? Hadn't we all had to take a full genome test before coming on this trip? What had caused the fatal brain bleed?

"Glad you could join us," Ty said, deciding to notice my entrance. I knew she had seen me when I first entered but continued her conversation with Dianna.

I didn't reply and took a seat in a comfortable reading chair by the galley. I tried to relax, though I could feel tension in the air. Ty might be well rested, but I could still feel the team's agitation.

"This memo doesn't make sense." Ingrid tapped the top sheet of paper.

"Yeah, but see, this memo says the same thing," Sam said, pulling another sheet out of the pile. "The record shows the delivery of twelve motion sensors, more than sufficient for each of the teams with spares."

"So what happened?" Ingrid said, sifting through the folder.

Before Sam could answer, Ty stepped forward and spoke. "Our split schedule and the amount of work we've been doing have given us little time to really discuss what's been going on. A lot of information has become available, and I think it's time we discuss the facts as a team rather than one-on-one."

There were some murmurs and some nods of agreement.

"What killed Amy?" Dianna asked. "Was it from something any of us did? Or didn't do? Did we fail her in some way?"

"Interesting questions," Ty said. "Christina, do you want to explain this one?"

Christina glanced at me before directing her answer to the group. "There was nothing any of us could have done. It was a ruptured brain aneurysm. Even if we had found her and provided her with immediate medical help—surgical attention—there was a ninety-five percent chance it would have killed her anyway."

"What's the deal with the plant found in her hand? Could the plant have caused this?" Miho asked. "There are many dangerous and toxic plants, but we don't have them in our aeroponics lab or in our foodstuffs."

"The pathologist doesn't mention the plant in his analysis. I think Amy just grabbed out as she fell. The aeroponics lab is full of plants," Christina said. She'd gripped the back of my chair so tightly that her knuckles were white.

"Didn't we all have a genome test?" I asked, turning in the big chair to stare directly up at her. "Shouldn't she have known this was a possibility? Shouldn't GICE have known?"

"That was in the report," Ty said. "There were no indicators. This was a complete unknown."

"So why now? What could have caused it?" Rue asked.

Ty turned to Christina, who nodded.

"Any number of reasons. Her consumption of four cups of coffee a day. The stress she was putting on herself, trying to make everything perfect." Christina looked down at me when she said the "make everything perfect" comment before continuing. "Anger, vigorous exercise, sex, constipation, blowing your nose too hard, even being startled, can cause an aneurysm in someone susceptible to them. Traces of Covid antigens were found in her system. There have been reports of strokes in people who have otherwise shown no symptoms or affects. It's not a hundred percent clear what caused it. Does anyone remember Amy complaining of any pain behind her eyes or vision problems? Dizziness, vomiting?"

"She mentioned having a headache for several days. I told her to go see you. And, well, I think you intimidated her so she didn't… and she said that she'd taken some Tylenol," Rue said. "I didn't think anything of it. With the elevation and the dry cold, I thought it was just, you know, normal. I've had a few headaches."

"Amy wasn't one to complain. If she said her head was hurting, she must've been in a lot of pain." Dianna turned back to Christina. "Why wouldn't she have gone to you?"

Christina shrugged.

"I think Christina has an air of isolation about her," Ingrid said. "Amy never wanted to bother anyone."

"If anyone has any medical concerns, physical or mental, please come see me," Christina said. "I'm sorry if I seem standoffish. My normal patients are usually brought in on stretchers and my bedside manner may be wanting." She looked like she wanted to say more, but her lips compressed, as if not allowing any more words to flow. Outwardly she looked calm, but I knew she was taking Amy's death hard.

"So that's the first item. Amy's death was tragic but not caused by anyone," Ty said. "But it highlights a huge problem." She looked around the room and her eyes came to rest on me. "We are all used to doing things alone. We spent a week in Switzerland and we spent a few weeks off and on in the last year training, but we haven't learned to count on each other, not really."

I slumped in my chair. I could tell what Ty was leading up to and I wasn't sure what to say. I had always been a loner like Christina. I had learned to count on myself since I was seventeen. I was always moving fast, an adrenaline junkie. Motion silenced my mind. I could see now, looking at it through the lens of these last few months. It had affected my personal life as well—pushing away some of the brave souls who had struggled to be near me. Before I could devolve further into my pity party, Ty's next words broke through my chain of thought.

"Before we talk about the unscheduled trip outside, I'd like to let the group know what I heard from GICE with NSF approval." Ty paused. The only sound was the hum of the air flow and the refrigerator burping out some ice cubes. "With Amy's death being ruled accidental, we've been given the choice of staying or leaving."

"Is it an all-or-nothing decision?" Ingrid inquired.

"Yes, if any of us want to leave, they'll pull the whole team. A nine-member team is acceptable. Anything less puts the mission in jeopardy," Ty replied, scanning the room. Her gaze hesitated ever so briefly on Miho before meeting mine and passing over the rest of the team.

"Before I answer, I want to know what Jo and Christina found outside," Elisabeth said. "And can we talk about the missing and failed sensors? There is more than one mystery and I think the lack of discussion and communication has been part of the problem." Her normal smile was missing from her face and voice. "That's a lot of pressure to put on any of us. One person can pull the plug on this adventure, this mission?"

Sam pushed forward on the couch. "Amy was driven. We all know it. She put so much pressure on herself to be perfect. She put it on us too. Sometimes it made us better people, sometimes it was just stressful." She shared a look with Ingrid and then continued. "Ingrid and I have found some strange information.

GICE bought the sensors. Twelve of them. We have the inspection reports and they look clean. Each group was supposed to get three units. That leaves three spares at GICE. Each group doesn't have these numbers and there are no spares in the warehouse. No one seems to know where they are or what happened to them. That's still a mystery and I don't think it's one that's going to be solved in the short term." She sat back, a frown creasing her brow. She was normally gregarious and lighthearted, but like the rest of us, mysteries were to be solved, not to be shoved into a back corner.

"What about the fuel?" Elisabeth asked. "Dianna smelled jet fuel in the aeroponics lab with Amy." She stared at me, her blue eyes intense. "Jo dragged Christina out in a snowstorm to check out our fuel depot. What did you find, Jo? Was it worth it?"

I could feel the burning intensity of all the eyes on me. Moment of truth and I felt small and stupid. Even though the weather was clear when we left, I had still shown poor judgment and made a bad decision. And this after telling myself, I wouldn't do that again. As I tried without success to make my mouth form words, Christina came to my rescue once again.

"At the time we went out, we didn't know that Amy's death was an accident. Jo remembered Amy had been outside right before the incident in aeroponics. Dianna's mention of the jet fuel smell and the strange readings we were getting from the sensors pointed to something being wrong. We wanted to check out the area before any trace evidence was erased." Christina stared down at me, her eyes narrowing. "I just didn't know that the reason the evidence was going to be erased was due to a snowstorm. Or that we hadn't gotten our final load of fuel." She looked back up and directed her comments to the group. "It's a good reminder of why we shouldn't go outside without talking to Ty, and also, weather can be unpredictable." She smacked the back of my head.

I was so surprised I squeaked my indignation.

The group laughed and the tension was broken.

We spent the next three hours discussing all the pros and cons of staying versus leaving. The maintenance crews from Pole Station would perform the final top off of fuel. There were still several issues, including the hate mail from SpaceGen, but we all agreed there wasn't much we could do about those things. We'd identified the problem to the team leads at GICE and they could handle the investigation from there. Our job was to complete our study. Everyone agreed. We'd be staying.

After all, if nothing else, we were all risk takers. There wasn't a woman here that hadn't had to challenge the status quo, mess up, fail and then get back up. Most of us had to fight hard against people—men and women—who didn't want us to succeed. I felt that pressure now. That external pressure that there were those who didn't want us to succeed, but we hadn't gotten this far, only to roll over now.

I think Miho was the only one who wasn't one-hundred-percent happy with the decision, but she wasn't about to throw away her shot at this incredible opportunity to winter over. Few people could do it, and she wanted it as bad as the rest of us.

Amy's death had been explained. The threatening emails and letters were out of our control. Most of the questions on everyone's list had been explained. But not everything. What happened to the spare sensors? What or who had damaged our sensors? Both were still mysteries.

CHAPTER SEVENTEEN

February-Antarctica

Once the decision was made, everyone seemed to settle down. Our fuel was topped off. No one had gone outside to watch as we were isolating, but we were informed during our contact windows when the South Pole Station crew would complete the fill. Once they had left, Dianna and Ty had gone out to confirm. Trust but verify. As scientist and engineers, it was a firmly believed motto.

With that last item checked off, we were officially under complete isolation. There were people at Pole Station and the two other isolation teams, but we were all separate and would remain that way. All incoming and outgoing traffic to the South Pole had stopped on February fifteenth, as planned. No outside contact until November. We were officially wintering over.

At first, this was hard. We had all understood isolation. Knowing this and actually living it were two different things. Since December, we had only seen two other people, the two people who had come to take Amy away—two more people than the other two teams. But seeing the people at South Pole station, or even the possibility of leaving, had still been possible. Now we were truly alone. No way out. The sun was still present almost ninety percent of the day. In the next month, though, that would change and we would move slowly into total darkness. So alone and in the dark with only each other and our work for company. The heart of the study was coming into play.

This change affected each of us differently, a similar rhythm to when we started, but now everyone made more of an effort. Ty seemed to come alive. Her dream of spending the winter in Antarctica had come true and she rejoiced in the accomplishment. Miho grew quieter, if that was even possible. I took to hunting her down and talking with her just to make sure she was okay. She seemed to like the quiet, and though she chatted with me amicably enough, she seemed relieved to have the conversations end, content to stay with her plants and vines. The others were between these extremes. Ingrid shared Ty's exuberance for Antarctica while Christina became more hermit-like.

We still had our shift works. Ty kept us meeting for morning shift breakfast/second shift dinner, forcing us to communicate. For dinner, I loved omelets even if they were made from a dried mix. Mostly Ty, Christina, Miho, and I ate what the day shift made or created. A hodgepodge of pastas, stews, casseroles, and salads. Now that the garden was producing, we had salads at every meal. Lettuce of every shape and hue, tomatoes, bell peppers. It was the color in our meals. None of our group was big on cooking or baking but we created great salads.

"Rue, bake me some cookies," I asked one morning as I tore lettuces leaves into bite-size pieces. "Your chocolate chip cookies are to die for."

Rue pushed her glasses up on her nose and frowned at me.

"Pretty please," I coaxed. "I have to review ice shelf data. Ty has finally gotten the NSF to send the data from Pole Station and the overhead satellites. I need some sustenance."

"Okay, I'll make some cookies. Hopefully, you'll get a few before the hoard descends," Rue said. "Why don't you ask Christina to help with the data? She's got a knack for it."

"Great idea," I replied, knowing I'd have to bite the bullet at some point.

I was nervous and scared, though. Since the smack on the head, she had withdrawn. She wouldn't make eye contact with me. There was no more flirting. I didn't want to acknowledge how much I missed the connection with her.

The data review was off and I couldn't put my finger on why. My sleep had been restless thinking about it. Finally annoyed, I jumped down from my bunk, deciding it was better to do something than toss restlessly. It was cool in the room. I shivered in my boxers and T-shirt. I paced to the window and flipped on the desk lamp. Sam's framed photo of her large family at a gathering in someone's backyard caught my eye. I had asked her about it and she had laughed and said the photo was of a party taken at her *abuela's* house, grandmother to a huge clan of family and friends. She talked endlessly about her family and their antics all lovingly rendered, even the arguments. Envy surged through me. There were no family pictures on my desk. Loss and isolation, my companions for so long, seemed even more present. Trapped here in this space with these women, I couldn't move from place to place, job to job. I couldn't hide behind activity. It was getting harder, not easier.

As I stared at the photo, a sudden jolt caused the picture frame to fall from its place of honor and smash against the floor, cracked glass scattering.

"What the…?" I jumped back. My feet were still bare and now covered in glass. "Ow." I stepped back and cut my other foot on a second piece of glass. My second scream brought Christina charging into the room. Noticing me sitting on the floor cradling my bleeding feet, she immediately moved to my side, glass crunching under her shoes. Rue peered around the corner but didn't come inside. Christina scrunched down next to me, let out a heavy sigh, and then scooped me up as if I weighed nothing. Knowing we were probably the same weight, I had no idea how she did it, but she just did. She didn't waste any time and strolled out the door and down the corridor to the medical lab. Rue got there before her and opened the door. She dropped me unceremoniously on the table before nodding at Rue, who left and shut the door behind her.

"The tremor." I grabbed her arm, noting absently that she didn't even seem out of breath from carrying me. She was fully dressed in yoga pants and a sweatshirt with an NSF logo embroidered on the front.

"I know," she said, sweeping her free arm to point around the room. A couple of cabinets were open and boxes and bottles lay turned over on the counters and the shelves. Nothing had broken here but I knew the hab had shifted, which meant the ice shifted. I needed to get to the data.

"I need to check my equipment."

"You need to get your feet looked after. What were you thinking?" Christina said in imitation of Ingrid's words when pulling us from the snowstorm. She pulled a blanket from a storage cabinet and wrapped it around me.

"Hey, I was getting ready for my shift. How was I supposed to know the frame would go flying? Or that there would be so much glass?"

I was babbling now. It had been a while since I had been so close to Christina, and the smell of her floral shampoo and soap played with my senses. When she was carrying me, I could feel her heart beating strong, and it had soothed me, but it had also awakened my senses and made me aware of our connection.

I watched the back of her head as she pulled a glass shard from my foot. Her black hair was caught up in a thick ponytail at the midpoint of her neck. A few strands had come free and with a quick hand, she pushed an escaped strand behind her ear. Moving over to the counters, she pushed through the scattered packages and pulled out gauze pads, some antiseptic ointment, and a wrap.

"How have you been?" I asked lamely.

She didn't answer. Working with clinical ease, she finished cleaning and bandaging the wounds on both feet. She paused, looking down at her handiwork before raising her eyes to mine.

"What do you want, Jo?"

I just looked into her eyes. I couldn't feel her heartbeat anymore, but I could feel the connection between us. I was confused. Ty had told me not to play with fire, but fire was what I felt when I looked at Christina. I was drawn to her.

I let it happen. No, I created it. I took her face in my hands and kissed her. Our lips met and the warmth and softness were intoxicating. It was a brief kiss, but the possibility had been opened.

Christina stepped back. Her eyes sparkled with the old flirtatious amusement.

"Well, okay then," she said, breathlessly.

I smiled back. "Well, okay then."

There was a knock and we both turned as Ty opened the door and looked in. Reality came crashing back. One didn't get into a relationship with one's doctor. It was a cardinal rule. I enjoyed taking risks, but I had made promises to Ty. To support her. To support the mission. One kiss and I was ready to throw all of that under the bus. Ty was the only family I had. My mind tried to find a solution and came up blank.

"What happened?" she asked.

"Misadventure with glass," Christina said, gathering the trash and extra materials together and putting them away, each to its precise location in the medical room.

Ty looked at me and I shrugged. "Sam's family picture fell during the tremor and I wasn't wearing shoes yet. Caught some glass in my feet. Christina finally got a trauma case to work—me."

"Can you move around? I need you to look at your equipment. What's changed? Can we expect more of these tremors? Was that normal?" Ty asked.

I put up a hand. "Christina, am I good to go?"

"Get someone to bring your slippers. I don't think the bandages will fit inside your sneakers. And you might want to get dressed. Other than that, I think you're good to go. I'll want to check the bandages at end of shift. You don't need stitches, but your feet will be tender. Don't walk too much."

"Right. Clothes." I turned back to Ty. "I'll join you in the science lab as soon as I'm dressed."

"I'll get Rue to bring you your slippers. She's hovering outside," Ty said, a puzzled look on her face. "Do you know anything about that?"

Both Christina and I shook our heads, and Ty left, closing the door behind her.

"Do you know why Rue is outside?" I asked Christina.

Christina shrugged and continued to straighten the boxes and bottles that the tremor had disrupted.

I waited. Two could play this game. She knew something but didn't seem ready or willing to share. Part of the draw to her was the mystery, but I wanted some answers.

"It's medical, and no, I won't be sharing information with you," Christina said, facing me.

There was a second knock on the door and when it didn't open, Christina called out, "Come on in, no orgies happening right now."

Her teasing smile made my stomach flutter. I could feel my cheeks heat.

Rue opened the door and tentatively came in the room holding my UGG boots. Thanking her for them, I put them on and slid to the floor, gingerly placing each foot carefully down before putting weight on my feet. Not too bad. Slight discomfort but no genuine pain.

"Okay, lab time for me. You two have fun," I said with a quick glance at Christina and a wave to both of them before heading past Rue, who was hovering at the door.

I heard the door click behind me as I carefully walked back to my room. It left me wondering what that was about. Christina said medical, so maybe she was treating Rue for some ailment. Not my business. The thought of Christina made me smile. Though the kiss had been brief, it had felt good and I could still feel a tingle down my spine. I sighed. I needed to get my priorities right. I was here to help Ty, not find a lover.

CHAPTER EIGHTEEN

February-Antarctica

Ty was sitting at her terminal with her back to the door, reviewing messages, when I entered.

"Anything from NASA or the NSF? Any other crisis in the lab other than me stepping on glass?" I asked, trying to read her screen.

Ty closed her email before turning to me.

"What? Not sharing? I thought we were done with that." I dropped into the chair next to her.

"Personal emails." Ty ran her hands through her short hair. Elisabeth had recently cut it for her.

"Elisabeth did a good job," I said. "Anything from GICE or the NSF?"

"No. Other than some spillage in the galley, you were the only casualty."

"That's good. I'm surprised I didn't have more visitors."

"I had them checking other systems before I tracked you down in medical. Anyway, our comm window isn't for another twenty minutes." Ty looked up at the digital clock on the wall that showed local time, Houston time, and UTC (Coordinated Universal Time—successor to Greenwich Mean Time (GMT)) used for the program. "I need you to write up our sensor findings. I've already put together a message. Beyond that I need to know what you think about—"

"Are you all right?" Sam asked, bursting into the room. "Dianna said you'd been hurt. Something about flying glass."

"News travels fast around here. I'm sorry about your big family picture. Seems it was a casualty of the ice shift."

Sam looked momentarily saddened. "My family has survived worse." She shrugged. "You okay?"

"Just clumsy. I stepped when I should have stood still. Christina fixed me up." I waved a booted foot at her. "Sorry, I can't replace the glass in the frame for a while. I'll clean up the mess when I finish here."

Sam shrugged dismissively. "Did Rue mention wanting to switch rooms with you? She doesn't want to be in *that* room anymore." Rue had been roommates with Amy. "She thought you might like the quiet of living alone."

"Trying to get rid of me?" I asked teasing. Inside my stomach churned. Discarded again.

"No, no, just she and I come from big noisy families. She's alone in that room and thought, well…"

"Sure, I can switch…You are so noisy even when you're not in the room, and I need the peace and quiet." I smiled. It was fake. I did it anyway. Even though I didn't see her a lot because of our shifts, her happy chatter about her family let me live vicariously. Usually, I was glad to get away from people. Have my space. But this felt different, more of a loss.

"Can we get back to the data?" Ty's question sounded testy.

Sam waved and backed out of the room.

I got up from my seat and moved over to my workstation. Pulling up the sensor data, I compiled it for Ty's message to GICE and the NSF. Our comm window was only fifteen minutes this time. It wasn't a completely realistic version of a trip to Mars. As with the earth, we'd have satellites orbiting Mars to relay the data back to the earth, so communication, though slow—a three- to twenty-minute delay—would be continuous. Here in Antarctica, we had to share a few polar orbiting satellites, so we had specific comm windows which changed daily.

The data showed a sharp motion with some minor shifts. Normally, the shift was slow and unnoticeable to humans. The sharp tremor had been an anomaly. I packaged up data from the sensors, including Dianna and Amy's hand-built motion sensors, and sent the package off to Ty via our local network connection. I felt a twinge of grief. Amy had been working on the 3D pattern. One more thing adding to her stress level. Had it been the last straw? I shook off the feeling. Recriminations weren't going to help.

"Sent." I stood stretching out my back.

"Any thoughts on the why?" Ty asked, swiveling in her chair to face me.

"Definitely an anomaly. The ice shelf moves. It usually doesn't move suddenly like that. I'm wondering if it has something to do with the construction of the modules or the chill we had last night. Temperatures dropped ten degrees from the previous day. If something in the construction had weakened the ice, it could have caused the shift." I shrugged. "I'll need to see the data from the other sites. I'm really interested in the satellite view. Can you ask GICE to expedite that information?"

"I can ask, but as you know all the requests for data have to go from them to NSF and back. GICE doesn't have direct access," Ty murmured as she uploaded my data into the message she had written. "Okay, sent. I don't expect a response for a while. It will take them at least twenty minutes to get the message, time to review, and then another twenty minutes before we get a response. I think with this, they'll break with protocols and not wait for the next window. But I don't know. Do you think we'll get more tremors?"

I shrugged and shook my head. "Dunno. I want to say no but I wasn't expecting the jolt we got. I've been concerned for a while that this is what would happen, but it's the wrong time of year. I would have expected it in the fall or winter, not in the spring when temperatures are falling in the southern hemisphere." Having spent so much time in the Northern Hemisphere, it was a constant mental adjustment to remember that the climate was reversed on this side of the equator. January was warm and July was cold."

Ty slowly swiveled back and forth as she thought. Finally, she took a deep breath and got up. "Nothing we can do for a while. Want some coffee?"

We headed down to the galley.

Everyone but Christina and Rue had congregated in the galley. It was late for the first shift crew but everyone seemed to want to be together. Dianna was attempting to make cookies and the rest of the group got in her way as she moved around the galley trying to collect ingredients. The team kept stealing the items she laid down and putting them away while her back was turned. Dianna was a horrible cook.

"Hey Jo, what was that tremor about? Should we be worried?" Elisabeth called to me as we entered the galley.

"Not enough data. But I'd suggest putting away breakables or at least making sure they're securely fastened down." Walking carefully, I waddled into the room. "Like my new walk?"

"You walk like a penguin," Sam chuckled, then sang out. "Put one foot in front of the other."

"And soon you'll be walking out the door," I chimed in, accentuating the waddle.

Ingrid laughed and then Dianna snickered, a real snicker that sounded more like a wheeze than an actual laugh. This caused Ingrid to laugh louder and Elisabeth to snort, which ended with the entire group laughing, giggling, snorting. Each time someone attempted to stop, a snort or wheeze would start everyone off again.

"Maybe I should do standup," I said finally.

Ty waved a hand as she tried to catch her breath. "Please don't, you aren't very funny."

Then Sam sang, "Walk like an Egyptian."

This set off another round of laughter. With some of the tension burned off, Elisabeth took over the cookie-making from Dianna, who was pushed into a chair by Ingrid.

"Has Evelyn sent anything on the investigation?" Miho said quietly. "Have they found my ex? Is he part of this nightmare? We had our issues but he wasn't crazy. I would never have expected him to join SpaceGen. We'd laughed about them."

"Yeah, I had meant to say something but the small ice quake made it slip my mind," Ty said, going over to the coffeepot. After a few head shakes, she set down the pot, picked up both cups, walked over and handed me one. "Evelyn says they're having difficulty tracing the IP location website on the emails. The addresses conform to the acceptable protocols so the emails are getting through the filters, but they can't prove they came from your ex. They've sent it to the FBI, as this could be considered domestic terrorism, even though we're in Antarctica." She took a sip of coffee and winced. "Who made this?"

"Have you received any more emails?" Ingrid asked, her words coming out in her precise English.

Miho shook her head in the negative.

"Anyone else?" Ingrid said.

"I have," Christina said, coming into the room. Rue trailed in her wake.

"And?" Dianna asked.

"I got an email challenging our right to participate in the study." Christina walked over to the coffeepot, poured the contents into the sink, and set about making a new pot.

"From whom?" Ty asked, taking a small notebook from her pocket. "Can you forward it to me? I'd like to get it to Evelyn to include in her discussions with the FBI."

"I can. It had a funky address. Almost like spam."

"What did it say?" Dianna asked, getting up only to be held in place by Ingrid.

"Don't help," Ingrid said.

Dianna looked hurt but settled back into place. "Hey I can bake. It's like engineering, very precise."

"Not chancing it," Ingrid said. "Your last attempt at cooking almost gave us food poisoning."

"People can we get back to the subject at hand?" Ty said with amusement in her voice. "Go ahead, Christina. What did the email say?"

"A lot of crap about a woman's place, taking jobs from real men, radiation and babies…the normal crap," Christina said.

Elisabeth blended flour into the batter. "I'm surprised the spam filter didn't catch it. I thought our email filter vetted every message to ensure it was from a real person…not spam."

"It is filtered for spam and addresses are checked, but the contents are private," Ty said. "It has to be coming from a legitimate email address, so you're correct, Elisabeth, and that's one question I'm going to put in my next message to Evelyn. I want to know how this is getting through or who is letting it get through." Ty emptied her cup of coffee into the sink. She then cleaned, dried, and put the cup away.

"Afraid your single dirty coffee cup will end up in your bed?" Ingrid asked.

"I don't agree with Miho's pranks, but it is effective. We all should be responsible for keeping the common areas clean."

I was glad I was tidy and hadn't had my dirty dishes or laundry stacked in my bed.

"Better watch out, Ingrid. Someone might put snow in your shoe again," Elisabeth quipped.

CHAPTER NINETEEN

February-May-Antarctica

"I heard Rue moved in with Sam," said Christina.

I jumped at the sound of her voice. New data had come in from the satellite feed and I had been correlating it with the previous week. It was a few days after the foot incident and I had been avoiding being alone with Christina. I was still trying to figure out the line between mission and sex with the team doctor.

She lounged in the doorway. Her hair framed her face, which had an easy smile. My heart sped up.

"Yeah, I'm single," I said and could have smacked my forehead. Dumb.

Christina grinned and eased into the room and hopped up on one of Dianna's stainless-steel tables.

"Yes, Rue was stressing out. It seemed easier. I can live anywhere." I was babbling and knew it. I took a deep breath and let fly. "Look, you're the doctor on this mission. I'm a potential patient...was a patient. I can't do this to Ty's mission." There I'd said it. What I hadn't said was just being in the same room with her was making me tense. The thought of running a fingertip over her full lips and then following the finger with my lips was intoxicating. No alcohol required.

Christina nodded, a knowing glint in her eye. "Can't do what?"

That wasn't clear? The words said no but the eyes…She was playing word games with me. She wanted me to say it. She wanted me to say that her mere presence was driving me nuts, and being trapped in a twelve-hundred square-foot area with constant exposure to her melted my brain.

"Rue knows I like my space. Her moving in with Sam gives me a room of my own," I said instead. There, take that. Frustration was getting the better of me. Two could play this game.

She watched me for a few moments, then hopped off the table. "Sounds like you got what you wanted."

I waited until she left to put my head in my hands. I wasn't very good at games. Just running.

A couple of days later, Christina knocked and then poked her head in my door. "You want some wine?"

"Sure." Maybe she wasn't giving up on me. I had been mostly content to hide in my data and listen to Ty grump about Evelyn, since we'd last spoken. "Come on in. Where did you get the wine?"

"Medicinal stores." The gleam was back in her eyes.

Maybe this wasn't such a good idea. But after another fruitless day of reviewing data, wine sounded great. I could keep my libido in check. "Why now?"

"Because I like you and want to spend time finding out your secrets," she said.

"There is nothing to know."

"Oh, I think there is. And I understand the rules."

We talked of inconsequential things, drank the wine, and Christina fell asleep on the extra bunk. That's how it started. Slowly.

As I pushed the door to my room open, I looked expectantly at her bed but Christina wasn't there. She normally beat me to the room we now shared. It was a gradual process, but by May, she had fully moved into my room. It actually surprised me in some respects, as she was such a private person and neither she nor Elisabeth spent much time in their shared room. Elisabeth didn't seem to notice her absence as she was enamored with beer production.

Elisabeth, our brewmaster, with Dianna, Rue, and Sam, were still trying to get the small batches of beer just right. The small quantity of hops, barley, and yeast they had gotten Ty to requisition as part of their food allotment was treated with reverence. The barley and yeast had been relatively easy, but the hops had taken some fancy footwork. I would have thought it easier and more productive to make vodka with a potato crop, but they were intent on the beer. Ty thought it kept them amused and out of trouble.

Christina's move had started gradually with a nightshirt and a change of clothes. Over time, her clothing and possessions had made their way into my room. It was no secret Christina was spending more and more time in my quarters. When Dianna singed her hand while welding another sensor for me, Ingrid had known just where to find Christina, rousing her from her bed. Ty hadn't said a word about the move, though she had given me a long look.

She was a part of my world even without the intimacy of sex. It was hard having her so close and yet off limits.

Not finding her in the room, I decided to get some of my mandatory weekly exercise. I changed into yesterday's T-shirt and mostly-clean shorts and headed back to the common room. Hopefully, no one would be on the treadmill and I could get in a run. Just as in space or on Mars, exercise periods were mandatory. Losing muscle in space could be debilitating. Mars's gravity was thirty-eight percent of Earth's. Between the trip to Mars, time spent on Mars and the trip home, muscle loss would be a serious problem. But problem or not, exercise was also a serious way to fight off depression and regulate moods. Ty had instituted a regimen for all of us which was posted on the wall in the galley. For the competitive among us, it served as a scorekeeper and incentive to keep us motivated and trash talking each other. For those who weren't athletically inclined, it was a painful reminder.

Miho was pedaling slowly on the stationary bike, reading a book. There wasn't much in the way of exercise going on, but it looked like she was putting in her time. I hadn't seen Miho in a few days, and her hermit-like ways made it hard to connect regularly.

"Hey, Miho." I moved to the treadmill and stashed a flask of water and a towel on the machine.

Miho started coming back from wherever the book had taken her. Checking her watch, she closed her book and stepped off the bike. "Good morning," she said.

"It's good to see you. How are things?"

"Fine." She didn't look at me.

"Have you heard from your kids? Your mom?"

"No."

"When was the last time you heard from them?" I asked, now concerned by her monosyllabic answers and her overall appearance. Her head was down and her hair, usually immaculate, hung lank and without luster, shadowing her face.

"Twenty-two days." Miho flashed me a brief glance. There were dark circles under her eyes and her cheeks looked sallow. "I was hearing from them at least once a week, if not more. I know they're busy with the end of school. But..."

Miho had moved from the far side of Houston to a ranch-style house close to Johnson Space Center and GICE with her kids and mom when she had gotten divorced two years before.

"Do you think there's a problem? Something with your ex?"

"I don't know. It's been a long time since we were together." It came out as a cry. Miho dropped into a crouch on the floor, her hands over her face, rocking back and forth. Silent sobs racked her shoulders.

I dropped next to her and took her in my arms, letting her cry as I held her and patted her back, trying in vain to soothe her. Ty walked into the room and saw me. I just shook my head. She stopped and leaned against the wall waiting as Miho cried herself out.

Finally, Miho sat back, her face calmer but showing the stress and fatigue of the past few days. I let her go but held her hand and gave it a gentle squeeze.

"We're all here for you," I said. "Ty, is there any way we can check on Miho's family? Could something be blocking her emails or something?" I thought of all the bad things that could have happened, including problems with her kids. I scrounged around in my head and came up with his name. "Have you heard from Jonathan?"

Miho paused, then shook her head. Her tear-stained eyes looked from me to Ty. "I have full custody of the children...after the divorce he didn't want responsibility...I spoke with a lawyer prior to coming. I signed legal paperwork to give temporary supervision and custody to my mother in my absence. Jonathan wasn't happy. He feels I abandoned my children and am an unfit mother."

I gave her hand another squeeze and a little shake. "Did he threaten you?"

She gave a noncommittal shrug. "He was angry. He's not a violent man. I can't imagine him harming the kids or my mom." She shook her head. "I don't know why he would go work for SpaceGen. His marketing and sales job at Lockheed had a lot of perks. Or at least he seemed to like it when we were married."

"I'll ask Evelyn to send someone out to your house to check on the family. I'm more concerned that someone is really playing with our communications," Ty said, running a hand through her short hair. "Some emails I should have been getting aren't showing up. If this is on purpose…Well, I've got a few choice words for our management." She shook her head. "I don't think Miho's lack of mail is on purpose."

I looked up at her from my position on the floor by Miho. "Those guys are twisted but this is wrong. We'd know on Mars if our communication was compromised. There might be lags but entire chunks of information wouldn't be missing." I stood up and pulled Miho to her feet. "There is a problem."

Ty gave a quick nod and headed out of the room to get what I hoped would be some answers.

"Are you going to be okay?" I asked not sure if I should push for more information or just be with her.

"I'll be okay. I have my plants. They comfort me," Miho said, her calm façade back in place. "I think I'll go work in my garden."

"Any luck with the potatoes?" I asked, trying to lighten the mood.

"Some but they aren't as robust as we'd hoped." She turned to go. "Thanks, Jo. I'll save you a potato for baking."

"Miho."

She looked back at me.

"We'll figure this out. I promise."

CHAPTER TWENTY

May-Antarctica

Christina still hadn't shown up in our room when I returned after an hour run on the treadmill. I hated treadmills but at least the unit had an interactive screen I could program to be anywhere in the world. That and the interval training made it bearable. I had cleaned up after my workout and was thinking of going in search of her. She had probably started meditating in medical or was helping one of the team with a medical issue or evaluation. She had said something about testing. Yeah, that must be it. Was I getting jealous or possessive? This study had no room for egos or hormones. I didn't know what I expected from the relationship. I knew it was getting harder not to act on my urges. Maybe I needed a cold shower.

I went to the window and tilted up the cardboard covering. It was dark outside. At home in LA, it would be sunny at this hour of the day. Not here. Dark, dark and more darkness for the next month. We wouldn't get sunlight even on the edge of the horizon until August. This was the most critical time here. We had been isolating now for almost seven months.

There had been a couple of flare-ups between the crew but nothing major. Anytime temperatures got elevated, another practical joke got played. The last one had been a kidnapping. Rue's penguin from the McMurdo outpost had been nicked and a ransom note left. It seemed someone wanted Rue to make her famous oatmeal chocolate chip cookies. It was a good thing there were still chocolate chips in storage, or Ty would have had to intervene again. Rue had gotten very attached to her penguin. It was like that with possessions here. With nowhere to go and no way to get anything new, what you had took on new importance.

My grandmother's quilt was like that for me. I wrapped myself in that quilt whenever I wanted a hug and Christina was not nearby to provide it. I had become more touchy-feely. My usual reaction to stress wasn't available. But I wasn't sure leaving was what I really wanted. I was starting to enjoy the comradery of the team.

Still, I didn't go looking for company. I pulled myself up on the platform to wrap myself in my grandmother's warm embrace. What would she think of this adventure? She wouldn't be getting down on herself like I had been for the last few days. Ty's statement about communications was rolling around in my head. My aunt and the letter popped into my mind. Did I really want to deal with that? I'd thrown it away and Ty had retrieved it. Hiding from whatever she had to say was the same as running, wasn't it?

Sliding off the bunk, I fished around in the bottom drawer. The letter was under my Save the Whales T-shirt. Staring at it wasn't reading. It was taking up space in my head. Space I didn't have to give. What did my aunt and I have left to say to each other? After finding me with my best friend, she'd thrown me out. Told me I wasn't worth her time. I was the reason her brother was dead. Everything about me was wrong. If it hadn't been for the scholarship and the money my grandmother had given me, I'd have been penniless and without means of support. My aunt fought me over the inheritance, but my grandmother had set it up well. After that, it felt like I had no family. No, that wasn't true. I had Ty. Ty was my family.

I should just rip off the bandage and learn what my aunt had to say. How could it be more devastating than being rejected as a seventeen-year-old?

Jo,

I hope this letter finds you well. I sent it to Tyson as I don't know your current address.

I'm sorry. I am sorry for so many things. That doesn't excuse my behavior. I was wrong. Wrong on so many levels.

Natalie

Tears blurred my vision. At seventeen, I'd needed and wanted acceptance. Half a lifetime ago. What did an apology mean now? Years too late. Was it enough? The cynic in me wondered what she wanted. I was still sitting on the floor looking at the letter and its implications when Christina came into the room almost at a run. I wiped my eyes quickly and stuffed the letter back in the drawer. She hadn't noticed my distress and started opening drawers and grabbing items.

"Problem?" I asked.

"Medical emergency." Christina grabbed a bag and shoved clothing and a few toiletries into it.

"What? Who? Where?"

"Dr. Charles, part of Col. Ride's team, has what appears to be a ruptured appendix. She has the classic symptoms and is in a lot of pain."

"Can't it be treated with antibiotics?"

"She's running a high fever and she can't operate on herself," Christina said testily, continuing to pull items out of drawers.

"Why haven't they asked Pole Station to assist? They have doctors and the means for getting to Col. Ride's hab way before you could get there." I still didn't understand why Christina was packing like she was going to go somewhere.

"I got the call," she said, looking at me for the first time.

"But why?"

She was silent and motionless until she finally murmured, "Why, indeed?"

"What's going on?" I took the bag out of her hand and pulled her toward the door. "We need a group meeting now." I wasn't going to make a decision without team input again. And I sure wasn't going to let Christina make that mistake.

As we went down the corridor toward the main area, I banged on doors. My new room was at the end of the hall by the emergency exit section. I could hit all the doors as I went. We had a few heavy sleepers, but it was during first shift, so other than Miho, everyone should be in the main areas.

Given our hab wasn't that big, the noise I was making with my banging had Ingrid and Elisabeth coming out of the science lab. I waved them to follow as I headed for the common room.

"What's up?" Ingrid asked, following on my heels.

"We need a group meeting." I didn't slow down. "Someone is messing with us."

I was feeling tired and a little cranky as it was late evening for me. But fresher heads should be able to figure this out or at least stop me from imagining the worst. I probably should have talked with Ty before doing this. Too late now.

Ty was sitting in the galley eating a colorful salad with Rue when I barged into the room, with the rest of the team trailing in behind me.

"Mutiny?" asked Ty as she forked up another bite of salad.

"Did you hear about the medical emergency with Col. Ride's team?" I asked.

"No," said Ty, putting down her fork with a harsh click on the table.

"Dr. Charles sent a distress message to Christina. She has appendicitis." I waved at Christina as if she were door number three.

"What?" Ty said. "Why would they ask Christina to go? Why not Pole Station? Why wasn't I informed?"

"Exactly my question." I looked around the room. "What's going on? And who is playing us?"

"Can we contact Pole Station? Or Col. Ride?" asked Elisabeth, her voice piping up from behind Ingrid's tall form.

Ty rubbed her chin and exhaled heavily.

"Not without breaking more protocols," Christina said, now looking more relaxed with her arms folded, leaning against the counter.

Ty nodded.

"Have you gotten any more data from Evelyn? Anything on the threats or on Miho's kids and mom?" I asked.

Ty shook her head.

Rue pushed her glasses up on her nose as she asked, "Are our communications compromised? Do you know if Evelyn is even getting our reports or emails?"

"Is there any way to check?" Pacing wasn't an option for me with everyone standing in the galley.

"Didn't you set up a key word with Evelyn? Something for problems?" Ingrid asked. When everyone else in the room stared at her, she added, "It's fairly standard. In case there is a mutiny or real problem, the leader is usually given a few keywords or phrases to use that no one else would know. Something to convey the problems without alerting the person or persons causing the problem."

"And how do you know about such things?" Ty asked, her eyebrows raised in question.

"My dad worked on projects he couldn't talk about, but he shared some of the trade craft secrets," Ingrid said, finally sitting down and stretching out her long legs. Several of the others took her cue and sat down at the table. Christina remained standing, as did I. With more room, I paced.

"Do you have a secret code with GICE? With Evelyn?" asked Miho, her voice soft.

"Do you have a code for 'our communication links are compromised?' Do you have a secret handshake too?" Elisabeth said with a trace of humor in her voice.

"I'm sorry to say I don't. The phrases I was given were for someone going a little crazy and freaking out," Ty said.

Ingrid nodded. "We need to find a way to communicate securely with Evelyn. And really know it's her. You have a working relationship with her. Ask her something about herself or a coworker that only she would know. We need to understand the problem we're facing. Is the communication problem all the time or intermittent?"

"There is another elephant in the room that no one is talking about," Christina said, straightening and setting herself to block my pacing without looking directly at me.

All eyes in the room turned to her.

Before Christina could speak, Ty said. "What if there really is a medical emergency? What if Col. Ride's communication link is compromised too? We need to confirm whether there really is a problem over there, and if there is a problem, is Pole Station working on it or does Christina need to go? We can't just sit by and let a fellow human die without at least trying to provide help."

The response to Ty's statements brought comments from everyone, and I couldn't keep track of who was saying what.

"How can you be sure it's not a setup?"

"You can't walk there. That's crazy."

"Pole Station has to help them."

"They just want us to fail."

A piercing whistle had people clamping their hands over their ears.

"Enough," Ty said. "We need more information. I think I can figure out how to find out if we have an actual link with Evelyn." She turned to Christina. "I need at least an hour."

Christina looked ready to argue. Then nodded her head once. "An hour. Then I'm going to help Dr. Charles."

Ty left with Ingrid in tow. The rest of the group seemed to want to continue the discussion, but I followed Christina back to medical.

"As a trauma surgeon, don't they usually bring the patients to you?" I asked, trying to ease the mood as I trailed behind her.

"I've done surgeries in the field," she said as she unlocked the door.

Medical was one of the few locked areas. Even our private rooms didn't have locks, which had always seemed slightly weird to me. It was also weird how the mind went off on tangents when it should focus.

"I didn't know that. There's nothing in your profile about it." I came in behind her and sat in her semi-comfortable desk chair.

She moved around the room precisely and efficiently, collecting items she wanted to take with her.

"Won't they have the supplies you need?"

"I don't take chances with people's lives. Not if I can help it," she said.

"What makes you so sure this is a real problem and not a ruse?"

"Gut feeling and something in the email message," she said, finally glancing at me. There was a hunted look in her eyes. "Most of her email was just about her condition and that she needed me. But there was a postscript at the bottom, almost like an afterthought. That code phrase that Ingrid was talking about."

"And it was?"

"Zeus knows."

I shook my head not understanding the significance.

"Zeus knows. It was a phrase a friend and I made up during that year in the field. It was our way of saying that doctors were all liars, thieves, and alchemists. The caduceus, the traditional symbol for Hermes with two snakes winding around a staff, was an ancient sign—"

"For liars, thieves, and alchemists. What does 'Zeus knows' have to do with that?"

"It was our code for knowing when something was wrong. A bad situation. Our way of saying that God knows the liars and frauds," Christina said. Her knuckles turned white as she gripped the bottle in her hand.

"If it's a lie, then why would you go?" I stretched a hand out to her, but she ignored it and walked over to the medicine cabinet, selected another key from the ring, and unlocked it. She selected a vial and then replaced it, took a similar one next to it, and added it to the collection on the counter. Done selecting items, she packed the bag methodically as if by rote with the materials she had collected.

"Why?" I asked again. "Does it have to do with Dr. Charles? Do you know her from before? You seemed very friendly at Pole Station."

"Yes and no." Christina let out a long exhale. "We have a good friend and colleague in common. Connie was in the Sudan with my friend from university the year after I was there. For me it was a rotation with a UN health organization, but for my friend…She's still working in hot spots around the world."

"You think your friend shared 'Zeus knows' with her?" I had more questions, like why her time with the UN wasn't in her profile, but I wanted to stay focused on the current situation.

"I don't know. It's just weird and my gut says something is wrong." Christina reached out to me then, and I took her hand with the long-tapered fingers and held it gently. "I'm afraid something is wrong over there and whether Dr. Charles has a ruptured appendix or there is some other problem, she was asking for me. Me specifically."

"You can't go alone. Ty can't go with you. She needs to be here. That leaves me. If you go, I go. Buddy system and all that."

She leaned in and kissed me. As kisses go, it was too quick. Her lips were soft and set off an answering ping down to my toes. Before I could respond, she turned to the door. "I don't think that's a good idea. But I'm going to take you up on it. I don't want to go alone and you were…a Girl Scout, Guide, Bluebird?"

"You mean, can I read a compass or a GPS?"

"Yeah, that."

"Yes, I can get us there if the weather is right. I can't if there is a storm. I'll go check on the weather and meet you back here before Ty's hour is up." I released her hand and headed for the door, then stopped. "You know, Ingrid might be a better person to travel with. She's got a lot of winter wilderness experience."

"True, but I want you."

CHAPTER TWENTY-ONE

May-Antarctica

It didn't take me long to determine that the weather would be clear for another twenty-four, then the wind, blowing east to west, would pick up significantly. We could walk a mile, even in these conditions, in less than an hour, so there was more than enough margin even if the storm came in a little early. It wasn't ideal, but given the darkness and freezing temperatures, it was the best we could hope for if we really were going to attempt this crazy trip.

Back in our room, I packed a small backpack for myself. No sense wasting time. And what was that phrase? "Be Prepared." Right. How prepared could I be for a hike through a pitch-black expanse of frozen wilderness with temperatures forty-five degrees below zero. It was insane. We had no vehicle. I threw another fleece in the bag like it would help. I hoped Ty would find there wasn't a problem or if there was a problem, Pole Station was handling it.

I knew I was building it up in my mind. I had never actually spent any time in these conditions. Read about them, yes. Read about Shackleton's voyage, all from the comfort of my living room chair in a nice warm house. It was only a mile. I could do a mile. And back.

I gnawed on a fingernail. Did I really want to do this? I had said I would. What was it Christina had said about lies, liars, and frauds? Who was behind all of this? And more importantly why? Was their intent to frighten or actually harm? Exhaling a tense breath, I zipped up the bag and slung it over my shoulder.

The team gathered in the common room to hear the news from Ty. Christina was looking pointedly at her watch when I entered. I thought she was angry with me, then noted that she hadn't noticed my entrance.

"Nothing," Ty said. "I can't get through to GICE or the NSF."

"Is our connection to the satellite up?" Rue asked. "I can try to reach Pole Station through the ham radio operator network. I know I wasn't supposed to do that, but I'm a belt and braces kind of person with communication links."

"The connection is up and it's loading files properly," Ty said, her brow creasing as she looked at Rue thoughtfully.

"Is it time to break out the emergency communication equipment?" Ingrid asked, glancing over at Rue before adding, "We have a secondary communication link with Pole Station besides Rue's ham radio set."

"If we use that one, it gets counted against us," Miho murmured, glancing around at everyone. "Well, it does."

Several heads nodded.

I walked into the room and sat in my usual chair by the galley. "Christina believes the email she got requesting help is real." I glanced at her. "Do you want to tell them or do you want me to?"

"What's this?" Ty asked, turning and looking from me to Christina.

Christina shook her head at me, as if she was disappointed that I had brought it up, but I had played this game twice and wasn't going to do it again.

"Christina thinks there was a message to her in the email from Dr. Charles." I glanced at Christina, who gave me another small head shake. "Something only she would understand and it gives her the belief there is a serious illness or a serious problem over at Col. Ride's hab. If you can't give us anything more to go on, I think Christina and I should go over there."

"It's forty-five below zero outside. Are you nuts?" Dianna said.

"What was in the email?" Miho asked.

"Both very key points," Ty said. "I take it you don't want to get into the cryptic comment in the email?" Ty had read the email. I wasn't sure if the rest of the group had.

Christina and I both shook our heads.

"I think this needs to be a group decision," Ty said.

Christina looked mulish and Ty raised her hand in a gesture of appeal.

"Miho is correct. If you go over there and there isn't a serious problem, you put the whole mission at risk." She raised her hand again, palm up. "That doesn't mean saving a life isn't worth this whole study. But there is the problem of getting there safely and not putting one or two more lives in jeopardy when we could contact Pole Station. They are better equipped for this."

"What's the wind speed?" Ty asked.

"Relatively calm right now." I hedged.

"Speed?" Ty repeated.

"Two to five miles per hour." I knew exactly where she was going with this. It wasn't just the temperature. It was the wind chill factor. The harder the wind blew, the colder the actual temperature felt and the harsher the effects on the body. "Yeah, I made the calculation. We have about twenty-five minutes before we are at risk of hypothermia or frostbite."

"Do you really think you can walk a mile based on a GPS device? No road, no path, in total darkness, in twenty-five minutes?" Ingrid scoffed. Ingrid had lived in Norway most of her life and knew about extreme cold. It was one of her many specialties.

"I brought two pairs of heated socks and we have enough hand warmers to place in strategic locations. I think we can bump up the time to thirty to thirty-five minutes with these adds."

Christina stared at me, her eyebrows raised in surprise.

"Not my first rodeo." I smiled at her. Of course, it hadn't been minus forty-five degrees and I'd had cross-country skis.

"Still, I think I might fare better at getting Christina there and back," Ingrid said, although I could read the tightness of her jaw, and she wasn't convinced.

"But why go at all?" asked Miho, her normally quiet voice sounding shrill. "You don't know anything is wrong. We haven't heard from GICE or from our primary contact, Evelyn. Why would you put the study at risk for some wild email that hasn't been substantiated?"

The room was silent except for the gentle humming of the heating system.

"While I'm less worried about the study…It's not like they can fly us out of here in the middle of winter…I have to agree with Miho about the email," Elisabeth said. "Can you share the hidden message and why you think there is a problem with Colonel Ride's team? Do you have another girlfriend over there?"

Christina rolled her eyes. "I don't have time for this."

Again, everyone waited. It had to be Christina's decision and the team understood Christina didn't share much about herself. Why that was, I was just starting to understand. She had been raised not to bring attention to herself. She was a child genius, had graduated early and often, with multiple degrees from multiple universities. It was all in her provided profile. But behind it all was loneliness and her solid belief that if you didn't talk about it, your friends and family would love you or at least not avoid you. Nobody likes a know-it-all.

It was a long wait. No one even fidgeted. The hum of the heater was almost soothing. Finally, Christina shared with them what she had shared with me. I'm not sure what finally got her to talk, but I think it was the patience everyone showed her. It's hard not to argue your point and push. It's hard to ask and then let the answer come in its own time.

"Be the good you want to see in the world," Sam said after Christina finished her explanation.

"What?" Rue asked.

"I think Sam is trying to tell us we need to do the right thing," Ingrid said, standing, her long frame seeming to tower over the group. "It doesn't matter whether or not there is a problem. What matters is we do what we can to help."

Several in the group nodded their understanding.

"How do we know it's the right thing?" Miho asked, her voice low but firm.

"We don't." I stood. "What we know is someone is trying to isolate us even further…by interrupting our communication. Christina believes—I believe—something is wrong. We need to go figure out what's going on and potentially save a life." I turned to Rue. "What kind of transportable communication devices do we have and will they work between here and Colonel Ride's hab?"

Rue looked surprised to be called on. She glanced around at the group and then at Christina before turning back to me.

"We have the SAT phone," she said hesitantly. The SAT phone or Satellite phone was our emergency communication device for the hab.

"Why can't we just call Colonel Ride with the phone?" Elisabeth said. "Wait, aren't we not supposed to use that phone except in cases of emergency? If we use it, we violate the terms of the study? But we're doing that anyway by even going over there."

"Yes, that phone." Ty rubbed a hand across her face. "We can't call Colonel Ride or Jason Von as we weren't given their phone numbers. We were told we wouldn't need them and to call GICE. If there was an immediate emergency we couldn't handle, Pole Station." She cleared her throat. "The unit works just like a normal phone. But on the good side, we have two of them and we know our own phone number. To Jo's question, we have a viable communication link."

Ty continued, "Christina, thank you for explaining the cryptic text. I was curious if it was from NSF or from someone on one of the teams. Is there any way anyone other than your friend or Dr. Charles would know what that meant? Could they access the information? Use it against you and through you, us?"

"I don't know," Christina said, running her fingers through her dark hair. "I've thought about that. I would have given an unequivocal no, but I didn't think my friend would have used our code either."

"Can you call your friend on the SAT phone?" Dianna asked, raising her hand slightly as if trying to get a teacher's attention. "Do you have her number?"

"I have the number of the World Medical Organization, but I can't be sure that they'll put me through to where she is. They keep that information private for safety reasons. The medical staff usually carry disposable phones and keep their personal phones locked up. I don't know when or if she'd get a message if I called her. If she's even using the same number from five years ago." Christina shrugged. "Look, I know this all sounds crazy, but I have to go now during the day cycle when it's slightly warmer, if you can call anything here warm, or I'm not going to have any chance of success in getting to Dr. Charles and helping her."

"And if she's fine, it's all fine and this is some aberration?" Miho said, still not sounding convinced of anything.

"Then you can say I went rogue, and you all told me not to go, but you couldn't stop me," Christina responded with some heat. "My job, my life's work is to save lives. I have to go. You'll have to lock me up to stop me."

"No one is locking anyone up," Ty said. "Jo, Ingrid, I know you both agree that Christina should go and both of you are willing to go with her. Does anyone, besides Miho, have any objections?" She silently surveyed the room. No one spoke. There were a few negative head shakes, but no one verbalized any agreement or objection. Ty nodded once then turned back to look at me, Christina, and Ingrid, who were all now standing in a group. "Jo, I'd like you to go. Ingrid, you'll be backup if something happens. We have the GPS coordinates for Colonel Ride's camp." She turned to Rue. After Rue nodded, she turned back to us. "The tracker should give you the path to get from here to there. Once you leave, you have twenty-five minutes to get there and check in. That's going to be hard, but you're both in good shape. Call before you enter their hab. That way if there is a problem, we at least know you made it. Once inside and you've assessed the situation, call again and give us status. What am I missing?" She surveyed the group, then checked her watch and then looked at Christina and me. "Good luck and I really hope you find nothing and come back to us before the wind picks up."

CHAPTER TWENTY-TWO

May-Antarctica

The first blast of cold air took my breath. We had donned multiple layers, including a full arctic balaclava and goggles, and still the heat seemed to leach from my body immediately. I felt like a poor excuse for a Michelin man with all the layers. We had already activated the hand warmers on our backs, arms, legs, and hands. My feet were still warm from the heated socks I was wearing. The day, if you could really call the blackness that surrounded us day, was clear and the sky was full of stars. It was beautiful and I wanted to stop and stare in wonder.

"Come on," Christina said, trudging forward in the white bunny boots. "Point the way."

Bringing the GPS closer to my goggled eyes, I checked the readings and took off in a northerly direction. We were all so close to ninety-degree south that everything was to the north of us. Colonel Ride's team was north and west of us. Our flashlights did little to illuminate the path in front of us. Tempting as it was to turn the lights off and navigate by starlight, the snow drifts were deceptive. It took us a while to get the hang of scanning the near horizon and detecting the path in front of us.

It was slow going. I pushed for greater speed knowing our time frame was limited. I didn't want Ingrid to have to come find us, though I knew her arctic weather skills were better than mine. I wondered why Ty had let me come instead of Ingrid. Christina and Ingrid had avoided each other. No outward hostility, just a subtle rivalry. Two very smart people watching each other. The flirting Ingrid had directed my way was halfhearted and always with an eye toward Ty—maybe to see if jealousy would work. It had stopped completely once Christina had moved in with me. I was friendly with all of my teammates and tried not to show any favoritism to Christina. It was hard in this isolated life not to group together, be it roommates, workmates, and even playmates.

I stumbled over another drift of snow and I could feel ice beginning to form on my balaclava from the heat of my breath. I shivered. The cold was ever present. We slogged on, not talking. Checking the GPS every couple of minutes kept us on the path. The night sky was so beautiful and so clear but the wind was picking up. At last, we came over a slight rise, and in the distance, a single light could be seen distinctly.

"I see their hab." I called back to Christina, the wind whipping the words. Her head was down, as she was concentrating on pushing through the snow, but it came up as I spoke. She was as covered as I was and I couldn't see her expression, but her pace picked up and she came up even with me.

"Let's get there," Christina said with enough force to be heard over the wind and through her own face coverings. "I'm losing the feeling in my fingers."

She took off at a crazy lope that looked like the gait of Apollo 11 Astronaut Neil Armstrong as he moved across the moon. It wasn't as bouncy, but it seemed as stiff and the landscape looked to be otherworldly. I followed quickly behind her. I was freezing and my body was feeling sluggish, but I got my feet moving and tried to mimic her movement. My feet got jumbled and I fell onto the snow. It felt good to stop and not move. I knew I needed to get up. I felt so tired but knew that we were almost there. As I crawled to my feet, I felt Christina grab my jacket and pull me up.

"Just a little farther," she said, grabbing my hand and pulling me forward. "Move."

It seemed to take forever. Like one of those dreams you can see where you want to go but never get there. Their habitat setup was an exact duplicate of ours. If I hadn't known better, I would have thought we'd just made a full circle and were back at our hab module.

Christina unzipped two layers to get to the SAT phone where it had been kept to keep it warm. The number had been pre-programmed in and she hit the send button. It seemed to take forever for the phone call to go through. Ty picked up after the first ring.

"We're here," Christina said.

I couldn't hear Ty's reply, but Christina nodded and said, "Will do." She hung up the phone, placing it carefully back in its storage pouch and fumbled the zipper jackets closed.

"Ready?" Christina asked.

"I wonder whether we're expected or if this is going to be a big surprise," I said. "Let's go, I can't take much more of this cold." My ears, even through four layers, were frozen and I could feel my teeth starting to chatter as any heat I had generated with motion was dissipating quickly.

There was a barely perceptible shrug before Christina pulled the latch and opened the heavy outer door to the mixed team's front entrance. As we stumbled into the vestibule, the difference in temperature caused us to shiver. We had made it. It had taken us twenty-four of the twenty-five minutes allotted.

I opened the door into the changing room and another shudder went through me as the heat from the room hit. I shrugged out of my backpack and began peeling off layers of outerwear. Christina did the same. I pulled off the various warming patches and stowed them in my bag. No need to be messy and leave our trash in their hab. Once we had divested ourselves of all the outer gear and stowed or hung it up to dry out, Christina turned to me.

"Ready?"

I nodded and she opened the door to their common room. It was a lot like our common room. The configuration of couches and chairs was slightly different and the artwork was completely different with fit military types instead of nature pictures, but the gym setup and overall layout was almost an exact replica. The smell was a little more pungent but that could have just been a first hit of a new place. A rangy, athletic woman was running on the treadmill with headphones on and didn't turn when we entered.

Christina made a soft chuckle as she approached obliquely to let the person see her as she approached. The woman's head turned. She stumbled before righting herself and jumping to straddle the moving treadmill. She slammed a hand on the emergency button and yanked off her headphones.

"What the hell?" she said. "Who are you?" And then answering her own question. "Aren't you from Blackwell's team? What are you doing here?"

"I got an email message saying that Dr. Charles had a ruptured appendix. I came to operate or do what needs to be done to help her."

"Dr. Charles has a ruptured appendix? What?"

"Well, I guess that answers that question," I murmured.

"Can I talk with Dr. Charles?" Christina asked. "My name is Dr. Christina Sohn. This is Jo Peterson. And yes, we're both from the women's team headed up by Ty Blackwell."

"I'll get Colonel Ride and let her make the decision. You guys aren't supposed to be here," she said, backing away from Christina like she carried the plague. She made a hasty retreat, and we were left alone in the room.

"Not an auspicious welcome." I fell into my normal chair by the galley. "Gee feels like home but not. What now?"

"We have a conversation with Colonel Ride and find out what's going on," Christina said, standing up straight and taking a deep breath as if to center herself. She didn't put her hands on her hips but her presence suggested she had. She was suddenly calm and in charge. "I think she will be very interested to hear about our lack of communication with GICE and the NSF. I wonder if they are having similar problems."

"I am very interested," Colonel Ride said from the doorway.

She was a tall woman, about my height, with a build more like Ingrid's—all legs and long arms. Her brown hair was short and her features seemed honed. There was no welcoming smile on her face. "What's this about a ruptured appendix?"

Christina removed a folded sheet of paper from her pocket, smoothed it out and handed it to Colonel Ride. "I got this three hours ago. We tried to contact GICE via our communication link and the SAT phones and we couldn't get through."

Colonel Ride hesitated before accepting the paper. Finally, she took the proffered paper and read the brief lines, making no comment on the last cryptic line. Returning her gaze to Christina's, she lifted an eyebrow.

"Tina, go get Dr. Charles," she said with a quick glance over her shoulder at the treadmill runner. "Maybe she can clear this up."

As Tina left the room, two men entered. One was short and slight with a pale face covered by an overly large mustache, which looked quite out of place in relationship to his overall size. The other man was my height, with a clean shave that included his head. His dark complexion gleamed under the fluorescent lighting. Neither man looked happy to see us.

No one spoke and it felt like a standoff in an old western movie. I stood and moved to stand by Christina; it didn't feel like a time to be casual.

After what seemed like a long time but was only moments, Tina came back in the room at a run.

"The medical door's locked and Dr. Charles isn't answering," she said in a rush.

"You stay here," Colonel Ride barked, pointing at us like we were trained show dogs, as she hurried from the room.

The two men eyed Colonel Ride as she rushed by but just remained in the room watching us. It was getting uncomfortable. I could tell that Christina wanted to rush down the hall and see what was happening, but I knew "Tweedledee and Tweedledum" would stop us before we got out of the room. I also knew I shouldn't think of these two men this way, but I didn't like the way they were eying us—like dinner on a plate or virgins to the slaughter. I wasn't sure, and I didn't know if I wanted to find out. I was ready to head back out into the cold. Dr. Charles be damned but I wasn't going to leave Christina. I was glad at least that I was next to her and not across the room. I also was aware I was giving into fear. These men weren't my enemies.

Christina didn't seem to feel the tension in the room. Her mind and attention were focused on the corridor. Like a runner poised in the blocks, she was ready to move as soon as she was given the signal. It came suddenly, like the shot from the starter's pistol.

Tina burst back in the room waving a hand at Christina.

"Come quick," she said, startling me and the two men watching us, mistrust plain on their faces.

Christina didn't hesitate and I did only briefly before charging after her to medical. I had to shoulder past a woman and another man who looked familiar, but when I reached the room, Christina was already at Dr. Charles's side, checking her vitals. The room stank of vomit and I wrinkled my nose. Christina glanced up briefly when I entered. I went to her side and we carefully lifted Dr. Charles's limp figure on to the metal table identical to the one in our hab that I had sat on to get the glass removed from my foot.

"Clear the room," Christina said to me, her voice carrying.

I turned to see several people had crowded into the room and the rest were in the corridor peering into the room.

Recognizing the dynamic in this team, I turned to Colonel Ride and said, "Please clear the room. Dr. Sohn needs to create a clean field in which to work. If surgery is required, we're going to have to sanitize the room as much as possible. We need everyone to respect that."

Colonel Ride looked frustrated. I knew she wanted answers but until we could see to Dr. Charles, we didn't have many answers to give. She nodded and barked another command to the team which had them scattering. She stayed in the room and closed the door.

"Why did she email you and not tell me that she was ill?" she asked.

Christina shrugged and continued her examination.

"I want a report as soon as you know anything," she said and not waiting for an answer left the room, closing the door softly.

"Do you know why she didn't tell Colonel Ride?" I asked.

"Maybe, but right now I just want to get her stabilized. And I think she's in shock. I wish she had contacted me sooner. She tried to deal with this on her own with antibiotics." Christina waved at a vial and syringe on the counter. "In the cabinet behind you are cleaning wipes. Start sterilizing the area, but first call Ty and let her know that Dr. Charles does need surgery. Be quick, I need you."

We got Dr. Charles—Connie—undressed, the table cleaned, an IV and plasma bag started, and the necessary surgical items sterilized and prepped. Her abdomen was bloated and she groaned every time Christina touched her midsection, but she didn't wake.

"Are you prepared to be my surgical nurse?" Christina asked, staring me in the eye.

I had taken courses in first aid and emergency procedures but I wasn't great with blood. But it was a little late to be asking now. Taking a deep breath to steady myself, I nodded.

"It's no shame if you can't," she said, "but I need to know now. I don't want two patients."

"I'll be okay," I said. I wasn't so sure about that, but I could manage my reactions. I wanted to help and this is what I needed to do to help. "What do you need?"

Christina began to give calm clear instructions, which I followed to the letter. Listening to her voice and not watching what she was doing, helped. When she needed something, I handed it to her or got it from her bag or the cabinet she indicated. When she needed an extra hand, I did what she asked with only an occasional shudder at the warmth or texture of what I held or pulled with my gloved hand. I had a couple of gag reflexive moments but controlled them, listening to Christina's calm voice. After what seemed like forever, Christina was stitching the wound together with quick, efficient motions.

"This all could have been done without major surgery if we had a proper operating room but that isn't feasible here or on Mars," Christina said to me conversationally, her hands coated in blood, her face covered by a surgical mask.

I wanted to pass out. The smells and the blood after the fact were now starting to get to me, even through my own mask now that the surgery was complete.

"Wash your hands in the sink, and sit down," Christina said. Her voice was still calm, in control and soothing.

I did as she asked and felt better immediately. As I pulled off the gloves and washed my hands, I couldn't help but think of Lady Macbeth and wonder if my hands would ever be clean again. I shuddered once more and put the thought out of my head. I had helped save a life.

"When will she wake up?" I asked from my perch on the medical stool. Christina continued to work, checking the stitches one last time, before applying some solution and covering the wound with bandages.

"It will be several hours before she wakes, and I'll need to monitor her for at least three to four days minimum, possibly as long as a week if there are problems. I think I got here just in time. Thank you for your help."

With that statement, I knew she meant more than just the help with the surgery. I had believed her and worked with her to get her where she could do the most good. That mattered to her and I knew it. I simply nodded and gave her a quick smile.

"What are you going to say to Colonel Ride?" I waved a hand at the patient who had morphed from "Dr. Charles" to Connie.

"As little as possible. There is something going on here. Connie should've let her know, and there must be a reason she didn't. Without talking to her, I can't know."

"Are we going to tell her our communication with GICE and the NSF is out or compromised?"

"I think that would be a good idea. Speaking of communication, why don't you check in with Ty and let her know our status. We'll have to stay until Friday minimum, that's four days. I plan to keep us locked up in here to not cause any more disruption than necessary. That should appease Colonel Ride and Ty." Christina began collecting the surgical tools. "It's going to take us a day just to clean up this room. It looks like we slaughtered a hog. It was good that Connie had a supply of plasma for us to use. I hope there isn't another need for it anytime soon."

I made the call to Ty but kept it to just the facts. Ty pushed for more but I was tired and didn't have anything more to give, so I cut her off, telling her that we needed to conserve the battery. I'd check in with her again as soon as I knew more.

After the call, I wanted to just lay down and sleep but the smell and the blood was something that would just cause nightmares. Sliding off the stool, I put on a new set of gloves and started cleaning up the mess.

The lull was too good to last and a knock on the door signaled that Colonel Ride wanted information. Christina motioned me to continue as she stood tall, rolled her neck on her shoulders, lifted her chin, and pushed out her chest. I would have laughed at this but the determined gleam in her eye stopped me. Power pose time. I hoped it would help manage Colonel Ride.

"Dr. Charles will be fine," Christina said as she opened the door to face the Colonel. "She won't be awake for several hours as the anesthesia needs to wear off and I don't want anyone else in here contaminating the environment."

Colonel Ride attempted to look over Christina's shoulder but she had angled the door and her body such that there wasn't a clear line of sight. I was completely hidden from her view.

"I wanted to let you know we couldn't raise GICE Corp or the NSF during our comm window or on the direct satellite phone. We did attempt to communicate with them prior to making the journey between habs," Christina continued in her calm but authoritative doctor voice. Just the facts ma'am. No emotion, very clinical.

"Why didn't you raise us on the SAT phone?" Colonel Ride asked her voice hard.

"A question that came up in our own discussions," Christina said. "We don't have your number. We were never provided it." She cocked her head to the side and continued. "Do you have the numbers for our team and the men's team?"

Colonel Ride didn't reply and I couldn't see her face. I wanted to peek around the door but stayed where I was out of sight, and hopefully, out of mind.

"You do," Christina said. She didn't sound surprised only justified. "Why is that do you wonder? That you have these numbers and Ty was never provided this information?"

"I'm military. I have a need to know," Colonel Ride said crisply.

Christina just nodded. She had used this technique on me before and I always had to stop and not babble answers. It was a good technique. Nature abhors a vacuum.

"I asked for the numbers before we left," she said. "I like to be prepared for contingencies."

"Prepared for contingencies," Christina repeated. "What kind of contingencies?"

There was a long pause but the Colonel didn't respond.

"I need to stay with Dr. Charles for the next four days to ensure there is no infection or any additional procedures required. Jo and I are prepared to stay in this room with her during that time to prevent further disruption of the isolation study." Christina paused, waiting for Colonel Ride to comment. When she didn't, Christina added. "Feel free to *call* Ty and discuss our communication issues with her."

Colonel Ride must have given some sign because Christina closed the door and turned back to me. She gave a brief shake of her head to indicate that I shouldn't say anything just yet and put her ear against the door.

I pulled out a small notebook from my breast pocket, which I carried for jotting down random thoughts and making lists. It kept me from obsessing over things. Writing quickly, I turned the pages to Christina.

IS THERE SOMEONE LISTENING TO US?

Christina shrugged. Stepping away from the door she came over to where I knelt cleaning up the last of the blood that had splattered against one of the lower cabinets. Surgery was so messy. I had to stop thinking about what I was cleaning or I would've been retching continually. How did crime scene cleaners do their work?

Christina took my arm, pulled me to my feet and turned on the sink so that the sound of water splashing filled the room.

"I think Colonel Ride has posted a guard on the door," Christina said in a soft voice that didn't carry. "We need to watch what we say but we need to have normal conversations so that they believe nothing is amiss."

This was getting stranger and stranger by the minute. Now that the crisis of Dr. Connie Charles's emergency surgery was over, I had time to consider the fact she hadn't shared her condition with anyone on her team.

Christina put her arms around me and gave me a comforting hug. I could tell she was feeling the strain of the last few hours as much as I was. Leaning my head down to rest on her shoulder, I snuggled into her warmth. Then I stepped back and laid a gentle hand on her cheek. I wanted to give her a kiss but we had set the rules. There had been a minor break. It didn't diminish the fact the mission was still in place and we were in someone else's space.

"We need sleep," I said. "We've been up too long. With the email, lively discussion, the trip to get here, and this surgery, I'm completely wiped. You must be too. I just helped. You performed a major surgery." I put a hand to her lips before she could protest. "I know you're a big bad trauma surgeon used to forty-eight-hour shifts, but you have to deal with anything that comes up with Connie." I nodded to the motionless figure on the metal table. "Sleep. I'll keep watch and wake you as soon as I see her coming around."

Christina nodded and turned to pull some supplies from her backpack, making a nest on a clean expanse of floor. I thought it would take time for her to fall asleep but she seemed to go out immediately. A true medical professional. Take sleep when it's offered.

I went to my own backpack and pulled out some fresh clothing. I washed as best I could in the sink and changed into a new pair of cargo pants and thermal top. It was colder in this room than in most of the rest of the hab on purpose. The medical supplies liked the cold and germs did not. I hadn't really warmed up from our walk outside; I just had stopped thinking about it. I added a fleece to my ensemble. I hadn't brought a blanket like Christina had and wanting to know if there really was someone posted in the hall, I opened the door and peered out.

The tall black man with the shiny dome looked at me. That answered another question.

"Do you have some bedding we can borrow? We need another blanket to cover Dr. Charles and maybe a pillow for her head. The table in here was never meant to be a sick bed."

He gazed at me thoughtfully without the hostility of before.

"I'll see what we can do," he said, his voice a deep baritone. "Do you need to use the facilities?"

I realized that I very much needed to use the facilities and nodded quickly.

He pointed down the hall and as I hurried down the corridor, he followed, passing me as I reached the restroom door to continue to the sleeping area. I made quick use of the facilities and as I emerged once more from the washroom, I found him in the hall waiting for me, several blankets and three pillows in his arms. We exchanged a nod and I headed back to medical with him trailing me. He handed me the supplies and shut the door in my face.

I let out a deep breath and decided that had gone well. Yes, there was someone posted to watch us, but the hostility I had felt when we first arrived seemed to have dissipated. I couldn't really blame them. How would I have felt if one of the other teams had burst unannounced into our hab, our mission?

I got out the SAT phone and its charger and plugged it in. My argument to Ty had been specious but it had gotten her off the phone. Then I placed a second blanket over Christina and set up

Connie with blankets and a pillow, before creating a nest for myself across the room from Christina. I was afraid I would wake her up if I got too close or if I fell asleep, I might end up cuddling with her. If we got a sudden surprise visitor, I didn't want them to have ammunition to use against Ty.

I checked on Connie again but all the vitals Christina taught me to watch for seemed normal and she was still asleep, so I pulled out my reader and tried to stay awake. My own exhaustion took hold as I let myself relax. I put myself in a semi-uncomfortable position and still found myself nodding off occasionally. I finally got up and started pacing quietly across the room.

One, two, three, four, five, turn. One, two, three, four, five, turn.

I tried to count as I walked to quiet my mind but all the worries and secrets over the past few days kept sliding into my mind one by one. Zeus knows. What was up with Christina and Dr. Charles? What problem or trickery was going on here or with the study? What was up with Miho's family? What was up with Miho's ex? Had the people at his new job somehow brainwashed him? And what was up with the communication system? No word from Evelyn or GICE or the NSF? Or the FBI? Why was Ty worried about the personal emails she had been getting? Were they personal or were they something else? The emails reminded me of my aunt's letter which I had compartmentalized. What did it mean? What did she expect me to do with her apology? My head was spinning and the room felt suddenly stifling.

Movement on the metal table.

I checked on Connie and saw her eyes flutter open. She blinked rapidly and her eyes focused on my face. She was scared. I didn't want her to flail around.

"Hi," I said soothingly, trying to use Christina's calm technique. "You're okay. I'm Jo. I'm here with Christina from the women's team. You're okay."

She relaxed a bit at my words. She tried to speak and her words came out as a croak. I decided she could probably use some water.

I stooped to shake Christina. She came awake immediately and I nodded over to our patient. As she got up, I quickly went over to the sink and grabbed a mug that was sitting on the counter that read "I am a doctor—to save time let's assume I'm never wrong" and filled it with water.

Christina took the mug I handed her and helped Connie take a few sips. Just enough to wet her throat.

"Quite a scare you gave me," Christina said, her voice quiet. "First the email, then being out cold when I got here. Why did you wait so long to get help?"

Connie's eyes flashed around the room.

"It's only me and Jo here." She rested a hand on her arm and proceeded to give her patient a medical rundown that went over my head.

When she was done, Connie visibly relaxed and her eyes shut.

"Is that normal?" I asked.

"Yes. She'll probably sleep for another couple of hours." She noticed the blanket over Connie. "I see you got some extra blankets." And seeing the pillow under Connie's head, she smiled. "And pillows."

"I left the room for a short time to hit the washroom and ask our guard to get us some supplies," I said.

"Why don't you get some sleep? I'm good for the next shift."

My sleep was restless. I felt I was shivering uncontrollably as I wandered through an ice landscape alone, believing with every rise, I'd find our hab module. People kept popping up to tell me my phone wasn't working but when I tried to talk to them, they just faded away like a snow flurry caught in the wind.

I woke up to the buzz of the SAT phone. Christina scooped it up before the third buzz and cradled it to her ear. After a brief acknowledgment, she just listened and watched me. The frown between her eyes deepening as the conversation progressed. She turned and walked to the sink, turning on the water, spoke softly into the phone, then she hung up. Shaking her head, she beckoned me over.

"Evelyn has been arrested. She was in league with whoever caused the sabotage and they think Miho's ex may be part of it. No information on Miho's kids or mom. And Jo, there's evidence that Evelyn modified information in Amy's medical record."

I rocked back, stunned by the words.

"Evelyn's been Ty's friend for years. How's she taking it?"

Christina shrugged. "I just got the facts. Not feelings."

"We need to tell Colonel Ride," I said.

Christina shook her head. "Ty is concerned that Colonel Ride might be part of the problem."

"What? Why?" I felt like I was still in my weird dream.

"We need to complete our work here and get back to our own hab," she said. "I don't want to be here any longer than we have to be."

"Has Dr. Charles said anything?"

"We had a brief conversation," she said, glancing toward the sleeping form.

"And?"

"I agree with Ty," Christina said, turning off the water.

I knew that was my cue to stop talking. We couldn't leave the water on indefinitely. That would be as big a giveaway as our conversation. And we couldn't waste water. I decided we could talk about our exit strategy.

"Any infection? How does the healing look?"

"Too soon." Christina glanced at me, shaking her head. She knew what I was asking and she couldn't give me an answer. It was too soon. "She was dehydrated when we got here and she lost blood due to the surgery. There is a limited amount I can do given where we are and what we have." She poked at the IV drip. We had already gone through three IV bags. The supply wasn't unlimited.

"You wanna sleep while I stay up with her?" I had a lot to think about. Evelyn's treachery could explain the lack of spare sensors, leaving Amy on the team, and the communications gaps with Houston. She was setting us up to fail.

CHAPTER TWENTY-THREE

June-Antarctica

It was a long four days. Dr. Charles slept through most of it and when she wasn't asleep, she and Christina conversed in low tones. Christina had made her walk the room. It was slow and painful to watch, but she seemed to get better each time. Colonel Ride showed up on day two to see how things were going. Our patient was asleep at the time and Christina wouldn't let Colonel Ride wake her up, citing Dr. Charles's need for sleep and healing. I didn't know how long that answer would placate the Colonel, and I was still hoping we would be leaving in another day. One way or another, Connie wasn't going back with us, and Colonel Ride would be talking with her soon.

I was getting tired of being put off too. Not being able to talk freely with either Christina or with Connie was wearing on me. I had a few tentative conversations with Christina about what she'd learned from Dr. Charles, but it was convoluted. Connie believed that Colonel Ride was monitoring our channels back to GICE and the NSF. Ride's team seemed composed of military personnel, except for Dr. Charles. Neither the men's team or our team had military included. That didn't make Ride's team bad, but I agreed it was strange and suspect.

After the first couple of days, I had gotten over my fear of being close to Christina. It was so cold in the room and we had limited bedding. We built a cozy nest against the back wall, after moving Dr. Charles off the metal table and onto the mattress her team brought in for her. We'd situated her on the floor opposite us. That last night, sleep didn't come easy and there was no way to burn off energy beyond a few sit-ups and pushups. Christina and I settled down to pretend to sleep when I couldn't take it anymore.

"Did she explain the 'Zeus remembers' comment?" I asked, keeping my voice low and muffled by the blankets pulled up around us.

There was enough light in the room with all the medical sensors, monitors, and devices, that I could just make out her features as she faced me. She didn't answer immediately but pulled me close so that my head rested on her shoulder and her mouth was near my ear.

"It was as I thought. She had worked with my friend Melissa in Ghana. Melissa had shared stories with her about our problems with some management and military not sharing information, potentially putting the medical teams in danger." Christina paused before continuing and took a deep breath. The air she released tickled my ear and made me shiver. She squeezed my hand and continued. "She knew using that phrase would get me here. She didn't trust that Colonel Ride would call for a doctor. She wanted me."

"Seems extreme," I murmured. "Wouldn't it have been easier to get a Pole Station doctor? This kind of emergency wouldn't have put the study at risk or put a dark mark on the Colonel's record. This team doesn't appear to be having our communication problems." I paused snuggling against her. "Does she know why we're having communications issues? Did she say anything more about Colonel Ride and not trusting her?"

"She wouldn't commit. She said she knew Evelyn was sending a lot of messages. The only one she saw had mentioned something about changing data sent for your ice shelf monitoring. She didn't remember the exact words and didn't write them down, as one of the team showed up while she was reading. She feels like an outsider among this military group." Christina shifted and my head moved down to rest on her chest where I could hear the steady rhythm of her heart and feel the soft cushion of her breast. "She was a last-minute replacement like me. The military doctor they had came down with a bad case of shingles."

"Ouch."

"Yeah, shingles in an adult can be very painful."

"Still, I would have thought they would have pulled in another military doctor."

"I guess she came highly recommended," Christina said. "I agree with you. Weird. Maybe they liked her world health experience." She paused. "It's been a crazy few days. I had meant to ask earlier, but why were you crying before all this happened?"

I sat up and moved away from her. I didn't want to talk about my past.

She put a hand on my back. "You can tell me. I have enough of my own baggage. I won't judge you."

Her tone was soothing and her hand was warm. "Tell me."

"My aunt sent me a letter. I received it before we left for Switzerland." I shook my head. "She threw me out of the house after she found me kissing my best friend in high school. Said I disgusted her and that I should have died with my parents. That it was my fault they'd died." Tears leaked from the corners of my eyes. "I agree with her. I wish I'd died. If I hadn't thrown a temper tantrum, I'd have been with them, or they would have left earlier and never been near that drunk driver. She's right, though. I should have died."

"What did she say in the letter?"

"She was sorry." I wiped my nose on my sleeve.

"How old were you when your parents died?"

"Twelve."

"Twelve? Did you ever talk with a therapist about their death?"

"No."

"Did you talk with your aunt about it?"

"No. She was always away traveling. Short trips but continuous, like she couldn't stand to be around me. She'd stare at me and burst into tears. They had been really close, her brother and her. Money was always tight and I was a burden." I wouldn't meet her eyes.

"And how old were you when she threw you out of your home?"

"Seventeen."

"Jo, she was wrong to blame you. She couldn't handle her own trauma and took it out on you." Christina ran a soothing hand down my back. "I'm glad you didn't die."

The tears flowed in a steady stream down my face. She pulled me close and held me until we fell asleep.

On the fourth day, Connie was fully awake and mostly mobile. She still had a drainage tube attached, but the plan was to remove it before we left.

Colonel Ride came with the dinner meal. Tina, the woman we'd seen on the treadmill back when we arrived, brought in the meal and then left without speaking.

"I've spoken with Blackwell. She makes a good argument for you coming unannounced into our isolation study. I'm still not happy, but I think Dr. Charles, my team, and me personally appreciate her recovery."

Her words came out stilted as if she wasn't used to saying thank you. She really hadn't said thank you but it seemed like that was all the praise Christina and I were going to get.

She walked farther into the room and over to the chair where Connie now sat.

"Why didn't you tell me you were sick?"

Connie flinched from the words. Her eyes darted around the room and then up at the colonel looming over her. She murmured, "I thought I could handle it with antibiotics."

Colonel Ride frowned at her. "You thought you could treat appendicitis with antibiotics." She glanced up at Christina for confirmation. Christina just shrugged. "So why when the antibiotics didn't work did you contact Dr. Sohn instead of coming to me?" Colonel Ride looked a mixture of angry, hurt, and bewildered.

Connie said something inaudible to me. Colonel Ride took a step back as if punched and braced as if another blow would come. "I would never put your life in jeopardy for a study," Colonel Ride said.

I could hear the honesty in her voice, and I could hear the strain of command. Of all the people in this team, Dr. Charles wasn't military. And just from the past few days, I could tell that Colonel Ride ran this hab with military precision. I didn't see the practical jokes and good-natured banter of our group happening in this hab. It was on the leader to build a team. Colonel Ride may have built an efficient organization, but it was very different from our group. Seeing this so clearly, I wondered if there really was a problem for to us deal with or just the stress affecting Dr. Charles.

I watched Christina out of the corner of my eye, wanting to see her reaction. Did Colonel Ride's statement change anything? Regardless, we were out of here in a few hours. They would have to sort out their own problems. I wanted to get back to our friendly village. Even though we had our own issues and stresses, it still seemed a more welcoming place with all the pranks and laughter.

"Dr. Charles is still recovering but will be able to fully resume her duties in a few days," Christina said, her voice professional and crisp. "I'm going to remove the last drainage bag today. Someone will need to help her with her bandages a couple of times a day."

Ride's face transformed. The Colonel was back. "Do you think that wise? If we have a medical emergency or Dr. Charles has a relapse, we need you here."

"We've spent as much time as we can here. Dr. Charles is fine to supervise or do basic medical procedures. We have our own team to support. We will be leaving in…" Christina checked her watch, "…two hours. Please clear a path for us to the changing vestibule."

Ride's brow furrowed as she contemplated Christina's words. She didn't look like she liked having her orders countermanded. Then she gave a curt nod and left the room.

I let out a breath I didn't know I was holding.

Dr. Charles just snorted.

"Get your stuff packed up," Christina said. "We are leaving. I'm sorry, Connie. You're on your own. Try to make friends or get used to your own company. Send me updates and I will reply if we stop having problems with our own communications. Use the medical profession and follow up codes if you get pushback from Ride. I really do want to make sure you're okay." Christina's lips quirked up. "It seems like a tough crowd here. Seriously, try to find a friend. This adventure isn't over for another five months."

The next two hours were a blur. I made a final call to Ty to check the weather and make sure the wind hadn't come up. That could have seriously derailed our planned exit. I wasn't looking forward to the trip back, only *being* back, and that was enough to get me motivated for the journey. Being trapped in our module with nine other people for the past seven and a half months hadn't seemed as stifling as being trapped in this room for the past four days. I was packed and had stacked our provided bedding, well before it was time to go.

As I assisted Christina as she made the final adjustments and checks on Dr. Charles's wound, I began to get a bad feeling.

"What if Colonel Ride won't let us leave?" I asked as quietly as I could.

Christina glanced at the door and then at Connie.

"You're concerned too?"

"Get the thought out of your head. We're leaving. Take care, Connie. We'll see ourselves out." Christina motioned me to follow as she headed for the door.

No one was there when she opened the door. I took it as a good sign as we threaded our way down the corridor to the common room. It appeared deserted. Then Colonel Ride stepped out of the galley, blocking our path. I almost ran into Christina's back at her abrupt halt.

"Thank you for your hospitality," Christina said. "Since you gave us your SAT phone number, we'll call and let you know of our safe arrival when we get back to our hab." Her emphasis on "our hab" was distinct and unmistakable.

"My weather officer says the wind has picked up to above fifteen knots," Colonel Ride stated. "I can't risk your lives."

I looked at Christina who looked back at me. I stepped forward to confront the force keeping us here.

"I checked the weather. It's cold, yes, but the wind is only five knots and expected to be steady for the next two hours. We have a window. It's time for us to use it before the weather does turn."

Before Colonel Ride could say more, Christina stepped around her and headed for the changing room and exit.

I thought Ride was going to stop her, but she just glared at Christina's back and ignored me as I hurried to catch up. I started to question myself and my conversation with Ty about the weather forecast but stopped myself. Ride was bluffing and it wasn't going to work.

We dressed quickly and efficiently, attaching the second set of warmers to each other and activating them. We were almost sweating in the room. Entering the outer vestibule, which was about twenty degrees colder than the changing room, we checked each other to see if any skin was exposed before we opened the outer door.

The cold hit us like a barrier but the wind was relatively calm just as I had known it would be. Head game indeed. As we cleared the building, I gasped in wonder. The dark landscape was lit up with the Southern Lights, aurora australis. Greens and yellows. Purples and reds. Eerie and inspiring. I stared, jaw slack.

"Come on." Christina took my arm. "It's truly beautiful but we'll look at it some other time—together where we can truly enjoy it. Right now, we need to get back to our own hab."

We set off at a brisk pace into the dark landscape lit with the spectacular colors. I checked the GPS device regularly to make sure we were on course. Being locked up in that room had made us antsy to be moving again, and even though the cold was intense and ever present, it was good to be moving. It was a weird feeling. I could feel the intensity of the exercise, like I was going to sweat, but it turned immediately cold and icy. I knew this could kill us if we were out too long.

Traveling in the dark with only the colorful sky and our headlamps to guide our steps, it felt like we were the only people in the world. The crunch of snow under my feet seemed to be the only sound other than the sound of my own labored breathing. I comforted myself by watching Christina cut a path through the snow with me calling a path change occasionally if she veered too far from our goal. I shivered and I was just starting to worry that the GPS was faulty when we crossed a rise and could see the welcoming lights of our hab. The team had pulled all the cardboard from the windows and the lights were brilliant. I could feel my eyes tear up.

We put on a final burst of speed making a beeline for the safety of our southern home. Before we reached the door, I took a last look up and sighed.

Christina turned at the sound. All I could do was point and shrug. She turned to the aurora and reached out a hand to me. As I came up beside her, she hugged me tight to her side. We didn't linger long. It was too cold and we had generated enough sweat that the cold was really starting to leach into our bodies. We hurried forward to the comfort of good friends.

CHAPTER TWENTY-FOUR

June-Antarctica

The welcome felt like déjà vu. Ingrid was at the door to the changing room and pulled us through. Then the room was crowded and we each had multiple hands getting us out of our winter gear. The laughter and the comradery were intoxicating after the last four days in the military zone. We hadn't experienced the other team's normal life and schedule, and we had crashed their world. But the guard on the door and Colonel Ride's controlling attitude had felt stifling to me.

Sam surprised me with a big, warm, inclusive hug once my coat and bunny boots were finally stored in my cubby. She knew how undemonstrative I was and yet she had reached out to show me how happy she was that I had returned. I hugged her back tentatively at first and then with real affection.

"Missed you," I said. "And all your crazy stories but not your surprise attacks." Not being her roommate had separated us and I sorely missed our interactions.

"Need to bring you up to speed. To the galley," Ty called over the din of conversation and laughter. "Slaves…"

"You couldn't resist," Elisabeth said, jostling Ty as she went by.

Christina and I moved with the group into the comfort of the galley, where we were pushed into chairs.

"Cookies?" Dianna asked, waving a plate before Christina.

Christina hesitated before reluctantly taking one.

"Don't worry, Dianna didn't make them," Ingrid said, taking a cookie from the plate.

Christina visibly relaxed as she took a bite.

"Hey, settle down and sit," Ty said. "We have business to discuss."

As everyone found spots, Ty jumped up to sit on the counter. Christina settled in the seat next to me. It felt good and comforting to have her close.

"How was it over there?" Elisabeth asked, taking a cookie from the plate being passed around. "How is the other doctor... Connie?"

"Connie is fine. We got there just in time. And the atmosphere over there is tense," Christina said as the eyes in the room swiveled to watch her. "I don't think they're having as much fun as we are."

"Colonel Ride runs a tight ship," I added. "They didn't know we were coming and there was a lot of tension when we first showed up."

Ty nodded. "I got that from Ride, although not in so many words. Did she really not know that Connie had a ruptured appendix?"

"She didn't know," Christina confirmed. "Connie was afraid that Ride would have had their psychologist, who's had some medical training, do the procedure. I really don't understand that. Colonel Ride is a bit of a stickler, but I don't see her as being so into the mission she wouldn't take emergency steps to save a member of her team." Christina nodded her thanks as Rue handed her a steaming cup of coffee and then one to me. "Although she may have worried if Dr. Charles had been evacuated to Pole Station, if she would've come back."

"It seemed like it's a military zone over there. Dr. Charles wasn't very forthcoming but she thinks Colonel Ride is hiding something. I'm wondering if she has a separate mission from ours," I continued, nodding my thanks and taking a sip of the brew. "Thanks, Rue. The cold outside is brutal. I really don't want to go out again for a while, though the Southern Lights were beautiful and amazing."

The team looked interested at this but Ty cut them off. "Enough time to see the Southern Lights some other time. Let's focus." Ty waved a hand at Elisabeth. "Elisabeth and I have been going over all the information the FBI has provided GICE since Evelyn," she grimaced at the name, "was arrested. It seems she was associated with a patriarchal religious organization set on keeping women in subservient, submissive roles. She hadn't reported her connection to the organization. They are still working to find out who else may have been involved, but so far, the count is five. GICE has been cooperating with the FBI to find these individuals and ensure they get them all. Both the head of GICE and the NSF personally reached out to me, emphasizing the importance of our work and their commitment to taking action. I might add that Amy's death is being reviewed again in light of the altered medical record."

"You've been friends with her for years," I said.

"Work friends. We never socialized," Ty corrected. "Though to be fair, I thought I knew her."

"Do they believe Amy had a medical condition?" Miho's voice was low and tentative.

"They didn't say, specifically," Elisabeth said, her blue eyes very serious as she turned to gaze at Rue who looked ready to cry.

Ty nodded and continued. "They still haven't been able to fully tie anything to your ex, Miho. A few of the emails Christina got, the ones that got through the spam filter, are helping. They point back to SpaceGen, the company your ex recently joined. We don't have much more than that."

"It's good to know we're not crazy," Ingrid said as she stretched a long arm across the table and neatly pulled the cookie plate back across the table just as Rue reached for a cookie.

"Are communications back up and functional?" I asked. Then remembering another conversation. "Miho's kids, her mom? Is everyone okay? Have you heard from them?"

Miho nodded, her eyes welling up. She covered her face with her hands. Dianna put a hand on her back and leaned down to whisper in her ear. Then the two got up and left the room.

"What happened? Did we just lose communication or was Evelyn actively blocking us? And how come we couldn't get through on off shifts when she wasn't there?" I asked.

"A combination of things," Ty said, taking a cookie from the plate Ingrid offered. "Two of the three shifts were Evelyn's people. The third shift was covered by a new person, who, though they weren't actively part of the plot, had been led to believe the data they were to provide or not provide, was part of the study. They didn't question it until our panicked communication on Dr. Charles. They didn't respond as they'd been coached but sent the message through to all the department heads."

"And that's when the shit hit the fan," Elisabeth said. "Evelyn hadn't covered her trail as well as she thought she had. John is livid. He called the FBI and found that no investigation was in progress." She sat back and smiled. "There is one now. The quail are starting to scatter."

"Quail? What do quail have to do with anything?" Rue asked, pushing her glasses back up on her nose. The group laughed at her puzzled look.

"I think she means that all of those involved in the conspiracy are getting flushed from their hiding places and the FBI is closing in on them," I said. "What about Miho's family, are they okay?"

Miho had left with Dianna but I still felt in the dark.

"We think the grandmother has gone into hiding," Ty said, the concern evident in her voice. "Miho has received word from her that she is okay. It has all the right phrases so Miho believes it is from her mother. Seems they had a code too. But there is a trust problem now. Her mother doesn't trust GICE or the FBI, so she's not saying where she is. Miho is worried that if her ex is still out and about, that they are all still in danger. We can't get her protection if we don't know where she is. We don't even know if she and the kids have been grabbed and the ex made her mother send the message."

"Has Miho told her what's going on, that Evelyn and her cohorts have been arrested?" Christina asked.

"So far they haven't tied anything back to the ex," Ty said. "Miho knows he's involved but doesn't have any details. It's a mess and she's getting more and more emotional."

"Yeah, the plants are getting plenty of water," Elisabeth said.

Ty frowned. "Dianna appears to have a connection with her and is trying to help her emotionally, but I'm worried." She rubbed her forehead. "We can't do anything from here except make phone calls and write emails," she trailed off and shrugged.

"What is GICE saying about all this?" I asked. "Have they informed the other groups? Are we at risk? Colonel Ride's group was acting like a military camp. I didn't think she was going to let us leave."

Ty shrugged. "The men's group has been told and GICE reports no problems or issues with them."

Ingrid snorted.

"Colonel Ride's team has also been told," Ty continued, ignoring Ingrid.

"Did her group report our presence or Dr. Charles's illness?" Christina asked, beating me to the question.

"She didn't say and GICE didn't mention it," Ty replied. "I didn't ask her or GICE about your extra-curricular activities."

"What now?" Rue said, her glasses had slipped down her nose again but she didn't push them back up.

"I propose we check and recheck all our systems. Check through our data reports with GICE and the NSF and make sure nothing is missing," Ty said, rising from her seat. "That's about all we can do."

"Until the next shoe drops," Ingrid muttered.

CHAPTER TWENTY-FIVE

July-Antarctica

Over the next few weeks, Ty communicated regularly with GICE on the study and with the NSF on the data we had collected on Antarctica. There was no additional word on the investigation or the location of Miho's family. The FBI was tracking Miho's ex but what they found or didn't find was a mystery to us.

The complete darkness outside coupled with the complete absence of information from our sponsors was disheartening. We didn't know if the lack of information was because they didn't have anything to share, keeping us in the dark was part of the study, or the investigation prevented them from sharing. We had no additional communication from the other teams. Christina had received one email from Dr. Charles a week after we had last seen her.

Vitals are good. Thanks for the support.

And then nothing. I questioned Christina but she merely shrugged and said Connie was fine. Since our trip to help Connie, Christina was more circumspect and it seemed Rue was frequenting medical more. I wanted to yell and throw a tantrum but decided the darkness and close quarters were getting to all of us. But like Ingrid had said, we all waited for the next shoe to drop.

I knew Ty wasn't sleeping. Ingrid was supposed to handle first shift unless there was a problem, but Ty was up at all hours. She was getting ragged around the edges, and I was about ready to get the team to do an intervention, when Christina slipped her a mickey. I wouldn't have believed it possible, and I was concerned that Ty would react badly when she woke up. The dosage wouldn't have put a child to sleep, but Ty went down quickly and awoke after sleeping twelve hours straight. She'd been so exhausted I think a suggestion would have put her down for the count. Christina wasn't subtle about what she'd done and the entire team knew. I was glad it was an open secret. We needed to pull together. When Ty realized what Christina had done, she was pissed, but Christina had just shrugged. We took our cues from her.

Miho's mood swings affected the entire team. On days when she received an email from her mom, she was up. When she got pictures or a video, she was absolutely giddy. Ty quietly acquired the emails to let the FBI trace them only to have them go quiet. Then nothing for days, and Miho's mood would crash, taking some of the team with her. Dianna and Sam were the most affected.

Sam worked with Miho in aeroponics. The plants seemed to be a safe haven for many of us. We had pulled a small couch into the area where the grow lights and humidity gave off positive energy. Hanging out with the greenery got to be such a premium that Ty had to create a sign-up sheet with time slots after complaints that Miho was sleeping on the couch when not actively working in the lab.

It came to a head one morning when Ingrid walked into the lab to find Miho sleeping on the couch. I was in the galley drinking coffee before I started work. There was a loud crash followed by shouting. I jumped up, nearly spilling my coffee, and ran into Rue, who had been taking yet another pan of cookies out of the oven. Rue controlled the pan but I got a searing burn across the arm. I yelped but the noise from the hall had me running toward the confrontation. I heard the pan clatter on the counter as Rue followed me.

Ingrid loomed over Miho's tiny form. It would have been funny if the anger on their faces hadn't been so real. Their noses nearly touched and neither gave a fraction of an inch. Miho's hands were balled into fists and it looked like she was getting ready to take a swing.

"Get over yourself," Ingrid said, her words crisp and controlled. "Get out of this lab. Do something...anything."

"Go away, leave me alone. This is my lab!" Miho cried. "My lab, my lab, my lab." She was almost chanting it like a child. She looked awful. Her luxurious black hair was matted and her eyes were dark rings. She looked like she hadn't slept or bathed in days.

Ty pushed me out of the way as she entered the lab. "Ingrid, back off. Miho, stop."

Ingrid turned toward Ty and Miho hit her. The punch never would've landed if Ingrid hadn't been distracted. But Miho's fist carried all of her fear, anger, frustration, and hopelessness, and it clipped Ingrid on the jaw right below her ear and sent her stumbling. Luckily the force of the blow pushed her onto the couch instead of into the racks of plants.

Miho covered her face with her hands and burst into tears at what she'd done. The racking sobs shook her whole body. Ingrid massaged her jaw from her prone position on the couch and just stared dumbstruck at Miho.

Christina pushed past me and Ty and took Miho by the arm, pulling her gently from the room and taking her down the corridor toward medical. "Come on Miho, you need to rest." Miho fought her grasp, trying to go back to the lab, but Christina's soothing tone seemed to strike the right note and she let herself be pulled away, feet dragging with each step.

Ty rubbed a hand over her face and then walked over to Ingrid. "You okay? I can't believe Miho knocked you down."

"Lucky blow," Ingrid said as she sat up.

"Probably," Ty agreed. "Jo, everyone is on edge and Miho more than the rest of us. What gives and what can we do?"

"All of our days are running together," I said. "Food, work, maintenance, food, work, repeat. And for most of us, either too much or too little sleep." I stared at Ty pointedly. She snorted and looked away.

"I think we could all use a couple of rest days," I continued. "Other than mandatory maintenance activities, we need a play day. All of us, together. And then we need to get all the concerns out on the table. Things have festered long enough. Miho has got to tell us what's going on and the rest of the group needs to share what they know.

"It's ten p.m. and most of the team is running on adrenaline. I think we all need some sleep. Can the night shift cat nap? I think we should go to a split shift: six a.m. to six p.m., noon to midnight. That way we can all be awake together most of the day. Nothing is happening from midnight to six a.m. anyway. I've got all the sensors on audible alarms and I can get Rue and Dianna to rig those alarms to my room. We need to be together."

Ty nodded.

I backed up toward the door. "I'll let Christina and Miho know the new plan. They should both be in medical. I think Miho is suffering from nervous exhaustion. The lack of information has got to be preying on her mind."

Ty shook her head, her eyes sad. "I should've done something sooner. When not in aeroponics, Miho has been hovering over Rue in the communication area of the science lab. I'll talk to the rest of the team. Go find Christina." She made shooing motions and I left to see about Christina and Miho.

I found them in Miho's room. Miho was in her bunk, the covers pulled up over her shoulders, her eyes swollen and puffy from crying. Christina administered a shot of something and stroked Miho's hair, talking to her in a low, soothing tone. Christina might not like groups, but she was great with individual patients.

I waited by the door until she finished getting Miho settled into a drug-induced sleep. "Exhaustion?"

"Among other things."

"Ty's switching up the schedule." I filled her in on Ty's plan.

"Probably for the best."

I could see the exhaustion in Christina's eyes. Something was bothering her. My inquiries were being met with vague and unhelpful responses. She worked second shift too, but she was on call at all hours and a lot of the check-ins and samples she took were during the day shift. We were all tired. The fluorescent lighting wasn't a mood enhancer and staring out into the dark was beautiful, but after so many months we needed light, real light. The vitamin D supplements were no substitute for the sun.

"Why are you rubbing your arm and wincing?" Christina asked. She turned over my arm and spotted the burn the hot cookie sheet had made.

"Rue was making cookies. She saved the pan."

"Let's get this cleaned up."

Christina and I got a few hours' sleep after three a.m. It was hard after the closeness we'd shared at Colonel Ride's hab to go to our separate beds. The bunk was big enough for two, kind of a classic full-size bed, if no one flailed around too much. But here it would be too easy to slip into intimacy. Even though we'd shared warmth at the other hab, the knowledge that we were constantly being watched had made it easier to keep things chaste.

"Up," Christina said, her lithe form beautifully faint in the dark room backlit by light seeping through the hallway door. She tapped a nonexistent watch on her wrist. "Breakfast. I'm starving."

I buried my head under the bedding.

"None of that." Christina pulled the quilt from the bunk and threw it over the desk chair. "Ty promised a play day. I'm curious what she's got planned."

The rest of the team was already present in the galley when we arrived. Elisabeth was making made-to-order omelets and Dianna had been relegated to pouring orange juice to the general ribbing of the group. Christina and I put in our orders to Elisabeth, while Rue played sous chef.

Christina then went over to Miho and plucked up her wrist taking her pulse. Miho didn't protest. She seemed a lot better after a good night's rest. She had showered and didn't have the haunted looked of last night. She still looked wan, but then we all did. No sunlight.

After the team enjoyed Elisabeth's wonderful breakfast and the galley was cleaned, we turned our attention to Ty.

"So, what's on the agenda today, Chief?" I asked, taking a sip of coffee and smiling.

"Snow people," Ty said.

"Snow people?" Ingrid asked, looking perplexed.

"Yep, we're going to treat it like a real snow day," she replied, pulling small bags out from a drawer. "Teams of three. You have twenty minutes to build a snowman or woman. Be quick and have fun."

We all piled out of the galley and headed for the coat alcove. I knew what was in store as Ty had conferred with me on the weather. It was cold at minus forty but the wind was calm at less than five knots. It would be a reasonable day to be outside, and the team might get a chance to see the aurora borealis.

It was the first time Miho, Rue, and Elisabeth had been outside since the van had pulled up to unload us.

There was some grumbling but everyone got dressed quickly, pulling on the rugged snow pants, bunny boots, and doubling up on fleece and coats. Handwarmers were passed around for mittens. Balaclavas and goggles were pulled on. We were all starting to sweat when Ingrid pulled open the door to the antechamber and we pushed through to the outer door and then to the dark Antarctica landscape. We immediately began to cool down.

"Move it people," Ingrid called in her clipped English, the phrase and the tone sounding completely at odds. "Dianna, Elisabeth with me." She snagged one of the bags from Ty's hand.

"Rue, Miho," Sam said, grabbing a second bag from Ty. "Let's show them how to do this!"

Christina and I looked at Ty and she waggled the final bag full of parts for the snowperson in front of us. We exited the warmth of the anteroom and plunged into the cold, dark night. Unbeknownst to us, Ty had removed the cardboard out of several of the windows and it lit up the surrounding area so we could see some of the local landscape. It was beautiful and stark. The night sky was brilliant and the light from the hab wasn't enough to take away the view of the millions of stars shining in the sky.

It was actually quite hard to build a snowman in Antarctica. Most of the snow was packed as there was only a light dusting of snow every year. We had to find drifts and pull the dry snow together compacting as best we could. We were so intent on our work that the first snowball took me completely by surprise, hitting me squarely between the shoulder blades. It was about fifteen minutes into our allotted time and our snowman was just starting to take form with two small boulders of snow. I was feeling the cold and the snow hit at just the right angle to blast snow between my outer garments. Turning I saw that Ingrid's team had built a snow wall instead of a person and was using it as a defensive spot to launch snow missiles at Sam's team and us.

Sam and Rue had been hit and Miho was hiding behind the snowman they had put together. They had gotten farther along than we had, and the next snowball from Elisabeth hit their snowperson, knocking the carrot nose sideways on their frosty face.

"For God and snow people!" yelled Sam. She scooped up some snow and ran directly toward the defensive wall.

Ty shook her head and shrugged. We scraped up snow and ran yelling at the lumpy ice fortress. Mayhem ensued as we all threw snowballs, dodged, and rolled in the snow trying to get away from each other. It didn't last long. The extreme temperature and the snow finding its way underneath our outerwear made us shiver, and we ran back to the hab module laughing like crazed children on too much sugar.

"That was really stupid you know." I pulled off my wet mittens, which covered a second dryer set below.

"Yeah, but it was fun," Dianna said, her nose red from the cold.

"And beautiful," Miho said softly.

"Our snowman was better than yours," Sam said, looking over at Ty, a big grin on her face. "Yours was a shorty and had no nose."

Ty raised her hands in surrender. "Ours still beat out the snow wall. It didn't have a head or body."

"We could have crushed your snow people," Elisabeth crowed.

"To the galley for some hot chocolate," Christina said. "We need to get some warmth back into these frozen fingers and toes."

CHAPTER TWENTY-SIX

July-Antarctica

"Which one, *Aliens* or *Captain Marvel*?" Elisabeth asked.

"*Captain Marvel*," Sam said.

"*Aliens*," Miho and Dianna called simultaneously.

"Both," Rue said. "*Aliens* first."

Ingrid grunted agreement from where she sat—facing Ty in a game of chess.

I filled a bowl with popcorn and settled onto the couch next to Christina who seemed uncharacteristically tense. "You okay?"

She gave a perfunctory nod and ignored the popcorn bowl I offered her.

It was nice to veg out with the team. Ty kept us all together until the late afternoon when we were all tired, sprawled on the couches and comfortable easy chairs. She had a final surprise for us.

"We've been together off and on for almost a year and a half. Some of us have known each other before that but most of us are new acquaintances. Our main mission, regardless of the stated parameters, was to see if a women's team can come together as a unit, be it for a Mars expedition or for any other exploratory adventure. That's why we're all here, but I think there's more to it than that. We're all different people with different backgrounds. Different strengths and weaknesses.

"We've been here for 229 days. A real year on Mars is 687 days, so we made it through a third of the expected mission on Mars. We've done well so far. Provided GICE, NASA, and the NSF with great data and analysis. We've faced adversity from possible sabotage, communication issues, death." Ty stopped for a moment and grimaced, then she nodded toward me and Christina. "A walk through the great Antarctic wilderness to help another team. We've dealt with the loneliness and isolation, each in our own way."

She walked over to a box sitting behind my chair near the galley. Bending over, she opened the lid and pulled out a bottle of scotch. From my vantage point, I whistled softly through my teeth.

"That's an eighteen-year-old bottle of Highland Park single malt whiskey," I said, reading the label.

"Nice," Rue said, smiling appreciatively. "Very nice."

"I thought you all deserved a wee dram," Ty said as she pulled our clear, ordinary juice glasses from the box. "Sorry about the glassware. It's what we had. Does anyone need ice?"

Rue made a hissing noise and shook her head, making her red hair flare around her shoulders. "That's eighteen-year-old single malt, not some bargain basement stuff. A wee bit of water if you must, but no ice."

Elisabeth jumped from her seat as Ty unsealed the bottle and began to pour the rich, amber liquid into the common glasses. She distributed the glasses as Ty poured.

Once everyone had a glass, we all sat for a moment admiring the dark, honey-colored liquor. Then Ty raised her own glass and we mirrored her.

"To Amy," she said soberly and took a sip.

We all nodded and followed her lead. A few seconds elapsed and then the silence was broken as Rue sighed in appreciation of the rare vintage.

"Damn that's smooth," Ingrid said.

There were a couple of shaky laughs. Ty smiled. "As I was saying, we know why we're here but I believe there is more to it than that. I'd like to know why each of you is here," she asked softly.

"Trying to loosen our tongues with fine whiskey?" Elisabeth asked.

Ty cocked her head in acknowledgment of the jibe. "Who will go first? Why are you here? What do you hope to achieve, find, or learn?"

Ingrid rolled the clear glass in her hands, warming the liquid as she contemplated Ty from her corner of the couch between Rue and Miho. "I'll start," she said, taking another small sip from her glass and staring at Ty. "I'm here because Antarctica is amazing and the chance to winter over here is a dream come true. Sure, the science is cool. The project, the Mars mission, is amazing. But Antarctica..." As she spoke, her gaze traveled around the room, before resting on Ty. "I'm here for Antarctica." There was an intensity in her eyes that she was there for more than Antarctica.

Murmurs of agreement spread around the room. Ty looked over at Dianna.

"I'm here for something similar. Antarctica, yes, but more than that...I'm here for the challenge. To test my skills against the needs of the team and nature. I've done many projects across Africa and a few in Europe, almost always with men challenging every decision and design I made. This is completely different." Dianna's hands made strangely intricate motions as she spoke. Her dark eyes flashed with intensity.

Again, there were murmurs of agreement from the team, and then the room went silent as the group thought about the two statements made.

Rue sat forward on the couch and raised her glass to her lips, draining the contents in a final swallow. "Any more of this?" she asked, waggling the glass at Ty.

Ty stood and added another inch of liquid to the glass. She continued around the room refilling glasses, before finally stopping in front of me. "Last drop," she said.

"No, you have it."

I motioned her to fill her own glass. She complied and then sat putting the now empty bottle of whiskey on the ground beside her chair.

"I'm here because I wanted to see the place where I've talked to so many people over the years," Rue said, leaning back into the arm of the couch, her clear blue eyes dreamy behind her glasses. "I've had a ham operator license since I was seven years old. I can still remember the first time I talked with someone in South America and then got patched down to Antarctica. I had a map of all the places I contacted on my wall." She pulled her glasses off and cleaned them on the tail end of her shirt and then put them back on. "I loved talking to those old guys. They had such interesting stories. I wanted to see those places they talked about, and I wanted to be that voice to mentor the next generation."

"How about you Miho? Why are you here?" I asked.

Miho didn't respond to my question. As the team had answered the question, Miho had seemed to shrink into herself. She had finished both fingers of the expensive whiskey, grimacing as if taking an unpleasant medicine. Her eyes were downcast, and other than a brief glance at each of the speakers, she had focused on her hands in her lap, which were still and motionless.

"Miho?" Ty said.

Miho couldn't look at her. Her fingers clenched in her lap. "I'm here for the science and the study," she said softly.

We waited for her to add to the story but she didn't say anything else. Ty and I exchanged a look.

"I'm here for the opportunity to be the first to brew beer in Antarctica," Elisabeth laughed, breaking the awkward silence.

"Are you sure you're the first?" Sam asked.

"I think you're late to the party. The Aussies have been home brewing over at the Casey Research Station since the 1960s," Dianna said, shaking her head at Elisabeth's statement.

"What?" Elisabeth exclaimed, pressing one hand to her chest and the back of her other hand to her forehead. "I guess I'll have to go to Mars and be the first." Then she broke up laughing.

Ty just shook her head and nodded in Christina's direction. "How about you, Christina?"

"I'm here because the GICE director of exploration asked me to be here," Christina said her gaze calm as she returned Ty's stare.

This got everyone's attention including Miho, who raised her eyes to stare at Christina.

"Why did John Steinman ask you to come?" I asked. I felt betrayed. My offhand comment about Christina being a ringer had been true and I hadn't seen it.

"He suspected something, didn't he?" Ty asked. It was less of a question than a statement.

Christina nodded her eyes on Miho. "There was a lot of pushback on this team. It was all very logical and seemingly reasonable. Budget cuts and feasibility."

"I thought Evelyn was supporting me," Ty said sadly.

"The director thought Evelyn picked you specifically because you are an out lesbian," Christina said. "She thought that would doom any results that came out. The public wouldn't stand for a bunch of lesbians on Mars, regardless of how competent we are. A team of men is heroic. A team of women, well, they must all be lesbians and man-haters."

"Hey we aren't all lesbians," Sam said. "Did Evelyn think you would corrupt us? Or that we'd all turn into lesbians through proximity?"

"Don't you feel jealous that Christina and Jo are having sex?" Miho said suddenly, her eyes hard and accusing. "None of us has a partner in this isolation study or in any all-female group that goes to Mars."

We were momentarily stunned by Miho's sudden outburst.

"That's pretty harsh, Miho," Sam said. "Romance happens."

"Harsh but not unrealistic given the political climate today," Ty said.

"We are not having sex," I said. "Christina is the doctor on this mission. It would be inappropriate unless we were a known couple going into the mission."

"Yeah, I'm a little jealous they could have a relationship." Sam sent me a sympathetic smile. "But how is that different from a men's team? Do you think men can't be gay or have relationships?"

"The men have never been outed," Ty said. "The only astronauts that ever came out formally were lesbians. Sally Ride kept it private. It came out in her obituary after her death. Anne McClain was the only active-duty astronaut who was outed during legal actions against her by her wife. It's considered a career wrecker, just as divorce or separation was for the Gemini astronauts. You need a happy wife at home to show stability and manly fortitude. Are women more honest than men? Is it societal pressure or reality?"

"Let's get back to the director," Ingrid said. "Why you? And what was the concern?"

"Just this," Christina said, waving a hand in the general direction of Miho. "He wanted to know about and protect against active or subtle sabotage of the study from this group."

Now we all turned to look at Miho.

"Whoa, whoa, just hold on a second," Dianna came to her feet with a burst of fury. "What are you saying?"

"Miho are you going to tell them, or am I? How much time do we have?" Christina said, her voice once more transformed into her soothing professional delivery.

Miho looked startled. "Tell them what?"

"About the explosives," Christina said softly.

Miho's brows drew together in confusion, like she couldn't process what Christina was saying. "I don't know what you are talking about! What explosives?"

"Hmm…Dianna, can you and Ingrid make a survey of all the pylons holding the hab module? I suggest you dig down at least a foot at the base of each," Christina said calmly in her best doctor's voice, as if it was a normal maintenance operation. "The items to look for will be well hidden and blend into the pylon structure. Be very careful not to damage what you find. It might set them off, which is why I'm suggesting only Dianna and Ingrid look for the devices." She stared at the two women. "You both have experience; the others do not. Mistakes can kill us all, or at the very least, kill any chance for mission success, though this mission seems to have gone off the rails already."

Now it was Ty's turn to sound alarmed. "What are you saying? Has someone or some group put explosives on our hab?"

Christina nodded. "If I'm correct, we had a precursor a few months ago when Jo got her foot cut. I think something set off one of them without triggering the others. I was hoping I was wrong, but I don't think that's possible now." Her gaze fixed on Miho.

"Why would I put explosives on the hab? I don't want to hurt anyone," Miho stammered.

"Do you know what kind of explosives?" Dianna's question was flat, abnormally calm without its usual hint of laughter or wry wit.

"Something that doesn't leave much of a trace, if not found within about twenty-four hours. And wouldn't be noticed if someone didn't know what to look for."

Dianna nodded. Her eyes somber in her dark face. She stared over at Miho. Her look was as flat as her voice had been.

"Okay, we have the what," Ty said calmly, "do we know the timing? Who is planning to set them off? Or are you saying that Miho is the one who would set them off?"

"That would be completely idiotic," Ingrid said, anger apparent in her voice. "She never goes outside. What would be her excuse to go outside when she activated the system?"

"That's the beauty. She wouldn't have to go outside," Christina said. "This fob would set off the explosives." A thin square box, enclosed in a clear plastic baggie, dangled from her fingertips.

"That's not mine!" Miho exclaimed. She lurched to her feet.

"Then why did I find it fastened into the lining of your backpack?" Christina asked, her tone not wavering.

"Why were you going through my things?"

"I only figured it out today. Something Connie mentioned after we learned about Evelyn's treachery." She looked at me and shrugged sadly. "She overheard Evelyn on a call back in Houston. She was talking with someone, a man, about the extra care required with the support pylons when setting up our hab. That seemed suspicious and John started reviewing all the paperwork regarding our team. There were irregularities and higher contract costs compared with the invoices with the other team's habitats."

"Couldn't that have been due to the later shipment of our hab?" I was hurt and confused. She'd kept this from me. Did she suspect me? And how did these invoices lead to explosives?

"The team that set up our hab had specialized knowledge and no longer works in Antarctica. In fact, all the individuals on that team are missing."

"Okay, but how does that point to Miho?" Ingrid asked.

"John sent me a message today. He confronted Evelyn with the information he had. At first, she was reticent to talk, but when she was confronted with manslaughter and conspiracy charges for falsifying Amy's medical records, she admitted to working with Miho's ex. She provided emails stating explosives had been planted on the structural pylons supporting our hab. She couldn't tell John exactly where they were or how they'd be set off, just that it would be with a close proximity detonator."

There was a stunned silence.

Christina lifted the bag with the fob. "I just needed to find the mechanism to set them off. The plan was to search everyone's gear. I just happened to start with Miho. I found this about an hour ago while you were all watching the movie."

Ty leapt to her feet. "What gave you the right to search our possessions?"

"The desire not to die and the fact John directed me to do so."

"Why would I blow up this hab module? What could I possibly have to gain?" Miho threw her hands in the air and stared at Christina.

Christina ticked them off on her fingers. "Your kids are missing. Your mother is missing. You can't fake the amount of stress you've been exhibiting. You've been moody and upset. I know you've had some private messages that have been erased."

Miho looked stunned or guilty. I wasn't sure which.

Christina turned to Ty. "I'm not sure she doesn't have a backup detonator, and until we do a thorough search of her room and aeroponics, she can't be left alone."

"We don't have a jail cell," Dianna said. Her voice going from flat to hostile as the impact settled in. "You played me. You played us all."

"I didn't!" Miho cried. "I don't know how that fob got into my things." She stared around the room. "It could have been put there by any of you."

My mind swirled with the implications. Surprise and terror mixed for supremacy. It didn't add up. "What does Miho stand to gain by blowing us up? She'd be blowing herself up too. That doesn't make sense. Why would anyone do this?" I asked, fighting to stay calm.

Ty put her head in her hands. "I have to call the mission."

"No!" The words resounded from everyone except Miho and Christina.

"We have another four months before the first plane lands here," I argued. "We don't have the facilities to hold anyone. We can't call Pole Station. That just plays into their hands too. We need to work through this problem. We need to do the investigation and make sure that we are dealing with real explosives. They'll prove sabotage. Then we need to resolve the issue and remove the explosives." I glared at Christina. "It's not clear Miho had anything to do with this, regardless of what Christina found."

"Agreed, but who is behind this? Who can be trusted?" Ty asked. "Who has your kids and mom?"

"I don't know," Miho said, resignation in her voice. "I'm not a hundred percent sure they've been taken. A few days after Evelyn's crime was discovered, communications stopped. If we had all gone home after Amy's death, would any of this have happened? If I had known about this, I would have gone home. I'd be with my children. If I wanted to kill the mission, I would have left after Amy's death. You all would've been pissed at me but it was a legitimate excuse."

"We'd have been considered weak and susceptible to hysterical women's vapors," Ingrid said with derision.

"Using incidents and our perceived fears to justify our inability to get the job done," added Elisabeth.

"All of it playing right into the hands of those who want us to fail…need us to fail," I concluded.

Miho smacked a table. "That didn't happen! I didn't go home."

There was silence in the room as everyone contemplated the ramifications.

Dianna jumped up and glared at Miho. "I can't deal with this right now. Ingrid, let's go look for the explosives."

Ingrid followed her out of the room.

"How do we know there isn't another layer we haven't uncovered yet?" I asked. "Ty, what have you gotten out of the director? Are we really safe in our communication?"

"I think so but how can we be sure? I've known Evelyn for years and would never have suspected she'd do what she did. I realize now you were right, Jo. She was actively messing with us before we even left Houston." Ty rubbed her temples.

I was angry. My comments back in Houston had been about my frustration at Evelyn's incompetence and the work it was causing Ty. I had never thought she was actively trying to stop us. She wasn't working alone

I stared at Christina. "Who can we trust?"

"I trust John. He's currently working with the FBI, but it's slow going. Evelyn is talking but she hasn't given names, except for Miho's ex." Christina shrugged. "I think there are still enemies at GICE."

"I think we need to go silent," I said. "If Dianna and Ingrid can find all the explosives, maybe we can set them off away from the hab. An explosion would give a reason for our silence."

"Not afraid of it triggering one of those ice fractures?" Christina asked me.

"I don't think so. Not if we control it. It won't be near the ice sheet and it's winter here. It just needs to be loud."

"But wouldn't Pole Station or the other teams come to investigate?" Elisabeth asked. "They have the motion sensor data same as we do. Plus, the noise—the pulse—would be noticeable. We aren't that far apart. I like the idea of going silent. I think NASA and the NSF are trustworthy but I agree with Christina. We don't know about everyone at GICE or the rest of our corporate sponsors. If we go silent, the perps might believe their mission succeeded."

"What about the American Polar Satellites? They go over every ninety minutes or so," I said. "That would give us away immediately. I'm sure they would have photographic or thermal evidence we're still here." There were nods around the room.

"Seems a lot to overcome to make the bad guys think we're dead," Rue said from her corner of the room. She had been silent so far, making no comment after enjoying her whiskey.

She didn't seem as surprised as the rest of us. Her trips to medical made sense now. She was Christina's contact point with John. My heart hurt.

"I have an idea," Ty said. "I'll need your help, Christina."

CHAPTER TWENTY-SEVEN

July-Antarctica

Christina's revelations had hit me hard. I swung from feeling betrayed and used to a fiery rage, and now a deep sense of abandonment. Never had I wanted to run so much, but to where? There was nowhere to go in this cramped twelve-hundred square feet full of engaged women. Ty and Christina huddled together to make plans. I was out of the loop. After making the suggestion, I thought I'd be included. But Ty didn't need me. She needed Christina. Everyone else was busy too. Miho and Sam worked to get the garden rejuvenated. Elisabeth and Rue crunched data for Ty and supported communication with the NSF and the FBI. And Ingrid and Dianna worked on removing the explosives.

"You were right," Dianna said as she cradled the steaming cup of coffee to her chest with both hands, letting the warmth permeate the residual cold from her body. "The explosives are well hidden. Without knowing they were there, I wouldn't have seen them, even when looking directly at them. I don't know that I would have seen them even knowing they were there if Ingrid hadn't pointed them out. The saboteurs covered them and then painted them to blend into the structure."

"Were you able to remove any?" Ty asked.

"We took a lot of pictures of them in situ, and after carefully peeling back the coverings, once we had them exposed, removal wasn't too difficult. I don't think they expected them to be found. We removed about a half dozen," Ingrid said, mirroring Dianna's stance, coffee cup cradled in her hands. "It's slow going. It's cold outside, even for me." She grimaced. Ingrid loved the snow. She was tough but the winds were making the cold even colder.

"How many explosive charges do you think are out there?" I asked, once Ty and Christina were out of the lab. I wanted to get in there to check on the weather for the next few days. Even after I checked the forecast, I didn't trust that it wouldn't shift. Change was the nature of weather.

"We checked out three of the ten pylons. We found eight charges on each." Ingrid looked to Dianna for confirmation. "That's what we found so far."

"We'll go slow and find them all. But probably eighty devices, I'd say," Dianna said, nodding at Ingrid. "We'll check again but I agree with Ingrid. Once we knew what we were looking for, the bumps on the surface of the pylon are noticeable. At this rate, it's going to take a few days to remove them all. It's a tricky operation and the fingers go numb fast. We've been trading off, warming our hands and using multiple hand warmers, but it's really slow. The gloves don't help."

"Can the explosives be reused?" Christina asked as she came into the room.

Dianna frowned, exchanged a glance with Ingrid, and then said, "Maybe. The six we pulled are completely disarmed but we could pull them without making them inert. Not as safe for the hab or for us. What do you have in mind?"

"How dangerous?" Ty asked, watching the two women carefully.

Dianna and Ingrid exchanged another look and then Ingrid answered, "I'm actually surprised there has only been one incident. This type of explosive…" Ingrid trailed off and shrugged. "How many do you want? It will take at least twice as long to pull a device without disarming it and we'd need a safe box to store them. It would have to be away from the hab or they would still be very dangerous to us."

Dianna nodded emphatically. "These explosives are no joke. If Miho had hit the button, we'd all be very dead."

"Hey, we don't know if Miho had anything to do with this," I said. "She'd be just as dead as we would and she has family to live for."

Dianna went on as if I hadn't spoken. "We could still be dead if Ingrid and I don't get them off. The one that went off was really a dud. It should've set off the others near it in a chain reaction." She placed her coffee cup on the counter. "I really don't like the idea of keeping any of these devices live, but we can do it. How big an explosion are you looking to make?"

Christina's lips turned up slightly. It wasn't a warm smile but a smile full of intent. "Enough to put on a good show."

It took six days to remove the devices. In the end there were seventy-one devices found on the ten support pylons and a couple more on the understructure of the hab. It was a miracle that they were located, but Dianna and Ingrid had become experts at finding them. Knowing lives were at stake, they'd done a thorough check of the hab. Eleven devices were arranged into a large metal packing box Elisabeth found in the storage area. I joined Elisabeth in digging a three-foot hole in the ice a hundred meters to the southeast of the habitat. It was away from both our hab and farther from Pole Station and the other habs. Dianna and Ingrid carefully tucked the box into its new home.

"Weird number of devices. Are you sure you got them all?" Elisabeth asked.

Ingrid shrugged. "It's what we found. Most of us are used to round numbers or easy multiples. Seventy-one is a prime number, which in and of itself makes both of us suspect that there may be more but that's what we found. Maybe the ordnance person has a sense of humor."

"A sick sense," Elisabeth said.

The group was once more together in the galley eating enchiladas that Sam had cooked up with the traditional assortment of Spanish rice and beans. She had made fresh salsa from the tomatoes, onions, and cilantro from the garden.

Now that the explosives were relocated and/or disarmed, Miho was once more allowed to spend time in the garden. The area had been checked for communication equipment or any potentially harmful devices. Chemicals were removed and doled out sparingly and always with someone else present.

Miho didn't protest. She spent all her time in the aeroponics lab. She concentrated on her experiments to improve yield and the hardiness of the plants under cultivation. This was one of the driving reasons for the mission. Small area, closed food production. I didn't think she was guilty but Miho seemed to close in on herself, resigned to the accusation. Still waiting to hear from her children and mother, she was unmotivated except when her hands were in soil or tending to the hanging plants growing in their misty worlds.

"It doesn't matter." Miho trimmed back a weak vine on the strawberry plant. "Dianna believes me guilty." She shook her head and setting down the clippers, took up a pre-cut length of cotton string to help support the strong vine that remained in its climb up the wire trellis. "I just want news on Alicia and Brandon. And my mom. Dianna's and the team's anger hurts but not knowing what's happening with my family is killing me."

I had joined her to enjoy the warm humid air and UV grow lights. The environment in the rest of the hab was dry to the point it caused my nose to bleed if I didn't drink enough fluids.

"How did you get the fob?"

"No idea. If Christina was right, anyone who had access to our luggage could have put it in the lining of my backpack." She interrupted me before I could speak. "But, unlike Christina, I don't think it was any of us. I think it probably happened at the hotel or either McMurdo or Pole Station. They are pretty careful about who is allowed on station with background checks. My bet is McMurdo or the hotel. My backpack was left in the conference room while I explored the facility and store with Dianna and Sam."

"With your kids and mom missing, it's easy to pick you as the weak link," I said from my comfortable position on the couch. "It's unfair for Dianna and Christina to pin this on you. The evidence is at best circumstantial."

Miho moved to the lettuces and carefully selected and picked the fresh leaves for the evening meal. She added it to the pile of tomatoes, cilantro, onions, and broccoli that were already in the basket. "They need someone to blame. I think Christina is still watching and waiting. Dianna is just angry. She'll come around.

She doesn't like surprises, and this was a surprise. And if Christina believes it, it must be true. Dianna is a ones and zero person."

"All or nothing?"

"Yes, no halfway for Dianna," said Miho. "She thinks I betrayed her. You and Ingrid have stood by me. I appreciate that."

"Tomatoes look good," Sam said as she plucked a couple from the basket and began cutting them into cubes for the salsa.

Miho joined her at the counter, washing the cilantro and using a towel to dry the green leaves.

The fresh produce was a welcome supplement to the dry stores we had. The expectation was that Mars explorers would use the same techniques to supplement their diet. What thrived and gave the most nutritional value would be utilized but variety counted too. Sam didn't cook often, even though she was one of the better cooks in the group. Her tendency to make a huge mess, using so many pots, pans, and dishes that the counters, sink and even the table were covered with the path of her culinary progress, made even her wonderful cooking less worth the cost to those having to clean up after her.

Usually, everyone made their own meals and cleaned up after themselves. It was a treat when someone cooked for the group even if it took a group effort to clean up the detritus afterward.

After everyone had eaten, Sam revealed a peach cobbler, made with canned peaches she'd found in a box at the back of the storage area.

"Man, oh man," Elisabeth said, her nose raised as she sniffed the smell of the cobbler that Sam pulled from the oven and waved in front of them. "How did I not smell that before now?"

"Had your head down scarfing the enchiladas. Nicely done, Sam. Smells terrific," Ingrid said.

I took an appreciative smell myself.

"We sure eat great for being isolated," Elisabeth said right before she took a big bite of the cobbler. "Do you think they'll eat this well on Mars?"

"A happy group is a well-fed group," Sam said, piling a second helping on Ingrid's plate.

"True but the cost of shipping food is probably going to be one of the biggest costs until they can achieve self-sufficiency," I said between bites. "You really outdid yourself, Sam."

"Now that you've all stuffed yourselves…" Ty gazed around the room at the group of happy eaters and the anxious Miho who had eaten little. "Time to take the next step."

CHAPTER TWENTY-EIGHT

July-Antarctica

It took several days, numerous emails, and several satellite phone calls directly with the NSF Office of Polar Programs. No one was completely happy, but they had nailed down a plan of action. The NSF would work with the military and NASA to control the flow of information. GICE wasn't in the loop.

There had been a long discussion whether Dianna and Ingrid had found all the devices and whether we should vacate the hab before setting off the explosion. It was probably the prudent course of action but in the end, we trusted Ingrid and Dianna's removal. Rue needed to be in the hab to shut down all the communication gear in sync with the explosion. If one stayed, we all stayed. No one had put up much protest after that.

Dianna tinkered with the fob Christina found in Miho's backpack to trigger the explosion. It was unclear if the removal of the explosives had made the device inactive or it had never been active to begin with. The radio frequency pinged the timer in the open box and destroyed the box and much more.

The explosion rocked the hab and rattled the windows. My sensors showed significant movement, but no one was injured and we were all grateful for that. Dianna and Ingrid's box of explosives was relocated from its nest to about five hundred meters from the hab, away from the fuel station and opposite the path that Christina and I had taken to get to our nearest neighbor, Colonel Ride's group. Even though the team knew it was coming, none of us had expected the devastation and there was silence as we reviewed the damage from the safety of our still-standing home.

Only eleven devices blasted a hole two meters deep into the frozen earth for a space of over twenty meters. If the seventy-one devices had exploded as planned, the damage to our habitat would have been catastrophic and we would've all been killed. With that amount of damage, how could the investigation have determined anything but sabotage? The only questions would be who and why.

"No more communication," Rue said. "To the outside world, we all just died and the saboteur's plan succeeded."

"Now, all of us are cut off from our families, just like Miho has been," Sam said. She looked at Miho and shook her head. "I don't believe you would kill us all. It's too hard to get my head around. But I'm not ready to trust you yet."

"I understand. I don't know what else to say to convince you," Miho said. "At least you know your families are safe. I don't have that luxury."

"Not just cut off, Sam." Rue pushed her glasses up on her nose. "They think we're dead. We just died to the outside world."

"If it wasn't for the fact our families think we are dead," Ty said, "it would be an excellent simulation event of the satellites and relay system between earth and Mars going down. Unlikely but not impossible." Ty stared out at the explosion site and sighed. "Let's just hope the FBI and NSF can figure it out."

"The Amundsen-Scott Rescue team will be here shortly to confirm our demise," Christina said. "Let's let them do their job in peace. The news will be released to the world. This should set the wheels in motion for whoever planned this. Even with Evelyn arrested, this should move the rest of the terrorists forward."

"Do you think they'll release Alicia and Brandon, and my mom?" Miho asked.

Christina shrugged. "Can't know. They'll have no reason to hold them unless they can expose their captors."

Miho's eyes went wide and tears welled at the corners.

I stared hard at Christina. "They'll be fine. The FBI will find them." I patted Miho's arm. "They'll be fine," I repeated.

Whatever happened, we wouldn't hear until the first flight in around November. No sending study data, no emails from friends and family, no news from anyone on what was happening back in the US. No one believed Evelyn was the head of the snake, and Miho's family was still at large and possibly in peril. The agreement was to go forward and keep those who knew the truth to a very small number.

After the meeting agreeing to the plan, Christina followed me to our room. "You didn't have much to say about being cut off."

"Everybody had a lot more at stake than I do." I opened the door and flipped on the light.

Closing the door behind her, Christina tilted her head, clearly asking for more.

"My parents are dead. I don't have any siblings. Everyone else has people. In the case of Sam and Rue, large families." I climbed onto my bunk and laid a hand on my quilt.

"What about your aunt?" Christina asked.

I shrugged. I still hadn't decided what I wanted to do about my aunt.

As Christina planned, the emergency team from Pole Station arrived as planned. There was no interpersonal exchange made. They would report the devastation and that no one could have survived. The emergency team wouldn't investigate further until a forensic team could be flown in on the first flight when the weather once again permitted ingress to this part of our frozen planet. Four months minimum.

The other isolation teams would be notified and told to stay put. GICE would have them check for any problems in their own habitats. No mention of explosives, just warnings to look for any faulty systems. They would ask their question and make statements alluding to an explosion in the fuel storage. We wouldn't know if they found anything. We were cut off and on our own. Radio silence.

It had taken some time to coordinate. We had to be sure of the audience at GICE, the NSF, the FBI, and the emergency crew from Pole Station. In the end only five people knew the whole story and a few others just had limited knowledge, like the emergency crew from Pole Station. It was a top-secret endeavor with "need to know" only in place at all levels. Christina and Ty had worked it out with the GICE Exploration director, John. He was Christina's contact and reported directly to the deputy director of NSF who was a long-term careerist and not a political appointee. Like Ty he was on loan from his home organization. Unlike Ty, he didn't work for the GICE CEO, Cid Balkner. Though Christina and Ty thought highly of the head of the NSF and of NASA, neither one wanted to put that trust to the test. John and the deputy director both knew about Christina. John had notified the deputy that he felt there was cause for worry.

Ty hadn't known any of this. She'd been blindsided, putting her trust in people she thought were there to support her and the team. Her faith in Evelyn had been misplaced. And it had come as a real shock for Ty to learn there wasn't just one plant in her group—Christina—but potentially there were two—Miho. Someone Ty had handpicked as a member of the team. Who was Miho? A killer? A plant? A dupe? And Christina, the spy and protector of the team. It was a lot to take in quickly.

I didn't know how Ty had pulled herself together and accepted all this. It had thrown me and the rest of the group. Ty, though, was resilient and a pragmatist. After the initial shock, she had just taken the facts and worked with Christina to devise a plan.

Now that the plan was in motion, I couldn't foresee the consequences. I didn't even know if our supposed deaths would be released to the public, or if, when they were released, would the news garner even an inch of column on page three of the *Houston Chronicle* newspaper? And we wouldn't know anything more until the investigation team showed up in four months and the evidence surfaced that we were really alive. I was sure the forensic and investigation team would be on the first flight, and they were experts at determining what went wrong.

Interesting question. What had gone wrong? And could we have done anything to fix it before it became a problem? I couldn't think of a single thing we could have done differently, other than play into the hands of those who would have stopped us from succeeding. Ty had known Miho for years. Could she have known she was allegedly the weak link and susceptible to extortion? Sure, the ex was a problem. He hadn't been crazy when they'd been together. Only after he'd fallen in with the SpaceGenesis crowd. Miho couldn't have known that, could she? Love was weird and fickle.

Christina was another fish entirely. Ty had only met Christina after the original team doctor had fallen and broken a leg. She was John's selection and had the perfect credentials. He was the Exploration Director and held sway over Cid. While Christina hadn't fit seamlessly into the group, she was competent and likeable. Most of us had introvert tendencies, Miho for instance. I guess it was the quiet ones you had to watch out for.

Thinking of Christina made me think seriously about our friendship or whatever it was. Wrapped in my grandmother's quilt in our shared room, I stared at the ceiling in turmoil. It had been such an intense, frenetic day. What did it say about our relationship that I hadn't known about her work or her agenda here in Antarctica? I thought she was like the rest of us here for the study, the science, and the adventure. In a sick sense, maybe she was here for the adventure part. Was our friendship real or part of the subterfuge? A role she put on to hide in place. My stomach felt queasy with that thought. My emotions rocketed from anger to loss to feeling used and back. I wanted to scream or run, the feeling of betrayal, the duplicity of being used as a stooge, surged through me in waves.

I was so caught up in my inner dialogue, I almost didn't hear the door open. I froze, wondering if I should pretend to be asleep and hope Christina would go away. I wasn't ready to deal with her or my emotions. I knew how to deal with loneliness; it was an old friend. It was confrontation that was frightening—being made to feel wrong, to be the object of pity, scorn, ridicule, not being valued.

Christina pulled the desk chair over to the platform bedframe and climbed up carefully. The dim light in the room hid her expression.

"I couldn't tell you, Jo. Even after I knew I could trust you, I couldn't. I was here undercover."

I was silent. Even now, in the near darkness, with the quilt pulled tightly around me and my face obscured, I could feel her reading my reaction.

She reached out and ran a hand through my hair. "You weren't in the plan. How could I have planned for you?" she said this last as if to herself. "I didn't plan to fall for you."

She must have felt me jump at her words and her soft chuckle sounded loud to my ears.

"Fall for me?" I didn't believe her words. Was this another game? She hadn't said love. Was I falling for her? Falling maybe. Trust? Maybe. That was so much harder.

"Yes, I don't quite believe it myself but it's true," she said, caressing my hair once more before reaching down to stroke my cheek with the back of her hand. "You bring out the protector in me."

I jerked my head back.

"Yes, yes, I know how strong you are and how resilient. I let you come with me to help with Dr. Charles when Ingrid would have been the logical choice. It was a choice. I wanted *you* with me. Your insight is something I value. I wanted to see how their study was going and if they were part of the problem. I could trust you to have my back."

"And?"

"I think they have their own issues unrelated to Miho's ex and his group of crazies," she said. "I know I need to earn back your trust. When this mission is over, I want a relationship with you. I want to be in your life. You may not believe it or feel the same way, but it's true."

I wanted to reach for her. I wanted so much to reach out, to trust. But I couldn't. I didn't know what to say. I wanted to rage but I didn't have words. She had blindsided my best friend, made some horrible accusations against a teammate. We still needed to have genuine conversations about trust and faith and friendship. But it was Christina and I wanted her. We had four months to figure out if we could survive as a team. This was completely separate as to whether this relationship could survive and if I could face my own feelings without running.

"I need time," I said. I couldn't give her more.

"I understand. Take the time you need," Christina murmured. "We're both tired and this day has been…draining."

CHAPTER TWENTY-NINE

August-Antarctica

Once more the group was assembled in our go-to location, the galley. Food was a comfort, and it gave everyone but Dianna and Miho something to do. As usual Dianna was banned from cooking due to her complete lack of culinary skills, up to and including the inability to cut up vegetables without screwing it up, and Miho, because her trustworthiness was in question, though that seemed to be fading over time for some in the group. Her surprise when the fob was found had been genuine. Aside from some emails she hadn't shared, she had done nothing untrustworthy. We all had emails we hadn't shared.

Ingrid, Elisabeth, Rue, and Sam were rummaging in the cabinets and twin stainless-steel fridges. They seemed to be putting together an assembly line for sandwiches and salads. The group looked chaotic, but in a very few minutes a respectable collection of fresh vegetables from the aeroponics garden, meats, cheeses, defrosted bread, and some newly opened cans of fruit had been set up. The team quickly made the rounds and settled to eat contentedly. Even Dianna couldn't mess up a sandwich, though she had to go back for the mustard she'd missed on the first go-around.

Miho was the last to go through and didn't put much on her plate. Her weight loss was obvious. She hadn't had much weight to lose and now her clothes hung on her. It was evident that waiting was eating at her. Now that we had taken the action steps to silence ourselves, would the waiting eat at us too?

Ingrid looked at Miho's plate with its meager contents and snatched it up. Taking it back to the counter, she added some cheese and more of the canned fruit she knew Miho liked. Coming back to the table, she placed it carefully in front of Miho.

"Eat," she said. "You're not helping yourself, them, or us by starving yourself. We've got four more months. You have time to convince us of your innocence. Ty, what's the plan?"

Ty nodded and put down her sandwich. "I think we should talk about how the lack of outside input is going to affect us all. In some ways, we're in a lifeboat adrift in Antarctica. We're on our own." Ty's words reflected my thoughts.

Sam looked pointedly at Elisabeth, who was addicted to social media and had been haunting the science lab at all hours, using every available minute on the internet that wasn't allocated for team business, studying up on minimalist brewing techniques. "Life in a bubble, real isolation from the outside world. No more podcasts or internet videos." Elisabeth scrunched her nose and then stuck her tongue out at Sam.

"Sam's not wrong," Ingrid said. We've all been looking to the outside for connection. We really haven't been looking for that connection within the team." She waved a hand before Ty could respond. "This is an isolation study. Yes, Mars explorers will have access to the earth, but the point of this study is to see how we connect." She made a circling motion with her finger. "Now we have that opportunity. Warts and all, we're all we have."

It was a few days later when the reality of our aloneness really hit me. Sam was staring blankly at the screen before her, tears streaming down her face.

I rolled my chair over to her station and laid my hand gently on her forearm.

"What?"

"My family thinks I'm dead," Sam said. Her voice was thick as the tears continued to course down her cheeks. "It may kill my abuela, my grandmother. My mother, father, sisters, and brother, my cousins…my friends. What will they think and feel?" A slideshow of family gatherings cycled slowly across the screen. Scenes of a large, happy, boisterous family played in an endless loop. Birthdays, holidays, graduations, celebrations big and small, but always in groups. There wasn't a single picture of her alone. Anyone alone.

"I can't tell them I'm still alive. I can't contact them at all and I won't hear from them. My sister is due next month. I'll be an aunt, maybe. She was having a hard time with the pregnancy. Oh God," she said, and her shoulders shook with the anguish of her thoughts and emotions.

Sam's family was so extensive, so much a fixture in her life. I was used to only receiving sporadic emails from friends and colleagues. I was used to being alone. I had sent out more emails than I had received in reply, but that was normal for me too. None of my emails were verbose. I said I was fine and included a brief note on the technical progress of my research. I felt tears in my own eyes as I watched with fascination and jealousy the closeness Sam had with her family, a closeness I had never felt anywhere in my life. Even my relationship with Ty had been sporadic. These last few months had been the closest I'd been to other people since my grandmother had died.

"You'll be a wonderful aunt." I squeezed her arm gently. "You can't dwell on this. Your family loves you, and you'll all come out stronger. Think of how proud your grandmother will be when she hears the story of how you foiled the bad guys."

Sam's laugh came out as more of a hiccup. She ran a sweatshirt-clad arm across her face, wiping snot and tears away.

"I'm such a crybaby," she said, trying to gather herself. "Miho must be dying inside, not knowing if her kids, if her mom is okay. It would kill me if anything happened to my family, anything I might have stopped."

I so wanted to tell her they were both lucky, she and Miho, that they cared so much and had people who cared about them, but I couldn't say it out loud. It was too painful, too real…too sad.

"Do you think Miho was planning to kill us?"

I shrugged. "I don't think so. It doesn't make sense to me. Killing yourself to save a family that you'll never see again."

"I'd die for my family."

She fell silent and I tried to contemplate killing these women I'd become fond of for a family I didn't have.

"What do you normally do when you're feeling low?" Before she could answer, I added, "Besides talk to someone in your family."

The laugh this time was more real, a little lighter.

"I cook," she said, looking at me with a sly tentative smile.

"For the big, noisy family," I said, catching the meaning quickly and feeling a small opening in my heart. "You've got a family here, too. And we love your cooking, so let's go put me to work as your galley slave and you create something grand for dinner tonight for this family of ours."

Sam wasn't the only to feel cut off from the world. Days seemed to run into each other. We continued our research, grew our food, maintained our environment, dealt with the elements, and shared with each other. The new schedule helped. The nine of us moved to work the slight split shift but even that mostly went away. We worked on whatever needed attention, when it needed attention, without thought to schedule.

No one had to be awake for scheduled GICE or NSF messages. There were no communications. I couldn't imagine the hoops Christina and Ty must have gone through to get them to agree to this. The NSF was so safety conscience, a plan for every contingency—every contingency except for this one. Maybe that was why John had sent Christina with us, as an inside safety net. And, if something did go truly wrong, we still had Pole Station two miles away and Colonel Ride's team a mile in the other direction.

"I want to understand," I said to Christina as we lay in our bunks. "When did you become the superhero, super spy? How did you get assigned to this mission?"

"Boring," Christina said, fidgeting in her bed.

"No, it's not boring, and I would really like to know."

I levered myself up to look at her across the small divide between our beds. Christina sighed. She liked to sigh. I think it was her way of expressing her exasperation with the world or me. I stayed silent but attentive, watching her struggle to answer my question.

"I don't know how much I can really tell you." She tucked one hand under her head and stared at the ceiling. "I guess I just fell into it. I finished college when I was sixteen. Completed medical school and my residency by the time I was twenty-two and then started working through a host of specialties. My best friend at the time, my only friend, conned me into doing this stint with this traveling doctor group. Mostly it was just hard-core medicine, problem-solving with little support or resources, crazy hard. I wasn't an emotional person. It was all about the medicine.

"I got a rep for being able to diagnosis difficult cases. There was this one kid. Cute kid in that way some kids have about them. I tried to stay focused on the medicine but this kid just wormed her way into my heart. Every spare minute I had, I worked her case. I needed an MRI machine but we didn't have that. I needed better blood sampling equipment. Didn't have that either. Her mom was there every day, trying to make her comfortable. She was in pain, you know? And I didn't want to just give her something to let her die. I finally worked out a course of action for her. I thought it was a parasite. We dealt with parasites all the time but this one didn't follow the norm. I didn't know what else to try and she was failing. She had such trust in me. The kids, the moms, the struggle, amazing spirit."

There was silence.

"What happened?" I asked softly, afraid of the answer.

"She lived. Another doctor came in from another group. She needed surgery. I got too close. I didn't work the problem. I didn't save her but someone did."

Christina sighed again.

"My first real failure. Oh, I'd had patients die. This was different. I wanted to quit. Quit being a doctor. Quit having people rely on me. Quit. Then I met a woman who wanted me just as I was. She brought me out of my funk and sent me on my way, healthier and more mentally stable. I thought I was in love but she said it was just therapy. Whatever it was, she introduced me to John Steinman and the projects they were working on. Trouble spots. She knew I needed distance from the emotional needs of these kids, these families. I was a great problem solver but not great with people. John embedded himself in GICE after some information had come through the FBI.

"I wasn't meant to go on this mission. But John needed a problem solver. I had the background and the experience of living in a hostile environment with crazy politics. I've operated with a gun to my head when I did surgery on an insurgency leader's son. If he died, I died. I didn't flinch at that one. But that girl."

"So here you are," I said.

"Here I am," Christina echoed.

"And now you're emotionally involved again." There were so many questions I wanted to ask but I had to trust that they would come in time.

"Yes."

I lay back and pulled my grandmother's quilt up to my chin. I could see the conflict. To watch or to engage. To solve problems or be a friend, companion, or lover. Christina, who had such trouble with emotional entanglements had said that I mattered. She had the courage to say it and mean it. Yet I held back, scared and fearful of making the commitment, of trusting.

CHAPTER THIRTY

September-Antarctica

The days moved with glacial slowness. We worked, slept, ate, and managed to move forward with the science we were there to collect. It was the science that absorbed me. I had brought several gigabytes worth of reading material and data on weather patterns and changing landscapes. Reading that material had seemed like a sound plan, given all the time I would have here in isolation but the longer we were isolated, the more I reached out to the people around me.

I liked people but I feared attachments. People came to rely on me, had expectations and then I failed them. If I engaged with people, I might become attached. And now I was becoming attached. To Christina. To Sam and Dianna. Rue, Elisabeth, Miho, even Ingrid. It scared me how attached I was becoming to these women.

Ingrid was still a trial. I wanted to like her but I was still angry at her for hurting Ty. They were so different and yet I could see what might have attracted Ty to her. She was smart, as in genius smart. Her mind was razor-sharp and her ability to communicate fluidly in multiple languages on an unending variety of subjects would've drawn Ty like honey. Ty was attracted to smart women. Smart, sexy women. And Ingrid was definitely that. Christina and Dianna aside, I believed Ingrid could do all of our jobs. She made me nervous. In that aloof, untouchable, superior way that some women had.

So when she came over to my weather station setup in the science lab, I froze like a rabbit, thinking that if I didn't move, the predator would move on to other prey.

"What's the weather forecast for the next eight hours?" she asked, her clipped accented English sounding loud over the hum of the computer systems.

I stared dumbly at her for a moment. Even after months of living in close quarters with her and knowing she was a real person, I had kept my distance. Not engaging.

She raised her eyebrows at me and tilted her head waiting for me to respond. In my seated position, she towered over me. I wasn't used to being intimidated.

I waved vaguely in the direction of the weather board I kept up to date with the two-, four-, and eight-hour predictions, as well as forecasts for the next several days. It showed all the data from our monitoring equipment since we didn't have access to the internet and NOAA. Dianna had to go out fairly regularly to do some maintenance outside and other team members used the data in their own studies. Ingrid knew this like everyone else. Why was she asking for the information?

"I want details." She dismissed the weather board, which included data on temperature, wind speed and direction, wind chill factors, humidity, and chance of precipitation.

"What details do you want that aren't on the board?" Her request mystified me.

"Tell me what I can expect outside over the next eight hours." She pulled up a chair and moved into my personal space.

Sitting she was less intimidating, but her proximity let me smell the heady fragrance of her shampoo and lotions mixed with her own body chemistry. This was a woman who knew her own power.

She must have seen my glazed look and the smirk on her face brought me crashing back to reality.

I swiveled back to my workstation and began refreshing screens. I read off information similar but not exactly to what was on the board. But she wasn't paying attention.

"What do you and Ty talk about?" she asked. "Does she talk about me?"

There was no one else in the science lab to overhear our conversation, but her words were so soft I wouldn't have heard her if she hadn't been sitting so close to me.

I turned to face her. "Ty?"

For the first time, I could see traces of genuine anguish in her face. She had always seemed so cool and remote, beautiful but aloof. She was hurting and lonely.

Ingrid glanced toward the door and then back at me. "Does she talk about me at all?"

I shook my head. I knew little about their relationship except for the highlights. They had met at a Swiss language school and after graduation had spent the summer together. Then Ingrid had just up and left her one day with a breezy, unemotional goodbye. I could see that Ty was devastated even though she hadn't said it. I wouldn't have known at all if we hadn't gotten drunk commiserating over my brief fling with a news anchor. She mentioned Ingrid and then sobered up and quickly changed the subject, but not before I had seen the hurt in her eyes. Why Ty had accepted her on this mission was a mystery except for the fact Ingrid was brilliant, a top scientist in her field with a lot of powerful supporters.

"Does she have a girlfriend? Someone waiting for her on the outside?"

Again, I shook my head.

Ingrid let out a deep breath that she had been holding, as if it was protection against a closely held fear. "Then there is still a chance," she said almost wistfully.

It was my turn to cock my head.

"I hurt her. I pushed her away when I should have pulled her close."

"Why did you push her away?"

She got a distant look in her eye and I wasn't sure she was going to tell me. I waited. I had gotten good at that. One of the psychology classes I'd taken mentioned silence was an awesome tool if someone really wanted to talk but was afraid. The words, when they came, rushed out in an angry torrent.

"I was young and stupid and didn't understand the wonder of what we had." She stared unseeing at the numbers on my screen.

"I thought...I don't know what I thought...maybe that it was too easy. I wanted to go places and do things and I wanted to explore the great wide world of women. I didn't know what I had. I want her back." There was real longing in her voice, which changed her tone and she sounded real and warm.

"Have you talked to her?" I asked gently. "Have you apologized? Or told her how you feel about her?"

She gave me a disbelieving look, her vivid blue eyes lost.

"What do you want?"

She shook her head, her blond hair swaying with the movement.

"You're going to have to make the first move," I said. "She won't do it. You hurt her."

She started to respond and Ty walked into the room. Ingrid jumped to her feet, which sent the chair rolling back into the wall behind her with a crash. She looked guilty.

"Smooth," I muttered under my breath.

Ty just looked at the two of us, then turned and left.

"Go." I pointed at the door. "Go after her now. It's now or never. She may reject you but don't leave her hanging again. You owe her."

Ingrid hesitated, but only for a moment. Her long legs carried her quickly from the room as she picked up speed.

I was glad Ingrid had come to me. It was about time for these two to make peace. Maybe she and Ty could have a second chance?

I found Miho back in aeroponics. Dianna, when she wasn't doing maintenance activities, had made it her responsibility to watch Miho. Miho roomed with Ingrid, but theirs had never been a warm relationship. Dianna had seemed to bond with Miho, which made the supposed betrayal that much harder for Dianna to take. She was taking her role as guard seriously, watching Miho with narrow eyes, waiting for any misstep.

Miho wandered listlessly through her beloved plants. She moved slowly almost painfully through the motions as if each dead leaf clipped was a limb she was taking from her own body. She winced with each snip of the pruning shears.

"Why don't you take a break, Dianna?" I moved fully into the room. "I'll stay here with Miho."

Dianna eyed me suspiciously and looked pointedly at her watch. "I don't have any maintenance activities."

I could feel her anger. It had grown with each explosive removed. She had taken Christina's statements as fact, and Miho's protestations had fallen on deaf ears. I wasn't really sure why, but the bond she and Miho shared had been destroyed as quickly and as effectively as the metal box containing the explosives. One moment a clean, simple design, the next a crater in a frozen wasteland. Dianna needed help too but first I wanted to deal with Miho. I needed some closure and I needed to pull Miho back into this group.

"It's okay, I heard Rue talking about some issue with the stove. Maybe you can take a look and see if the fuel line is clogged or something. I'd like to eat sometime tonight. I'm tired of sandwiches."

Dianna perked up at this. The group had made it abundantly clear that the only task Dianna could perform in or near the galley was cleanup or eating. She hadn't been called on for kitchen repair. The habitat's equipment was new and other than routine maintenance everything was running fine. After the missing sensors at the beginning of the mission, Dianna had gone over everything with Amy, system by system, part by part, to ensure that nothing else was missing or put together wrong. They had found nothing. Dianna had reviewed all of the systems again after Amy's death, and then again after the explosives were found, including the galley equipment. But this would be the first request for her to repair something in the room she was rarely allowed in. Dianna loved to tinker and fix things. And she, like most of us, needed to be needed.

Once she had gone, I turned to Miho who didn't seem to notice Dianna had left. She was starting on a new row when I walked up to her side. Noticing me, she jumped like a squirrel with a nut startled by a rabid dog, dropping the shears, which clattered noisily on the metal flooring of the room.

"Hey, it's just me," I said.

"I'm sorry, I'm sorry." She moved farther away from me until she bumped against the back row of plants.

I bent over and picked up the fallen shears and placed them carefully on the growing table next to the group of plants she was checking.

"It's okay, Miho," I said. "Why don't you come sit down with me on the couch?"

At first it seemed like she didn't hear me or didn't understand, then she stared up at me. She looked haunted. I knew she was spiraling and I wanted to work with her to interrupt the pattern. The blame, shame, and fear were getting to her.

"Come on, Miho, sit with me. I'm not your enemy and I want to help." I watched her carefully, even as I moved to the couch and sat down.

She remained motionless for a few seconds and then she moved toward me with none of her usual grace. I had always admired how, even being the shortest among us, her grace had always given her a strangely long-limbed, confident, easy walk. That walk was gone, replaced by an ungainly shuffle. She seemed to have aged five if not ten years.

As she sat down beside me on the couch, she wouldn't meet my eyes. Her hands settled limply in her lap.

"Miho, you need to have hope," I said. I didn't try to touch her. Her earlier actions made me hesitant. "We've done everything we could to make it appear the bombs exploded. I don't think these people want to hurt Brandon and Alicia. We don't even know if they have your kids."

Miho twitched slightly at the mention of her children but said nothing.

"With your death, there will be a memorial service. If your ex shows up with the kids and your mom, the FBI will nab him. The deputy director promised me they were getting the warrants based on the information you provided. They'll search his home and business."

"He's not the head of the organization," Miho said. I knew she was talking about her ex. "How can you be sure that the FBI agents or John hasn't been compromised?"

"At some point, you have to trust. I want to trust you, Miho. Can we trust you to not hurt yourself or us?"

Miho shifted in her seat, looking me in the eye for the first time. Her mouth set in a grim line. "I didn't have anything to do with the explosives. But there are people in this group, including Christina, that think I did, based on circumstantial evidence. Intelligent women. How can you trust someone who would take their own life and the lives of innocent people?" Her eyes watched me for any sign of what I didn't know. Belief, fear, contempt, hatred, anger, pity.

I showed only compassion, but my mind was churning with what she'd said. Did I believe that she could have done this? Could I trust someone who had broken faith with me? Someone who might have killed me and people I cared about?

Nope. I didn't know how the fob got in Miho's backpack, but she wasn't a good enough actress. Miho's surprise at Christina's unveiling of the device had been real. She might have done this for her kids but I didn't think so. The question was who could have put it there? What were they trying to accomplish? Was it to create infighting and distrust? Was Miho faking her concern over her kids? Her mom? Nope, she was a dupe. Someone had intentionally left a false trail. Someone to blame. Until we'd actually used the fob, which Dianna had to adjust, we couldn't be sure that the fob was functional. We hadn't tested it for obvious reasons, we couldn't be sure it would have activated the explosives. And it didn't make it the only one. Miho was dying a bit more each day, swirling in the facts: some of the team did not trust her, and she didn't know the whereabouts of her family.

Now she was facing the consequences of hiding her fears and concerns. She hadn't asked for our help. She hadn't trusted us. Yet we had changed the course of our lives for her, to help her and her family. Eight very intelligent, capable individuals would have supported her if she had just opened up and asked for it. We had known there were problems. We had known about her ex. The link was what we needed.

We sat in silence. I had offered an olive branch and Miho had rejected it but I was still there. Silent but supportive. I wanted her to rejoin the group and help us solve the puzzle. Her only failure had been in not trusting the team to support her. Miho had let the fear and the inability to protect her family cloud her mind and pushed her to hide those threatening emails. If we didn't pull it together, we were a broken, failed team, even if we survived to tell the tale.

"What do you want? Do you want to fall apart or do you want to find out who's behind all of this?"

The hum of the aeroponics kicking on and the drip of the water was all the sound in the room. I sat enjoying the humidity and smell of the plants and the earthy scents of dirt and potato plants. Elisabeth and Dianna had been working with Miho to cultivate those potatoes and to build a way to distill them. Ty hadn't been happy with the thought of so much alcohol, but she was happy the team was enjoying this project in their spare time.

"I need to tell the team about the emails from my ex." Miho sat up straighter. "I felt so isolated. I didn't know any of this would happen or I never would have come on this mission. The emails started after I lost contact with my mom. Just before we left, my ex said some very cruel things. I told my mother about him and then when I didn't hear from her or my kids, I panicked. He got to them somehow. I can't believe he'd hurt them. Not his own kids. But whoever is responsible for these attacks is crazy. I swear I didn't know anything about the fob or the explosives. I understand how some on the team could believe it. God, I hate this. The not knowing. I want my kids."

"We just have to stay hidden and let the FBI find your family, find proof of the conspirators. We need to trust they'll find Brandon and Alicia."

"I have to do something. I've been fixated on who could be behind this since Christina showed us the fob. The explosives had to be part of the pre-fab of our habitat and brought in already installed." Miho ran a hand through her lank hair and grunted. "I have to do something."

This time I reached out. Her hands were ice cold in contrast with the warm, fetid air of the lab.

"They'll think the plan succeeded and we're dead. If your ex does have something to do with this, what do you think he'll do now?"

She shuddered and took a deep breath, trying to regain some composure. "I don't know. Not now."

"If he has your kids and mom, will he release them? Would he take them to a memorial service?"

"The kids maybe, not my mom." Miho looked down at her hands. "My mom always hated him, or rather, she didn't trust him. I should have listened to her, but he said all the right things, made all the right moves. I thought I was in love." Fresh tears rolled down her cheeks. "If he's got them, I think he might hurt my mom. She'll turn him in and he knows it."

"Do you know his associates?"

"Some. I gave Ty and Christina the names of those I knew or suspected, but I've been cut off from my ex for the last two years, except for the last three months, when he tried to get a judge to give him custody of the kids. Two years after the divorce and now he wants the kids. If SpaceGen is part of this, they're using him because of his connection to me. I'm sure of it."

"What do you think they'll do now that he has no use to them?"

"No idea. That's what scares me."

At dinner, Miho apologized. She stood and faced us, her judge and jurors. "I know I've broken trust with you," she said formally. "I had nothing to do with the explosives. I didn't know about the fob. But I did keep information from you. I'm sorry I didn't trust you all enough to ask for your help." She turned to Sam and Rue. "I know how hard this situation is for you both specifically. You come from big, loving families. I know this is probably hardest on you and I really appreciate your sacrifice in going silent. Thank you." She looked around the room, her eyes finally landing on Christina. "As for secrets, I'm not the only one who has secrets." She took a deep breath and let it out slowly. "I know I have lost your trust and whatever boundaries you put on me to feel safe...I will abide by."

The faces that stared back at her were varied. Some showed understanding, others anger, and a few with no expression at all. But it was a start. Time would tell if it would make a difference.

CHAPTER THIRTY-ONE

September-Antarctica

The days were getting lighter. We were now beyond what was considered Civil Twilight, where the sun was at about six degrees below the horizon, and we were seeing the sun again. It both lightened the mood and upped our anxiety levels. Time was passing. Our teamwork was still tenuous. No pranks or fun ransom notes had been sent since the explosion. Elisabeth and Sam had both formed a tentative link with Miho. It was awkward but they went out of their way to include her in their movie marathons and rummy card games.

Dianna was still ignoring Miho. If Miho talked to her, she would turn her back and leave the room or talk to someone else. Miho gave up trying. She would participate when asked, but otherwise she would sit quietly in whatever room a group of us visited.

Ty hadn't mentioned Ingrid's apology, but I had seen them together in the galley, heads inches apart, going over the documentation on the explosive removal. It was a work in progress. After Ingrid had asked for my help, the regret evident in her voice, I'd been rooting for her to break through Ty's shell. I knew Ty feared it was just a passing fixation, and as soon as we were no longer isolated, Ingrid would leave again.

I was tired of the trust issues. Since I had shared with Christina, I felt lighter. What to do with my aunt's letter still hung heavy. Seventeen years was a long time to carry the disdain and guilt. This team, though, was filled with intelligent women. Why couldn't we get it together? We'd all lost something with this mission, with the revelation about Evelyn, Miho's ex's connections to SpaceGen, with connections between friends and family, with trust. If we couldn't figure our shit out, was there much hope for me and my aunt?

I was feeling worn out, rung dry, tired. Days were filled with science and data reduction, conversations with Ingrid and Dianna and Rue on weather, climate, geology, wind and water patterns. But the evenings were hard, especially the nights. Christina spent most of her time in medical. She came in late and didn't wake up when I left the room, giving me space and time to think and reflect. I missed our closeness.

I tried to read some of the books I'd brought, thinking I'd have all this free time to enjoy them. Instead of reading, I just stared at the wall or sat in the dark room watching the light play on the frozen world outside. The wind swirled and pushed the snow against the fuel storage structure, only to take it away the next day. The temperatures crept up and the time passed slowly. We all seemed to be in a holding pattern.

A few days later, Ty and I were alone in the lab, each working on reports. I asked, "We've got two more months before the first flight comes in, and then our secret will be out. Do you think our gamble paid off?"

She shrugged. "The team is failing. We're doing great science but we're not coming together. This thing with Miho. The secrets."

"A nice dysfunctional group."

Ty snorted. "How are you doing with Christina?"

"We aren't in a relationship, if that's what you're asking." Dysfunctional indeed.

"And after the mission?" Ty asked.

"I could ask you the same thing. Are you going to give Ingrid a chance?"

She glanced over at me and then stared at the computer screen. She swiveled the chair to face me. "Would you take back someone who dumped you?"

"You blazed too brightly and you scared the shit out of her."

Ty rubbed her face and then ran her hands through her hair, causing it to spike. It made her appear younger. "You didn't answer my question."

"Christina lied to me." I felt my chest tighten and shoulders hunch.

"She didn't tell you something she was required by her job not to tell you. She kept a secret, secret."

"You're right." She was. Running was what I did when I couldn't handle a situation. I had taken Christina's subterfuge personally. She had told me what she could. She put the mission over the personal. Would I have done it any differently? My desire for connection with Christina had blinded me. And scared me. Living in the same room, seeing her every day, longing to touch her, and not acting on my desires was frustrating on so many levels. It had skewed my perspective.

"What? I don't think I heard you."

I ignored her and went in search of Christina. As anticipated, she was in her domain—medical. I expected her to be working on reports but she was seated on her meditation pillow.

I walked in and closed the door. "Destressing?"

"Trying." She gave me a slow smile, leaned back against the wall and stretched out her legs. "What's up?"

"I've missed you. Missed being with you and..." I sighed. "I understand why you didn't tell me about your other mission here. You were right. I wouldn't have kept it from Ty. She asked me here to support her." I watched her face for any sign of emotion. "Look, I'm sorry. I took it personally and it wasn't."

"What do you want, Jo?" There was no hostility in her soft question, only longing.

I wanted to throw myself at her but there were still rules. Distance helped me keep those rules in place even if I didn't want to. "I just wanted you to know, I understand what you did." I turned to go before she could see just how much more I wanted.

"You know Jo, hugs can be considered medicinal."

I choked out a laugh. I let her envelop me in a full-body hug, hoping it would say what I couldn't put into words—yet. It was heavenly while it lasted.

CHAPTER THIRTY-TWO

September-Antarctica

Two days later, I was pounding out steps on the treadmill. Christina and I were talking again. The tension was back as if we both knew how much more there could be, given time. In lieu of action, I craved motion. Only a few of us had kept up with the workouts prescribed in the study. I hated treadmills, but I hated inactivity more. I almost veered off the side when Ty's voice came from the doorway.

"You'll be ready for a marathon when this is over with all the running you've been doing, and at altitude, no less." She leaned against the wall, away from my sweat-coated body.

I lowered the speed but didn't stop. "What's up? I have another three miles before I'm done."

She leaned against the wall more comfortably. "We're getting more daylight each day."

I didn't reply as it wasn't a question and I was still pushing hard even at the slower speed. Sweat slid down my face and I grabbed my towel to wipe away the excess before it got into my eyes.

"I broke the team," Ty said.

I jumped to the sides, allowing the treadmill to continue before I smacked the off button. The room was suddenly very quiet without the whirl of the machine and my steady stride.

"We made the decision as a group to play dead."

"Yeah, but we were struggling before that...Amy's death. I know that Dianna and Rue are still struggling with that. Even Miho. Then there's my utter failure to keep us safe. Christina found out about the explosives and got Dianna and Ingrid to remove them. You got them to save some."

"And you came up with the plan and got Christina's connections to help you execute it."

"Yeah, we're playing dead because of me. Because I didn't solve the problem before it became a problem."

"No one said you had to do it all on your own. It was your job to lead, not be all knowing. We're still here, and doing the science we all wanted to do, despite all the efforts to get us to leave. Things none of the other teams have to deal with."

Ty scrubbed her face with her hands. Her tired eyes were unsure. "The team still feels disconnected."

"What are you going to do about it?"

"I don't know."

"I think this has been our problem the whole time. We each think we have to solve problems by ourselves. I could name a situation where each of us has had a problem and tried to go it alone only to fail. Each time we've asked the group for support, we've succeeded or at least haven't made the situation worse." I shrugged. "I'm including myself in that assessment. Maybe it's time to ask for help?"

"That sounds scarier than finding explosives on the hab or emergency surgery," Ty said with a snort. "Elisabeth will want to brew beer and Dianna will think of a mechanical solution."

"You do the group a disservice." I stared down at her. "Remember, you're the collaborative one."

"Yeah, I remember where that got me in Switzerland. There was almost a mutiny."

"You asked for our support and you got it. You just have to step up."

This time we met in the science lab. It wasn't as comfortable as the common room or as homey as the galley, but the lab set a more business-like tone. There weren't enough chairs for everyone so Ingrid and Rue grabbed a couple from the rooms and dragged them in. Just like in Switzerland, small groups had formed within our team and it was evident in the seating arrangements. Ingrid and Rue. Sam, Elisabeth, and Dianna. Only Christina, Miho, Ty, and I stood separate. Or maybe we formed a group as well. It was hard to tell.

We all looked a bit scruffy with clothes we had rotated through for weeks and looked frayed around the edges. There were spaghetti sauce traces on Sam's favorite sweatshirt no amount of washing would remove. Ingrid, whose clothes always seemed pressed and crisp, had finally lost out to time. Miho's neat appearance was noticeably absent. She was sleeping and eating, but the vibrancy she had early in the mission was gone. Sam and Ingrid were the only ones who still wore any makeup and that was down to just an occasional lipstick and mascara. We had the appearance of castaways convening for a board meeting.

"We are gathered here today," Elisabeth said in her best southern Baptist drawl, which sounded ludicrous when adding in her slight German accent.

The tense mood lifted slightly as Sam laughed and Dianna smiled at her attempt at humor.

"Yes, yes, we are gathered," Rue said as she rolled her chair to her normal workstation and proceeded to log into the system. "But for what reason? Haven't we talked ourselves to death?"

Ty had stationed herself at the back of the room and walked to the doorway, where she could see the entire room and everyone could see her. Her brown hair was longer than she normally wore it and the ends curled up around her ears, making her look younger than her thirty-six years. Her hands were in the deep pockets of her slacks and she rocked slightly forward and back on her toes.

We went silent, our eyes focused and attentive. Under our watchful gaze, she stilled and took her hands out of her pockets.

"I need your help," she said simply. "I want us to be a team. You're exceptional individuals. We've made a few group decisions, but right now it seems we are existing, not thriving. There also seems to be, if not anger, resentment in the group."

Dianna and Rue glanced at Miho who sat looking at her hands. Sam glared at Christina.

"Ingrid said it best a few weeks ago. We're all we have." Ty shook her head slightly and frowned. "In less than two months, the world will know we're alive. Our family and friends will know we're alive." She let her eyes rest briefly on each person. "We came here to do hard science and to show the world an all-women team could hack it. We've had some formidable obstacles thrown in our path. We lost Amy." She paused. "It was no one's fault but she's gone. We've had our study sabotaged. We've dealt with another team's problems. And we've experienced betrayal. I don't think we've really processed how far we've come. Yes, we're alive, healthy, and we have accomplished some great research, but have we formed the bonds necessary for an extraordinary team?"

She waited and I took a moment to glance around the room at my colleagues. Ingrid and Christina just watched impassively. Dianna seemed annoyed. Rue and Elisabeth looked expectant. Miho watched Dianna.

Sam sat forward in her seat. "What does an extraordinary team look like?"

"On paper, we are an extraordinary group of women," Christina said. She was in her usual position, leaning casually against a wall, away from everyone else, her arms folded comfortably in front of her. "But I agree with Ty, I don't think the trust required in a team is present." She turned to Ingrid. "I believe you are the most experienced outdoor winter survival expert we have. You were the logical choice to go with me to save Dr. Charles, yet I didn't ask you. Was I wrong?"

Ingrid flicked her Nordic blue eyes to me before returning her gaze to Christina. She frowned and appeared thoughtful but didn't answer. I could tell from Ingrid's lack of comment that she knew she had been the logical choice. We had discussed it at the time.

"You think I made the choice because you think Jo and I are sleeping together?" Christina tilted her head in question.

Ingrid shrugged but didn't disagree.

"Jo volunteered and I knew I could trust her to follow my lead. Jo can lead or follow. You're a leader. Type A through and through. I didn't know if you could or would follow my lead. I know now that you might have because of the way you worked with Dianna to defuse the bombs."

"Dianna is the expert," Ingrid said, her gaze flicking from Dianna to me and then back to Christina.

"Yes, you trust Dianna's expertise but you see me as a rival first and a doctor second."

"Wait, what does this have to do with building an extraordinary team?" Rue asked, watching the byplay, then turning to Ty for an explanation.

"Christina is making a point, I think," Ty said as she glanced between Christina and Ingrid. "So what you're saying is that we might trust a person in the group to do their job but we don't really trust the group."

"Just the opposite, I think we trust the *group* but we don't really trust each other. Oh, I think all of us trust an individual in the group. I trust Jo implicitly. I trust you to make decisions in the best interests of the group. I respect Dianna's ability to keep us safe and the equipment maintained." Her eyes focused on Ingrid. "I respect the fact we are all experts in our fields. But I don't know about trust." Her gaze flicked to Miho and then back to Ingrid. "Miho has never tried to destroy the aeroponics lab. But we watch her now. We watch each other expecting…what?"

"Faith has been broken," Dianna said, folding her arms and shifting in her chair, as if uncomfortable with the conversation.

"Has it?" I asked. I looked at the two women. "Miho has stated that she didn't know about the fob. Other than finding it in her backpack, has she done anything else to betray your trust?"

Dianna glanced at Miho and then back at me. Her eyes narrowed and she glared at me but didn't say anything.

"Obviously, someone or some group doesn't want us to succeed. But we don't know who or why," Elisabeth said.

Tension permeated the room. All the loneliness and anxiety of the past ten months was coming into focus. I wanted to get up and pace but there was nowhere to go. I turned to Christina. "You lied to us too. Pretending to be something you weren't."

"I am a doctor." Christina's tone didn't change, nor did she betray any emotion in her face or body language. Still. Waiting.

"But that's not all."

"Yes and no." Christina said with a slight shift in her shoulders. "If nothing had been amiss, I would've been just the doctor."

"That would've been a lie," I said, not quite sure how I felt about it, even after working through the necessity for days. "Why do you trust me implicitly?"

Several people chuckled and Christina just smiled at me.

"What?" I glared around the room.

"You are transparent," Rue said. "I understand why Christina didn't clue you in on her deception. I missed it too, by the way, even while I was being the go-between with her and John." She shrugged. "And I'm suspicious by nature. We could all see how hurt you were, so we knew you were as clueless as the rest of us. Christina played her part brilliantly. We would have never known."

"Does this matter?" Elisabeth said. "Christina's point is we lack trust. We've spent a lot of time with each other, in Houston, in Switzerland and now here. And we still don't know each other or even why we should trust each other." She glanced over to Rue. "I trust Rue and Dianna, my partners in beer brewing. I trust Ty to lead us. I respect Ingrid and I don't think she'd do anything to harm me, but I would have said the same about Miho. I want to trust that Miho wouldn't have hurt us, but I don't know." Elisabeth shot Miho a sympathetic look. "So where does that leave us?"

"I think we're all missing the point," Ty said. "The mission is that we show NASA and the NSF that a team comprised solely of women can be a successful, fully evolved team. There is a myth in people's mind that women cannot have successful teams. That we destroy ourselves with backbiting and infighting. One reason why we never had a female Mercury astronaut was for that exact reason," she added with a distant look.

"Huh?" Dianna said. "What do Mercury astronauts have to do with us?"

I settled back in my seat. Ty's knowledge of NASA and the history of the astronaut program was extensive.

"Thirteen women passed the same tests as the Mercury 7," Ty said. "Thirteen. The women were lighter, used less oxygen, withstood isolation, vibration, heat, noise, and discomfort better than the men, yet they were denied the right to serve as astronauts."

I looked around the room and all eyes were watching Ty.

"Men," Ingrid said with disdain.

"Partially, but the infighting of the women didn't help. The group that fought for women to be seen as equals wasn't unified. Jackie Cochran, Jerrie Cobb, and Janey Hart, who became the spokespeople of the group, were at odds. Even these three dynamic women didn't work with the other women, who also had strong views."

"You're saying we did ourselves in?" Elisabeth said.

"I think so," Ty said. "These women were the superior candidates in almost every facet, yet they were shunted aside. Part of that was the time period, the early 1960s, but the women, if they had been united, could have changed history."

"Is history repeating itself?" I asked. "Is that what you're most afraid of?"

"I feel like I've failed you all. I should have seen the forces set against us and taken precautions. I shouldn't have let the outside divide us so easily," Ty said. "I don't know how to pull us back to our mission. We are a fantastic group, but we are divided."

The group was silent. The hum of the computers was low and soothing.

"Somehow I don't think team-building exercises and falling back into each other's arms is going to help us with trust issues," Dianna said finally, running a hand over her headscarf. "Trust is hard. All of us have been betrayed in our lives. Yet, we trust again."

"I think we need to think like family," Sam said, looking at Rue.

Rue smiled and nodded.

"Family?" I asked.

"A big messy family. We fight, we play, we love each other," Rue added and then laughed. "You have to believe in the family."

I knew these two had large extended families. The accusation against Miho rested on the belief that she would do anything, including kill herself, to save her children and mom. I didn't have any family left, except my aunt. And I didn't know what to think of her. What did I know about families?

What did it take to build a family? Commitment and making the group your highest priority. Committing to the group happiness and strength. Feeling affection and common purpose. Coming together under crisis and stress. Maybe, after more than a year with these amazing women, I was finally starting to understand.

CHAPTER THIRTY-THREE

October-Antarctica

I woke up freezing. A small amount of light shown beneath the cardboard-covered windows illuminating Christina's shape bundled in covers. My fingers were numb as if layered in ice. I could see my breath in the air. The clock read three a.m.

"Christina, wake up."

"Hmm?"

"No seriously, wake up, something is wrong."

Her head came slowly out from underneath the covers. When the cold struck her, she burrowed back down.

I tried again. "There is something wrong with the heating."

She mumbled something but I didn't understand it. Since I could see my breath, the temperature had to be below forty-five degrees in the room. I needed to find out what was going on and if our room was the only one with the problem. I took a deep breath, pushed off the covers, and jumped to the floor in a fluid motion. I scrabbled into my clothes, pulling on a thermal shirt, two sweatshirts, and an extra thick pair of socks before finally putting on my shoes. Christina peered at me from underneath her blankets. I took pity on her and threw her clothes up to her.

Ty and Dianna were in the galley, huddled together in their outerwear.

"What's up?" I asked, my arms wrapped around me to hold in what warmth I had.

"Power plant is down," Dianna said, glancing up as I entered the room.

"Sabotage?" I asked, a hint of fear in my voice. Cold could and would kill.

"We don't know." Ty waved me over to review the hab diagrams spread out on the big table.

"I think there is a blockage or a pressure problem in the line." Dianna nodded and her fingers ran over the lines in the schematics.

"How can I help?" Despite the double sweatshirts, I shivered.

"I need someone to go out and check the pressure gauges and sensors in the fuel storage area," Dianna said. She handed me and Ty walkie-talkies before clipping one to her belt. "I don't know if this will work below ground. You may need to check and then come back up to let me know what you find."

"What will you be doing?"

"I'll be in the power plant getting the backup generator started."

"Why didn't you do that already?"

"I need the information from the fuel station. I was getting ready to make the trip myself when you showed up. The process for starting the backup generator is dependent on what you find. Are you okay going alone? Ty is going to be our relay."

Even though I knew there was nothing to fear, I remembered my last trip down the metal stairs to the fuel tanks. It had been creepy and dank. I didn't relish the thought of going alone but I had volunteered to help.

Dianna noticed my hesitation and frowned. "We need to hurry. We've got about three hours before plants die and pipes freeze."

I moved.

First, I checked the weather. I had a good feel for what it would be, as I had checked all the sensors before bed the previous night. The wind had picked up and was stronger than expected at fifteen knots. The temperature was a balmy minus forty, but the early morning was clear and would pose no problem to the hundred-meter walk to the bunker.

Ty met me in the coatroom to help me get outfitted. I kept the extra sweatshirt on and began pulling on the additional outer layers. Just as I was pulling on my hat, Sam showed up.

"Want company?" she asked, knowing without the question I would be happy for the companionship.

"Get your stuff on. I'm sweating in all this gear. Plus, Dianna is concerned about pipes and plants."

Even with the cold temperatures in the hab, the first smack of the Antarctic night wind swept in to hit us as we opened the outer door. We didn't hesitate and crunched down the steps and toward the small building that housed the stairs to the fuel storage tanks.

I pulled the heavy door open. "You been down before?"

"No, not one of my regularly scheduled adventures."

"Take an air filtration mask," I said as I took one off the peg for myself. My goggles went on the now empty peg until we finished our task below. "We probably won't need them as there shouldn't be any gas buildup, but safety first."

Once I was sure she had taken a mask, I grabbed a flashlight from the rack and then flipped the switch for the lower-level lights. I started down the steps to the tanks and suddenly stopped, Sam almost running into me.

"The lights went on. We have power here so the fuel system generators and air handling equipment must have power. Let's check our communications." I pulled the walkie-talkie out of my coat pocket and thumbed the on button. "Hey Ty, can you hear me? Over."

"Five by five. Over," came the reply.

"The fuel station generator is working. Heading down. Over."

"Good information. Okay to proceed. Over."

I pocketed the walkie-talkie and nodded to Sam. "Let's go."

Some ice had formed on the steps and it was well below freezing, but with no wind. Our steps were loud and echoed. The overhead lighting cast eerie shadows. Now the noise from the fuel generator could be heard rumbling below us. The noise got louder the farther we went. As we completed the last turn, I heard Sam's footsteps stop.

"Wow, this place is enormous."

"One great big hole in the ground for the tanks, though you'd never know it from the tiny building up top. Remember if the smell gets too much for you, use the mask. Let's check the numbers and get out of here. This place gives me the creeps."

"I can see why. If you got locked in here, you'd be a frozen person-sicle by the time anyone found you."

I shivered. My thought exactly.

I moved down the row to the first tank, shining the flashlight on the multiple dials. Dianna had coached me on what to look for in the vast array of dials and switches. She wanted me to make note of the tank and line pressures, and told me the acceptable ranges for each. Tank pressure looked to be ten psi with the line at 0.27 psi, which looked acceptable. The next two tanks read zero. The last tank was in series with the first tank. The tank pressure was four psi but the pressure was zero.

I pulled the walkie-talkie from my pocket. "Ty. Over."

No response.

"Ty. Do you read me? Over."

No response.

"Let's go tell Ty and Dianna what we found." I strode to the stairs.

At the top, I tried again. "Ty, Dianna, do you read me? Over."

"What did you see? Over." Dianna's voice crackled over the speaker.

I gave her the information.

There was a pause before Dianna said, "I need you to check some switches and then I'm going to start up the backup generator. The two tanks are empty and it looks like we've lost pressure to the next one in the link."

After she gave me the changes she wanted, Sam and I once more retraced our steps down to the tank floor. I had Sam check my work as we reviewed the switches. Then I sent Sam back up to relay the information to Dianna while I stayed put to relay information or make any additional changes as required. I was worried I'd do the wrong thing. I didn't know any other way of doing this quickly and Dianna had already told me we had limited time. Under my multiple layers of clothing, I couldn't see my watch and had no sense of how long we'd been at it. Anxiety made me want to move, to get out of this dank space.

There was a loud bang from above.

"Sam, can you hear me?"

Sam didn't respond. The noise had sounded like a door slamming shut, but I couldn't be sure with the generator noise. My anxiety building, I called out again but got no response. I was getting ready to go up when Ingrid appeared above me on the stairs.

"Sam can't hear you and was getting too cold. I'm going to relay to Rue." Ingrid flashed me a faint smile.

"We're playing telephone," I said, concerned about the added layers of communication and potential for misinformation.

"Don't worry so much," Ingrid huffed. "We'll take it slow and only repeat what you say."

I didn't have a better plan and I was happy to see Ingrid. She didn't frighten me so much now that I knew she was really human.

"Stop staring at me. Dianna needs you to cycle a few switches and provide more readings. She wants to start the backup generator."

The next fifteen minutes or so were excruciating. We relayed information and instructions via our human communication chain. Checking and re-checking to ensure each step and check each reaction.

"Dianna says she's got the backup generator functioning. Time to head back."

I was never so happy to hear those words from Ingrid. I hadn't realized how cold I was until I stumbled on the way to the stairs. My legs were stiff and I could feel the cold in my bones. I shivered and my teeth chattered.

Ingrid was halfway up and I pushed myself to follow her. My legs warmed with the movement. Gripping the banister, my hand strength weak, I steadied myself and moved up the stairs as fast as I could. I kept trying to flex my fingers, blood flowing through them again but they didn't bend very well. It seemed to take forever. Even though we had been sheltered from the outside elements, this cavernous room with its small anteroom, housing the gear and stairs wasn't heated or insulated from the cold that permeated everything. The heat from the tank generator elevated the temperature some, but it was still below zero. The cold had sapped much of my energy.

Ingrid was waiting for me at the top. Her normal impatience was missing. She looked concerned. "You sound like death," she said as I came around the last turn. My breath was coming in ragged gasps.

"I'm tired and cold," I said. "Guess standing still in front of the instrument panel for the last hour didn't help," I said, taking my goggles from the peg and replacing the mask I thankfully hadn't needed.

"That's why Rue and I were sent to replace Sam. It's colder up top."

"Thanks for waiting for me," I mumbled. Lacking sleep and breakfast, I felt exhausted.

"We still need to get you and me back. You ready, or do you need a minute?" In her clipped tones, it wasn't so much a question as a push to get me moving forward.

I was having trouble concentrating. Even after the climb up the stairs, I was shivering and I couldn't seem to stop. "Hope the heat is on in the hab."

"Dianna's focused on getting the temperature right in aeroponics," Ingrid said. "Looks like there was some loss but they think they can save most everything. If you're curious, the potatoes are fine. Seems dirt is better than water at retaining heat or maybe they are just hardier plants."

"Guess Elisabeth is happy." I could tell she was trying to distract me.

Ingrid was more elegant in her re-entry into the hab, looking like an alpine hiker coming in from a successful expedition. I just stumbled in, the feeling in my extremities a thing of the past. I knew I wasn't hypothermic, but it was a near thing. My feet felt like bricks.

"Let's get you out of your gear, into bed, and warm you up." Ingrid pushed me onto a bench and pulled off my bunny boots. She left my double layer of socks in place after checking to make sure they weren't damp. I just sat like a lump still shivering intermittently. I could tell from the air coming through the room vents that the backup generator was working hard to push out the cold that leached into the building when the primary generator had gone offline.

"Main generator?" I asked.

"Dianna's working through the primary generator system to figure out if we can get it restarted. Until then, we're shutting down some areas to conserve power since the backup generator, as you know, doesn't have the power capabilities of the primary."

I didn't want to move but I knew I needed warmth and rest. I shook myself. I shrugged out of my parka and snow pants and stowed them in my cubby.

"Come on, Jo. Ty let me know that they've set up the common room. Looks like we'll be bunking in there until Dianna gets this figured out."

The couches, chairs, and exercise equipment were pushed against the common room walls, leaving the space in the middle open for mattresses pulled from the bedrooms. There was a slender two-foot path around the mattresses and a single path down the middle for access. The room was warmer than the coat room but not by a lot. I shivered again.

"Jo." Christina stood up from the couch. "Ingrid, bring her over here." She waved to a mattress near the galley pass-through where I could see my grandmother's quilt spread out, giving a splash of color against the otherwise drab blankets provided.

Ingrid kept a hand on my arm, steering me around the perimeter of the mattresses. It was a good thing, as my feet seemed uncooperative, and I weaved a little. The quilt looked so inviting. I wanted to lie down, get warm, and not move for a long time.

I burrowed under layers of blankets with the quilt making the last layer. Then, Christina was at my side pushing a steaming cup at me.

"Broth," she said, helping me to sit up. "Drink this and then you can sleep."

The broth was flavorful and not too hot to drink. It soothed my throat and felt good going down. Christina took the cup from me and helped me back under the covers.

"Sleep."

And I did.

CHAPTER THIRTY-FOUR

October–Antarctica

Noise and yelling woke me.

"I'm not sleeping without someone on watch." Dianna's voice sounded shrill.

Rubbing my gummy eyes, it took me a few seconds to figure out where I was. I had no idea what time of day it was or how long I'd been asleep. It had always been easy to lose track of time in the hab. With the darkness and the full light of Antarctica, time was for clocks and our bodies got out of sync with normal circadian rhythms.

"Dianna, Miho isn't going to do anything to harm us," Ty said, her voice calm and reasonable.

"Right, and how did that work out for us?" Dianna's voice was sarcastic and hard. "How do I know that it wasn't Miho who clogged the vent line?"

I sat up and could see that all of us were present in the room, Christina in her usual position—leaning up against a wall, Sam in the bed nearest me, also looking like she had just woken up to the argument as well. Miho was at the far edge of the room, straight across from me and far from the corridor to the hallway and the galley, labs, and washroom. Her head was down, her black hair hiding her face from view. She was statue still.

"Hey Jo," Sam said. "You okay?"

I nodded but before I could say anything, the argument continued.

Ingrid's voice came from the far side of the room. "You don't know that. Personally, I think the fob was planted. Something to divide us. Miho has been nothing but kind, helpful and diligent, since Houston."

She hadn't always supported Miho. Their personalities were too different. Ingrid was fair, though, and as Ingrid's roommate, she had spent more time with her than the rest of us. "Christina found the fob...what, four weeks ago?"

Dianna looked ready to protest again.

"Could the clog have been there for four weeks? And why would Miho have clogged the vent if she was going to blow us all up?" Sam said.

"I don't think we should let our guard down," Dianna grumbled.

"Are we back on the primary generator?" I asked, my voice coming out rough. I cleared my voice and continued, "What is our status?"

Ty spoke before Dianna could interject again. "Dianna's got the primary generator running again. From the readings you and Sam provided, we have plenty of fuel. Dianna found a clogged vent that tripped a safety, which shut down the system. No harm, no foul." She gave Dianna a bright smile.

"Why are we camped out if everything's back to normal?" I was puzzled.

"What? You don't like my company?" Sam asked, rolling from her bed onto mine and snuggling up against me. She was a physical person and showed her affections easily. It was something I'd been forced to deal with when we'd roomed together.

I patted her head before giving her a slight push to create some space between us. "I like you just fine, although I wasn't expecting a slumber party."

"Ty thinks that if we're all together, we'll bond better," Christina said. She didn't sound happy about the prospect. Christina liked her privacy. She'd probably find a way to hole up in medical. Her eyes drifted to mine and I could see a question in her eyes.

I turned to look at Ty. "For a month?"

"For a couple of days, until Dianna finishes her checkout of the system. We may need to go back to the backup generator, which is why we did this." She waved a hand around the room. "If we can stay on the primary, we'll all go back to our rooms. We can still do our research and all the things we normally do."

Christina snickered. It was unexpected from her and it made me smile.

"Most of the things we normally do," Ty amended smoothly, not looking at either of us. "Dianna will let us know when it's safe to go back to our rooms."

"Shall we call her Mother?" Elisabeth clasped her hands to her breast and tried to look penitent. "Mother Dianna, may I have permission to visit my potatoes?"

Dianna looked like she wanted to remain angry but Elisabeth's friendly gibe made her relent. She waved her hand at Elisabeth in an exaggerated sign of approval and Elisabeth headed out of the room, a skip in her step.

I thought I knew about these people, but sleeping in the same room was another level entirely. Ingrid snored. It wasn't feminine, sexy, or appealing. It was epic. A gasp, a snort, a wheeze. Slow and rhythmical. It was so regular it would have been hypnotic if it hadn't been so loud. I was at the opposite end of the room from her. Maybe it was the acoustics of the room that accentuated the sound, but I couldn't imagine how loud it was next to her. Had it been that bad when she and Ty were together? Either Ty really loved her or she was deaf.

Also, nine women living in the same room was taking on the smells of a locker room. The room had already had a faint odor of sweat and rubber from the exercise area, but the proximity of bodies in the twenty-by-twenty-foot area of the common room was overworking the air filtration system. Rue hadn't helped the situation.

After Dianna had gotten the backup generator online, Miho and Sam had worked hard to save as many plants as possible, harvesting what they couldn't save. This had led to an overabundance of broccoli and kale at a few meals. It had caused everyone some problems. Rue's digestive tract hadn't fared well and we were all dealing with the smell. These were the kinds of things you had to learn to deal with in close company. I couldn't imagine sharing about one tenth this size space on a one-year trip to Mars with a crew of eight to ten. No privacy to speak of and the interesting smells. I wonder if they let individuals that snore on the mission?

"I've been thinking," Rue said to the room at large two nights later.

"Is that wise?" Elisabeth asked, her eyebrows raised in mock concern. She was lying on her stomach on her mattress next to the easy chair Rue had commandeered next to a wall outlet.

Rue made a face at her. "I've been sorting through all the emails Miho got from her husband, rather ex-husband," she said, sending an apologetic glance toward Miho who was lying quietly on her bed. "As well as the emails Christina and Ty got, and I've found some interesting correlations."

Now she had everyone's attention.

Ty strode into the room from the galley and moved to stand beside Rue. "Don't keep us in suspense."

"It's the email addresses used." Rue looked down at her laptop screen. "At first, they all looked random but I think I've found a pattern. Also, I've been looking at the sentence structure and word usage."

If anyone could find a legitimate pattern, it was Rue.

I looked up from my reader. I was lounging on one of the couches pushed up against a wall, my feet in Christina's lap. "Anything that points back to SpaceGen?"

"Yes and no," Rue said, her brow furrowed as she scrolled through screens as if searching for something specific.

"That's helpful," Elisabeth quipped.

Ty gave her a quelling look which Elisabeth missed entirely.

"What data points to SpaceGen?" Christina said, coming out of a meditative state.

"I think the most specific is word choice," Rue said. "I analyzed the words used, number of uses, word combinations, spelling mistakes, use of, etc."

"We get the point." Elisabeth interrupted Rue's laundry list. "What does it mean? And why do you think it points to SpaceGen?"

"Capitalizations. With Christina's help, I correlated what we had previously found on the SpaceGen website—letters from the

CEO, and promotional materials. Christina had the foresight to grab the data before we went offline." She pushed her glasses back up on her nose and gave Christina a nod, which Christina returned.

Ty looked at the laptop screen. "Similarities?"

"See for yourself." Rue pointed to something only she and Ty could see.

"Seventy-two to seventy-nine percent," Ty said. "I can see that there is a correlation. How can you be sure that isn't random? Have you looked at that?"

"I've looked at our sponsors, NASA, and the NSF for correlations and it's marginal in comparison…between twenty to thirty-seven percent. Some words and combinations are just normal." Rue looked up to scan the room and all the faces looking back at her. "Some of the word combinations only come from newsletters, as if someone were parroting some rhetoric."

"Okay, why then, if you are finding so much correlation between the emails and the SpaceGen documentation, are you questioning the data?" Christina pushed my feet to the side and stood. "It seems like you're convinced it was them."

"I can't be sure if it's the entire organization or just a few specific people," Rue said, scrolling through data again. "I'm still working on the who."

"Who cares anyway?" Dianna asked. "It's the FBI's job to figure this out."

As she said this, she glared at Miho as if it was all Miho's fault. I wasn't sure how to help Dianna with her anger. It was festering.

I put down my reader. "I think it's our responsibility to do all we can to help. Even if the FBI has figured it out, as you say, any evidence we could provide would ensure the convictions of the saboteurs." I glanced at Miho. "Yes, there is a limit to how much we can do, but I think we could do a lot more."

"Such as?" Dianna said, glaring at me.

"Have you examined the explosives? I know you've worked with them before. Do we know what they are? Where they might have come from? You and Ingrid did a great job of disarming them and then exploded some of them for us. What could they tell us?"

"You mean like fingerprints?" Ingrid asked. Before I could speak, she waved a dismissive hand at me and continued. "No, I don't mean actual fingerprints. If there were any, we've probably destroyed them. I mean manufacturer or identifying marks, lot, serial number, etc. Sometimes unique lots are built and can be identified."

"Exactly." I smiled, my first actual smile in a while, glad that someone was following my train of thought.

"Dianna, this is something you know a lot about and I know a little. If we put our heads together, we might come up with something useful," Ingrid said, looking at Dianna but I could see she was trying to get Ty's approval. Ty wanted this mission to succeed, and Ingrid was happy to find something she could actively do to help, even if it meant pushing Dianna.

"Maybe," Dianna said, nodding slowly as if she wasn't happy with the idea.

I knew time was getting short. We only had a few more weeks and tensions were running high. We were all ready for it to be over and yet not. Had our ruse worked? Had the FBI located Miho's mom and kids? Who were the saboteurs? Were we missed? Cocooned in our little world, we were immune to the troubles in the outside world. No news feeds or social media. The only dramas were the ones we created.

Rue, a data junkie who'd been cut off from her data stream, found her outlet in parsing through the data available to her. Ingrid maneuvered to get closer to Ty, with Ty responding like a skittish colt, making Ingrid work for every step. Elisabeth pranked everyone and played the class clown. Sam gave random hugs, even to those who didn't like them. We were all learning to trust and work together. Ferreting out clues and details were what we were good at, usually as individuals, but now as a team.

CHAPTER THIRTY-FIVE

October-Antarctica

I knew it was bound to happen. We moved back to our individual rooms and some of the tension of living on top of each other had ebbed, but Dianna had been stomping around for days. She worked well with Ingrid and they learned more about the explosives. Without the internet, they had to go from memory, experience, and the research articles and manuals, they had both brought with them. I thought it would be enough of a distraction, but every night, Dianna would march into the galley for dinner and her eyes would immediately seek out Miho.

Miho was sitting at the end of the big table, making herself small and trying to blend into the background, her eyes darting around the room but not settling on anything.

"Why didn't you stand up for yourself, for us?" Dianna exploded, stalking over to Miho.

Miho didn't say anything, her shoulders hunching as if she expected a physical blow.

Dianna threw up her hands. "What? You think I'm going to hit you? Really? Really?" Her voice was getting louder and louder with each word. "This is the problem." She waved her hands at me and the rest of the assembled group. "You see this. She won't stick up for herself. She didn't stick up for us. She just rolls over." She turned back to Miho. "You're pathetic."

"Cut it out Dianna," Elisabeth said, exasperation clear in her voice. "Stop yelling at Miho. She doesn't know how to fight. Can't you see that?"

Dianna glared at Elisabeth working herself up to include her in her anger.

"She's right," Miho said.

We were all stunned. Even Dianna turned to stare. This was the first time Miho said much of anything since the fob incident that wasn't related to her plants.

"I don't know how to fight or to stick up for myself. Confrontation frightens me."

I hated confrontation, too. Running was my tried-and-true method of avoidance.

"Confrontation doesn't mean that you don't love someone or aren't friends. Some people like to argue for argument's sake," Sam said, looking pointedly at Dianna.

Dianna gave her a "who me" look.

Elisabeth laughed. "Hey, Dianna, you know you tried to kill us," she said, her German accent fading a little as she drew her words out.

"What?" Dianna turned to face Elisabeth, a surprised look on her face.

"You tried to kill us the second week we were here," Elisabeth said, examining her nails with exaggerated concern before sending a sideways glance at me and Miho.

"I did not," Dianna said, her brow furrowed and crossed her arms.

"You tried to poison us with your cooking. You said you were a fabulous cook. It says so in your bio. Doesn't it, Rue?"

Rue raised both hands, the corners of her mouth twitching slightly as she tried not to smile. "Don't get me involved."

"The woman who is so detail-oriented yells at anyone who so much as puts a tool back in the wrong slot, can't tell the difference between cinnamon and cayenne pepper."

"Hey, Ingrid said she liked the bread better with the cayenne," Dianna said, looking to Ingrid for support.

Ingrid just shook her head.

"Yeah, but you almost killed Miho," added Elisabeth in a superior tone.

"How was I supposed to know she would have an adverse reaction to cayenne pepper?" Dianna said, glancing at Miho, whose eyes were focused on the hands in her lap.

"Did you ever apologize for almost killing her? Noo, you just brushed it off. And did she get angry at you, call you a horrible cook, or accuse you of trying to kill her?"

Dianna looked guilty; her mouth was in a tight line.

Elisabeth looked around the room and held up her arms in victory. Then she went over to Dianna and laid an arm around her shoulders. "Love you, my beer buddy."

Dianna accepted the side-arm hug and then pushed her away. "All right, all right, Miho," she said, her voice conciliatory. "I'm sorry that I almost killed you. But I'm still angry that you didn't come to me about those emails. I thought I was your friend!"

Miho looked up at Dianna. There were tears in her eyes. "I was afraid, afraid you wouldn't understand. Or that you would understand and do something that might make it worse. I'm worried about my children. And my mother. I wanted to tell you," she said sincerely.

I could tell Dianna was struggling with her emotions. It was a hard decision. Did she trust that Miho wasn't a part of this sabotage? That she had been set up as the fall guy? Even Christina had come around. Dianna and Miho had been tight before the incident. Dianna had built and tweaked designs for the aeroponics lab she and Miho had worked out. They had spent a lot of time together, laughing and tinkering. Miho had been an integral part of the beer and vodka making using the potatoes. I hadn't known you could make beer with potatoes but Elisabeth, Dianna, and Miho had worked it out and it wasn't bad. I knew Dianna missed Miho's company. Elisabeth was too much of a class cutup. Dianna needed Miho's calm stability.

"Well," Dianna said, her voice calmer but laced with sadness, "You should have told me." Then she turned away and left the room without dinner. It wasn't closure but some of the tension had dissipated. Dianna would work through it.

CHAPTER THIRTY-SIX

Early November-Antarctica

Our time in the hab was getting shorter and expectations were rising. I was getting edgy myself. I wasn't ready to go back to the real world, and yet, in less than a week, reality would be upon us. I wasn't sure what to expect. This mission wasn't what I'd expected either, more drama and less science, but I think it was more realistic. We were definitely here for the science, but the true mission was really about human interactions. Could we live and function as a unit?

Rather than focus on the tension within me, I worked with Ty to push on the team to learn more about the people trying to make us fail. Ingrid and Dianna had found several serial numbers and a manufacturer's mark on the explosives. Rue's work with Christina on categorizing the data gleaned from the emails had generated some pointers to key individuals. Still it was the conversations that pulled it all together.

"Remember Cid's party in Houston?" I asked Ty one night at dinner.

Ty looked up at me, a fork full of lettuce and cucumber glistening in an olive oil and balsamic vinegar concoction she liked to use.

"Wasn't it George Weller, the men's Houston lead, that made the snide comments about our team? You were really mad."

"George with Todd at his side. That was after Evelyn came by," Ty said, putting down the fork. "I forgot that."

"Miho, did you hear or see anything? Or later in the offices. You spent more time at GICE than the rest of us."

Miho looked up from her plate. Life had gotten better. Still, she kept to herself. "I didn't think about it much. I heard similar comments from a few of the men. They always couched it to sound like a question rather than an accusation." She looked at Dianna and then away. "Why would you want to live in such a harsh environment? What about your children? Shouldn't you be home with them? Are you one of 'those kind?' said with a wink and a nod. They did try to get me to talk about Ty." She shook her head. "They wanted something to use against her. I just said Ty was a good leader and ignored them."

"Do you remember who these guys were? Names? Dates? Was there any escalation? Did anyone put a stop to it?"

"George Weller was one of them. Also Todd Schwartz. Peter Bennett came in on one conversation and told the guys to cut it out, though I'm not sure he didn't agree with them."

"Why do you say that?" Ty asked, her eyebrows coming together in a frown.

Peter Bennett was one of the three GICE Corporation vice presidents that had no direct responsibility for our mission. He was slated to move to the second spot when Dr. Carroll, the VP, stepped down. Balkner was grooming him with more responsibility and special projects.

"It was the look he gave the men. It didn't feel like he was standing up for me or for you so much as he was unhappy with the fact they had brought up the subject at all," Miho said. Her gaze shifted to the distance, as if she was trying to see the scene again. "Maybe I just imagined it."

Christina and Rue exchanged a look.

"What?" I asked.

Christina nodded to Rue.

"We started analyzing some of the emails and reports from GICE," Rue said.

"And?" Ty asked.

"Emails from Bennett's office use some of the same wording. The correlation isn't as strong but it's still there."

"So you think Bennett is part of the conspiracy?"

"It would make sense. He was in charge of the procurements. All the module's design and building would have come through his office."

"But it's all conjecture. Do we have any proof?"

There was silence in the room.

"Does anyone know of any connection between Bennett or Weller and SpaceGen?" I asked.

"Yeah, Bennett and the president of SpaceGen were both at that party. That was before SpaceGen's investment was rejected once their misogynistic policies were uncovered," Ty said.

"More circumstantial evidence," I said. "Did you hear any conversations between them?"

Ty shook her head.

Were we building mountains out of molehills? Looking for connections that weren't there? It was so frustrating having theories and conjecture but not being able to do any real checking. Instead of a locked door murder, we were in the locked room.

"That's weird," I said as I looked over the data Dianna and Ingrid had compiled on explosives. "You sure?" It was a day later and we were in the science lab.

"As sure as we can be with our limited data pool," Ingrid said, her long fingers tapping through screens.

"Have you run this by Ty?"

"Not yet. You were the one pushing for the information so we brought it to you first." Dianna drummed her fingers on the desk and sat back in her chair.

"When you first found the explosives, you said they were built into the habitat pylons," I said. "Do we know who built the modules? They must have been really expensive."

Dianna nodded. "Yep, flying a pound of cargo sent to the South Pole is almost as much as sending it to outer space. That's one of the main reasons they built the South Pole Traverse. Also the size and weight were prohibitive, especially the power plant modules."

"I call it the forty-day highway, nothing but snow and ice and freezing temperature for the forty days it takes to get between here and McMurdo. But it can also support bringing in the bigger stuff, like the pre-made habs which were shipped from the coast. They wouldn't have fit in planes."

"How could the explosives not have been found? Don't they have dogs?" I asked.

Ingrid shrugged. "I don't know. It wasn't brought on a US ship, I know that."

"The inner mechanisms remind me of the Chinese devices used in Africa," Dianna said.

"What? You think the Chinese are involved?"

Another shrug, this time from Dianna.

"China has been very busy building bases and icebreaker ships," Ty said from the lab doorway.

"How long have you been there?" I asked, looking from her to Ingrid.

Ingrid's eyes were fixed on her. Ty watched me.

"At the various donor meetings, we were briefed on the Antarctica Treaty which prohibits mining, military training, nuclear explosions. We were also informed the Chinese had been making noises about mining operations."

"Rumor is they've had military exercises too," Dianna said. "Obvious violations if true."

"You think they want to start an incident to break the treaty?" I asked. This was way too crazy. "Are you thinking that SpaceGen is a front for the Chinese?"

"Or the Russians?" Ty pondered. "But more likely the Chinese. And no, I don't think SpaceGen is a front. From everything Rue and Ingrid have pulled from the data, the CEO of SpaceGen and their organization have pushed fundamentalist values. Women should be silent. No women until it's safe and then only in supportive roles. They needed money to be part of the study and I think they got the resources through the Chinese, possibly without knowing it."

CHAPTER THIRTY-SEVEN

November-Antarctica

With twenty hours of sunlight a day, we knew the end of our mission was approaching. Even Elisabeth, who thought everything was a joke, was tense. Miho had gone so far as to put on her outdoor wear and pace outside the building, watching the sky.

"What's first on the agenda once we're alive again?" I asked.

Sam looked up from the keyboard. "My sister. I want to find out if she's okay and if I'm an aunt. And how is the rest of my family doing? Did my abuela get her hip replaced? Did Mom and Dad get the new car?"

Ty walked into the lab. "Any news?"

"Nope," Sam said.

"You know the first flight in is solely for resupply and fueling of Pole Station," Ty said as she logged into her own workspace.

"It will give us warning. The next one will have an investigation team," I said.

"Do you think John Steinman will be on the flight? If he sent Christina, he has to be one of the good guys, right?" Sam asked.

"Why are you cleaning?" Dianna's angry voice came from the corridor outside the science lab where I was yet again reviewing data. I had jumped at her words as I thought she was talking to me since I was indeed cleaning up my files.

"Stop, it's not your job," her voice was louder now, more emphatic. "I said stop!"

There were the sounds of a scuffle in the hallway and I jumped from my seat to intervene. Dianna was trying to take a mop away from Miho and Miho was putting up a fight. Ty and Sam were right behind me. Ingrid and Rue joined from the crew quarters and Christina and Sam rushed in from the galley.

Miho wrenched control of the mop handle and whacked Dianna on the shins. Dianna, undeterred, came back with a vengeance. Miho was winding up to take a golf swing at Dianna when Christina grabbed hold of the handle and yanked it from her grip.

"What's going on here?" Ty asked, moving to stand between the two women who were now glaring at each other.

"She was cleaning," Dianna said.

"And that is a problem...why?" Ty asked, looking between them. They were both still breathing heavily as if ready to come to blows again.

Dianna huffed. "She's not on the schedule to clean this week. I'm sick of her poor pity me, I'll take all the shit jobs, sad sack act."

"Sad sack?" Ingrid said to Rue who was standing next to her.

Rue shrugged.

"It's from an old American cartoon from the 1940s. The main character is hopeless and fails at whatever he does—sad sack— became a catchall for someone who is clumsy and inept," I said, remembering how much my grandmother had liked that cartoon.

"I am not inept," Miho said, glaring at Dianna.

Elisabeth snickered. She had come in from the common room and was still holding the tablet she had been reading. "I think Dianna would agree you have a pretty good swing."

Dianna massaged the shin Miho had hit.

Trying to maintain a frown, Ty's lips twitched as she repressed a smile. "Miho can clean if she wants to, Dianna. Although if she wants to use the cleaning implements as weapons, I'm not sure I want her cleaning either."

"Give it up, Dianna. Miho isn't trying to kill us. I, for one, don't think she ever intended to. It was all too convenient." Rue looked between the two of them. "Shake hands and make up. Don't let whoever is doing all of this divide us."

"Sorry," Miho said, but she didn't sound sorry, she sounded mad. "I'm tired of all your pity."

Ty sighed and ran her hand through her hair. "Look we're all a little on edge. None of us know what the next few weeks will bring. I do know that the first flight in with passengers will have our investigation team. I think John will be on that flight but we don't know who else. Nor do we know what they have discovered."

"Yeah, but we do have a lot of information that can be used to prosecute the perps." Elisabeth bumped Ingrid and grinned. "Like that...prosecuting perps?"

Ingrid glowered down at her.

"That wasn't funny?" Elisabeth asked, holding her hands up.

I guess we were ready for this adventure to be over. We were definitely getting on each other's nerves.

The day we had anticipated and dreaded became somewhat anticlimactic. We heard the first flight come in and knew the next flight would be our investigators. We started gathering our gear together in anticipation of the investigation team's arrival, although we weren't really "packing" as we'd stay put until our actual flight out as space at Pole Station was limited and we didn't know if they'd want to keep us separated from the other teams. But rather than John and the investigation team, two vans arrived with drivers. They hadn't look surprised we were alive, nor did they share any information other than Mr. Steinman was waiting for us and to leave all materials at the hab. We informed them we had been collecting data, but they again stated that we should leave all materials in place.

We were driven to a large outbuilding a hundred meters away from the main Pole Station complex. It looked like the polar equivalent of a tropical Quonset hut half buried by drifted snow with a tunnel cut to allow for entrance into the double metal doors. I followed Ty and Christina into the building.

Ty's protests and request to see John and have him debrief us on the investigation and Miho's family went unheeded. By this time, Miho was frantic and Dianna was by her side, silent but supportive. She might pick on Miho, but no one outside of our team was going to get the opportunity. Our drivers only asked us to wait as they shepherded us quietly but firmly into our separate rooms.

Ever since the drivers arrived, I felt a building anger toward John for not having the grace to meet us himself. We hadn't anticipated this, not in all of our sessions trying to determine what would happen and how we would present our finding on the munitions, the symmetry between the wording on the threatening emails, and the SpaceGen documents. We had agreed to hold our conclusions about how our corporate sponsor, GICE, might have been infiltrated by SpaceGen collaborators and the possible Chinese connection. Now I was being held in a locked room. The lock snicked into place as the driver of my van shut the door on my room.

After a year of being together, this was the hardest punishment of all. Sure, we all had private time, but in an area so small we had always had someone close by and a quick call out would bring a response, even if it was an annoyed one. Now, we were really isolated. I sat in the hard metal chair at an equally hard metal table in a small room with nothing on the walls and thought Christina was probably enjoying this. She's probably using the time for meditation without Elisabeth coming in twelve times to see if she's done yet. It brought a brief smile to my lips before the door opened and two men entered the room.

"Ms. Peterson, Joanna Lynn Peterson?" The tall one consulted a file folder, though I was sure he didn't need to review what was in it.

I hated my full name and no one, not even my grandmother had used it. "Yes, I'm Jo Peterson," I said, my voice flat.

"Ms. Peterson, I'm John Smith and this is my colleague, David Jones. We're with the GICE legal department." The shorter of the two, with the chubby cheeks and a fringe of brown hair, said. "No charges have been filed but we need to get a complete understanding of events, specifically the explosion that occurred four months ago."

"Charges?" My heart skipped a beat. Were we under threat of arrest for our actions? My second thought was Smith and Jones? Really?

"Antarctica is a protected area." The taller man introduced as Jones interjected smoothly. "We need to understand your rationale for performing such a hazardous and illegal activity."

His words hit me like the icy wind outside and I grew calm again. They had divided us up on purpose. They wanted us to blame and make statements they could use to destroy the mission and our friendships. I knew I hadn't created the actual explosion but I wasn't throwing Dianna, Ingrid, or Ty under the bus, nor was I going to throw the team under the bus for making the decision to do it in the first place. While this scenario wasn't anything the team had discussed, Ty had mentioned that they might try to challenge the team in our formal reports on the mission. I just watched the two men patiently wondering what they would do with my silence.

"Ms. Peterson," the chubby-cheeked Mr. Smith said. "We need to understand what happened. Your insight is invaluable."

"Wait, we've been isolated for a while and I'm a little concerned about my friends. Can you tell me if Miho's family is safe? Her kids, her mom?"

The two men exchanged a look.

"I want some answers too and it doesn't look like either of you are prepared to give me any. I'd like to talk with John Steinman. I know he's here."

"Ms. Peterson, we need to go over some of the statements in your team's report," Chubby said.

"I'm not the team lead. Ty is. And I don't appreciate being locked in this room. I have nothing. *Nothing* to say to either of you until I get some more information."

There was a loud noise in the hallway and then I heard a shout.

"Get your fucking hands off me."

It was Dianna. I jumped up from my seat. Chubby Cheeks tried to block my path to the door, but I sidestepped his grab and shoved him into Tall Dude. Seemed the moves Sam had taught me were coming in handy. Wrenching open the door, which the two had failed to lock on their way in, I stepped into the corridor to find a man trying to corral Dianna.

"What's going on, Dianna?" I called to her as I hurried down the hall.

"This goon tried to get me to sign some bogus paper saying that Miho is a criminal." She batted away the arm that reached for her. "Ty was right. They are trying to get us to rat on each other. Well, I'm nobody's stooge."

The man reached her side and attempted to herd her back in the room that she had escaped. "Get away from me."

I could hear doors rattling up and down the hall. "How did you get out? Mr. Smith and Mr. Jones forgot to lock the door. Does your guy have a real name? Why is this all so cloak-and-dagger?" I asked.

Chubby Cheeks and Tall Dude were now out in the hall and Dianna and I were trapped between the three men.

"Great question," Dianna said, reaching for the nearest door and opening it. It seemed that the door locks were on the hall side instead of the room side. "Hey Ingrid. Want to join us out here?"

I did the same on the other side and found Sam. Now we were four against three. We all headed for additional doors when John came out of one of the rooms Ty behind him.

"Ladies?" John said.

We all froze like guilty children.

"I need you to go back to your individual rooms and answer the questions given you."

I looked at each of the women around me. We shared a nod.

"I don't think so," I said, speaking for the group. "We need… We *expect* some answers. Where is Miho? Is her family safe and has she been given that information?"

Dianna, Ingrid, and Sam had formed up behind me. I saw Ty slightly nod over John's shoulder. John must have been interviewing her. I could see her but the three men in the hall could not. She wanted us to protest.

John frowned. He didn't want to give us answers. Sam and Ingrid had moved to open the other doors while Dianna stood firm and supportive at my side.

I waited him out. I didn't want to justify our actions to him or anyone. It would come out eventually. We deserved some answers and I was sick of playing games.

"You set us up didn't you? Miho's family is fine and the sabotage was a setup to see how we'd react?" It was a shot in the dark but the thought came to me with sudden clarity. So many things had gone wrong and the response from corporate hadn't been decisive or helpful.

I felt the team's eyes on me. Was I right? Had this all been part of the mission?

John seemed to sense his carefully laid out mission debrief was unraveling. He shook his head at the men who were edging closer to us.

I scanned the corridor and the whole team had assembled with the exception of Miho. "Where's Miho?"

"Yeah, where's Miho?" Dianna rocked from side to side as if she was getting ready for a mad dash, to what I didn't know, but I felt the energy vibrating off her.

The rest of the team started to mutter when John held up his hand.

"She's in conference room one, talking with her kids over a video link we set up for her."

Dianna relaxed slightly but then blurted out, "How do we know you aren't lying?"

John sighed and shook his head. Turning, he called over his shoulder, "Conference room two."

He led the way and we trooped obediently after him. The three stooges following. When we got to the room, John waved off the men and shut the door.

John walked to the front of the room, and we all took seats at the conference room table with the exception of Christina who took her normal spot leaning against the wall near the door. Ingrid started to take a seat and then decided to lean against the wall opposite of Christina.

All attention turned to John, who eyed us warily. There were bags under his eyes and his face was pale under the fluorescent lights.

"Miho's children and mom were in jeopardy. That was never part of this mission."

"And the explosives? Were they part of the mission?" I asked, still pretty angry at having to deal with the two men who hadn't give me their real names.

John shook his head. "No, they weren't part of the mission either. I don't know how they got shipped here. Explosives, while not specifically illegal by treaty, are highly regulated here. We are still trying to figure out how they got shipped here and how they were installed. But, yes, each group had a stressor added into the mission. Yours were the sensors that you, Jo, had created and worked so hard to get."

"And the other teams?" Ty asked, giving John a hard look.

"Colonel Ride was given instructions to run the mission like it was a military operation."

"She knew what their stressor was, but not me?" Ty pushed. "And since when is living in a hostile environment not enough stress for any group?"

"She's military. You're a civilian and the higher-ups didn't think you should have been given the job at all. They decided to make it fair. You wouldn't be told and that would be part of your mission."

"Experiment is more like it," Elisabeth said. "Rats in a cage. Steal the cheese and see if they bite each other."

"What did the FBI find out? Was Miho's ex arrested? Is her mother, okay?" Dianna leaned forward in her seat, her full lips a flat line and her brow creased.

All good questions we wanted answers to. John looked like he'd rather be anywhere but sitting in this room. He tried to meet Ty's eyes but couldn't and ended up fiddling with a pen that had been left on the table. "Miho's mother is dead."

There was a cacophony of noise as we reacted to the news.

"What happened?" Ty's voice was loud over the tumult.

I shook my head in dismay but I glared at John as if it was his fault specifically that this had happened. I wanted the explanation as much as Ty.

"Both she and Jonathan Pierce were shot during the planned rescue mission." John didn't elaborate.

Miho's ex and her mom are both dead. Where was the justice in that?

"By whom? What went wrong?" Ty pressed.

"There was a mix-up with the communications," John said wearily. "It shouldn't have happened. The kids were safely out, then Jonathan used Miho's mom as a shield and well, there was a miscommunication, and they were both shot. There is an ongoing investigation."

Miho had seemed to know her mother wouldn't survive. A miscommunication. What the hell did that mean? Someone's life was lost because someone said the wrong thing at the wrong time? These were trained professionals.

"Does Miho know?" I asked.

John nodded sadly. "While Cynthia Uyekubo's death was tragic, it isn't our most pressing concern at the moment. The international community is in an uproar over the use of explosives and violence here in Antarctica. China is making the loudest noises. The

Antarctica Treaty conference started last week. Your deaths and the explosions have been hot topics."

Dianna and Ingrid shared a look.

"What?" John pounced on this exchange.

"We filmed the explosives in situ before we removed them," Ingrid said. "And we did a detailed review of the ordnance we pulled off the habitat pylons."

"You analyzed the explosives?" John frowned, his face and body tense.

"We didn't explode all the ordnance, only eleven," Dianna said. "We examined the rest for markings and even did a chemical analysis on one of them. We even got a few latent fingerprints. There may be DNA evidence as well. We didn't have the tools for that analysis."

"And?" John said.

Dianna looked to Ty. Ty nodded and Dianna continued. "Some of the components could be of Chinese manufacture."

John stood up as if propelled from his seat. "Are you sure?"

Dianna looked at Ingrid and shrugged. "We only had the information we'd brought with us or downloaded before we cut ourselves off, but I think so. I've dealt with Chinese munitions before in Guinea West Africa. They have a huge iron ore mining operation there. I'm familiar with the timing and triggering devices they use."

"We'll need to go over the data and evidence you accumulated," John said, looking at Dianna with interest and speculation.

"Before we turn over all of that, what assurances do we have that it will have proper review by qualified experts?" Ty interjected. "I don't want all of this to get shoved under the rug when it points to places that our company or the US government doesn't want to point to."

"And how do we know that people you brought with you aren't compromised?" Sam said into the momentary lull as John tried to formulate a response to Ty's injunction.

"Yeah, we have concerns about George Weller," Elisabeth said.

"George?" John asked. "He's here to coordinate with the men's team and hasn't been part of your mission except for normal all-hands meetings."

"When did he find out that we were alive?" Christina asked.

"I briefed the team after we left McMurdo earlier today," John looked puzzled by the question. "I needed to get the team ready for the debrief."

"And what was his reaction when you told him we were alive?" Christina continued.

"He was overjoyed," John said but he didn't seem as sure of himself now. "The whole team was. They thought they were going to have to deal with frozen corpses."

"Was he overjoyed or just shocked?" Christina pushed.

John didn't say anything. He gazed off into the distance as if trying to reconstruct the scene in his head.

"You told them all on the plane, right?" Ty asked.

John nodded.

"Did anyone make any phone calls or try to connect to the outside?" Ingrid asked, her voice a low growl.

"I don't know. I don't think so but I was focused on giving out assignments on the actions we needed to take once we landed." John looked like he'd tasted something bitter. "After all the secrecy around this, I never even considered it could be one of us. And I still don't think it."

"Where is George now?" Ingrid asked.

"I sent him out to check on the blast site. Like I said, the international community has been furious about the explosion and the fact that they weren't given much information. I wanted him to take photographs and detail the damage."

"You mean he's at our hab?" Elisabeth asked in alarm.

"Is the forensic team with him?" Christina asked, turning to share a look with Ingrid.

John nodded his head. "We brought Todd Schwartz to assist with the initial review. The FBI forensic team comes in tomorrow. There was a mix-up at Christchurch and they didn't make the original flight."

Dianna jolted to her feet. "Wasn't Todd Schwartz one of the creeps who gave Miho a hard time in Houston? He's knowledgeable on explosives. He and George are cronies and shouldn't be left alone in our hab."

"Our data!" Rue cried out and then relaxed slightly as her hand groped for something under the table. She must have made copies of her data and put it on a flash drive. She was very protective of her data and wouldn't have left it behind, regardless of what we had been told to do.

Christina and Ingrid exchanged a look and headed out the door at the same time, barreling through it. Ingrid hit Mr. Smith, who must have been eavesdropping, hard enough to send him sliding a few feet on his ass.

No one stopped to help him up as we charged toward the outer door and our outerwear. One of the two vans that had brought us here was still parked nearby and we piled in, Christina driving. Christina had the van in motion before we got the door shut.

CHAPTER THIRTY-EIGHT

November-Antarctica

The hab looked like home in the bright sunlight of November. Christina jolted to a stop next to the other van and the team piled out. The place looked peaceful, serene even.

Christina made it to the front entrance, just in front of Ingrid. They both entered with the rest of us following quickly. Ty and I were behind everyone else, and before I could enter the hab, Ty grabbed my arm and pointed. A thin stream of smoke was escaping above the right side of the module but dissipating quickly. The wind was strong. I estimated it at over fifteen knots, which wasn't unusual.

"Rue, Dianna, possible fire in the hab. Warn the others!" I shouted the last and waited until Rue appeared in the doorway and gave me a nod, before following Ty to the side of the hab nearest the fuel storage area.

The smoke was more evident as we made it to the side of the hab module. It wasn't clear where the smoke was coming from, though it seemed to be from the storage room. At first, I had thought it was the power plant module, which frightened me as there were a lot of flammable chemicals in that area. Seeing the smoke from the storage room didn't make me any happier. The two modules were side by side with only a sealed door between them. The thick, insulated walls would be a barrier, but given time or a different path, the fire could destroy our entire hab quickly.

"Is that smoke actual fire or just a fog from the heat differential?" Ty said.

"Can't tell."

"Let's get inside and see what's happening."

"Let me get the respirators from the fuel storage area." I jogged to the storage shed and grabbed an armload of the air filtration respirators. If there was a fire, these would prove vital.

After making it through the second door we didn't stop to divest ourselves of our snow gear. We didn't know if we'd need to make a quick exit through the front or the back of the hab. The coat room and living area were empty. Loud voices could be heard down the corridor.

We arrived just in time to see Sam frog march George Weller out of the science lab. Some of the team followed in her wake, their faces showing various degrees of anger and satisfaction.

"You've got the wrong guy," George said, trying in vain to pull free of Sam's firm grip. "I'm on your side. I've been investigating the sabotage and I think you guys have the information I need."

"Hey, Dianna, any issue with the generators or storage area? Did you find a source for the smoke coming from the building?" I called out over George's continuing protests.

"Just normal venting, I think. I'll run a couple of air checks. Visual inspection showed the storage area is clear and there is no live fire anywhere in the work or living areas," Dianna said.

Ty and I exchanged looks. She looked relieved and I thought my face showed similar relief. Fire wasn't to be taken lightly here. Too many ways to destroy buildings and precious resources that weren't easily replaced. People's lives would be at stake, science destroyed.

"Where's Todd?" I looked beyond George to the rest of the group. My relief at hearing there was no fire evaporating as I scanned the faces in the room.

"We didn't find him," Ingrid said from the corridor. "I'm going to go back and check the emergency exit. Elisabeth?"

Elisabeth followed her back up the corridor, almost jogging to keep up with Ingrid's long strides.

"Any sign of damage or theft or sabotage?" Ty asked Rue.

"No," Christina said, coming up behind Sam. "I don't think he had enough time. He was trying to log onto the system when we found him. I don't think any of the boxes were disturbed."

"I'm telling you," George said. He'd finally stopped fighting Sam's hold. "I'm not the source of your problems. Where is John? Where is Miho?"

"Miho's talking with her family," Dianna said.

"You don't have to answer him," Elisabeth said. "He's just trying to cover himself."

"Ask John about the China connection," George shouted.

This got our attention.

"Did he have time to find that in our data or lab?" Christina asked, looking around at the team.

There were a lot of shaking heads and shrugging shoulders. Looked like the consensus was no.

"We can't whipsaw around on this," Ty said. "Jo, let's head back and find John. The rest of you stay here and figure out what George knows or thinks he knows. Rue, can you get us that set of walkie-talkies we used before? Will they reach to the station?"

Rue nodded and ran off to get the gear.

"They were trying to mentally divide us up," Christina said. "Are you sure this is a good idea to split up? Shouldn't we stay together?"

I couldn't tell from her expression whether she meant what she said or didn't want to be separated from me again. She had kept her eyes fixed on Ty when she'd made the statement.

Rue arrived with the walkie-talkies and handed one to Ty and one to Christina.

"We can talk over these. Check in every fifteen minutes. If either team finds something of note, we communicate immediately. Don't wait," Ty said, turning the walkie-talkie on and then clipping it to her belt.

"What if one side doesn't answer?" Rue pushed her glasses up on her nose. "What then?"

"What if we don't want someone on the other side to hear our conversations?" I asked. "Do we have code words for safe to talk or problem? Are we sure the walkie-talkies will reach all the way to the station?" I could feel the tension in the room. Christina was right. They had tried to divide us up. Had John been honest with us?

What was George's deal? After our lives moving slowly and only with each other, now we had a whole host of characters and places. The tingling in my stomach was akin to panic, and I couldn't shake the feeling that our problems weren't over but just beginning.

"Hey, I'm concerned too," Ty said. "We need to split up. Find Todd, find Miho and make sure she's okay. Secure our data and get some actual answers out of John. We need answers out of George too. That will be your job." She nodded at the women she had asked to stay at the hab. "That and collecting the evidence we've pieced together. Don't worry about the hab. This isn't our home anymore."

Home. We'd all been thinking of it. Back to parts of the world that had trees, dogs, and birds and restaurants. Everything but the restaurants sounded great. A professionally cooked meal sounded wonderful, but I didn't know if I was ready for large groups of people and not knowing everyone in the room.

"Let's compromise. We'll pack up our stuff and the evidence we've collected and use the second van to move back to the station," Rue said. She didn't look like she wanted to remain at the lab any more than Christina did. Her normally cheerful, round face was pale and her eyes darted from George to Ty and back. George watched her intently.

"There's no room for us at the station. The summer crews are starting to come in and they don't want us there when we have perfectly good rooms here," Ty said.

We all knew this. It was in our original briefing package and she had reiterated it several times over the last couple of months. We had all been a little stir-crazy and had said that eating out at the Pole Station cafeteria would be a treat when our study ended.

"Enough," Ty said. "I need more answers out of John."

As if uttering his name conjured him, he walked into the common room. He was still wearing his outer gear and Miho was with him. She appeared sad but resolute. Her gaze tracked through the group until she found George.

"How much did they pay you?" Miho said, her voice no longer soft and compliant.

George would have backed up if Sam hadn't had a firm grip on him.

"What are you talking about? You're the one who's guilty. You were going to blow up the hab," George said but his voice lacked conviction.

"You collaborated with SpaceGen. You fed them mission information and details. You helped them bring the explosives into Antarctica! Most damning of all, you introduced the Chinese contacts to SpaceGen. They didn't know where the money was coming from, did they? They only knew that it was flowing in easily. They thought it was from Americans who shared their beliefs. Saps. But you aren't a sap, George, are you? You went in eyes wide open. Was it greed or power or something else?"

George's eyes darted around the room. "You're crazy," he stammered.

"No, I'm not," she said as she moved toward him. "Alicia might be young and small, but she's got an excellent set of ears. Jonathan talked a lot. He knew there was someone high up in GICE and it all points to you. I shared this with John and he's already got people working on checking your records. You do know that all of your phone calls are tracked. Even the one you made from the flight here from McMurdo."

George had a ruddy complexion but the scientist in me marveled at the way the color drained from his face. I had always thought it was just an expression. I glanced over at John to see his reaction. His facial features seemed to go from shock to anger. He obviously hadn't truly believed George had been part of the conspiracy. They had worked together for years, and if office gossip was to be believed, they had close family ties as well.

"Damn Miho," Dianna said. "I see you found your spine."

Miho glanced briefly at Dianna before returning her gaze to George. "You had my mom killed. I know it and you know it. I'm not sure how to prove it yet, but the Chinese are going to want to silence you too, you know. You're a hanging chad. The FBI might be able to protect you, but I have no idea why they might want to."

George seemed to collapse in on himself. He shifted his focus to John. "John, buddy, you gotta protect me."

"If we didn't need the information, you probably have, I'd let the Chinese…" John trailed off, the disgust in his voice clear. "I trusted you."

Running steps could be heard from the corridor and then Elisabeth burst back into the room. "We think Todd egressed through the emergency door and he's got a couple of boxes of parts," Elisabeth panted. She hadn't been big on exercise and the short run had winded her. "Ingrid went after him but the wind is really blowing and has kicked up the snow. Visibility is bad."

The explosive devices had been disassembled into their component pieces with the actual explosives stored in a metal box some distance from the hab and the fuel storage area. We hadn't wanted any unfortunate accidents. The box wasn't exactly obvious, though it wasn't hidden either. We had marked the location, drifting snow covering most of the area. It would take a concerted effort to dig it out.

"The explosive material isn't in those boxes," Ty said, expressing my sentiments out loud. "What can he do with the parts?"

"Destroy primary evidence. Dianna and Ingrid took pictures but the boxes contain the real evidence," Christina said.

"But where can he go?" I asked. "It's not like he can escape the South Pole. There are only two ways in and out: by plane or by the transverse highway on a cargo puller, both highly watched. He can't sneak aboard a plane, especially if people are watching for him. There is literally no place to go. No one is going to rescue him if he tries to walk or ski out of here. He has no supplies."

Dianna looked thoughtful. "Do you know which boxes he took? If he took the detonators, and he found the explosives, he could build something. It would be extremely crude and it would probably kill him if he set it off."

"We need to go after Ingrid," I said. "With the wind up, the temperatures are going to plummet and Elisabeth said the visibility is bad, which means she could get lost if she strays far from the hab."

We all knew that would mean certain death without shelter. It looked like we were going to divide up anyway. The thought of shelter gave me a queasy feeling.

"Hey Dianna, when you checked the hab for explosives, did you check the fuel storage area?" I asked.

Dianna shook her head. "Ingrid and I just checked the hab and support pylons. Everything we found was on the pylons. We did a cursory check of the fuel storage structure but didn't go down into the fuel storage area. That was probably dumb but I didn't think the signal would carry down there."

"Nobody else thought of it until now either," Ty said.

"I suggest we check there first." I pointed to all the filtration masks Ty and I had grabbed. "Ingrid is smart enough not to go down into the main storage area without a mask."

"Even if there aren't any explosives there, with detonators there is enough fuel for him to create a huge explosion," Dianna said, looking around the room. "I think everybody should clear out. Take the remaining evidence and go back to Pole Station. I'll go find Ingrid and get her out," Dianna said. "If Todd wants to blow himself up, that's on him. As Jo said, he can't leave this area without real assistance."

"I'll go with you to find Ingrid," Miho said. "But I want to stop Todd too. I don't trust the Chinese government. Someone put that fob on me. They may have subverted Todd. He may be on a suicide mission."

"More reason to get everyone away from the hab," John said. It was his first time speaking since Miho's bombshell and he looked frightened by the prospect. "We need the evidence you all have gathered and George needs to be questioned by the appropriate authorities. I'm sure the FBI and possibly the State Department will have questions."

"I'm not leaving Ingrid either," I said. After a quick glance at Christina, I grabbed a filtration mask and headed toward the door. "We don't know where Todd is or what his plan is. First on the agenda is checking the fuel storage area. I think of everyone I've spent the most time there and know the hiding places best." I didn't want to go back into the cavernous space again. It was cold and dank and noisy but it was also a good bet this would be where Todd would be hiding.

"I'm coming with you too," Dianna said, taking another of the masks and tossing it to Miho before taking one for herself. "Miho may be right and be able to talk him down, but I'm the best person to disarm any bombs."

Before anyone else could volunteer to go after Ingrid and Todd, Ty cut them off. "Be careful and stay together." She took the walkie-talkie off her belt and handed it to me. "Stay in continual contact with Christina. Sam, please watch George and make sure he doesn't do anything stupid. The rest of us will get the evidence and our gear into the vans. We aren't staying here even if we have to share tight quarters at Pole Station."

Ty continued to give out instructions as Miho, Dianna and I headed for the front door of the hab. Ingrid was outside and so was Todd.

CHAPTER THIRTY-NINE

November-Antarctica

The wind had picked up and I could feel the bite as the cold found pathways through the layers of protective wear. Even though it was sunny, the high winds were causing the snow to swirl, limiting our line of sight. Then I stopped thinking about the cold. The door to the fuel storage shed was open and Ingrid was lying in the doorway, her long legs stretched out in the snow and her torso lying across the threshold. I didn't stop to think; I just ran.

She lay on her side, wedged in the doorway with the door pushing against her back. Blood streaked her forehead. I checked to see if there were any other visible injuries but didn't find anything other than she was cold, not dead cold, only exposure cold. She had dressed warmly in her outerwear which had helped, but no one did well lying in a freezer. The shed provided some protection from the wind but she needed to be warm—soon.

"We have to get her back to the hab," I said to Dianna and Miho who had run with me to the outbuilding. Ingrid was a tall woman but slender. Still it took the three of us to maneuver her out of the shed without doing more damage.

I shook her shoulder gently to see if I could wake her. She murmured and her eyes fluttered open and then quickly shut again against the sun. She tried to sit up and we helped her.

"What?" She put a hand to her head and her glove came away with blood on it. She looked at her hand and then up at me. Her eyes gaining a measure of comprehension. "How long?"

I shook my head, then glanced at my watch. "You've been outside for about fifteen minutes but we don't know when you were struck. Can you walk? We need to get you out of the cold."

She looked like she might protest, then shrugged, and we helped her to her feet. She swayed and her knees buckled but she gripped my arm firmly and steadied herself.

I looked from Dianna to Miho. Ingrid needed help getting back to the hab and I didn't want to go searching for Todd alone. Then I remember the walkie-talkie at my waist. I pulled it off my belt and thumbed the talk button.

"Christina, Ingrid's been hit. Dianna is bringing her in. Over."

There was static then "Got it. Ingrid's been hit. You're coming in. Over."

"Dianna's bringing her in. Miho and I are going after Todd. Over."

More static. "Not a good plan. Bring Ingrid in and let's get out of here. Over."

Miho and I exchanged a look. Miho shook her head.

"We're going after Todd. Take care of the team. Over." I clipped the walkie-talkie to my belt, knowing that it wouldn't work once I started down the steps. I wasn't running away from this.

I felt bad for ignoring Christina's request. Thinking of Christina sent a pang through me.

Dianna glanced at Miho before she gave me a quick nod and moved to help Ingrid.

"Miho, you still up for finding Todd?" I asked.

Miho nodded, her dark eyes showing no fear.

We pushed the fuel shed door all the way open, making sure that Todd wasn't waiting for us. No one was in the room and we moved inside and then I pushed my balaclava out of the way and pulled the air filtration mask over my mouth. Miho did the same and we exchanged a nod before moving to the stairway. Before we hadn't needed the masks, but I really didn't trust Todd and didn't know what we'd find below in the vast storage area.

We were going down to confront Todd without any weapons, only words. Probably stupid but I didn't think he had a gun, only the wrench he'd taken from the wall and used on Ingrid. It wasn't getting any warmer, and if we were going to stop Todd from doing anything stupid, we needed to move. I grabbed a flashlight from the rack, noting that one was missing. Ingrid at the fuel shed with the flashlight. And then shook my head, she wasn't dead and this wasn't a game.

We tried to move quietly down the metal stairs but they creaked with every step. I decided that speed was better than stealth and started taking the steps two at a time hoping that the noise from the machinery would cover our descent. Miho's short stature didn't lend itself to the two steps at a time approach, but she was quick on her feet and right behind me.

When I hit ground level, I didn't see Todd in the immediate area. Either Todd or Ingrid had turned on the lights, but the illumination was still low as had been the case on my prior visits to this space. I stopped to orient myself and Miho came beside me and pointed to the left. I followed her finger and saw a faint light that looked like a flashlight beam. I nodded and moved parallel to the massive tank, edging closer to its end. The instrument panel showed this tank was still at fifty-seven percent capacity. I knew it held the last of our fuel and that the others were empty or close enough to empty to have triggered the cycle to this last tank.

I peered around the edge. The tank was at least fifteen-feet long, nine-feet tall, including its structural base, and about five-feet wide. From my vantage point I couldn't see to the other side. I motioned Miho to stay put and slid around to look down the long side.

Todd had his back to me and was adhering some wires to the tank with a grayish material. Tools lay around him, including the wrench. The flashlight had been taped to the wall and pointed toward the tank and the grayish material. Was that explosive material? It wasn't from our hab. The explosives we had found weren't malleable. How had he gotten them here? Moment of truth...Did we confront him here or did we try to get out and report back to the others and get trained professionals to deal with this?

All I saw was a flash of motion next to me before Miho ran by me and crashed into Todd feet first like she was going to climb over him. She was half his weight but the momentum of her explosive action knocked him to the floor. That same momentum left her off balance and she landed awkwardly. He must have been expecting something because he recovered too quickly, rolling and grabbing for her. I froze in place. Then Miho screamed, I scooped up the wrench laying on the floor and aimed a swing for his head. I wasn't normally a violent person but I was angry and frustrated and he was hurting Miho.

My strike missed his head and the blow landed on his shoulder. He grunted, thrust Miho away from him and turned to me. I didn't have time to see if she was okay before he came at me. I was tall and medium-size, but he was about six-two and muscular and his outerwear made him appear bigger still. Some of the wrench's impact must have been absorbed by his clothing because all it had done was make him mad.

Miho had mentioned talking with him but it didn't look like that was an option anymore. I tried to remember what Sam had told me about balance and using the attacker's energy against him. He grabbed for me and I dropped the wrench. His eyes followed the move and I grabbed his right arm and rotated around him. The space between the wall and the tank was limited but I ducked under him and yanked his arm up, my foot coming down on the back of his calf sending him to the floor. He yelled and tried to struggle, but for once, I had a good hold. I continued to lever his arm back and up, forcing him to either remain down or dislocate his shoulder.

"Stop struggling and it won't hurt as much," I grunted. "Miho, you okay?"

"Yeah, I'm fine," she said as she rose from the floor, holding her side. "That was probably stupid on my part but I wanted him away from the wires."

Todd was moving his other hand to his pocket and I wrenched his arm higher. "Stop. I really don't want to dislocate your shoulder but I will." Turning to Miho I added, "I'd ask you to check his pockets but I don't think you should get near him."

Miho examined the setup attached to the fuel tank. "He looks like he was just about done."

"Get Dianna and Sam and something to restrain this guy," I said. It was uncomfortable holding him down. He was in pain but

I wasn't sure how much of that was faked for my benefit and how much was real. I needed Sam. I wasn't confident enough in my skills to get him up and moving now that I had him down on the floor.

Miho took one last look at me and then took off for the stairs.

As soon as she was gone, Todd turned his head trying to look at me, shifting his weight. I just added a little more pressure and he stopped. "Let me up. I'll make it worth your while." His voice somewhat muffled by the ground and the machinery.

"How so?" Information at last. I was curious what he'd promise me.

"I'll give you a hundred thousand if you let me complete what I started and I get out of here," he said, again trying to turn to look at me.

I didn't budge. "And how do you plan to get away? This is a closed site and people are already looking for you."

"I got friends who will get me out."

"I don't believe you."

He made a sudden thrust with his body toward me and I almost lost my grip. I had braced myself, fearing that if he was willing to dislocate his shoulder, he might be able to get loose. I stomped down on his back and added more twist to his arm.

He yelled out and stopped moving.

"I knew I shouldn't trust you," I said. "Are you working for SpaceGen or the Chinese?"

He went very still. "I don't know what you're talking about."

"Only that they are responsible for the explosives on the hab." I decided for a swing in the dark.

"Take the money. I'm good for it. Let me up. I gotta finish what I started." He was struggling again and I could feel the joint starting to give. He really wanted up and if he was willing to get hurt, he could throw me off. I dropped down, my knee driving into his back and he grunted.

"Stop struggling."

"You don't understand. They'll kill my kids. I have to do this." The fear was evident in his voice and even with my full weight and his arm twisted up behind him, his struggles were starting to push me off. Where was Miho with the rescue team?

There was a slight noise behind me that overrode the sound of my own breath and the noise in the chamber. Then Sam's welcomed voice.

"Nice hold but your grip is slightly off. That's probably why he's about to throw you off. Slide your hand up to the small bone in his wrist."

"This isn't a coaching session," I groaned, trying to move my fingers as she had indicated. "Did you bring something to tie him up with? I'd like to stop this."

Instead of helping, my movement had divided my attention and he rolled over, taking me with him. I smashed into the wall and he was up and running toward the back of the storage area.

"He's got a detonator!" Miho screamed and took off after the him, Sam right behind her.

Dianna leaped over my sprawled body and grabbed a handful of wires, sorting through them, and pulling out one connected to a strip of metal adhered to the tank and above the plastic. "Hand me the wire cutters."

From my position on the ground, I rolled to my knees and groped in the box of tools Todd must have taken from the storage cabinet. Finding a pair of cutters, I slapped them into Dianna's waiting palm, her attention fixed on the explosive setup. She continued to pick through the wires before cutting several.

"Is there a putty knife in the box?" she asked, staring down at me before returning her gaze to the bomb, her calm voice making this sound like an everyday task.

I rifled through the box and came up with a metal putty knife. "This do?"

"Hmm. Is there a plastic one? I don't want to scrape metal on metal if I don't have to."

My review of the box's contents was interrupted by the ring of metal against the tank near Dianna's head. Neither Dianna nor I had seen the wrench coming and it ricocheted off the tank and smacked her in the head. I caught her about the shoulders just before she crumpled to the ground. Another flash out of the corner of my eye and I saw a flying kick from Sam take down Todd. Miho used the flashlight in her hand to club Todd on his now vulnerable head. He slumped to the ground.

"What were you guys doing?" I shouted.

"We were playing tag around the tanks and he got by us by a couple of steps," Sam said as she knelt to check on Todd.

Miho rushed to my side and took Dianna's head in her lap. She pulled off her balaclava to stanch the gash on Dianna's temple. Dianna groaned and opened her eyes. "I need to finish with the bomb."

"You need to lie still," Miho said, taking the bloody cloth away from the wound and showing Dianna the blood before reapplying it with pressure.

"I can do it," she said, making to stand and then slumping back down. "Okay maybe not. But it's still dangerous as it is now."

"What needs to be done?" I asked and stood, looking at the mess of wires and plastic still attached to the tank.

"I've removed the wires and the detonator, but the explosive material still needs to be removed from the tank." She tentatively raised her hand to her brow and groaned. "What's with that guy and hitting women on the head?"

With instructions from Dianna, I got the explosive material off the tank and into a plastic container we found, probably the one it came in, though how Todd had gotten it was still a mystery.

"How is Ingrid?" I asked. With all the excitement down here, I had forgotten about Ingrid and the rest of the team.

"Christina said she'd be fine," Sam piped up, coming over to stand by the tank. "By the way, she's pissed at you. Said some really choice things. I think she likes you."

I wasn't sure what to say to that.

Sam continued, "She didn't think Ingrid had a concussion but she wants to get her over to Pole Station and their facilities. Ingrid wants to get up and help with the move. Christina's not having any of it and has threatened to restrain her. It was kinda fun to watch."

Sam tied Todd up. Either Miho hadn't hit him that hard or he had a really hard head. By the time I finished, he was swearing and pleading with us in equal measure.

"Not really how I expected to end my all-expense paid vacation in Antarctica," Dianna grumbled as Miho helped her to her feet.

CHAPTER FORTY

December-Antarctica

There is no police force in Antarctica. There are firefighters, which seemed weird in this frozen land, but fear of hazardous chemicals and fuels required to live were a much more prevalent anxiety than espionage. Even though John tried to keep everything contained, it was too small a community and too juicy a story. So everyone knew or thought they knew what was happening.

The summer crew filled the Pole Station corridors and burst into cheers as we entered. There were a couple of ribald jokes as the two handcuffed men walked through, everyone making guesses as to where the handcuffs had come from given the lack of law enforcement on the base.

Our survival was big news. The team they had sent out to check on us kept the secret. They deserved Oscars for their performance and grief at our deaths. We got quite a few nods and a couple of backslaps and fist bumps as we headed for our first meal outside the hab in thirteen months. No one stopped us but the excitement of our return was palpable. The other two teams had already been transferred out to McMurdo, to Christchurch, Houston—and home. Our turn would come but there was still time for questions and arrangements to be made.

The FBI had arrived and taken George and Todd into custody. George had been singing for a lawyer but the closest one was about two five-hour plane flights away. I wondered if they'd set up a Skype or Zoom call. He wasn't our problem anymore, though he was probably safer at the South Pole than any place on earth.

Todd had gone silent. After stating that his family was in jeopardy and they needed protection, he had stopped talking. Miho tried to talk with him, but he just turned away and stared at the wall. He knew what had happened to her mom. Miho understood he feared for his family and had some sympathy for him but not much. I just hoped that the FBI would figure out Todd's getaway plans. With over 950 miles of open, frozen, hazardous, mountainous terrain, it wasn't like someone could just live off the land. There was nothing to live off and the conditions changed daily if not hourly.

The FBI had accepted our data and written statements into evidence.

Before our farewell dinner, John asked us to join him in the conference room where we started our first day at Pole Station. I had begun with such high hopes and was feeling flat. We'd done the science and wintered over in an unforgiving environment. I should be excited to get back to civilization and my freedom, but instead I stared at Christina's back and wondered if I'd see her once we left Antarctica, or if we'd wasted precious time. Would the feelings between us still be there with distance? My mind skittered at the thought and I focused on the group. Ty leading. Ingrid following. Elisabeth telling jokes. Rue and Sam ignoring her. Dianna bending close to hear Miho's quiet words.

As Ty opened the conference room door, I could hear cheering and whoops. Following in behind Dianna, the conference room table and chairs were the same but a huge screen showed the smiling faces of the team's families.

Sam stalked right up to the screen, as if she could walk right into the tableau of her family scrunched together in a square. "Gail, did you have the baby? Are you good?"

A dark-eyed woman with a mass of black hair smiled and held up a swaddled bundle. "Yes, I'm fine. Meet your namesake, Sammy. You owe her big-time."

The other squares on the screen were filled with other family members smiling and waving to my friends who smiled and waved back. There were more call-outs and questions, but it was hard as the line only let one person talk at a time.

John cleared his throat. "You will all have time to chat with your families later. We've set up times and lines for each of you. But before all of that, I'd like to direct your attention to NSF Director, Dr. Amanda Bridgestone, in the top left of the screen."

Framed by the National Science Foundation logo behind her, Dr. Amanda Bridgestone was camera ready with carefully coiffed brown hair, intelligent gray eyes, and a warm smile ghosting her lips. "Thank you, John! Ladies, speaking for myself, my staff, and other interested parties, I'd like to thank you for your service to your country."

Dianna started to protest, and Miho elbowed her in the ribs. "Leave it."

Dr. Bridgestone continued, "The Antarctica Treaty Consultative Meeting is in session. Some countries…" Her lips thinned. "Some countries are using the recent incidents to indicate that the United States shouldn't be responsible for Amundsen-Scott South Pole Station, that our role in Antarctica is suspect, believing the explosions and your supposed deaths are due to incompetence. Some countries…are looking to open up Antarctica and the waters around Antarctica for exploitation and potential mining operations. With your resurrection and the findings of sabotage, we've been able to push the conversations back to protection and conservation. We don't have proof…" Her gaze flicked to each person in the conference room. "…of any specific country's interference in our territory. But please be assured that we are taking the investigative work you've done seriously and following up. Now, take the time to celebrate with your families and know your work over the last year has moved many projects forward. I appreciate this work, but I also appreciate that you found a path forward in spite of all the obstacles you endured. Please know your efforts pushed the Antarctica Treaty back on a positive path. Thank you." With a final smile, she left the conference call.

The room was silent for a moment. Then a small voice piped up from the conference room mike. "Are you getting a medal, Mom?"

"You deserve one," Dianna said. "For putting up with my sh…."

Miho bumped her again.

"Shenanigans." Dianna bumped her back.

I chuckled with the rest of the group. I thought of Amy and wonder how she would have taken the praise. She probably would have frowned and explained why what we had done was part of the mission. No more, no less.

Gazing around the room, I noticed Christina near the door, out of direct view of the camera. Scanning the screen, I didn't see anyone I thought might be her family. Ty's mom was there, and it seemed everyone else had someone linked in as well. No one for Christina or me. I had thought my aunt might be there. She'd reached out to me but I hadn't responded. Maybe it was time to stop running and talk with her. Maybe get some closure or maybe even a new start.

Christina's eyes met mine. She tilted her head to the screen and raised her eyebrows.

I walked over to her. "No one here for you either?"

"Nope."

"No family?"

"No, I have parents and siblings. They just don't know where I've been."

It was my turn to raise an eyebrow.

Christina shrugged. "Not everyone's family is Rue's or Sam's."

I started to say something and she laid a hand on my arm. "And that's okay. We build our own family."

I smiled down at her and took her hand in mine.

"Dr. Bridgestone wasn't kidding. Our return from the dead caused a lot of frenzied activities," Ty said before she took another bite of fried chicken.

Initial debriefs completed, family meetings held, we were now sharing a final dinner before our flight to McMurdo Station, Christchurch, and our respective homes. I was heading to Houston with Ty, but that was only temporary.

"Did they figure out why the FBI missed the flight to McMurdo?" Ingrid was sitting to Ty's left, still watching and wary.

Ty glanced at her before looking over at me and around the table. "George gave them the wrong times. He tried to pawn it off as a misprint, but John isn't buying it. Neither is the FBI. George's phone gave him away and they issued a warrant and found a laptop hidden at his house."

"Does it implicate the Chinese?" Miho asked. Her mom's death had hit her hard but seeing her kids alive and safe had done wonders for her.

"Not directly," Ty said. "George's cutout was a Chinese national but with no ties to Beijing or their military."

"Are they following the money?" I asked.

"It wasn't definitive," Rue said as she ate another fork full of salad. "They found links on George's computer to the dark web. Following the link, many of the tracks just vanished. Wiped away via computer viruses and system lock ups similar to ransomware but without any suggestion of a key to reopen. Various US government agencies are now looking hard at the data but without traceable proof back to the Chinese government, nothing can be done. Sam and Miho, your salads were better."

We all stared at Rue.

"What?" she said looking at us. "They were."

"No, where did you get the information?" Sam asked.

"I overheard some stuff while I was working in the communication center," said Rue. "Better internet there. I had a lot of catching up to do."

Sam laughed. "You would find a way to snoop and catch up on your sitcoms at the same time."

Rue beamed and ate another bite of salad. "Based on the information I got from the FBI, the thought is that China was funneling money into SpaceGen to create additional chaos as they build up their own space programs. The US's space program garnered a lot of goodwill around the world. Everyone loves an astronaut and space travel is cool. Giving NASA a black eye and making the US premier Antarctic outpost look incompetent is a win-win for them."

US funding for space programs hadn't really changed in years. Yet every dollar spent on NASA, yielded between eight and fifteen dollars in return, but the government and the taxpayers only saw it as a program to cut. With the application of commercial companies like SpaceX, Virgin Galactic, and Blue Origin, interest had again flooded the imagination of kids and adults alike. That was how GICE had gotten funds to work on the manned aspects of long-duration timelines spent on other planets, Mars being the primary contender. If China could do anything to hamper or create confusion between commercial enterprises and NASA and/or the US government, it was money well spent. It made my stomach hurt. We had been disposable. Just a cog in a wheel.

"China used the chaos to erode The Antarctica Treaty discussions," I said. "Maybe it wouldn't have happened at this conference, but China plays the long game with events carefully managed over time. Breaking down the trust and legitimacy of the treaty…So much upside for them making the US look bad, and so little down."

Everyone was still thinking about what had been said.

Ty rose to her feet, wineglass raised. "We survived. We did what we set out to do. We proved that we can handle the mental and physical stresses. We lost Amy due to a medical issue we couldn't have known about." She paused. "But we overcame all the crap they threw at us both intentionally and unintentionally. We built a team. A family. I call that a win."

We raised our own glasses. "Family."

"Did you find yourself?" Christina asked.

I added a few last items to my bag and took a final look around the Pole Station room, giving myself a few more seconds to put my thoughts in order. We hadn't returned to the hab after capturing George and Todd. This room was a single with none of the charm Christina and I had worked into our shared space. We hadn't discussed the future or our relationship. There had always been some crisis or another and both of us had evaded the topic.

"I found a family I didn't know I needed," I said, finally turning to look at her.

"Am I part of that family?" Her question came without her normal bravado.

The question was real. We had made no promises. So much had happened. She had withheld information and her accusation against Miho had sewn discord. It had driven us apart and then strengthened us as a team. I wondered even now if she had used my naïveté to hide behind. It hadn't stopped me trusting her or wanting her. Looking across the room, her eyes were pleading.

"Yes." The answer was simple. I still didn't know what it meant. We were both adventurers and liked our own company. Depending on others had never come easily for either of us. For all of that, I hadn't felt this way about someone in a long time, if ever. I wanted more.

A slow smile brightened her entire face, striking a matching chord in me. "What's next for you?"

"Ty offered me a follow-up contract in Houston. She's picking up back at NASA and it seems NASA's Mars division needs someone to watch the weather. And there is interest in commercializing the sensors I worked up with Dianna and Amy. They actually have a few interesting things my original design didn't have. And GICE doesn't own the design." Zipping my bag closed, I looked up into her expressive eyes. "And you?"

Her smile broadened. "John wants me for some job or another back in Houston. Not sure I'm really keen on going back there. It's awfully hot and humid in the summer."

"Houston in the summer isn't very appealing. Got any better ideas?"

She moved toward me and pulled me into her arms. "Oh, I have lots of good ideas and I think I'll start right now."

"I'm all in. Mission is complete. Rules don't apply."

Christina ran her hands up my back. This time, instead of soothing, I could feel the heat and my reaction to it. Lowering my head, I did what I had dreamed of since Switzerland and kissed her. It was better than I imagined. Her lips were soft and warm. All the pent-up need moved the kiss from soft to intense in a flash. The feel of her body against mine was intoxicating. She pushed forward until my legs hit the bed and I pulled her down on top of me.

A loud knock at the door made me turn my head. Ty opened the door and stuck her head in, grinning. "Planes wait for no one, people. Time to leave this iceberg."

More Titles from Bella Books

Hunter's Revenge – Gerri Hill
978-1-64247-447-3 | 276 pgs | paperback: $18.95 | eBook: $9.99
Tori Hunter is back! Don't miss this final chapter in the acclaimed
Tori Hunter series.

Integrity – E. J. Noyes
978-1-64247-465-7 | 28 pgs | paperback: $19.95 | eBook: $9.99
It was supposed to be an ordinary workday...

The Order – TJ O'Shea
978-1-64247-378-0 | 396 pgs | paperback: $19.95 | eBook: $9.99
For two women the battle between new love and old loyalty may prove
more dangerous than the war they're trying to survive.

Under the Stars with You – Jaime Clevenger
978-1-64247-439-8 | 302 pgs | paperback: $19.95 | eBook: $9.99
Sometimes believing in love is the first step. And sometimes it's all
about trusting the stars.

The Missing Piece – Kat Jackson
978-1-64247-445-9 | 250 pgs | paperback: $18.95 | eBook: $9.99
Renee's world collides with possibility and the past, setting off a tidal
wave of changes she could have never predicted.

An Acquired Taste – Cheri Ritz
978-1-64247-462-6 | 206 pgs | paperback: $17.95 | eBook: $9.99
Can Elle and Ashley stand the heat in the *Celebrity Cook Off* kitchen?

Printed in the USA
CPSIA information can be obtained
at www.ICGtesting.com
JSHW022354150224
57425JS00006B/1